STORIES AND ESSAYS OF MINA LOY

Library of Congress Cataloging-in-Publication Data

Loy, Mina.
[Selections. 2011]
Stories and essays of Mina Loy / edited and with an introduction by Sara Crangle. -- 1st ed.
p. cm.
ISBN 978-1-56478-630-2 (pbk. : alk. paper)
I. Crangle, Sara. II. Title.
PS3523.O975A6 2011
818'.52--dc22
2011017150

Partially funded by the University of Illinois at Urbana-Champaign, as well as by grants from the National Endowment for the Arts, a federal agency, and the Illinois Arts Council, a state agency

www.dalkeyarchive.com

Cover: design and composition by Danielle Dutton,
cover photo Mina Loy, ca. 1905 by Stephen Haweis, courtesy of Roger L. Conover

Printed on permanent/durable acid-free paper and bound in the United States of America

STORIES AND ESSAYS OF MINA LOY

EDITED BY SARA CRANGLE

DALKEY ARCHIVE PRESS
CHAMPAIGN · DUBLIN · LONDON

OTHER WORKS BY MINA LOY

Songs to Joannes (*Others* magazine, 1917)

Lunar Baedecker [*sic*] (Contact Editions, 1923)

Lunar Baedeker & Time-Tables (Jonathan Williams/Jargon Press, 1958)

At the Door of the House (Aphra Press, 1980)

Love Songs (Aphra Press, 1981)

Virgins Plus Curtains (Press of the Good Mountain, 1981)

The Last Lunar Baedeker (The Jargon Society, 1982)

Insel (Black Sparrow Press, 1991)

The Lost Lunar Baedeker (Farrar, Straus and Giroux, 1996)

TABLE OF CONTENTS

Introduction / vii

I. STORIES

II. DRAMA

INTRODUCTION

Born in London in 1882, Mina Loy was an artist, inventor, novel-ist, actor, and prose writer, but as yet, her foothold in modernist history is secured by her poetry. Loy remains best known for a collection of poems entitled *Lunar Baedecker* that she published in Paris in 1923.[1] The title poem is a travel guide to a lunar land-scape that is decadent and deteriorating, a heady combination of modern and ancient. Here, "Delirious avenues" are

> lit
> with the chandelier souls
> of infusoria
> from Pharaoh's tombstones

Loy's cityscape contains not a red-light but a "white-light district / of lunar lusts"; the moon hosts a desire strangely bled of colour

---

1   The misspelling of "Baedecker" (it should be "Baedeker") went uncorrected by the publisher, Robert McAlmon's Contact Editions.

and vitality. As the poem nears its conclusion, its setting is likened to a "fossil virgin" and a " 'Crystal concubine' " (*Lost LB* 81–2). This moon encompasses the prehistoric, petrified remains of plants and animals, as well as a state of inviolate chastity, a newness and naïveté; Loy's is a celestial object made of a substance so pure and transparent it is associated with prophetic powers, but is simultaneously akin to a "kept" woman sullied by her dependency on a man. This poem shows Loy at her oxymoronic best; in part, it is her fondness for surprising, even disorienting juxtapositions of high and low that defines her writing as modernist. These self-same practices arise time and again in *Stories and Essays of Mina Loy*, a volume that aims to broaden awareness of a writer and her era.

Mina Loy was unquestionably immersed in the key events and radical aesthetics of her time. She studied art in London and Berlin respectively, becoming a member of the prestigious Paris Salon in 1906; in 1913, Loy befriended the leaders of Futurism, F. T. Marinetti and Giovanni Papini; in World War I, she nursed the wounded in Italy; in 1916, Loy moved to New York and immediately became part of the circle of avant-garde artists regularly entertained by Walter and Louise Arensberg, a group including Dadaists Marcel Duchamp and Man Ray; in the 1920s, she started a lamp-making business in Paris with the financial backing of the American art collector Peggy Guggenheim; in the 1930s, she worked as the representative for her son-in-law, Julien Levy, purchasing surrealist art in Paris for his New York gallery; in 1959, on the basis of six decades of creative productivity, Loy received the Copley Foundation Award for Outstanding Achievement in Art.

Loy participated in artistic communities on three continents, and even the most cursory list of her associates reads like a compendium of modernist greats: among many others, Loy knew Djuna Barnes, Natalie Barney, Basil Bunting, Joseph Cornell, James Joyce, Alfred Kreymborg, Robert McAlmon, Marianne Moore, Alfred Stieglitz, Gertrude Stein, Carl Van Vechten, William Carlos Williams—and, pivotally, her husband Arthur Cravan. Throughout her life, Loy wrote avidly: her work appeared in era-defining periodicals such as *The Little Review*—the journal that first published extracts from *Ulysses*—and *The Dial*, which debuted T. S. Eliot's *The Waste Land*. Loy's work was reviewed and praised by Eliot and Yvor Winters; she was lauded, edited, and published by Ezra Pound.

Loy's widespread recognition suggests that her place must be firmly anchored in twentieth-century literary history, but as "modernism" became an aesthetic construct, Loy did not become part of its canon, a fate she shared with many of her female peers. Loy died in 1966 having published only two books: *Lunar Baedecker* (1923) and *Lunar Baedeker and Time-Tables* (1958).[2] As explanations for her waning popularity, critics point to Loy's reclusiveness, as well as her disinterest in self-promotion and publishing in her later years. However, it should be borne in mind that Loy was only ever well known within avant-garde circles, and even there, she often remained on the periphery. Although associated with Futurism, Dada, and Surrealism, she remained, as Kenneth Rexroth writes, "like those kings whom history has always given a bad press because no party wanted to claim them"

---

2 *Lunar Baedeker and Time-Tables.* Highlands, North Carolina: Jonathan Williams, 1958.

(70–1).[3] One of Loy's most ardent fans, Rexroth triumphantly—and prematurely—announced Loy's return to the cultural map in 1971. "She has been rediscovered," Rexroth writes, "and when the present generation—the counter culture—can find her poems, they are read with enthusiasm" (72). How can a writer's work be reclaimed if it cannot even be located?

This difficulty was addressed in part in 1982, when Roger L. Conover edited the third volume of Loy's writing, *The Last Lunar Baedeker*. This edition, now out of print, remains the most complete; it contains Loy's long autobiographical poem, "Anglo-Mongrels and the Rose," as well as a great deal of previously uncollected poetry and prose. In 1996, Conover published another book, entitled *The Lost Lunar Baedeker*. While shorter than the 1982 volume, the later collection is the most widely available and accurate to date; it restores, for instance, the layout and punctuation of Loy's celebrated poem sequence, "Songs to Joannes".[4] Alongside these primary sources emerged criticism such as Virginia M. Kouidis's *Mina Loy: American Modernist Poet* (1980), Carolyn Burke's biography, *Becoming Modern: The Life of Mina Loy* (1996), and the essay collection *Mina Loy: Woman and Poet* (1998). Loy is increasingly found on university curricula, and her

3   Kenneth Rexroth, *American Poetry in the Twentieth Century*. NY: Herder and Herder, 1971.
4   Loy published "Songs to Joannes" on four different occasions. In 1915, under the title "Love Songs," the first four poems appeared in the little magazine *Others*; in the same journal, in 1917, it appeared as a thirty-four poem sequence called "Songs to Joannes". In 1923, an abbreviated thirteen-poem version with the original title, "Love Songs," was included in Loy's *Lunar Baedecker*; this shorter sequence was reissued in *Lunar Baedeker and Time-Tables* in 1958, and is also usefully included in the "Appendices" of Conover's 1996 *Baedeker*.

work has been explored in recent doctoral dissertations addressing subjects as varied as abjection, satire, and avant-garde poetics. The growing body of Loy articles has led to a second set of essays: *The Salt Companion to Mina Loy* (2010). Indeed, should her popularity continue to grow, Loy may well become the next "representative woman modernist"—a vexatious title, both laudatory and reductive, that has alternately been assigned to Virginia Woolf and Gertrude Stein over the past few decades. And, although a quintessential modernist in many respects, Loy is increasingly perceived as a writer whose scepticism and indeterminacy anticipate postmodern aesthetics.[5] In the twenty-first century, everyone wants a piece of Mina Loy.

As the publication of this volume indicates, the reclamation of Loy's oeuvre is far from over. *Stories and Essays* includes the vast majority of shorter prose stored in Loy's papers at the Beinecke Rare Book and Manuscript Library at Yale; not one of these writings has been collected, and most of them have never been published. But this book is by no means a complete survey. A number of Loy's key prose writings are already available in Conover's two *Lunar Baedeker*s, which include Loy's "Aphorisms on Futurism," the much-anthologised "Feminist Manifesto," and landmark essays such as "Modern Poetry".[6] Additionally, Loy generated a number

5   Jacqueline Vaught Brogan, "Postmodernist Crossings: Aesthetic Strategies, Historical Moment, or a State of Mind?" *Contemporary Literature* (42:1) 2001, 155–59.
6   The pieces listed above are located in the 1996 *Baedeker* along with "Preceptors of Childhood" and "Auto-Facial-Construction". Conover's 1982 *Baedeker* includes the following prose works: "Collision," "CittàBapini," "Summer Night in a Florentine Slum," "O Marcel . . . Otherwise I Also Have Been to Louise's," "Feminist Manifesto," "Aphorisms on Futurism," "International Psycho-De-

of novel manuscripts: early works such as *Brontolivido* and *Esau Penfold* (written during or shortly after Loy's later years in Florence, 1914–16), and mid-career narratives entitled *The Child and the Parent*, *Islands in the Air*, and *Goy Israels* (products of the late 1920s and early 1930s).[7] Loy's only published novel is *Insel*, which was written in the 1930s, and is not currently in print.[8] Again, the availability of her writing, and lack thereof, has had a considerable hand to play in the shaping of Loy's reputation.

This dearth of published material has meant that most readers remain unaware that Loy the poet was an equally active writer of narratives, criticism, and cultural commentary. Loy wrote her first poem, "The Beneficent Garland" in 1914; in this same year or the next she began the play "The Sacred Prostitute"; shortly thereafter, she embarked upon another drama, "The Pamperers". While dates of composition are rarely given in Loy's papers, certainties include 1921 for "The Stomach" and "The Oil in the Machine?" as well as 1925 for one draft of "Gate Crashers of Olympus—". Loy's lecture "Gertrude Stein" was given at Natalie Barney's salon in 1927, and there exists good evidence that "In Maine: Green's Colony" was written in the late 1920s or early 1930s. Loy's thoughts on William Carlos Williams were mailed on June 5th 1948, while "Tuning in

mocracy," "Auto-Facial Construction," "The Artist and the Public," "Phenomenon in American Art (Joseph Cornell)," "Pas de Commentaires! (Louis M. Eilshemius)," "*Little Review* Questionnaire," "*View* Questionnaire," "Aphorisms on Modernism," "Notes on Existence," "Notes on Childhood," "Dante Gabriel Rossetti," "Ladies in an Aviary," "Arthur Cravan is Alive!" and "Gertrude Stein" (which differs from the lecture of the same title in this book).

7   Carolyn Burke considers the latter three manuscripts a single novel with multiple drafts (*BM* 375).

8   *Insel*. Ed. Elizabeth Arnold. Santa Rosa, California: Black Sparrow Press, 1991.

on the Atom Bomb" is evidently a product of World War II or its immediate aftermath. Lastly, Carolyn Burke claims that "History of Religion and Eros" was written during the years that Loy lived in New York's Bowery District, namely 1948–1953 (*BM* 422–23). A completely accurate chronology of the narratives and essays in this volume may never be compiled, but these dates alone clarify that Loy was writing a great deal of prose from the outset of World War I until the 1950s—the very period that encompasses her most productive writing years. Ideally, this book will thus contribute to a realignment and expansion of Loy's poetic legacy.

Stories and Essays will certainly confirm Loy's standing as a modernist. Loy directly addresses topics shunned by her forebears or considered anew by her contemporaries, including abortion, aesthetics, avant-gardism, the body, class, consumption, evolution, gender relations, genius, iconoclasm, metaphysics, power, sexuality, subjectivity, transcendence, and war. Artistic and ideological movements like Futurism, Imagism, and Dada also make appearances. Loy's criticism continues these preoccupations, and extends them to figures central to the shaping of modernism such as Brancusi, Braque, Eliot, Havelock Ellis, Freud, Joyce, Lawrence, and Picasso. But more than these ready associations with the modernism to which Loy is so often allied, these works illustrate how Loy gradually came to question twentieth-century mores. Some readers may be surprised to discover Loy taking a religious turn not unlike that of Eliot; while this interest clearly defines "History of Religion and Eros," it is also apparent in the Socratic dialogue "Mi & Lo," where Loy's philosophy, like Plato's, is informed by the human relationship to the divine. The religiosity of Loy's late oeuvre does not mesh comfortably with the scabrous hijinks of earlier satirical fictions like "The Stomach"; nor does Loy's faith sit easily with our presumptions about modernist secularism. But this facet of her writing has only recently begun to be addressed, and is part and parcel of a conversion to Christian Science that Loy enacted well before she started writing (*BM* 117).[9]

Just as Loy's religiosity is not simplistically modernist, it might be argued that there are a number of pieces in this book that reveal a latent Victorianism. "The Crocodile without any Tail" is a children's fairy tale that ends happily-ever-after; the plot of "The Three Wishes" is virtually Dickensian in scope; Loy's ballet "Crystal Pantomime" foregrounds a heterosexual relationship potentially disconcerting in its allegiance to stereotypical gender roles. Perhaps worse, Loy occasionally proves intrigued by rendering lower-class dialects to a rather painfully extensive degree. Yet each of these more "traditional" writings contains deliberate, disruptive absurdity; how many character lists of fairy tales, for instance, include children named 1, 2, 3, 4, 5, and 6? At the heart of this nameless naming is a suspicion toward language consistent throughout Loy's works, resulting in the linguistic play that is the foundation of so much of her originality.

---

9 The years ascribed to Loy's conversion vary slightly, but consistently predate Loy's first poem; Carolyn Burke suggests the period 1907–10 (117), while Virginia Kouidis cites 1913 (7). While observing that Loy converted alongside many other artists in her expatriate community in Florence, Burke does not give specific names. Notable modernist adherents to Christian Science include the American writer Hart Crane, and Loy's close friend in later life, the American artist Joseph Cornell. For recent writings on Loy and Christian Science, see the essays of Richard Cook and Maeera Shreiber in *Mina Loy: Woman and Poet*, and the work of Tim Armstrong and David Ayers in *The Salt Companion to Mina Loy*.

Loy's concerns about the communicative aspect of language come to the fore in some of the more obscure elements of *Stories and Essays*, and particularly in her persistent return to the figures of the sphinx and the asterisk, who surface in seven pieces in this collection.[10] "The Library of the Sphinx." is a critique of modernist literature, and begins as follows:

> While the sphinx retains her secret, who shall reveal the unconsummated significance of the asterisk—
>
> Notwithstanding that the secret of the sphinx is not conveyed in words—the asterisk is an assumption that the secret is possessed by each of us and therefore need never be mentioned—
>
> the asterisk is the signal of a treasure which is not there.

For the Greeks, sphinxes were gendered female. The most famous sphinx guarded the gates of the city Thebes, asking a riddle of those who wanted to enter; an incorrect answer resulted in death. Robert Sheffield appears to be the only critic thus far to comment upon Loy's frequent mention of the sphinx in her papers; he quite reasonably claims that "Loy's point of departure is Oscar Wilde's *The Picture of Dorian Gray*, in which the decadent Lord Henry Wotton dismisses women as 'Sphinxes without secrets.'"[11] For Loy, a countering femi-

---

10   References to the asterisk and/or the sphinx arise in: "All the laughs in one short story by McAlmon," "Gloria Gammage," "Lady Asterisk.," "The Library of the Sphinx.," "Pazzarella," "The Three Wishes," and more obliquely, in "Tuning in on the Atom Bomb".
11   Rob Sheffield, "Mina Loy in Much too Much too Soon: Poetry/Celebrity/Sexuality/Modernity." *Literary Review* (46:4) 2003.

nist aesthetic is at stake. In "Pazzarella," the female protagonist is alternately likened to a void or an enigma; when she insists that she contains an incommunicable "'secret truth'", her suitor Geronimo retorts that *he* is the solution to her riddle. Certain that he can see into Pazzarella's confused "female soul" Geronimo reflects:

> In the divine manner, it was from this chaos I drew my inspiration. At once I grew enormous—omnipotent. After centuries of mystery, I had found the solution—a solution that lay in myself. The secret of woman is that she does not yet exist. Being a creator, I realized I can create woman. I decided to "create" Pazzarella.

The sphinx, then, is not silent because ignorant, but because she has yet to formulate herself, let alone her riddle. Via the ancient sphinx, Loy contends that although an extensive history of Western civilisation has already unfolded, women remain in the infancy of their attempts to identify themselves and be recognised. Like any good parody, "Pazzarella" is part cautionary tale: women must express their "secret truth" or be defined yet again.

While Loy's sphinx implicitly undermines the advances of the first wave of feminism, it notably foresees the identity politics that shaped the second wave of feminism in the 1960s and 1970s. Loy extends the image of the sphinx to present women's lack of identity as strength and opportunity. In "Gloria Gammage," we're told that the protagonist "keeps a no man's land of meaning in these sleek stroking corners of her eyes" and that her lover "who will never be able to construe its significance—is anxious that no man else ever shall—". As Loy's narrator states, Gloria "[i]n this way—keep[s] the secret—of the Sphinx." And amid the general hilarity of "All the laughs in one short story by McAlmon," one woman smiles "sphinxly" and with quiet authority. The contemplative silence signalled by the sphinx corresponds with Loy's asterisk, "the signal of a treasure which is not there." While the asterisk can be used to indicate an unsayable obscenity, in Loy's hands, it denotes a more commonplace inarticulacy, as when, in "The Three Wishes," she describes a beaten-down couple as follows:

> They both seemed only with the years to be scrupulously washing themselves away.
> Like millions and millions of us, they were living off a literature that has worn down to asterisks.

Here, the asterisk marks a distinctly melancholic marriage that is devoid of any defining passion. For the sphinx and her followers, absence is secret and potentially powerful; for others, it is an empty wordlessness only obliquely aware of its unfulfilled promise.

The writings in *Stories and Essays of Mina Loy* contain complexities in terms of content, narrative structure, diction, and punctuation. Confusion arises when the toothless and tailless crocodiles are inexplicably conflated in "The Crocodile without any Tail". More often, though, this confusion is neither accidental nor gratuitous; for instance, a ferociously disjointed paragraph of dialogue in "Hush Money" concludes with the protagonist's proud claim that "he could keep up a racing, hurdle-leaping intercourse"—here form and content work symbiotically. Adding to the reader's perplexity is Loy's love of coining neologisms: Loy's word "millionheir" is both apt and consistently used; similarly expressive is the "*Introspeculates*" of "Mi & Lo". These terminologies are part and parcel of Loy's insistent treatment of language as a vital, living thing. Loy retrieves archaic or foreign phrasing and layers it with playful, modern meanings, as when, in "Gate Crashers of Olympus—" she uses the French word for break—*casse*—as a homophonic allegiance between Pi*casso* and his revolutionary "destruction" of the artistic techniques of his forebears. Still more unusually, Loy has many unorthodox forms of spacing and punctuation, and perhaps most notably, an odd approach to dashes.

In the handwritten drafts from which so much of this volume was transcribed, Loy has scope for a real range of dashes: sometimes they are very low or high on the line, sometimes they are broken up into short, repeated hyphens; quite often they are extraordinarily long. The significance of handwritten dashes has become something of a sore point in the study of Emily Dickinson's manuscripts and poems, and I want to steer clear of unduly fetishising Loy's dashes here.[12] Indeed, Loy's dashes often stand

---

12   Jerome McGann is perhaps the most celebrated critic who asserted that Dickinson's work could not be fully understood without recourse to the original holograph manuscripts that preserved variations such as the specific slant of her dashes. McGann is frequently cited in the ongoing debate about the sanctity of Dickinson's handwritten punctuation, which some critics dismiss as irrelevant, even as others suggest it is key to understanding the fundamentals of her writing, such as her line breaks (see, for instance, Domhnall Mitchell's "Revising the Script: Emily Dickinson's Manuscripts." *American Literature* (70:4) 1998, 705–37). Loy's dashwork may well instigate a similar critical debate; most recently, Andrew Michael Roberts argues that Loy's erratic punctuation and spacing could be central to her writing, as both pivotally "enhance the physicality of [her] poem[s]" ("Rhythm, Self, and Jazz in Mina Loy's Poetry." *Salt Companion*, p. 122).

for an incomplete and unedited thought process. Consider, for instance, the following sentence, which is drawn from the handwritten draft of "The Sacred Prostitute": "Love – is a feminine conception – spell't Greed — with a capital G – – this is female – alright!" In the typescript edited in Loy's hand, the same sentence shows a marked reduction in dashes, and a return to more standard punctuation: "Love is a feminine conception spelt 'Greed' with a capital 'G'—this is female, all right!" Although the number of Loy's dashes usually diminishes as editing gets underway, there can be no doubt that the length of her dashes is meant to signify either an extended pause, or on occasion, an unspoken word. Loy also incorporates some odd punctuation in her writing, as in her essay "Conversion" which includes "+++++++++" as well as a series of exaggerated dashes; in this instance, both of these typographical tics intensify the willful choppiness of her prose. In short, these aberrations quite regularly serve the content of Loy's work; as such, I've done my utmost to maintain these variations in punctuation whenever possible.[13]

A fidelity to Loy's revisions is particularly important, as ample evidence exists that she was serious about preserving and perfecting these works: Loy frequently endeavoured to have her handwritten manuscripts typed (and some instances, typed again), she extensively edited drafts both typed and handwritten, she signed her name to many pieces, and she tabulated precise word counts throughout some of her prose, and the stories in particular. A number of these narratives, however, remain incomplete, a problem that is compounded by a degree of disorganisation in Loy's

13 Throughout, short, repeated, broken hyphens are transcribed as en dashes, while longer dashes are transcribed as the more common em dash.

papers, which contain folders of improperly labelled or unidentified, fragmented writings. With careful sleuthing, I have been able to reassemble some of the stories; whenever uncertainties about narrative chronology remain, or parts of a text cannot be located, I detail as such in the editorial notes at the end of the book.

Everyone who explores an archive becomes a voyeur of sorts; alongside typescripts and handwritten drafts, Loy's papers yield lists of expenses, doodles, some deeply personal, diary-like scraps, and a constant return to a game whereby she tries to make as many words as possible out of the letters of a single word. As I articulate the ways and means that Loy seems to envision an audience for her work, I'm aware that my claims act as excuse and consolation for what must necessarily be an invasive exercise. But while there are more in the way of Loy's prose musings in her archive, every piece in this collection is either titled by Loy or bears a title page upon which its contents are summarised; each of these gestures suggests that Loy saw the work as an approximate, functional whole that could be encapsulated. In her essay "Conversion" Loy tells us "[t]he aim of the artist is to miss the Absolute"—so too, by stark necessity, must this be the aim of the editor. While not entire, *Stories and Essays of Mina Loy* offers insight into the ribaldry, the pathos, the occasional bathos, and the experimentation in Loy's prose stylings. It is a book that shows us a Loy truly contemplative about, and occasionally sentimental toward, her fellow human beings. Here Loy recognises Picasso's foundational role in twentieth-century art, takes her male contemporaries to task for their sexism, questions the popularity and limitations of psychoanalysis, ponders ways of rectifying poverty, and tries her hand, ambitiously, at numerous genres. These fictions, dramas, essays, and philosophical and religious tracts affirm and extend what we know about Loy from her poetry: as it turns out, Loy is every bit as astute, original, interrogative, and witty in her prose.

EDITORIAL PROCESS

First and foremost, let me clarify that *Stories and Essays of Mina Loy* is not, and should not be considered, a critical or definitive edition of these writings. Having said that, the manuscripts I've been working from are often handwritten, or are typescripts that have been edited by hand. As Loy did not have the opportunity to view final proofs and corrections, some notation of the changes made to the texts seemed absolutely necessary. In choosing to track Loy's revisions in the editorial notes, I follow the dictates of the well-known bibliographical scholar, Fredson Bowers, who asserts that the reader's awareness of textual revisions offers valuable insight into an author at work.[14] The need for this insight is inarguably compounded in this collection by the fact that the majority of these writings were left as works in progress.

Scholarly editions track every change made to manuscripts, while practical editions leave those decisions unremarked and in the hands of the editor. In the editorial notes to each piece contained in this volume, I offer an amalgam of these two approaches: I rarely note where I have corrected inaccuracies of spelling or punctuation, and a very few small revisions (regarding prepositions or articles, for instance) are silently incorporated into the

---

14   Fredson Bowers, *Essays in Bibliography, Text, and Editing.* Charlottesville: University Press of Virginia, 1975, p. 310.

text. Nor do I always detail instances where Loy has crossed out words that she reinstates elsewhere. On occasion, the illegibility of Loy's editing has made it impossible to verify a given change—either through scrawled handwriting or severe blacking out.

However, substantial differences within texts are listed, as are significant editorial alterations; by design, the latter category occurs rather rarely. Changes Loy made to her scripts are indicated by the word "was," as in the following, from the notes accompanying "Brancusi and the Ocean":

"evolved by" was "that has evolved through"

Editorial changes are indicated by the word "reads", and are followed by "—*ed.*" as in this example from "Gate Crashers of Olympus—":

"revaluation of values" reads "revaluation values"—*ed.*

I have made a point of noting changes between Loy's various drafts when they contribute significantly to the understanding of the gestation of the piece; when these distinctions are included, I have stated as such in the editorial notes. Loy's marginalia and speculative changes are also listed; Loy occasionally offers an alternate word, followed by a question mark, and these tentative edits are noted, as in this instance, from "Gate Crashers of Olympus—":

Before "disjuncted" reads "disjected?"—*ed.*

In situations where there is additional material that does not form part of the draft used in the body of *Stories and Essays*, I've given examples of this supplementary writing in the editorial notes. When this material is added at the back of the book, Loy's earlier phrasing appears in square brackets. For example, from "The Agony of the Partition":

> "the only illusion [for recovering] of resuming it, is to cling to those others who knew him also"

Here, the bracketed "[for recovering]" signifies crossed-out words in this portion of the text.

When words cannot be deciphered with complete assurance, these vagaries are denoted by: [*unclear word*], or with a specific identification of the illegible word, as in the notes for "Brancusi and the Ocean" which read:

> "intriguing comparison"—"intriguing" is unclear—*ed.*

Tears in Loy's manuscripts occur on occasion, either due to holes or wear; these disruptions are observed with: [*torn page*]. Only where absolutely necessary, and with the joint interests of foregrounding Loy's intentions and readability as fully as possible, have I added or removed question marks, brackets, full stops, quotation marks, colons, and commas. In some cases, Loy's use of quotation marks leaves the speaker ambiguous, and I have let this ambiguity stand. Loy's erratic applications of double and single quotations—often within the same piece—have been standardised. Unless otherwise stated, all of the structural divisions or sections within Loy's narratives emulate the manuscripts; whenever possible, the punctuation Loy uses to demarcate these breaks has been replicated.

Each of the editorial summaries indicates where the manuscript of the work is located. Excepting "The Pamperers," all material comes from the Beinecke Rare Book and Manuscript Library at Yale, and the specific location in that library is signalled as follows: (6:175). The first number represents the particular box in Loy's papers; the number following the colon refers to the folder within that box. Additionally, my editorial notes offer information about the state of the manuscript in question, occasional commentary on Loy's more obscure references, useful critical contemplations of the piece, and any extant indications of the date of composition. Because so many of these dates remain speculative, the works of *Stories and Essays of Mina Loy* have been arranged by genre, and then again by alphabetical order, rather than chronologically.

ACKNOWLEDGMENTS

Firstly, I would like to thank Loy's editor Roger Conover for permission to undertake this project. Without research grants from Queens' College, Cambridge (specifically, The Weil Fund) and the University of Sussex, this book would not have been possible. The longer French translations—namely the entirety of "Gertrude Stein" and the correspondence in "Pazzarella"—were kindly provided by Martin Crowley, a Senior Lecturer in French at the University of Cambridge. Finally, I'd like to extend my appreciation to the dedicated and attentive staff at the Beinecke Rare Book and Manuscript Library at Yale University.

SARA CRANGLE, 2011

ABBREVIATIONS

Last LB	Loy, Mina. *The Last Lunar Baedeker*. ed. Roger Conover. Highland, NC: Jargon Society, 1982.
Lost LB	Loy, Mina. *The Lost Lunar Baedeker: Poems of Mina Loy*. ed. Roger Conover. NY: Farrar, Straus and Giroux, 1996.
BM	Burke, Carolyn. *Becoming Modern: The Life of Mina Loy*. New York: Farrar, Straus and Giroux, 1996.
ML: W & P	*Mina Loy: Woman and Poet*. ed. Maeera Shreiber and Keith Tuma. Orono, Maine: The National Poetry Foundation, 1998.
Salt Companion	*The Salt Companion to Mina Loy*. ed. Rachel Potter and Suzanne Hobson. London: Salt Publishing, 2010.

STORIES AND ESSAYS OF MINA LOY

STORIES

THE AGONY OF THE PARTITION

I.

In this old apartment, spacious rooms had been sliced to cubicles where the staccato chatter of the inmates, relayed like tom-tom messages, mingled with the crash of irreconcilable radios. For the moment it was so quiet I thought to be alone in the place. The unlifting evening of back rooms in crowded areas deepened. The page I wrote upon become hazy; resting awhile, I looked up at my bit of ceiling. The moulding, like a monorail into the unknown, streaked through a false wall into the visibility of other lodgings.

Above the bolster I leaned against, my idle head came into contact with the partition. Flimsy to vibrancy, it had hardly the resistance of a solid, and as I lolled on the divan in the precocious dusk, behind my shoulders the vibrancy of that shallow plane seemed slowly to concentrate, to rhythmically accentuate, until in my drowsiness it was as if the partition were breathing. A breath that, as it rose and fell with mine, filled me with unaccountable anxiety. I was drawing-in dread. I was made heavy with responsibility; and soon, under those feeble winds I could feel a stranger's heart beat on my compassion. Its convoy of breath heaved through the partition as through a second breast. Varied, at intervals, to a râle from a chamber of torture.

For some days this percussion of inattributable emotion, my only company, transmitted its load of sorrow to some receiver within me extraneous to sense, which Mrs. Nome later, when we became acquainted, decoded.

It was like assisting at the presentation, without action, of a play whose protagonists projected onto the stage only an emotional abstract of the plot; a suit at law without evidence of any claiming. I might have been reading a tragedy, describing in phraseless parentheses, episodes undefined. Sometimes in its immeasurable alteration, it seemed to accord me the perfume of a rose, posthumously, or to poison me without a means. And always after a rarer agony, it would be as if a sugar of the heavens poured. The partition functioned as a vast Ouija-board without letter or number printed upon it.

I had no key to its communication, a contact so tenuous it is no wonder I did not realise at once that someone in the next room had chosen the spot corresponding to mine, to lean against.

When first I caught a glimpse of Mrs. Nome it was to see her vanishing – – – into a dark recess that obscured her door. A glimpse so brief it was not before she had passed I attributed her amorphous shape to her burden of ungainly packages. I hardly registered the passing of a taller figure ahead of her.—

Having so much to hold she fumbled at the lock, a glimmer of light striking the lower muscle of her jaw. At once a voice from the shadows hissed at her, "Insane old hag; it takes you a week to unlock a door." In the wake of its murderous inflection, out darted a tense hand. Cruel as a claw it dug deep into that illumined muscle, and giving it a vicious twist did its best to wrench it off. Half the parcels fell to the floor with a moan. The door opened and closed.

I returned to my cubicle. The false wall resounded with arpeggios of curses and shrieked bitches. A nerve-wracking invective, yet it seemed to issue from no heart-felt conviction; rather, as if a self-trained robot, glib with practice, were testing how great a tonal strain its metal lungs, its wire vocal-chords could stand. Or a child's bravado had run amok into adulthood, before an amplified converse. After dishing out a few platitudes from a daily broadcast, she reflected gently, ". . . for if we fail to reap to the full Unity's advantages it is because we do not get up early enough in the morning."

Without ado, the landlady's daughter seized a heavy iron deep-fryer and flung it at the philosopher standing almost beneath her. It missed the head of Mrs. Nome which, all I could tell of her appearance, was covered with wispy hair the colour of faded carrot.

A clatter of iron, a hop off the ladder, the girl's yells for mother to protect her. I stayed where I was. The landlady with her prowling gait of a limp orangutan, approached.

As she learned—of the brutal insults heaped by her lodger on a girl she despised for her kinship with one who rented out rooms—her critical sneers, her undue familiarity—she seemed to grow taller.

"And her foul language. Do you allow this woman to treat me like a servant?"

"This is *most* serious . . ." the landlady pondered on the back of Mrs. Nome, which rigid with astonishment did not stir.

"Most serious—" she stalled for time, herself quite as astonished, but proudly astonished: here was her daughter appealing to her.

I noticed that the door of the cubicle facing Mrs. Nome stood ajar. And now it was I who was astonished. It was not for helplessness before the onslayer that she had attempted no *volte-face*. Through that aperture peered an eye. Mrs. Nome's entire astonishment focused on the fortuity of her having a witness.

Out of her cubicle stepped the hairdresser from Killarney, her own black curls wrapped in an emerald scarf – – – to tell what had actually occurred.

"Can you beat that?" She panted for laughter, as she and her protégée found themselves, as they thought, alone – – –

"I can," said Mrs. Nome, impersonally, "at any minute. All my life I seem to have been the eternal 'innocent-accused.'"

"And always will be so," the Irishwoman assured her, taking in hers her hand. "I have seen the psychic mark of the cross on your poor forehead."

"I can't get over it," Mrs. Nome almost stuttered in her bewilderment, "you are the first one ever to testify – – –"

"You might have been killed—"

"Oh, no," said Mrs. Nome, "it's *always* by a hair's breadth."

II.

Cassandra laid her cheek against her mother's – – "the kiss of a skull. The ashes of love had petrified to a white ossification, her motor-power become an inhibition." Trying to describe her pallor, the voice of Mrs. Nome fell lower. "I caught a parting wisp of dim phosphorescence leaving the face that was once so luminous. It is so," she mused with qualities eclipsed, "one almost perceives their ghosts disperse from the person; yet I could feel that ineffable sweetness, which, always a component of her Nature, although denied me, still cling to her."

"As soon as she left the house," resumed the distraught creature, "to take the bull by the horns, I turned to Mrs. Moppet."

"So that's the effect Gabriel Schwartz has on a woman?"

"Schwartz?!" exclaimed the secretive looking matron with the finality of keeping a promise. "We don't know anybody of that name." Then deciding I looked sure, she hurriedly modified her connivance.

"Well *yes* – – – You see your daughter is in love with this man who loves someone else."

With these few words, spilling the insane love-affair, whose hallucinatory situations I had so long taxed my brain for a solution, into the commonplace, Mrs. Mop immediately widened the discrepancy.

"Have you no pride, I begged her?"

" 'I love him,' Cassandra would whine," in this friend's mimicry, erotically.

Shaken with my too sudden readjustment, I tried a casual, "Would you say the thing got so far as an actual liaison?"

"O, I shouldn't think so" she answered; a reassuring flicker on a mouth which operated smiling as an incessant buttoning up and unbuttoning. "It wouldn't have been safe; she's so inexperienced."

Soon Mop's married daughter Ilya strayed in, slimly took seat; a fragile silhouette in the temperate autumn glow of the window. She lay back in her wicker chair, silently measured me, and, chance iteration, sighed

"What that man has done to Cassandra!"

Her face was somewhat aimlessly reminiscent of screen stars—having suffered a certain erasure of feature: the unfaded fading of the nocturnal youth of New York. Her sympathy was soft and fair as the floss of her hair, as if anything that touched her must, slightly, turn to gold.

"I feel so badly about it," she pleaded in helpless regret. "It was I who gave him quite a build-up before introducing him to her. Cassandra whom we so wonderingly admired for being the opposite of what she turned out to be. Her strangely brutal arrogance to the men she attracted made us hold our breath, her aloofness – – – was matchless."

"It has been awful," continued Ilya, "*Every way* that sadist contrived to torture her. Her suffering terrified me. There came a time when she was actually insane."

My bruises at once absolved, "I had dared to think so," I proffered, "the violence of her behaviour – – – and there was *no one* with whom I could consult."

"Pooh," exclaimed Mop, her expression of slightly rowdy beneficence not changing, as she disappeared into the kitchenette.

"I soon put a stop to it, whenever she began getting violent with me."

"I hate him! I hate him!" moaned the girl, pounding the plaited arms of her chair— "None of us will have anything more to do with him," she assured me. "And we had been such friends—all through college."

"Things might have turned out differently," commented Mop, returning with coffee, "if, when he was here she had made any of the brilliant remarks she makes when he is not there; but no, she just sat without a word; goggled at him like a love-sick moo-cow."

"It was love all right," Mrs. Nome reflected sorrowfully.

"*She* didn't love him," contradicted Mop, "over and over again I told her, 'If you got him, you'd be sick of him in a month.' What she *wanted* was to get him away from the other girl."

"She'd wake up in the night—and rage – – 'I'll kill her, I'll kill her!' "

"But nothing, nothing she could say, would ever interfere with my recognition of my daughter's love for the man whose face I had never seen." Mrs. Nome seemed pleading with me to back her up.

That face they brought out for me now from among a miscellanea of photos.

Beach. Naked. An amateur Tarzan. Questionably picturesque, having a certain Greco-Woolworth grace, he had strung about his neck a scatter of sea-shells.

Under handsome hair he gazed from his paper effigy as in a momentary arrest of shifty eyes. Weak for any definite destiny, his mouth, a shapeless snare, thin; contractile as a sting.

"What mean beauty," cried Mrs. Nome in her surprise.

"I do not remember," mused Mrs. Nome, "which one of that *sub rosa* family revealed how Schwartz had made all arrangements to marry my Cassandra over a certain weekend, and disappeared on the eve, to join the other girl who played in some barn theatre. But I knew at once that sunbold summer morning when I crept into her room against the pressure of her grief—should have been her wedding-day—that, then, I had found her lying upon her incomparably betrayed bed of a bride.

"Like those corpses excavated from Pompeii, who in lightning overthrow, sheathed in the lava of Vesuvius, retain the rounded contours of bodies erect, seem to be bounced upon the horizontal, she appeared not to flatten on her mattress; but unsupported, to be stretched out rigid on the axis of her contractile agony. A centripetal demolition of despair, defiant of gravity as if she were too heavy to fall, endowed her with an insane levitation of sorrow become lead.

"On her lovely long body, the facing curves of the inner thighs whispered like marble to the instinct for form. The corner of a sheet she had, in an inalienable reflex of modesty, wafted across her midst, also incompliant to the planes of its location, traversed her as a fallen bar of folded stone.

"Vertical her derouted feet stood to the air, the mounds prominent on the sole as if released from treading further. Noting the guard of her forearm across her eyes, I drew the shades.

"Cassandra cursed me," concluded Mrs. Nome, looking as she always did, perplexed.

In the mind of the blonde, some unholy imperative attached to her necessity for convincing Mrs. Nome of things inconceivable – – –

"After she got rid of the baby, they forced your daughter, in a dangerous condition of haemorrhage, to sit up all night, every night, dragging her with them half dead to – – –" and now I could see this blonde's description of a den of vice projected as it were in television onto the centre of the clapboard; in her aerial colouring, a place suspect to the police, the sale of unlicensed alcohol, with Cassandra, crematorially white, a bleeding jitterbug in the arms of over-familiar negroes. "And they actually had the nerve to invite *me* there, she spluttered. "Nothing on earth would induce me . . . ."

"I know I promised to pay the rent," she reiterates, "But I am really under no obligation—Cassy is no longer the girl I could be friendly with—she'll never again be able to mix with decent people after that low crowd she's got in with so deep – – she's become just like them – –"

"On the contrary," countered Mrs. Nome, in an absent-minded impulse, 'in spite of all' to stick up for her offspring—"it was only the other day she told me how on finding herself once more in the Manhattan *monde*, she was surprised how easily she readapted."

III. Mrs. Nome

Yet for Mrs. Nome, and others also remembered it, there was a sweetness at the core of Cassandra. To this sublimely dulcet nucleus clung the vindicatory faith of this mother, although in its occasional effusion it never reached to her. The beneficent upsurge would well up, overbrim pouring itself in an angelic graciousness on her casual acquaintances. In spite of her having, herself, so fastidiously selected the pedigrees of the pets with which her mother had delighted companion her—it was as if among moral humans, her heart craved curs and mongrels—to gather them in her arms and rudely protect them from a woman intent on doing them (with herself) some unguessable harm. As if, identifying herself with them she must vilify her mother on their behalf.

Mrs. Nome perhaps plausibly suspected that the fleshly bond between mother and daughter does sometimes deposit disgust in the daughter's subconscious—that this might warrant the young withholding their sex confidences from their progenitors. This, she had modified, might, on the other hand, be due to the average parent having reduced "sex" to the humdrum atmosphere of disappointment pervading their home or degraded it in the dirt of false proprieties, contrasting so drastically with the budding faith in the life of their offspring.

—But was this disgust?

The sex-conversation of hospital nurses is even notoriously practical. And this woman who sniffed at *her* daughter in an effort to disparage the object of her rejected love for her alleviation— "Why, Bundy wasn't even man enough to get you pregnant"—to *her* bulge of hip and bosom the inaccessible Cassandra resorted as to the uttermost fount of the humanities.

Had her involvement in the hideous carnality of that prenatal murder endowed her with some warm pulsating motherhood congenial to Cassandra? A woman convinced that Cassandra's adoration of Schwartz was merely "pique" for his chosen girlfriend.

Mrs. Nome, repudiated mother, listened in an amazed agony as Cassandra lashed her the conceptual mother with hideous insults, while hugging close in her torn armchair, the mother of her selection. Their faces pressed together, the younger etiolate, the elder slightly bloated with her specialised contact with life – – – Mop seemed to be discreetly covering a bed-pan she might carry as offertory to her own biological gods . . . .

Cassandra in some crafty excitement this woman alone she elected as worthy to share with her—ever more agitated, insisting; Mop, ever so evasively placating—the girl almost hilariously angry; each, although obviously at odds, fully enjoying a tussle in cupidity.

Of what nature, Mrs. Nome wondered, was this transferred filial devotion, that slid so wantonly from lip to ear, that leaned with such suspecting trust upon this stranger's obesity, this gleam of parity in point of view, that suffused Cassandra with a tittering affection?

My presence, mused Mrs. Nome, in the physical world seems a signal for conspiracy; but in the ideological world how gloriously all pernicious sociability turns to my advantage as if—eliminating the dross from actuality one extracted a supernal essence.

It is when my helplessness allowing me to be crushed, leaves me not even the power to resist; when the wonder-worry of self accusation having failed to solve the mystery of my responsibility;— Pain and penury, the bruises and denunciations drop from me. Something innate to myself has all the while had no share in the evil events as if the arena of embroilment rejected this over-anxious outsider's intrusion—

I am left insensate, anaesthetised by that secret essence human society unknowingly distils for me.

"Here," pressing her hand to her brow, "where I find myself so 'otherwise' alone—and invulnerable," said Mrs. Nome gazing somewhat witlessly upon me—"from some vast distance I have all the same been audience to The Most Beautiful love-affair the passions of our world have ever brought about."

THE CROCODILE WITHOUT ANY TAIL

Once upon a time there lived a crocodile in a river. All day long he lay pretending to be an island and longing for the little children coming home from school.

One day a little boy was running along the bank of the river and the crocodile thrust his nose out of the rushes, and – – nearly – – snapped off the little boy's leg.

All the children were very sad. They thought they would be much happier playing by the river if there was no crocodile there. So they went to the fairy and asked her what to do.

"A very simple matter," said the fairy, "what you need to do is to pull out all the crocodile's teeth."

"How?" said the children.

"My dears," said the fairy, "if you like I will do it for you. I can make myself invisible which is far the safest way."

That very night the fairy flew into the crocodile's mouth while he was snoring, and gently *drew* out all his teeth with a *bone-magnet*.

He felt nothing. He went on peacefully dreaming of Charley-chops and Sirloin of Sammy and it was only at sunrise next morning that he awoke to find that a deep change had come over his nature. Somehow or other he felt much more tender and when later in the morning the little children passed him on their way to school, he felt that in the future he could only want to kiss them.

For the first time he felt lonely too, and wished that he had some kind friends, on whom he might in times of trouble, rely.

The land seemed to him suddenly much more attractive than the river which had never happened before.

When the children came back from school they wanted to see how the crocodile looked without his teeth.

He greeted them with the kindest smile, and offered to give them a ride on his back.

The gentle crocodile floated down the river with half a dozen darlings shouting "Gee Up" and flogging him with grass.

Which made another crocodile with teeth so jealous that he bit off his tail the same night.

The children said, "Oh poor crocodile! We will make you a kite tail." So they made him a tail of tufts of lovely pink and yellow paper.

When the wind rose the crocodile rose and went sailing over the house-tops with his tail floating. But when the wind dropped he dropped onto a kitchen chimney pot.

The children brought a long ladder to save the crocodile and they were only just in time for a spark from the chimney had set fire to the paper tail and they had to cut it off with a pocket-knife.

The children and the crocodile were now the greatest friends, and the children called the crocodile Grandpa and introduced him to their funny Mamma.

Their Mamma was funny because she was never surprised. She loved, she said, to see the children "express" themselves. And as she had nothing to do but ring for the maid to clear up after them, there was really no reason why they should not.

The funny Mamma said she was pleased to meet Grandpa and asked if he took sugar in his tea.

She also helped the children to throw the buns into his mouth. They all had a delightful time, and the funny Mamma said, "I think if you were to attach a Christmas tree to the crocodile for his new tail he would be both useful and ornamental."

The crocodile was delighted with the idea and kept quite still while they tied the Christmas tree to him. Then he practised walking nobly with his tail straight up, and when Christmas Eve came the children decorated the tree with coloured candles, fruits and crackers, and beautiful toys. They led him through the streets all lit up, and when they came to dark and narrow streets the crocodile walked in at the doors of the old houses and climbed up the stairs.

The poor cold little children huddled together on the landings and were delightfully surprised to see a Christmas tree walking up stairs.

On every landing the crocodile stood quite still and his candles shone and his toys twinkled while his friends gave toys and sweets to the cold little children who clapped their hands and gurgled with joy. And the funny Mamma who had trundled along behind with a great big wheel-barrow heaped with knitted woollen clothes of green and red, of yellow and blue, dressed the children most cheerfully and they felt much warmer.

Then the Christmas tree and the wheel-barrow went downstairs and visited every house where children lived who were likely to require them.

Now when the crocodile had got home and all his candles were burnt out and his tail tidied up, and he had been put to bed in the children's nursery, and the funny Mamma came to tuck them all in, she found her children pillow fighting and the crocodile sobbing dismally but softly all to himself. It took the funny Mamma a long time to find out what was the matter, but at last the crocodile sobbed out, "I want a doll."

The funny Mamma kissed the crocodile and said, "Of course you shall have one." And after chasing her children to bed she telephoned to Father Christmas for a big doll with real hair. But next morning, to her surprise, the crocodile looked just as sad, and when the children gathered round him he confessed, "This doll is no good to me – – I want a crocodile doll."

Each child ran in a different direction to buy a crocodile doll, and each returned with a nice green stuffed flannel crocodile.

The crocodile was happy at last and was a pleasing sight trying to eat its porridge holding in its arms its six long dolls.

All these children were the children of Mr. and Mrs. Happy Go Lucky and lived in Jollyville where their wise parents had chosen a house with lots of twisty turny passages in which to play Hide and Seek, with a few rooms opening off them in which to live, and a large garden whose trees had been specially trained for climbing. Indeed they held out branches invitingly in just the right places.

And these said the funny Mamma would not be too rough on the children's necks.

One afternoon the crocodile took his six green dolls out for an airing in a doll's perambulator, when suddenly it began to rain. The thoughtful crocodile tied the pram to a tree, and clasping his children in his arms, jumped into the river to keep out of the rain.

He was very much upset when he came out to find his children all sodden with water, quite spoilt. And he arrived home to tea in a most desperate frame of mind.

"Now cheer up," said the funny Mamma, and stirring the fire to a fine blaze she laid all the crocodile dolls around the fender, and when tea was over they were quite dry, and were soon pulled and patted into shape again.

The crocodile was growing more human every day. In this democratic household where all who chose to come and live were sure to be accepted on terms of perfect equality, the crocodile's better nature expanded under the sympathetic treatment. It was not long before he could scarcely tell the difference between himself and a child, and the funny Mamma would often lift him into her lap and only realised her mistake when she found that most of the crocodile was still sitting on the floor.

The crocodile became ambitious, he felt that if he could not be a child he could at least be as like one as it was possible to be. In fact the crocodile wished to go to school.

The children were called 1 2 3 4 5 and 6 because as their funny Mamma said so few children approve of the names their parents choose for them when they grow up, she had not thought it worthwhile to do anything more than number them until they were old enough to decide for themselves.

So 1 2 3 4 5 and 6 went to the school master and said, "Please Sir, the crocodile wants to come and be taught."

"Taught what?" said the school master very hurriedly.

"Lessons," said the children, "may it?"

"No," said the school master.

"Please," said the children.

"It is quite against the rules to receive pupils with even three legs and as for four! – – It would be a most unseemly example to the children, they would become dissatisfied with the number of legs apportioned to them and would probably quarrel with arithmetic."

"Sir!" said 6. "This crocodile has no teeth. He is quite accustomed to children. He sleeps in our nursery and lets Mamma tie on his bib."

"Well," said the school master, "you may bring him tomorrow to try, and if he is intelligent enough to pass his exams, which I very much doubt, I will accept him as a pupil."

"Oh thank you Sir," said all the children, "we promise you the crocodile will be perfect."

On Monday 1 2 3 4 5 and 6 took the crocodile to see a singing master. They waited nicely in the parlour and did not put their feet on the chairs. When the singing master came into the room he gave one look at the crocodile and dashing into the garden he climbed up the nearest tree.

The children followed him with the crocodile and called to him to come down. The singing master was trembling so hard that all the apples fell off the tree and the children were able to fill their pockets. And surrounding the tree they told the singing master that if he could not give a singing lesson they could.

"Now," said 1— "if you're a singing master, sing."

"B-b-bu-but," stammered the singing master quaking with fear.

"Sing," said 2. "Sing," said 3. "Sing," said 4 and 5.

And to each in turn the singing master only answered "B-b-bu-"

"We are going to stay here till you sing," said 6.

The poor singing master seeing there was no help for him tried his best, but the words would hardly come and the tree shook more than ever. He tried to sing "It's a Long Way to Tipperary" which somehow came into his mind, but it sounded more like somebody after a cold bath.

"Just smile at him, to encourage him," said the children to the crocodile.

The crocodile lifted up his head and opening his mouth – – – – – – . The effect on the singing master was magical, he quite regained his voice and the tree stopped shaking.

"Excuse me," said the singing master, "I was just looking for a bird's nest."

They went into the music room and the singing master sat at the piano and struck a note.

"Sing C," said the singing master.

The crocodile opened his mouth once more to sing – –

But this time the singing master was just as frightened as before he had been comforted at the sight of his open mouth. Indeed it was a strange sound the crocodile made.

"I think," said the singing master, "it is a doctor not a singing master that your friend requires." And bowed them to the door.

One day the children had a fine idea. They cut two fine rows of teeth out of white cardboard and fixed them in the crocodile's mouth.

There was a fair in Jollyville and the children had decided to make their fortune as well as the crocodile's so they put up a tent and hung up a big sign.

"Sixpence to see six little children put their heads in a crocodile's mouth."

The crocodile who would do anything to please his little friends, played his part as prettily as possible, and looked exceedingly ferocious when they put their heads between his teeth.

The news of this extravagant heroism spread through the fair, everybody came to visit the tent, not only the thousands of sightseers but also the very stall-holders of the fair themselves.

As you can imagine the children earned a large fortune.

GLORIA GAMMAGE

Gloria Gammage had arrived at Palms with regulation social intentions—her palace was tremendous and stuffed with things bought in the hurry of a woman with taste—and scattered around in the harmonious untidiness of temperament—erratically weeded in accesses of surfeit it was changing gradually to an ordered setting for what was most durable in her personality—

You could see Mr. and Mrs. Gammage from the States out at official receptions—Mrs. Gammage driving in the park with the most ungetatable dowagers—Mr. Gammage advising young dukes on the treatment of blight on wild oats—Mrs. Gammage spending with other young matrons of her millionheir class—Mr. Gammage drinking at the chosen confectioners where the ripe male generation of Palmian who's whos ruminated on the women and the cars behind in glass ambush—while the younger coroneted generation leaned up outside supporting the façade—while construing female biology.

But Gloria was one of those who exhaust modes of being in bursts of emptiness—and are early thrown for salvage on their instincts— And her big normal wide-eyed husband had his leisurely life put to it—to see that her instincts didn't get the better of him.

Having exhausted this marriage and the social prestige in Palms as inspirational agents she flopped herself on the chaise longue—and refused to budge.

She was more organically conscious of the men than most women who are, under their daily ritual of complex sophistication—so rudimentary that they have failed even to get into conscious connection with their own organisms—and function in a tepid pulp—of distantly removed irritations of longings they cannot sensitize—

Gloria's instinct had come to desire to stuff everything into her vulva to see what marvellous creative modifications it had undergone in the process—before chucking it away—

She had the divine female quality of lending to every latest science or philosophy no matter how mathematical or how austere—a ribald flavour of lubriciousness—with her insidious interest—she at this time was passing round "Bergson" to her friends—discoursing on it with those luscious eyes searching lovingly over their spiritual persons—that seemed to assure them that being was indeed as they had long suspected—an infinite orgy.

To Gloria, life, if only she get under the crust, was a pie, probably sweet—she wanted to stir and dip into it with her fingers—and pull out a plum.

She gave out that strong magnetic current of the "whole vitality" that calls to men and women alike—they required her to varnish their romances with her fuller interpretations—

She was the only woman who had conquered Palms—blown herself up for a voluntary ostracism—in which she could pick out some more bizarre ingredients from which to compound her inquisitive career—nourishment for her inquisitive soul.

She reached out for things and rid herself of them with the selfsame amplitude and never meditated on her actions—

The assurance of her states of mind came to her with lightning certainty—when she was bored she was bored—

Between her and Felicity—the little tweeny lawful furbelow bedfellow of the big—(hog-faced) X—who was most her equal in age provenance income and transatlanticness—there had long been a breach—on account of Gloria's eccentricities— The two husbands being of the same degree of social parity as their wives—were with the slower sociable processes of the male—still in the condition of intimate friendship—and had at last congratulated themselves on engineering a reconciliation between their respective beauties—

Gloria dines with Felicity—

On the evening on which Felicity is to dine with Gloria—she phones her—

Are you going to dine indoors or in the *pergola*—because I don't know whether to wear a heavier wrap—

Oh—that's of no consequence—don't bother to come at all answers Gloria—who has already acquainted herself with the ultimate possibilities of Felicity's reactions.

Felicity is still interested in Paris frocks—Gloria has just thrown her Paris frocks all over the bedroom floor—because they have no emotions—and offers them to any of the impecunious types with which she has begun to salt her entertainments—

"It's all nonsense," says her husband—standing—extending his pockets—over her chaise longue—where Gloria is smoking herself into a jaundice—"it's a question of making up one's mind—anyone can go to bed with anyone—if they have to"—

But Gloria all covered in priceless lace—in which she delights to drop hot ashes—has arranged to fly at midnight with the Ducca degli Cacciatori—and is listless to her husband's wooing—

She keeps a no man's land of meaning in these sleek stroking corners of her eyes—and Antony—who will never be able to construe its significance—is anxious that no man else ever shall—

In this way—keeping the secret—of the Sphinx.

And so it comes about that Antony that night—pounces upon the Young Cacciatori with a shotgun—which is not required—so precipitate is his withdrawal—leaving Gloria with something quite circumscribed in its potential "rowiness" to discuss with her Antony.

Now Gloria's income—though large enough to strike the population of Palms with terror for their prestige—is derived from the pleasure of a fabulously opulent Pappa with the universal dislike of scandal— And Antony's pleasure is a formidable weapon in Pappa's hand—

Gloria, knowing that she has invoked a crisis, takes the only possible means of gliding over a crisis—by invoking a more alarming crisis—one in which even such a crisis as that of matrimonial integrity shall pale in significance—and carefully measuring an enormous overdose of something frightfully dangerous—commits suicide—and is horribly sick.

With this commotion of the intestines she has fully paid the debt of threatened honour. The commotion in her extensive household is more than sufficient to drown the promptings of Jealousy—

Antony and Gloria—lounge about on her convalescent bed—
and decide that in all probability—her nerves would have been
more normal—if only they had had a child—for every month—
finds Antony mooing around the golden bedroom—and any stray
member of the house party is informed—that Antony is "the cow
mooing for its lost calf—"

HUSH MONEY

Daniel had come home to see his Father, whose handwriting had given out when he had been about to fulfill the only patriarchal action that he had been able to fulfill for some time. The signing of a cheque.

This at last produced in his wife signs of consternation.

Sir Somebody Something, the most expensive luxury Mrs. Bundy had ever enjoyed, pronounced upon examination with a ——oscope that Mr. Bundy's brain was rotten away "in patches," and that he would, after a rapid running down of the clockwork— lie like a log in his bed.

Daniel with a beating heart entered the spare bedroom where the father, *hors de combat* for the eternal conjugal polemics had, as it were, been put out to grass.

There was about him a sublime and hoary unconsciousness that made Daniel feel for a moment that he was looking at God.

But he was only a volcano that had exploded and fallen in, strewing itself with ashes.

Mrs. Bundy was appointed by the trustees to sign the cheques; she felt herself at last to have achieved what was due to her and rattled her keys.

+

Mrs. Bundy wrote very indignantly to Daniel on the departure of the seventh male nurse, the one who Daniel had known. He had endeavoured to protect his patient, already overexcited by the drugs prescribed for rotten patches, from the still more exciting persuasiveness of his wife— The poor half imbecile face sunk in the powerless shoulders became almost sane with apprehension at her approach.

And stripped by the expert insults of Mrs. Bundy's attack which forced all her adversaries to retreat for protection to their final justification—the truth—had enforced his diagnosis of the patient's necessity for peace with a report of her son's corroboration.

I—driven him—driven him indeed she wrote.

Daniel did not deny it. Her next communication was incredible—a cheque for £50.

Daniel realised that her consciousness, unfathomable calms of her conscience, had not been ruffled. She was buying an indulgence.

+

Daniel stayed with filial superstition to watch the clockwork run down. Mr. Bundy with two male nurses expounded at such times when he was not "worse" the marvellous intricacies of the simplest processes of the human mechanism, when he tried to use a fork.

When he was restless, he seemed always to be being led *away* from something by the two male nurses—all over the house. Once Daniel saw them shoving him hurriedly past his daughter, but all he heard was a mumbled

"She does, why shouldn't I?"

And yet Mr. Bundy had always shown a very marked horror of bad women—

The patient knew nobody present but was extremely occupied with the absent and he preferred to retire to those early years when things had not been wearing on him for so long—

When he was worse he would scream terribly, once at Daniel smoking at a top window, "You are catching on fire! You are catching on fire!"

He had been so anxious when Daniel was a boy that he should not begin smoking.

It was when he perceived anything actual, as in this case, a glowing at some distance, that his delirium became momentarily frantic. The sudden cognition of anything that was really *there* tortured him; within his world of fitful and reflex reactions he was only fidgety and ill at ease.

Daniel in his filial superstition sat hours upon the bench at the end of the garden under a row of aspen poplars that Mr. Bundy had planted as saplings in the early years of his misery—and had now grown very tall to rattle their eaves.

Mr. Bundy next to him, the "male" nurse on the other side.

Mr. Bundy and Daniel had been the members of the family who when addressed upon a particular subject had not retorted with a hot remark upon another subject. Conversation between husband and wife was like a game of tennis in which the husband served the ball gallantly to his wife—the wife retaliating with a lump of coal or a potato. Eventually as each ball had rolled away the balls became exhausted. And if it may take this imaginary game of tennis to symbolise a discussion of the children's schooling, the disposition of an income—the preparation for the holiday—we can understand that the Bundy family was a disordered one.

+

Daniel had developed that delicate feminine intuition of poets and often of men who have had mothers like Mrs. Bundy. In them nature seems to attempt to substitute the mother they should have had "outside" them with a mother inside.

He had acquired a vision of those signs and portents that men so often miss.

He felt as he sat by his father not that he was changed, not that he was absent, but that the centre of him had slipped inwards inwards and was buried under constantly dissolving currents of semi-lucid mud.

He had lost the thread of his life's discourse.

Daniel who could remember his father's repetitive reminiscences as he could remember the sky and the streets found that by pouncing on a remark—for his grandmother had been a South American woo'ed as a palliative on a business journey by his grandfather—while Mr. Bundy still smacked his lips—and answering it before the remark had dwindled into an anxiety as to the daughter's matrimonial prospects—she had now been married five years in spite of the mother's opposition—that he could keep up a racing, hurdle-leaping intercourse, for if the father intimated some story in his memory, the son could answer as if the complete narrative had been explored.

Gradually the eyes of Mr. Bundy assumed a partial peace. Sometimes they almost twinkled with the well-being of men sitting round the café table.

The more surprised to find himself answered, the more loquacious he became. The conversation became more connected—the frantic nightmares much more rare. He held his son's hand, and sometimes looked up peacefully at the trees.

And Daniel understood, that all his life—this man had had no one to speak to. He leant over and kissed him, and this man who Daniel had been told no longer knew anything about anything put his arms about him in terrible supplication and wept.

"Its extra-hordinary," said the male nurse, "the way 'e's pulled 'imself together since you been with 'im."

"Do you believe," asked Daniel—that anybody could be 'nagged' mad?"

"Do I berlieve—" answered the man volubly, as if he too had found a long-awaited audience— "Why—she can't let him alone even now—

"It sounds as if she were always 'opeing for a lucid moment in case she 'adn't really convinced 'im—as 'e's the bigger fool than 'er—

"Argue, argue, argue—and lookin' as though she feels 'er advantage—'im not being able to answer back any more—

"She'll come down in the morning so dignified and all—given' 'im that narsty look - -"

"Yet the specialist says his brain—"

"These 'ere specialists—they come in and 'ave a look around for 'arf a hour. Chock full of theories about some man as doesn't exist—

"They can't know nothing about people wot really 'ave to be alive. For these sort o' cases you'd a got to live in the family same as we do—we're the ones as finds out what's the matter.

"That's it. Nagged mad—and," he said significantly— " 'e ain't the only one—there's hundreds of 'em. You wouldn't believe—why even in yer own neighbourhood," sweeping his hands conclusively towards the narrow green gardens bumping their behinds into each other with their pantry windows and tradesmen's entrances steady as blind eyes—

"It's these 'ere little brick 'ouses—regular conservatory I'd say—

"You take it from me, your father ain't no more going to lie like a log—than I am.

" 'E's going to get better— More's the pity for 'im."

"But the specialist said his brain was rotten in—"

"You bet, they want to be so nice—got into serciety they have, they 'ave to prasoom that these 'ere married men wot shrieks at nothing at all, 'as been sitting all their lives in a angel's lap, while they just 'appened to rot away."

INCIDENT

A ridiculous little accident that happened to me just after World War I, while crossing the Place de la Federation, was the cause of a most significant experience.

I was hurrying to a tea-party with a friend. We were walking very quickly; arguing humorously, when, laughing, I nodded my head with what turned out to be exaggerated emphasis, which, as I was to realise later, dislocated my cranium from the spinal column.

Suddenly, I found myself "nowhere."

"Fool," I anxiously upbraided myself, "you've gone and let 'it' drop off"; spontaneously, as if it were quite usual for me to look upon my body as merely an instrument with which to contact one's universe, rather than my whole circumscribed "self."

An impression of physical discomfort where my neck "had been" soon ceased, but, for some time I seemed inescapably stuck in a solitary desolation: consciousness, with, never again, anything to be conscious *of*. This gave rise to terror so vast it exceeded my capacity for endurance, stemming from an uninter-ruptable impulse to contact, deprived of any contactual organ-ism. A terrified *conviction* of eternal existence while left without means of conveyance.

My preoccupation with this terror of long duration was so in-tense, I was unaware at what point it diminished, only, at last I realised I was at ease, free, unafraid, serene in an empty universe.

Very gradually, very low down, on an horizon in profundity, a faint, dark light began to penetrate the nothingness; a sombre lu-minousness I compared to the bluish base of a steel J nib that had fascinated me in childhood.

My ease became absolute, transcending any ease of the body, as if I had entered an ultimate safety-zone, I looked forward with placid curiosity, to the different gamut of experience I *knew* awaited me. I felt no concern for the world I was lately involved with. That world had *ceased*; the way a radio-television programme, once turned off, would no longer be conveyed to one.

I was stimulated by an innate assurance of high adventure for consciousness, when my rapt attention, focussed on that incipi-ent light, patient for the intuited revelation, seemed slowly to be drawn aside toward some issue of little consequence.

The cause of this interference was the dim forewarning of a "click"; as if an echo should precede, rather than follow on a sound, a sound which, about to be audible, seemed to herald the arrival, at some distance from the point where I was receiving impressions, of a form, whose proximity gradually increased. Suddenly, a shaft of rushing "force," with an impact-potential of incalculable tonnage descended from above upon that form. On

37

its approach, I reflected, "The whole force of the universe! It will crush that body to infinitesimal fractions of atoms." I *knew* the form was about-to-be-a body, for although I had no organs of sense, I *saw* it out there in the dark, its contours so vaguely phosphorescent, just as I could *hear* the tornado-like thunderous onrush of, infinite force.

I did not associate the body-contour, which had had no existence in my emptied universe prior to the annunciatory "click," with myself at all, as I waited, totally disinterested, for the expected collision; but as that shaft of force contacted the area on top of the cranium which at birth is open, at once ceasing to be cognisable by me, it slid easily, ethereally through the brain, down the spinal column, as lightning down a lightning rod, only, instead of running into the earth, it reanimated that body, now standing beside me not more than a yard away.

At the same time, the click becoming more immanent, my liberated self, the body-contour and the intervening space telescoped into one another. While *knowing* what was about to happen, I inwardly exclaimed, noway surprised, disappointed or elated, for this "other" condition seemed devoid of emotion, only of absorbing interest, "After all I am not going to find out this time," as though any time, owing to inevitability, would do.

The click concluding, I found myself "coming alive" again, as my leg, lifted in taking a hurried step, depending from a body that had lost control, crashed to the pavement, throwing my skull back again, as I heard it click (the almost timeless click of our usual time-perception) into its habitual relation to the vertebrae.

My companion, ―― ―― turned anxiously toward me was asking, "Hadn't you better lie down?" in the middle of a public square! "All at once you actually became a corpse. It's inexplicable. There's no mistaking a corpse."

"Actually, I must have dislocated a vertebrae," I laughed rather shakily, "Just for a fraction of a second."

During my disjunctional nod of humorous acquiescence my blood had already almost frozen; as if one's circulatory system functions somewhat in accord with that other measure of time. For quite a while I could *feel* the unbelievable force and celerity with which it zoomed from the top of my head, over my shoulders, down my arms, in glacial cataracts; and, biological curiosity, I could have sworn that a block of ice, little over a square inch, had been neatly inserted in either elbow; just, by the way, at the seat of the funny-bone.

– –

So this was Life; being a sort of magnet to a sort of universal electricity, while in some deeper stratum of consciousness there lies embedded a familiarity with eternal existence withheld from our every-day consciousness; but the origin and nature of *that*, which, retaining its identity, experienced all this, remains as great a mystery as ever.

It so happened that some days later my baby's nurse, reminiscing on her hospital work, mentioned how rare were cases of survival after arrested circulation. She also told me, how, in the few cases coming under her medical observation, there was invariably evident one outstanding phenomenon. Every patient entertained the illusion that blocks of ice had been inserted in their elbows. This, without my telling her of my strange little accident or having in any way brought up the subject.

LADY ASTERISK.

The Russian ambassador—and King Edward's mistress at the
prime minister's dinner table—
    Said Mrs. Birthright—
I can't imagine your reason for refusing promotion—
    And the ambassador—
I prefer to remain. You Englishwomen are the best bedfellows
    in the world—
Pure—so perfectly abandoned
I am proud to be able to say—
I have possessed every woman—
    at this table—
My wish is never to leave London—
There isn't a woman amongst us who hasn't committed adultery—
    And—mine—they
    turned such a lovely pink!—
But Mrs. Birthright belonged to the old school—

She always spoke of her life as if she had "not been there"
   had caused more scandal! – –
And she was unassailable—
The only thing that gave her away for the least of her peccadilloes—
Was the stamp of royalty she bore upon her—
   It never wore off—
More queenly than the queen as I watched her age—
   She never faded—
but receded—somehow—ceremoniously—
   Behind her regal presence
   The avoidance of wrinkles had made her callous to the expression of the emotions—
And she was so damnably kind—
But when we reviewed the moral of the after-war
   I could see as a cloud drifted across her eyes—
   That she regretted having at least wasted—*half* her time.
   The finest analysis of the moral order—
   Is in these older women's eyes
   You can see them thinking
   How frightfully unnecessary were all those lies—
   From so many degrees of virtue—those women who mustn't be found out—and the women who came to do it in Paris—and the apostles of England's new criminal offence—
   How different it all is—
   They usen't to dare
   be *seen* with a man—
   And now if there is no man they must at least consort with "something" that wears half his clothes.

And even the Night has lost its prohibitive mystery having become—the frenetic nursery of youth.

The jailor-mother has disappeared—and the problem of enforcing chastity.

"My dear that 'difficult' period with our girls—"

Galahadism for our boys?

They have solved the sex question.

Nothing much need happen all you have to do is to keep 'em jumpin'

And cocktails make fine wooers—but they take all the kick out of love philtres—

If we are to preserve our Civilisation we must avoid climax—

Keep 'em jumpin'—

And jazz is such a stimulus to memory—

right back to when you were nothing but steam in a coal forest—

We can recapitulate our reproductive history—

through the saxophone—

without an effort!

You can remember everything only you don't know what it was—

Everything's changed—

But *nothing* officially— That gives us the slant on political freedom— Everyman his own soul—if he won't mention it. The Bolshevik—is such a mutt he can't *play*—

So he doesn't want anyone else to—they'll have Pegasus cleaning out his own stable—

Moral social and intellectual supremacy—is the sense of humour

Well—the King hasn't got a sense of humour—

No but that's just our sense of humour—

And Bernard Shaw hasn't got a sense of—

No but believe me it was one—twenty-five years ago—

Dekobra bagged his Bolshevist—

When their minister crossed himself and muttered his prayers when the peeress proposed to him—

This was long before the war when only the aristocracy explained themselves—

It was about the time that George Moore—

Said dear lady—Asterisk

I should so much like to have you – – –

   "No?"—

– – – well perhaps another cup—thank you!

This stirred the London intelligentsia up—"So *brilliantly* casual – –"

And then there were all those eminent beauties

Chewing the cud of the latest divorce scandal—

And Eve got up and stamped

What's the use of all this humbug?

Tearing that poor woman to shreds

George Moore—has forgotten how to read—he says nobody has got any talent any more—George Moore knows that he knew how to write—because his father was a gentleman—and then he stuffed all his mistresses with "literature"—

None of them ever came forward to explain what really happened—they belonged to the generations of women who suffered in silence—

And now he himself lies buried in the last Bustle—

The highest culture of the upper classes is the study of the lower classes through art.

Creation, simply—was destroyed by the concept Art.

Art is a grimace of creation.

Creation—is the making - - -

Art is the aping - - - -

A critic who should say— Men are as yet so inexperienced that they are in all their most practiced pursuits—ignoramuses—

That even great literature is the supreme confession of ignorance—and that love is a factory—where all employees bungle their jobs—

But take heart—and do not kill that critic—for he will also explain it to you—

That it is not you the individual that is inadequate—

But tradition—

There is certain proof that love is a closed book—for if it were not so— Novels would not be written—

If the engineering of love were acquired—

The sex-psychology of our era would become immediately meaningless

IN MAINE: GREEN'S COLONY

For Maine is clean.

There are no corners where it may hide, space patrols every side of every house, and has not so far separated them that the eye of your neighbour's window—cannot pierce the eye of your own. There they are always sweeping something away, they are always shaking something out, they trade, they bank, they "ever" prosper in a modest way—

That Satan still—some mischief "may not" find—for idle hands to do.

There is nothing more rigidly occidental than the deportment of Maine—

Yet Maine is always backing away from an onslaught with prohibiting and perpendicular palms—as in a certain oriental dance.

It is certain that Maine has never known it—

Maine has never unbent—to behold itself into the inner mirror of its consciousness.

Maine still wears corsets and starches, whitewashes because of what is underneath.

But Maine has never routed its origin—that impetus that stirred the steaming swamps to life—it has retained the tradition, and swept it off, onto his neighbour's grass plot.

But I know that when I tried to smoke in the son's den, which had been converted into a lodger's room, the eye of the opposite window was fully aware.

The den had a different atmosphere than the rest of the house, sporting a rep drapery, where the mystifications of adolescence positively lurked and a volume of Plutarch's *Lives* in which I read—

"It is dangerous—to incur the enmity of a people who have the gift of song—"

John Straher was about 50—he had his own land, and sent his wife and family away on vacations, but John was not above doing a little sweeping, or a little chopping to oblige a neighbour.

He was so well preserved that it was a foregone conclusion that in another ten years he would blossom into that belated adolescence of the 100 percent clean American, who fumbles at young women with the postponed courage, the desperation of dissolution.

He would probably find his affinity.

It is doubtful however if John Straher would ever grow up to such a word—he had once travelled with the circus as a sword swallower—he could even now—my impression is a little vague—but I believe it was—push a grass blade up one nostril and pull it down the other—he could appreciate—he could drive a fast horse and buggy in a jaunty manner but he could not speak.

This was particularly trying for me as he had chosen me for the confidant of his "clean" passion for Lucy.

Lucy was all that Maine unconsciously potentially typified. She spent her winters raving in sanatoriums—in summer she had the most astounding mixture of the complacency of a cow and the brightness of a robin— In summer although she lived in the going on, fastest set in New York—she was the cleanest thing I have ever met. She always looked as if she were about to sing in the church choir, but in the sanatorium, even the interns were said to have learnt from her.

Maine responded. Although the mind of Maine was differently divided, keeping its sanatorium within and not without, perpetually and not intermittently—it knew at once that Lucy was like itself—quite clean.

Maine adored her—she also was never averse to lending a hand, at a little sweeping, a little shaking out.

John Straher would switch at his horse and chew a wisp with such dynamic meditation that it was painful to set within range of his knit eyebrows—

He would wag his beautiful iron-grey head in horrible perplexity and say,

I do like Lucy, I do like Lucy, gosh how I do like Lucy. She's a nice girl is Lucy—I never saway a nicer girl than Lucy. She's a clean girl is Lucy.

His chest would heave with a bewilderment that was tearing it. He would even whip his horse.

Then his eyes would clear with a potential poetry, that filled his conception of Lucy with the fleeing beauty of the laden autumn hedgerows—and his silence. And when he could bear it no longer, he would strike his knee with his twitching corded hand—and say—

I do *like* Lucy.

A short conversation for a long drive; other men with the same kind of faces had made me their confidant, they had told me how "her" body was a vase of fairest alabaster, and how they had longed to break it and sprinkle the ruby wine of "her" warm young life upon the altar of eternity— One had told how he had clasped her beautiful throat and pressed her head down, down—(nearly)—into the glowing embers of the hearth—because they were both seekers of new sensations.

These things are difficult for such as do not read the smart set to understand— John Straher was after all more lucid— Yet one wished for his own sake that he had a word or two to spare. A tremendous deal of shy sympathy—for Lucy was idiotically delightful—and a superhuman wrestle with his mind—at least achieved his fullest measure of expression.

I feel, I feel, that if she were ever sick, I should take her home to my house and nurse her— Yes! More, I should give her the best there is.

I do like Lucy.

Gosh she's a nice girl is Lucy—

If she were sick I would nurse her.

This is a clean thing mind you. I could look her husband in the eyes any day.

But *suppose* she were to fall sick when her husband was in New York— Why shouldn't I take her home and nurse her? I never seen such a nice girl as Lucy.

With nothing but a pocket vocabulary a man that looked at you like that—could have done horrible damage. As things were, it was his pleasingly redemptive doom to disappoint woman at once—but not later—

Lucy did just wish he had lived in Manhattan—

Love can talk to its "each other" with many couplings of languages as Malayan and French—but not in the language of Maine—to Maine.

I have tried to imagine how Mr. and Mrs. Granger for instance whose enlarged bridal portraits hung over the cottage grand had initiated the honeymoon with

Gosh you are a clean man—

Say but you're a clean girl

—there was the son in the den to account for.

This stranger, this guest entertained unawares whose incognito Freud has forever unveiled. The worthies of Maine in banishment from their own breasts preferred to have taken murky refuge in their neighbours'.

They denounced "it" for they knew it must be somewhere about.

The ray of the clean mind of Maine swept through its habitations like a search light, in which those poor stark unprotected wooden houses gave a perfect representation of living "morally" inside out.

The guest that lurks even as it lurked in those steaming swamps of a yet unpopulated planet—in the hot mud and the primeval bottom of the Maine consciousness.

We were driving back. John's horse was hoofing up a cloud of dust and John having relieved himself of his unpronounceable aspirations, his Maine masked *élan vers l'idéal* had his reaction. He became voluble. He was talking about the neighbours.

He told me that Mrs. Granger's son had syphilis—that he was a devil with the women—and had imparted it to every school girl—in the village. Where every moment of everyone's time was so meticulously "counted," where every door and every window—so collectively and so incessantly watched—where everyone one with every reason had ascribed that particular attribute of God—allseeing—to the villagers.

Young Granger had violated the innocent who returned from school along the short straight roadway under the long straight eyes of the Maine mothers watching from their well scoured stoops. He had walked diabolically abroad when doors were doubly locked and dogs barked—and grandparents slept lightly.

He had lived "conquering" while his mother's manifold chores had to be accomplished, his spirit like the werewolf—had miraculously emanated while he sat nightly by the window of the den without shades, transparent curtains in the bright light of the lamp, fondling his fraternity relics on the wall—and learning the danger of incurring the enmity of a people that have the gift of song.

When John Straher sang his song of Young Granger, he had that same suspicious, half tame gesture of self protectingly pushing something out of him into anywhere—no matter where else—with which I had seen Young Granger regard the women from New York, and indeed everyone except his excellent Mamma.

This black magical quality seemed according to my raconteur to be inherent to every inhabitant of Maine—and gradually as we neared the village post office where from so very far away—we could descry the most fearful miscreants leaning, as they did every night against the wooden posts and door jambs, dangling

51

their unformulated legs from the fence—chewing their wisps of chaw—and looking seemingly out onto the infinite horizon of blind men—

As we neared this post office, I learned that some members of "our" party had already, after an unwilling stay of 48 hours, become intricated in the local saga.

The Prince who divided his attention seemingly between his monocle and his motherless boy—had issued out upon the evening of our arrival—at such time as he was actually telling us ghost stories round the log fire—to patting John Staher intimately on the back—"the filthy libertine" enquired, "Where can I find one about here?"

And had been directed to the only thing they had of that description—

"Bad Mary of Maine."

Bad Mary was pretty bad—she was old angry and dusty and when I saw her, she was tramping up from a great distance with a basket of raspberries as her official presentation to the visitors, and she also proffered her desire to sweep anything up, to shake anything out.

There had been, according to John, nobody who had not benefitted by the embraces of those branchlike work-ridden arms and hands—the glances of that slightly glazing eye.

It was widely known that she preserved the portrait of a Spanish sailor who had once lain low with measles in her husband's shack—and had moreover received a letter of thanks from him on his subsequent voyage.

The Strumpet!

Though this underworld could never become very real to me there was yet a mystery which spurred my curiosity. On the road from the village to the lake woods—I passed a crazy sign.

"Green's Colony"

What is Green's Colony I asked in turn of everyone in the village—and of each one in turn I received—the answer of a deadly silence. It cost me great pains to discover the grim secrets of this colony of Greens.

Well you know said my informant most reluctantly, what a moron is—what a cretin is, what a degenerate is?

yes—yes—

Well that's what they are in Green's Colony—

Having at last decided on telling me, he meant to tell me really well. And as if the subject were one too vast for him he called together a few of his friends to help—

They presented it to me surprisingly well.

Nobody any longer dared to take that menacing path beyond the crazy sign—it was more than one's life was worth—

But they could remember. Now things were getting more and more fearful, someone had once unwittingly strayed there and had not returned—either at all—or at least not what they were before.

They were not very clear as to which.

These degenerates were a race sprung from an unnatural brother and sister and had in a few filthy hovels continued to breed prodigiously in the same biblical manner—

They were dwarfed, they were hunched, some of them were web-footed, some web-fingered and from the half demolished hedges of that ostracised domain—their microcephalus heads with bulging eyes would "start out at you". Their major impulse was murder then minor rape. They bred at deplorably infantile ages—their lives were spent in one long loathsome lust. In one infested lair, you could find if anyone dared to go there, five generations, forming the seraglio of the same pappa.

They had their own fearsome language of signs and snarls.

A tremendous interest in this race of dithering imbeciles supporting, clothing, protecting themselves without a keeper sprang up in me.

I must go and see. It was hard to take no heed of the frightened admonitions and vehement warnings—for one who finds it good sport to be alive—I should be flayed by the first prowling maniac for they were superhumanly strong, and then I should remember what they had told me. But my curiosity refused to die—by what amazing instinct did they light fires for themselves against the rigorous winters, who wove their clothes— How breed those more decently domestic animals on whom to feed— I enquired of many details— but was assured they were absolutely witless with their heads the size of an orange. They only knew how to kill and fornicate.

I asked and asked, I never found a strong man to protect me, but at last the fragile wife of a painter took up the idea with enthusiasm—we would go together—only a very genuine succession of vile headaches threatened to postpone our adventure indefinitely—and I went out to it alone.

But I did take a very stout walking stick to beat them off a little—in case – – – –

It was after all not such a long way, I wondered how it was the "dangerous" people never wandered—

A peaceful place.

The sunrays seemed to be zipping through the humming bees over the vibrant flowers of light— Everything smelt sweetly of everything else.

The riot of summer before it has succumbed to its own heat— the very dust was like a carpet in heaven—

It was impossible to feel afraid on such a day.

And after all they seemed to have their keepers, for at the outpost of the colony there stood a beautiful house covered with honeysuckle.

From the door onto the garden where a venerable old gentleman sat over the soup-tureen with his napkin tied over his magnificent white beard, a melodious tinkling of china issued like the call home from Wonderland that ended Alice's dream.

The wife who also issued out of the honeysuckle was just as well starched as Mrs. Granger, but she had not the same damning aspect, her human nature like her skin was one "you love to touch."

I almost shouted with joy at the way they called good day to me—

I prowled around to see if there were any strange children—

There were none at all—

So I walked along toward a roof on a distant hill, passing on the way a dilapidated house at which I knocked.

There was nobody at home.

Nobody starting out of the hedges – – –

The house on the hill was built of stone and banged against the sun—its meadows sloped away from it into the shade, where an ancient ploughshare lay under an apple tree and a few white fowls pottered among the gleaming dandelions and daisies—

* * * * *

Everything around the place is just something to play with—
You see the school house is too far off— Thanks be to the Lord.
And we aren't for putting any kind of notions into her head—
God's the best schoolmaster for her kind—said Grandfather Green stretching his toes further out in the sunlight—while his old wife nodded to him.
Do you see anything of the people in the village—
Eh what—? *Them* newcomers— Nope—never set eyes on 'em— our little bit o' tradin', we do with the town over t'other side.

* * * * *

On my way home, I found the door of the dilapidated house wide open, and Bad Mary of Maine shading her glazing eyes with her hand invited me in—
She cleared me a space among the indescribable gimcracks of her poverty.
The place was not clean, those branch-like arms had begun to wither—sometimes she would stumble up a lame wooden staircase—to take stock of her bedridden husband—whose face seemed to have stuck fallen forever onto the flyblown linen of the pillow—
everyhow

MONDE TRIPLE-EXTRA

Contes Tommy-Rots

A couple of estimable parents who had believed in the establish-ment of a Moral Order became so disheartened with the proceeds, that they brought up the fag-end of their family atrociously.

With the result that while all the elder children are now work-ing in factories, the last daughter married a prodigious profiteer, and the last son grew up with a certain little lift to the left corner of his mouth when he smiled —————

This son Jove Ivon Corvon I found one day seated under a hedge meditating upon his adolescence.

"Mina Loy," he cried on perceiving me, "You know something of life ——— Tell me how to live."

"I know only this," I replied, "That he who cannot live on his smile, lives not at all."

It was not long before Jove Ivon Corvon had heaved himself into the highest society, and his fame spread to the four corners of the cosmopolitan world. And every night when he came home, his spacious halls would look like a harem or a ——— So many women of fashion awaited him.

Jove Ivon was of a playful nature and loved to tease these wakeful aspirants to his favours.

Some nights when the place teemed with aristocracy and stars, he would enter with an anaemic flower girl, or a flimsy waitress, and guiding her with hovering devotion through the ignored exasperated crowd, would disappear with her through a heavy door in the mysterious distance.

Upon which there would follow a great scuffling of footmen and blowing of whistles for taxis. For as the psychologists tell us War would be impossible were not each soldier convinced that the soldier beside him, and not himself must fall; so had each eager lady dismissed her chauffeur confident that she uniquely would no longer require him.

It was a sight to see Jove Ivon Corvon fondling a stray kitten he had brought home with him in the bosom of his idyllic overcoat, while he watched the effect on those ladies attending upon his moods.

Magical slips of women, who in their brief and careless gowns, appeared to possess no human forms at all.

But on investigation revealed a firmness of ivory-coned bosom, and fluent curve of rosy thigh as would persuade us to believe that all modists are hypnotists.

Jove Ivon Corvon fondled his thin kitten with so genuine an ardour, stroking its muddy fur with such affectionate legerdemain, that the sensibilities of his uninvited seraglio succumbed to the torture, and several swooned.

But Jove Ivon persisted in stroking his kitten to the cosmic rhythm, while a galaxy of wistful eyes swayed with his wandering fingers.

"Tell me, Jove Ivon Corvon" said *la petite* Duchesse de Da Da, "Why is it that you can be so kind to a kitten, when you are so cruel to women?"

Jove Ivon lowered his eyelids in a subliminal uprush of pudicity, and answered with a blush and a whisper

"Because the kitten does not desire me."

On hearing this reply of Jove Ivon Corvon —— the ladies arose in silence and deserted those halls. Some of them arrived home safely, a few, entirely disheartened, eloped with Apaches, one or two withdrew to the convent of the Sacré Coeur.

And at the next performance of the Opera exquisite creations in kitten fur were strongly in evidence.

This *geste négligent* of Jove Ivon Corvon's was not entirely a pose, for he was in a fair way to become blasé.

All the women he knew were too beautiful, and his passion had become glacial.

He was notoriously the worst lover in the world, which in view of women's disposition towards self-sacrifice and reform work was not the least of his advertisements.

But this state of soul could not last.

The very next morning Jove Ivon arose early and donning a dressing gown of hummingbird's wings embroidered with emerald Catherine wheels, he wandered among the marble pillars of the lobby, we can only surmise, urged by the presentiment that a few corpses might be lying in the shadows.

When his eyes beheld, not dead, but alive, and of unfamiliar animation, a woman such as he had never seen.

Of a new shape, refreshing to his eyes, the full curves of her bust meandered into the folds of a skirt revealing only her feet (so much larger than the insignificant little things he was so weary of—). And her loose slippers flapped rhythmically to and fro as she walked.

In her hands she held a great sceptre or wand decorated at its lower extremity with a mass of soft wisps matted together like a mermaid's hair and of the colour of twilight.

This she was waving about in mystical arabesques upon the tessellated pavement, driving before her a shallow flood of beautiful water.

Like a cloud in a wind her grey figure would curve hither and thither. And as Jove Ivon watched her he saw how she conjured the beautiful water with her wand from out of a circular receptacle made of a metal that was most probably dead silver from the craters of the moon. While the pillars reflected in its contents danced in zig-zags of sky white.

The soul of Jove Ivon Corvon was exalted and when he discovered that some of her hairs were made of light, so purely argent they shone, in spite of his fear that the vision would evaporate, he revealed himself. And allowing his smile to steal—like dawn—across his lips, lifting ever so little that left corner ——————— he waited for it to take effect.

The vision entirely overcome by his garment of humming emeralds, planted one hand on her hip —— a powerfully archaic gesture —— and cried in a voice unlike other voices

"Lookit the guy!"

"O rarest of women," said Jove Ivon Corvon, "My name is not Guy, but if such is the appellation you choose to bestow upon me, you have only to baptise me with that beautiful water, and under that name I will live and die."

And stretching out his arms towards her in the great longing of his newborn heart, he did indeed receive a shower of the marvellous liquid on his impassioned brow.

With this supreme encouragement he gathered the unearthly creature to his breast, whereupon she with her magic did something passing strange to his head with the wand; allowing him the privilege of perceiving in their brilliancy an undiscovered constellation of stars.

And even as he reflected that here was a super-woman Good Fortune had trailed across his triumphant path did he become aware that she evaded him ———— was fleeing away from him!

As he gave chase he could observe the captivating detail of her clothes. Beneath the back of her bodice was arranged a peeping space of folded white and two fluttering ends of some unshining ribbon tinged like ancient alabaster, enrapturing his pursuit.

As often as he caught up with her she would repulse him, and Jove Ivon Corvon was soon leaping at her in a shower of iridescent blue feathers and sparkling emeralds, while the object of his Adoration swept him off from her with the mop of matted twilight, or jerking the wand with lightning dexterity among his feet ————

Jove Ivon, elated with these Eleusinian mysteries incident to his introduction to the favours of his super-woman, hopped in and out of the beautiful water with ecstatic alacrity.

The super-woman, to the syncopated accompaniment of her wand upon the pavement, chanting meanwhile

  "Young manile

  Aveyouno

          asima lidy
          Iāmm"

How long it was before Jove Ivon Corvon lost consciousness, or
if that Monde Triple-Extra ever learned that its most elusive idol
was vanquished by a matutinal charwoman, I do not know.

Should you protest that owing to his origin which I have touched
upon, Jove Ivon Corvon in his youth must have been only too familiar with middle-aged women who earn the rewards of virtue
by mopping other people's floors, which renders her metamor-
phosis in his imagination glaringly improbable, I can only suggest
that Youth is occasionally incapable of aesthetic reaction to wom-
ankind prior to adolescence.

Thus she was enabled to appear to him in the light of a virginal
visitation.

NEW YORK CAMELIO

Camelio has disappeared————
he is sitting upon the table of the ladies' cloak room holding his
bronze flame in his hands—the bronze flame suffers horribly—
apparently—from champagne.

A woman with a horse's face her lips coloured crooked—and a
dirty toby frill—has taken Camelio in her arms—

Darling, wails she, I cannot bear to see you killing yourself—

Camelio crawls down the tremendous marble steps and splashes
goldenly into the gutter.

Camelio is unconscious—

A big fat motor is backing into Camelio—

Woman attempts to drag him out of the gutter, unconsciousness is heavy—

Within an inch of the wheels Camelio somersaults onto the
sidewalk—

He is stuffed into a taxi—

A woman puts her little finger into Camelio's mouth—
he sucks it like a young calf
The woman is meditating primevally on how unconsciousness
relapses to the tremendous suction of life that drew man out of
chaos — — — —

Do you suppose asks Camelio that you can behave yourself at
least while we are in the elevator—

Camelio profile of a Bach prelude is lying on the table like a plate.
The woman with the toby frill whose mouth is now on her forehead—is moaning over his approaching dissolution—

It is known that Camelio has—Camelio has heart disease

PAZZARELLA

There was once a woman, and some golden hair is all the incognito I shall allow her.

In her boudoir, where I found myself by chance, the long windows opened on to a garden so overloaded with foliage that the infrequent flowers seemed to invite reproof for being gaudy. This Pazzarella, for so I have named her, succeeded in diffusing in the atmosphere a vague evaporative quality so illusively irritating that it exasperated me as nothing had ever done before.

Surrounded by fading colours and clouded mirrors, seated before the tarnished gilding of a dilapidated clavichord, she let her idle fingers under their crepuscular jewels crawl over the keys, evoking tired melodies that sobbed and slipped into the silence without defining their complaint.

When she was unoccupied she was just as disturbing. Her eyes resembled two bewildered swallows flown by accident into her face and caught in lines of suffering as yet undefined. Eyes that, being lost, had become fixed in patient expectation of clairvoyance, neglecting the present to search for the unknown. There was something about her of a plant that has matured in a cellar as though she had had to draw her alimentary light from an enduring twilight.

She spoke but little, replying to the remarks addressed to her with a desperate finality as if for some inscrutable reason she had been forbidden to speak.

The indiscernible traces of agony predicted on her youthful face provoked my ire—I was spurred by a desire to see them defined. Her unrevealing conversation filled me with a wild necessity to silence her, once and for all.

Her fragile body, whose voluptuous frustration seemed to evoke the couplings of butterflies and reptiles, rather than seduce the full-blooded male, forbidding in advance any possible illusion of satiety, congealed my veins in a glacial passion.

I approached her with the full intention of throwing myself upon her, when in the nick of time I recovered my reason. One possesses a woman out of desire; there is no known biological law that forces a civilized man to exterminate a perfectly amiable hostess for the sake of a couple of musical grimaces between two cups of tea.

I launched myself on a philosophical argument to thaw my arteries, which my companion punctuated with occasional gleams of intelligence, and little by little I began to feel safe in my superior acumen and the obvious appreciation of my audience.

My fantastic fury died down as I entrenched myself in my lucidity. It seemed as if, after all, there were definite points of contact between myself and this disquieting person. The butterfly fluttered away, the reptile undulated into oblivion, and I was beginning to feel quite at ease with her when, after apparently listening to all I had to say, she suddenly exclaimed, "But whatever *is* philosophy, and why do your eyes strike off such icy green sparks?"

Ah, then there was no withholding myself, and I did throw myself upon her. In a sadistic delirium of destruction I determined to put an end to her. When I regained my calm, I found I had only possessed her.

"I am so fond of you," she sighed.

"The worse for you."

"My affection—"

"But are you mad?"

"I am a woman."

I lifted up her face to take a good look at it. The prognostics of sorrow were effaced, the resuscitated roses of her lips bloomed in a contemptible beatitude—and God! how she chattered.

Evidently her impact with the male had shattered her silence. She flooded me with universal trivialities pouring from her cerebral confusion into an indefinite concept she reverently referred to as "love."

I rose to depart. But Pazzarella entreated me to stay, drawing me after her by my two hands, with the air of leading me on in some portentous expedition which made me sufficiently curious to let her have her way.

Graciously she led me through her apartment where an intrinsic sense of void produced an impression of vastness, and solemnly she would stop before the door of each chamber, whose furniture seemed to haunt its pitiable emptiness, and on entering each one with me, embraced me ceremoniously as if she desired to obtain a "fixation" of our presence "together" in every desolate enclosure of her home.

This sort of procession intrigued me immensely. I could not catch its significance until all at once the Pascal Benediction recurred to my mind. The Parish Priest accompanied by his acolyte visiting the houses of the devout at Eastertide to asperse their rooms with holy water. Was my passing intended to bless those vacuous lairs of my guide? Their solitude seemed hardly prepared for a blessing—it must be for an exorcism that my services were required. An involuntary shudder ran through me—how fearful must be the blank expanses of Time shut into those charming rooms, that this living enigma had the pretension to be rid of in consecrating them to a man who had just raped her.

"I have waited so long—so long—"

"Why?"

"Just waiting," she murmured.

"For what?" I insisted.

"Ah, if only I knew. Probably I shall never find out what I am waiting for, nevertheless I can make my choice."

"Oh—then you believe in the *Libre Arbitre*?"

"No—I merely choose. That is quite a different thing, for the confirmation of my choice is beyond my power."

"And may I ask what it is you have chosen?"

"You," she cooed quite contentedly, and her face fell onto my waistcoat.

"Evidently the *Libre Arbitre* doesn't come in there."

"It is several years since I began to love you."

"But you didn't know me."

"I have never known you—I shall never know you—but I have seen you."

"But—?"

"If you knew what countless numbers of my similars have never even seen the man they love."

"You're only raking up a platitude, 'In love with love.' Where does a man come in?"

"And yet I believe a man—"

"No—you trust in love."

"One must believe—love IS."

"And," I smiled, "*L'amore come si fa*— How is love made?"

"*L'amore si fa*— One makes love."

"Listen to me," I said, "and take this advice. If you really want, not love, but to *be* loved, leave off choosing—let somebody choose *you*."

"*You* have chosen me!"

"Chosen! Pazzarella—try to understand me—You are the most irritating creature I have ever come across. You irritate me to my very marrow."

"Your intimate irritant—"

"Intimate!!"

"And to think there are women, poor things, who do not even succeed in *irritating* the man they love."

A certain ambiguity in the triumphant inflection of these last words, vaguely disturbed me. I looked sharply into those feminine eyes, but they told me nothing. They were beginning to wander again.

"So you have not chosen me after all—"

"Decidedly not."

"Still, all the same—when you—isn't that what is called possessing a woman?"

"Ah—yes!"

"Why?"

"Because there's nothing in it."

In those intelligent eyes a reply began to twinkle, but her lips grimly closed upon it.

"Tell me," I insisted.

"It is the coronation of masculinity," she prevaricated, entirely taken up with interlacing her useless fingers with my unruly hair.

"Good-bye, Pazzarella."

"Forever?"

"Let us hope so."

"Who knows?" she mused.

"Pazzarella," I burst out, "I am not a beast—I am *MYSELF*."

"I know," she acquiesced, kissing me tenderly.

"I only want what is best for you."

"Then *you* give *me* a kiss."

"That would be hardly relevant."

"Good-bye," I called out, "give yourself to the first man who chooses you. You'll get your love." With this I left Pazzarella safely behind the door and I could breathe in freedom again.

The same evening a note was brought to me by hand, and this is what was written in it— "Why must a lump of female flesh, separate me so completely from all that is dear to me in the world—"

On the morrow I left for Paris and the only news I received of the amorous experiment I had prescribed for her, were these two lines

"O Geronimo, save me from this man who has desire as a dog has thirst, who makes love with the address of an able surgeon."

Never, have I been so offended, as by that spirited analysis. Not content with being unfaithful to me, she made light of her accomplice, and this attitude of hers so closely allied me with him, that I ceased to be clear as to whether it was *my* war or his I must henceforth wage upon her. Was he not my brother in arms? So obvious it was that a common enemy attacked the sacred and inalterable front of masculine solidarity.

I decided to pay her another visit on my return.

When I saw her again, she had greatly changed, having acquired in the short interval a certain audacity. Her eyes no longer sought for anything. Her clothes were extremely attractive, and she was even more beautiful than before, with that fixed and useless beauty some women assume out of mere contrariness when the longed-for fruits, rewards of beauty, have been withdrawn.

"But you," I exclaimed ironically, "are getting on magnificently."

"There is no denying it," she laughed. "I have revived. I am exploiting my soul whereas formerly my soul exploited me." Then with a profound *moue*, "Please, Geronimo, say—'Woman *has* no soul.'"

"You are monstrous," I cried. "A genuine cerebral masochist—does it give you such very great pleasure to have a man insult you?"

"We-ell, it does make it more difficult for him to impress me."

The call to arms was sounding. Giving no sign that I was aware of it, I continued, "It is for that very reason that woman can so easily penetrate the soul of others."

"You mean, that having none of her own, there is no obstacle," she laughed once more.

"Yet nevertheless," I said, my voice trembling with feigned emotion, "you were not able to penetrate mine. You could not understand that I in no way resemble other men, although it was for that you loved me, is it not so? You could not see that I loved *you*, nor understand that I, who am the man who overturns everything, must overturn even love itself."

While I was saying this, I observed my prey with the utmost attention. Pazzarella's face underwent an incredible evolution on my first sentimental inflection. The drama of a whole life took place in her eyes:—birth, hope, happiness, disillusion, ire, shame, revenge, desperation, callousness, death—purification, and as I drew her slowly towards me, she attained, through this impassioned conflagration, to a virginity of spirit that in her ignorant maidenhood she could never have approached. A pitiful virginity offering its whitened pain to nothing.

"How could you bring yourself," implored my shaken voice, "to betray me as you did?"

Pazzarella, petrified, listened to the useless echoes of her aspiration in my reproaches.

"I do not reproach you," I went on. "You have taken vengeance on yourself—outraging your true nature *in extremis*. Poor child," I whispered, taking her in my arms and stirring her with over-sensitive caresses to which her subtle sensuality responded automatically. "The touch of any hand but mine must martyrize your flesh—" And from between her white teeth and her underlip broke a single bead of blood.

"Incredulous monster!" I murmured in that fainting ear, "Had it never occurred to you that love, which flowers in beauty among promises and ecstasy, dies unassuaged and bruised under the blow of desertion?

"What, then, could be more logical for illuminated lovers than to let love be born lamenting, without any illusions whatsoever in the callous hour of abandonment? What could be easier after that than for love to mature, insured against all deception for the paradisiacal spasm on arrival at its goal— I thought I had detected between us of that sort of spontaneous affinity—" Here Pazzarella embraced me convulsively.

"Do not kiss me," I begged her courteously. "I feel the breath of the thirsty dog."

"Oh, you ordinary woman," I taunted her, "who conceives the lover as being of that species of idiot who, arriving with a bunch of roses and a gold bangle, after playing his messy little tricks, takes nostalgic leave and, on getting home, writes three pages of eulogy to begin all over again on the following day. You, with your conventional infidelity, have ruined the most promising love affair that ever —— you odalisque of an able surgeon!!"

"On your recommendation."

"The *humblest* beggar," I retorted, "refuses advice."

"God forgives," began Pazzarella.

"And, doesn't exist—"

"Only think," I meditated aloud. "Once past the period of growing antipathy, of reciprocal lies—the physical repugnance of satiety, which in our case would have become steadily less—*Think* what a lover I should have made—"

"I know . . . . I know," she burbled, brushing the palm of my hand with her lips.

"—exactly that 'something' you so long—so long had waited for. Think, if it turns your head when I treat you badly, what under heaven might have happened to you when the time came for me to grow fond.

"Think—in the theatre of the flesh, how endless a romance would have been ours according to *my* program which eliminated any possible denouement.

"Imagine the role you would have played under my—"

"Geronimo!" screamed Pazzarella, "If you don't clear out, I shall murder you."

It was some time since I had given a thought to Pazzarella when I met her one evening out in the rain. The lamplight shone on her extinguished eyes under their perfect eyebrows. Once more, on beholding her pale passivity, that insupportable sense of irritation tore at me until impalpable filaments floated out from my body, meeting nothing to attach to and which I could not cast off.

I offered her the shelter of my umbrella and, without speaking to me, she drew my hand that was free into her enormous muff and went on walking.

At last—

"Yesterday," she confided to me, dreamily, "I wandered— wandered far out of the creaking city into the indelicate night, where, finding myself alone with Nature, I asked her—'Why Geronimo?'"

"And what did Nature answer?"

" 'It's useless addressing yourself to me,' she grumbled. 'I'm *such* a brute—'"

"As far as you are concerned she has every right to be."

We had reached her house. Pazzarella closed the front door and, all tremulous in the shadows, held up her face to mine. Ah, the pleasure it would give me to suck away her entire life through those questing lips. It would be too acceptable an end for her. I threw her off.

"Your kisses are too sensitive."

We entered the warm brightly lit room. I sank into an armchair, and Pazzarella perched herself on the arm.

"Will you answer one question frankly?"

"As far as frankness is concerned, I'm a fellow who easily gets involved."

"Do try just this once."

"Well?"

"This sentiment of yours in regard to myself—is it inspired by a personal antipathy, or a theoretical ethic?"

"There are cases in which Futurist ethics come in very handy."

"Are you a Futurist?"

"For the present, and the present you may have noticed is the time for accomplishment—while the future—keeps you waiting."

"Bah—you show as much contempt for men as you do for women—with your system of postponement."

"Men are more easily satisfied the longer they have been kept waiting—"

"And woman who has always waited?"

"I'll make her a present of the future when I have finished with it."

"Mafarka having meanwhile snatched it from her womb."

"I having meanwhile desecrated her—"

"Yes—in *that* article you were really *too* bawdy—"

75

"My bawdiness was more favourable to woman than anything that has ever been written."

"So much so, that she blushed?"

"Because I have gagged the other men, or rather that not being able to go any further in that direction one will have to turn back—"

"To me?" enquired Pazzarella hopefully.

"For you," I snapped, "if you don't stop fiddling with my eyelashes—there is instant castration."

"And yet," she reflected, measuring my nose with my forelock, "I should so much like to have a son of yours."

"Not for anything."

"Oh why?"

"Firstly, because that 'son' might be born a woman."

"While I," she sighed, "am hardly even a woman. I am only the scapegoat to carry the load of your spleen induced by those tasteless females who won't admire your funny nose—while I dote upon it," said she kissing it on the tip——

I slapped her face and let myself out of the house.

When the European War broke out I received the following hysterical explosion:

> Incomparable man,
> You will go to war, as of now I am out of your life—reduced to the primal elements of offence and attack. And if at night under the stars on the hard ground, you ever recall a few hours of divine pleasure in Florence, you will only reproach yourself for this weakness. Woman woman

has nothing to do with war—and yet there might have been something for me to do, I might have, now that half the male population is to be wiped out, I might have had your son, but Mafarka forbade it.

The learned's cries are in vain.

I send you my love in a kiss because to understand all is to forgive all. Perfect lover, will they remove your—not my "riccioli"?

Your——

Pazzarella—

If war sweeps a considerable number of men off the earth, it has this advantage: it effaces the current value of his parasite completely. But how promptly she reappears in the starched costume of devotion, wearing the new and lighter cross dyed in the colour of blood upon her breast, and bustles about as if nothing had gone wrong. With what courageous self-discipline she attends to the soldiers' splintered bodies. With what passion of inhibited caresses she massages their inoperative limbs, fixing her cheated eyes on chimerical Duty.

I gloated over the desperate impotence of Pazzarella that forced her to the extremity of imagining she could substitute a newborn infant for the "missing man" of her own generation.

She didn't give up the attack. Some days later, hedged in with piles of newspapers, letters, manuscripts, I was sipping my coffee when here we are again—!

"Love I have pondered for three full days—I adore you and feel all too empty of you. I couldn't care less about Futurism. The child the future needs is the child of the two of us—you won't think I'm right but I am. If you can spare half an hour of your intoxicating inner life for this important work, I will come to you wherever you may be—"

Certainly she is forced to defy the thing she is most afraid of—otherwise she would wilt with discouragement—

– – – "If you will lend me the money for the journey—we are all penniless for the moment if you are too I will scrounge it somewhere. Tell me if or not—if not it matters little—I can also do without being benefactress to all humanity.

"You needn't discuss this with your fancy companions—it's something I take *very seriously*."

> Geronimo,
>
> You are the only man who is man enough to dominate me absolutely the only one strong enough to keep me all for himself—the only one Alas—who is hard enough to crush me—
>> Your Pazzarella
>
> In memory of an absent lover—of the freshness of your spit.
>> Good-bye.

She had right on her side—but no money. That incubus of desire who attaches herself to the male with all her impertinent passion for reproduction, unable to attain her ends unaided, could not do otherwise than take the affair seriously, even to the length of begging for a subsidy.

There was also a mosquito humming around my face, most likely another female who had no doubt some portentous plan for the future to further, in inspiring an infinitesimal drop of my life.

But to Pazzarella's request I must reply. To ignore it would be too simple. Pazzarella herself would not be surprised if I took no notice. War is all very well up to a certain point, but tradition has after all lent a certain glamour to motherhood.

This was an occasion requiring an answer, in the negative, that goes without saying, were it only for the question of economy. A decisive reply was imperative, only it must be tender—very tender. Nor could it be confided to the postman. It would be more considerate to present my answer in person. However, the air was cool up in the mountains, and it was late autumn when I eventually decided to go to her.

This time Pazzarella looked a trifle faded, laid out on a sofa lapped in her silken gown and propped with cushions, occupying herself as usual with her tea things which were set on a low table. This body gradually desiccating for want of caresses, this potential mother empty of fruit, must necessarily continue throughout her steady undoing to distribute her circles of amber and sugar gewgaws. A woman resigned, who, while her life was ebbing from her, seemed ceaselessly to be pouring it out from a silver pot for casual callers with hands that were livid with calm. What else was she likely to offer to Death when it should come but a cup of tea?

I kissed her reverently, assured that, in spite of the cataclysm of my presence and the wounds with which I should lacerate her, in the conventional breeding she would merely reply—"Have another biscuit, *caro*?"

Certainly this was a day on which conversation was not in order. Rather must I sustain a tacit expectancy of imminent collaboration between us—expression of eyes and inflection of voice stressing the *entente* of accomplices.

Pazzarella relaxed in the security of anticipation, while I laid my head in her lap where my undisciplined hair incubated that rapacious womb in a promising warmth.

A mushy autumnal temperature of vegetation dropping its seed invaded us from the garden. It impinged on every nerve in her sensitive body, become one with the earth, the air, the season. Her breathing languished and was wafted away to the most distant *podere*. The richest of harvests ripened within her. I could feel the long prepared impassioned nest palpitate beneath my ear.

Tenderly I related my infancy. I had brought a photo of myself, still wearing a little skirt, in my pocketbook—and before the rites of my showing it to her she sat with receptive eyes and folded hands. But when I told her of my mother's saintly consecrated gestures, sweetened by anachronistic jealousy, she could not resist, and interrupted me—"But don't you know, Geronimo, that *I* am your mother?"

"Now we come to it," I cried, leaping to my feet, "A lot you care about the future! For you the child is a makeshift for the *tame* man."

Sexual emotion in woman is of familial extent, the impulse of three generations—mother, wife, daughter—and as there is no relationship among women, the daughter responds to the maternal embrace only in the arms of a father, but a father who has not committed incest with her mother, therefore the lover, in whom woman takes root, flowers and finally disappears.

As I had not yet finished with her, I took her in my arms again and, rocking her, felt the entire abandonment of a being who has such radical aversion to reliance on herself.

Now in this atmosphere I had spread about us a receptive somnolence closed in upon her breath, and the Eucharistic eyes of Pazzarella glowed in the twilight. Probably she would *still* be waiting, if the cry of a newborn child from a house across the way, a shrill surprise, had not split up my promising silence, even dispersing the indolent pulsation of the falling dew.

My burden started with a shuddering ecstasy.

"Vampire!" I hissed, "In your terrified enjoyment of the first cry of that dolent life, you are so intent on drawing from one man to impose it upon another."

But still she clung to me, not able to withdraw herself at once from her hallucination that a mystery was about to be conceived.

"It is the hour," I concluded, liberating myself to bow to her ceremoniously, "for me to take leave of you *Signora*," and I parted from all those empty circles—the tea cups—the woman.

Six months later I passed Pazzarella on the street. Without a greeting we both stopped for a while to observe each other reciprocally, and then pursued our ways without exchanging our impressions.

"*Caro*—don't be discouraged if I don't seem to have died. I have, really. Only the business of daily life necessitates the continued functioning of the mere machine— Excuse me!"

Such was the message I received the morning after our meeting. Another interview was imminent.

I entered. She had aged. Her eyes had grown dull, and her taut nerves distorted her face in a rigid resignation. She moved as she walked towards me with an angularity that must have irked her limbs. She looked so funny that I hugged her close to me, to stifle my titters while covering her with sarcastic little kisses, until I felt her tension relax.

"Oho," I said, seeing her revive among the roses I had planted. "How goes love?"

"Not so badly, thanks to your having employed the wrong tactics."

"– – – – – – ?"

"All is clear to me— Because I irritate you, you wish to do away with me. That is natural—quite understandable. In your place I should feel the same. But you tried to destroy me through my pride, whereas I really loved you, and into love pride does not enter. If you are determined to succeed, there is only one way—you must make me die of love. Do you get me?" she enquired with a flicker of hope.

"Your game is pretty strong," she continued. "The first stroke a whiz—and so on, increasingly. But entirely miscalculated. You should have duped me long enough to inspire my confidence, and then, after some days of intimacy, when my love should feel secure—ah, if you had left me then, who knows but that I really should have succumbed.

"Oh Geronimo," she pleaded, enlacing my torso with the constriction of a serpent round a tree. "Try a little intimacy, I am practically certain you will succeed."

"Indisputably you suffer from suicidal mania. In the beginning it astounded me that you made not the slightest effort to save yourself. Now you are even helping me. You are incomprehensible."

"Dearest, you enjoy the *secret* distinction of being loved by the biggest imbecile in existence."

"Obviously that is a lie. Nevertheless, I have not yet been able to make out why you take the line of action you do, or rather why you don't take any line of action."

"Am I not *Passivity*?"

"And that's why you are odious to me."

"It is to this your intellect condemns me."

– – – – – – – – –

"I, falling in love with just a man, as any girl of the people has a crush on the barber's assistant's beautiful moustache, found I had bumped into an intellect, the male intellect that reduces me to absurdity. I weighed in advance my possible coquetteries, dignities, the fictitious value I could assume, the pretentious gestures I could make in the luckless position of being—what am I?

"There seemed nothing to be hoped for, nothing to be done. I could be unfaithful to you? A lot of impression that made on you. Enhance my beauty? You are short-sighted. Lie? You could do it better than I. Dishonestly hew myself a niche in your animal propensities? Not to be thought of—you have yourself so thoroughly in hand.

"You might suppose that I should have surrendered to total discouragement. But no. In spite of all, I existed for you. I, woman, irritated you for that very passivity you impose upon me. I irritated you to such a degree that you could not keep your hands off me! Have you not often confessed to me how utterly I irritate you; to the point of wanting to conquer me?

"But you did not guess that if there are difficult conquests that inflame a man, and conquests so easy they rattle a man—you did not guess, that I could imagine a conquest *so easy* that it staggers the intellect itself. Do I irritate you?" she inquired.

"Sufficiently," I answered.

"*Amore, caro*," burbled Pazzarella, "Can't you *see*? If you had been an ordinary man, with no great intellect—that irritation you feel whenever I come near you would have been love! You would have loved me at night to return in the daytime to see if I was still on earth. You would have taken me by the hand and together we should have run against the blowing wind to show how beautiful and how young we are. But as you are only an intellect—"

"You think perhaps I have done the worst I can to you? But if I have shown you an outrage on elemental womanhood, there still remains the civilized woman, whose death-rattle lasts much longer in an agony infinitely more complicated. I can extend the scope of your sensibility until it comprises a universe, and this universe being myself, can disappear from one moment to another. I can animate your latent voluble wit, nourish your vanity, and, when growing ever more beautiful, more debonair, you are sure you have arrived at a state of security, can unexpectedly remove your animator. I can play any tricks upon you I please while you will rest assured they are the natural working out of Destiny—because I can give you what you want. In short, I will love you, if you feel equal to it?"

"I have only the strength of my longing for you."

"Take warning. There will be moments when you will look into my eyes and see your salvation—moments in which my one preoccupation is to enjoy you, as you enjoy me—in which defence, irony, paradox, disdain, suspicion have vanished. We shall exchange the limpid glances of newborn seraphim in a celestial innocence of mutual possession. You will have the illusion of all barriers being overthrown, of the 'unknown' being revealed, in-equalities being razed—in that sweet and absolute union which is —— ephemeral!

"But beware of that moment following when you are suffused with the glow of my weakness from which, in a triumphant spasm, I have liberated myself. *You* will remember. *I* shall have forgotten.

"My regard scarcely recognising you will be fixed anew in the eternal urge to know. This is the wound in woman which never heals, even in subsequent ecstasies. This is the knowledge the last mother to dwell on earth will not dare to impart to the ultimately so-phisticated maiden when preparing her for the last honeymoon."

"How beautifully you talk."

"You haven't understood anything?"

"There are things a woman understands without accepting," re-plied Pazzarella, settling down in my arms with a smile of relief.

"You certainly have an indomitable courage."

"I feel so *cozy* with you."

"Now that I have taken the road to Death," she continued.

"Which leads through felicity."

"Do you mean it?" clapping her hands.

"Indeed, this is to be the happiest time of your life."

"Yes, I feel sure there is some elemental truth concealed in woman's love that men do not suspect, but which will some day make amends for our monotony. It is my ambition to reveal it to you, and so be more to you than what you expect of me."

"My dear, I ask nothing better than to vary that monotony. I give you *carte blanche*. I am here for a whole evening— Let us sample a little of this brimming secret reservoir in woman of which we men disdain to take advantage. See, I, in my turn, am passive. Profit by it!"

Pazzarella broke into a laugh of joyous discomfiture. "I can't."

"Ha?"

"Forgive me if I fail you at this crucial moment—it has just occurred to me—Womanhood cannot be consummated without a collaborator."

"Pazzarella," I asked her, "do you feel like making a little love this evening?"

"Actually, when one talks so much about love as we do, one hardly thinks of it."

"Ah—if one comes to think of it, it is such a comical business."

"So it seems to me," she made friendly assent.

"Then for once we agree."

"Miraculous!"

"And yet," I pursued, "every now and then we shall find ourselves invaded by this indefinable yearning."

"Fortunately," she sighed, closing her eyes then opening them again. "Geronimo, you are delightful—you look like a little boy hiding in the corner with a lump of sugar."

When at last we let go of each other Pazzarella fell into meditation. "How mysteriously designed is love— Here are we, the fundamental enemies whose dearest desire is to be rid of each other— yet when the flesh unites, how exquisite— It really tempts one to believe in a power above us."

Only some minutes later, a complete change had come over her, so that eventually I was led to demand, "Why the depression?"

"After all, it's idiotic loving you—there's no reason for it—I didn't want to—I don't know where passion comes from—I *object*."

I wondered how she would make defensive love—for day by day I found my enemy paler, her eyelids darker, but steadily fortifying herself in a new dignity.

"Be on your guard," she greeted me at last with a smile of great reserve. "I begin to feel the need of saving you."

"From yourself?" I inquired, "That is hardly your concern. I am perfectly capable of taking my own precautions."

"Don't interrupt me," she went on with majestic severity. "I have got to talk to you. I am more serious than you think. I am a superior woman—you, also, are a superior man. That being the case, do you suppose that this, our love, is worthy of us? Do you think it is *moral* that I, knowing very well that *you do not understand me*, should say to myself, 'I don't care, his embraces content me,' and let it go at that? No! You, being so supremely sophisticated, think there is enough to satisfy a woman in physical super-refinements and in your virility—above all your virility." Then, as it were, in parentheses, "I am worn out. For the last two days I have lain on this sofa."

"Forgive me," I begged her with much solicitude, "is it possible I have failed you, that I have not rightly divined your tastes? Tell me, my dearest, how many ways of making love have I taught you?"

"There is," murmured Pazzarella, counting on her fingers, "the one of the first time—that of the sacred Tuesday then yours, then mine and then the other ones."

"And which do you prefer?"

"All of them," she replied without hesitation. "That is to say," her eyes catching mine fixed on her hypnotically, "All, up to a certain point. But there is a spiritual aspect of love; woman was not created uniquely to serve as man's ——" I was looking at her still more intently, "created uniquely to enjoy herself," she caught herself up breathlessly. "We have a higher mission. I feel an absolute necessity to save you."

"Woman," I said, "Can you possibly suffer under the delusion that having followed the profession of literature for so many years, I had run into no female saviours? At least until now you had not exhibited the doubtful taste of echoing too often my other lady-loves."

"You must have patience. We have also, we others, our traditions—classical traditions. There are the women you pay and the women who save you. Every decent woman tries to save at least a couple. Up to now, none of the men I met seemed worth the trouble—they needed saving—so I was not interested. Men who require help, you will agree with me, had better be left alone. Whereas you who do not require any, are just my affair."

"Exactly. You want to 'save' me to save you."

"Oh," she reproved me, "Why won't you follow the rules of the game—leave things to me."

"Little one," I condoned with her, "You are pale, you are under the influence of a physical reaction. Evidently it is for the first time I observe with a certain amount of pride or you would not take it so hard—you're tired. If it relieves your body to weigh upon my spirit, I am only too willing."

"No," she insisted, "You may laugh at me, spit upon me—nothing will make any difference—I am determined to save you. Answer me. Do you not feel by any chance that your soul is become clouded, smirched with the pettiness of daily life? Have you arrived perhaps at the turning point where it is difficult to distinguish clearly *which* path to follow? Do you not long to feel a confident little hand in yours, to guide you?"

"Why such theatrical gestures when you're turning your back on me?"

"I am invoking the ideal."

"Oh, I thought this harangue was addressed to me."

"There's nothing to prevent you listening if you feel like it—but how satisfied actresses must feel before a *whole* audience. You, who have read all there is to read, wasn't there *anything* you could not discover in that universe of volumes? Even in your own colossal intellect, is there not lacking perhaps some other trifle?

"Trust in me—I am your redemptress. In all humility—"

"Murderess!"

"When one has exhausted everything else, one must turn to the simpletons of this world. When the great man soils his soul, even a prostitute may serve to cleanse it—and this simpleton," her voice trembling with emotion, "this prostitute, is perhaps myself! I feel really moved," then, her eyes imploring me, "Self-abnegation softens the hardest heart."

I flicked the ash off my cigarette.

"You are really opposed to being saved?" asked Pazzarella, subsiding onto my knees.

"Try by all means, perhaps I can even assist you," said I, declaiming as she had done. "Being unable to justify myself before my superiors to give any reason for my existence. Having no intellect I will save an intellect, to free myself of my annihilating sensation of emptiness and inutility."

"Nonsense," she rejoined, "it's ever so much simpler than that. Can't you imagine the vicious pleasure in being impertinent, for one who is frightening herself out of her wits?"

It was a long long time before I saw her again. When I did, it was evident my task was drawing to an end.

Pazzarella lay in a great bed where, among incredible flowering on the coverlid, a printed monkey climbed towards her heart, while the grey mist of empire mirrors reflected her waning life.

She was reading a little evangile of Saint John—too preciously bound.

"If only you could look at me once with the passionate glance you cast on books—" and no sooner had she said this than she spread her book open on her face under her eyes, and lay watching me. "There, you see, I have caught a look of adoration." Then she opened her mouth to speak again. "Listen—" And the word crept round the room like a dumb crowd.

How often before she had clutched her hand to her heart trying to tear out of it the confidences of her eternal non-impartation—as if she suffered from something incommunicable, rent by a secret she imagined she had been called to life to share with me.

"In the long, long, lonely night I call to you; we make the supreme discovery together—only your bodily presence makes me mute. Nevertheless, my secret is so vital to the world's destiny, it almost seems that the world would come to an end should I fail to confide it to you. It is so simple, a moment would suffice for the telling. So obvious— Quick, I am losing it again. Look in my eyes, perhaps you will discover it—feel the beat of my heart, that may convey it to you—"

As a matter of fact the heart *was* irregular.

"There it is, I see it again. Can't you come over *on my side* to look at it? Geronimo, I could describe it to you only you are over there on the *opposite* side. You can see nothing of how it appears from over here. I am in possession of a secret truth. Fate commands me to reveal it to you. I *will* tell you. LISTEN! Geronimo— Woman—"

"The riddle is solved, my poor child," I said, pressing her down by her shoulder. "I am your secret. Now lie in peace."

She let her heavy head drop on the pillow. A shadow spread across her face, enhancing in beauty the last spark of a life I had extinguished with my negations. Of every instinct that flowered towards me I had snapped off the stem. Every fire that warmed her I had put out. What a facile success!

Needing to stretch my legs after sitting so long by that inarticulate deathbed, I took up a candle and moved about the room. Some unaccountable impulse stopped me before the mirror and I found myself staring, this time, into my own eyes. How queer, they returned my gaze without recognition. Those steely discs might have looked out of a stranger.

Wondering what had happened to them, I peered into their brightness for some time. At first I could make out nothing, but gradually I became aware of a putrefying mass, a turbid residuum lying at the bottom of their wells. Luminous sepulchres of vanquished emotions, of petrified humanity, such had been my eyes. But now, beneath their inflexible logic, the effrontery of their wile, lay the decaying remains of an embryonic spirit, an almost imperceptible reflection of Pazzarella's dying. Had this wretched creature contaminated my very soul, insinuated her tenacious interrogation to the very stronghold of my wisdom?

Fuming, I returned to the bedside. "Creature! Are you not dead yet?"

"I don't know—"

"What a way to answer a straight question. Even a lie would be too direct for you."

"Very likely—for I who have been so confused in life, am not very clear about death."

"Darling," I exploded, "have you not often declared you loved me?"

"Yes."

"More than your own self?"

"Surely."

"Then, disappear now—at once. I command you!"

"I should be delighted."

"Then what are you waiting for?"

"To put an end to my life."

"There's no need for you to wait."

"But my life?"

"Yes, your life."

"But my life? Where is it? You have confiscated it. Where *can* you have tucked it away?" Feverishly Pazzarella patted my clothes, searched under my curls—to fall back once more, extenuated upon the pillows. "Tell me what is there, what is there about you that so satisfies me when I touch you?"

"Maybe that is your life?"

"Therefore —— ?"

Her pulse had become imperceptible—I admired the sensitive hollows under the cheek-bones, sculptured by the sophisticated compromises of my lips.

"If you really cared for me, you would tell me what it is sustains you in so miraculously remaining alive."

And Pazzarella murmured this incredible word in my ear.

"Hope."

"But my poor thing, what could you hope for? Even if I had not already completely spoiled you, you so fine, so fragile—you are not my type."

"Really?"

"Hadn't you realized it?"

"No. I thought it was just your way of amusing yourself."

"There is also a little of that," I laughed in answer to this gleam of intelligence. "But that alters nothing," I went on decidedly.

"So be it," and taking what I prayed should be her last look at me, she arose from where she lay, and all tottering, blindly left the room.

"What are you up to?" I called to her.

"Can't you understand that I shall never be able to die as long as you are near me?" And so saying, she threw herself on the stone stairs as if seeking a refuge unquestionably kinder than my adamant embraces.

I settled down comfortably and lit a cigarette. What peace. The bed, scarcely disarranged by its lethargic occupant, was a razed plane, clear of all insoluble enigmas, and the primitive monkey seemed to look at me in quite brotherly fashion from the Javanese stuff.

But this peaceful interlude did not last long, for all at once, the silence, my obedient and compatible silence, so unlike the gravid, disquieting silence of woman, was broken by a supreme sob—an irruption of cardiac blood and boiling tears—it was Pazzarella. She was crying at last; for the first time, outside on the stairs whither she had retired to vomit her soul on sordid blocks of granite.

"I don't care for that noise," I cried.

"I don't care for it myself," she spluttered. "I feel like the heroine of a melodrama. Couldn't you have found anything better to do with me? This business of dying is so extremely usual any charwoman goes through with it—it's not at all as you *litterateurs* seem to believe, an agony reserved for their mistresses."

I was thoroughly frightened. The contrariness of woman! Her voice was actually growing stronger—a shade of enmity was creeping into it. She could not die at my side, yet had she not once confessed to me that in my absence her love for me diminished? If she was to die of love, there was still some danger that she would not succeed even out there on the cold stairs. I was desperate, fearing that at a few yards' distance I lost some of my power over her.

However, the crying continued, and every outburst seemed to blow up her being. What a catastrophic result of all my labors. Could there not exist a more aesthetic conception of "finishing off" a woman? Was there perhaps something wrong with my method, when it came to naught but a horrible noise?

As a painter, struck for the first time with a higher conception of his art, regards his "earlier" work with disparagement, I contemplated my *Pazzarella de le Scala di Pietra* critically. How could I have failed in such an academic manner? Such sticky technique! This mixture of quivering mucous and clammy flesh running with tears!

I seated myself beside her and began tracing with my forefinger the swelling festooned from the arch of her nose across her hot wet face, leaving her bloodshot eyes in a purple pit.

Pazzarella, quieting under my touch, sank into a state of coma, leaving me at liberty to investigate. I picked her up and carried her back to bed. Then I arranged myself in such a position as best to contemplate her.

After all, even if she loved me, she was still a human being. And in that propitious hour when she could neither talk nor cry nor appear so pitifully conscious of being inarticulate, I could consider her case at my leisure, impartially.

Set free by this state of coma, this female soul presented itself clearly, for closer observation, and with every star that vanished from the night the mysteries of her silence likewise vanished, one by one.

This female Buddha sensed my power over her better than I myself. This was the reason for her calm eye and her *laisser aller*. Her pardon before the act and her maternal irony. There was no possible doubt but that she had understood. She must have cogitated every possible means of escape—theories of the laws and harmonies of sex, the rights of women which, once having been won, leave woman as solitarily woman as before. Pazzarella had known all along what she was—woman aware of herself. This seductive creature who was so feminine, so tender, found herself stranded with the awful certainty that intellectual self-respect for a woman is a juggling with lies. She had nothing more to say to other women or to men, either. Intrepid pilgrim of enlightenment, she had found one truth, and this one sufficed to render her immune to all illusion.

To me, keeping company with her coma, it seemed as if, her spirit having come apart from her, I could hold it like an object in my hands. It had the translucent opacity of an oyster, and, on looking into it deeply, I saw a flux of nebulous matter stirred by internal currents and countercurrents. The vital rhythm was disjointed— Ideas, facts, form and sound advanced, receded, grew large, then small, bright or dim, louder or fainter.

Every now and then a spark engendered would for a flash illumine the whole inside of this soul with a crazy half-light without ever throwing anything particular into relief. For always, on the verge of definition, the contents confused, spun round and round at a flighty velocity to evaporate at last in a vortex of mist—in which my *enemy* disappeared.

In the divine manner, it was from this chaos I drew my inspiration. At once I grew enormous—omnipotent. After centuries of mystery, I had found the solution—a solution that lay in myself. The secret of woman is that she does not yet exist. Being a creator, I realized I can create woman. I decided to "create" Pazzarella.

Until now she had nothing but her breath and the everlasting attraction toward man, lacking an axis about which to revolve. I am man and I shall be her axis. All this while she had lain at my flank, weak for the want of "a life" I could make for her, waiting for me to impregnate her mind as I impregnate her body, to organize that revolving chaos which is the source of variety among the individuals begotten of it. For she being identified with "everything," partakes of that universal "unity" sought by the mystic; with this paradoxical result that if man is promiscuous physically, woman is promiscuous spiritually.

But such reflections were powerless to deter me. I had found a fresh instrument for my intellect, a raw material with which to create; material so plastic in its untouched condition, that it offered untold possibilities of formation.

Stirred with a new enthusiasm, all the passion I had hitherto devoted to pen and paper welled up in my heart—

- -
Manuscript long ago lost.
- -

Pazzarella, arisen, her exhausted voice transformed for the future to the trill of a bird, is twittering to the dawn. To my surprise, like the hero of an ancient fable unexpectedly endowed with the understanding of the conversation of animals, I find no difficulty in interpreting the language of a creature so dissimilar to myself.

The End.

Note sent with M.S.S.

Sympathetic Enemy

One night I set to work and composed the gigantic opus for the vindication of feminine psychology with which I had threatened you. Whether it is that truth is more powerful than determination, or fantasy less fantastic than truth, or that woman, being incapable of thinking, reads the thoughts of others. However that may be, this is how it turned out.

Your affectionate

PIERO & ELIZA.

Like a drop of arsenic falling upon clay, he appeared among the lethargic clients of the café, as they crouched at sundown over their cheap vermouth.

His face was painted a greenish white, a mask of experimental irony, on which he pushed his bands of black eye-brow upwards to an insolent interrogation, crushing his eyes to slits of quizzical survey. His mouth was an arrogant crimson blot, and he cherished an ebony cane with his white kid gloves.

"*Gia*," said the *camerieri*, "he used to be a musician, but he is now a gentleman, for his uncle died and bequeathed to him his vineyards."

For perhaps half a dozen evenings he pirouetted among the café tables, wriggling in his frock coat which tweaked his waist and spreading to broad lapels bore in the buttonhole a pistachio-coloured carnation.

And always as he left he would bestow upon the company an impenetrable glance of assumed evil.

He had returned from Paris, a solitary decadent having lost his *ambiente*.

Eliza Blane was a middle-aged English girl of middle-class morality, with a hankering after the arts as a social outlet.

Into her life he frolicked like a sinister kitten.

Every woman continues to want a man in her life, and after some decades of inhibition her desire seeks merely a living symbol of unproven curiosities. In old maidenhood she achieves a paralysis of the instincts, with the result, to put it simply, that should Eros approach her, "she wouldn't know what to do."

There was something in the arsenical Piero that wanted a mother; something in Eliza that wanted a lover—a lover who would open the flood-gates of her fantasy, and leave her body where it belonged—rigid under the ashes of her accustomed inhibitions.

Piero played to her his mincing music, and tended this platonic conquest with playful quirks and humouring caresses.

They became inseparable.

She warmed the blast of emptiness that swept her palazzo to a home atmosphere, where she fed Piero with zeal and performed the ceremony of darning his socks.

Eliza, in the Venetian moonlight, romanced to him of the purely spiritual obligations of love, which he accepted graciously as a hitherto unsuspected form of abstract vice.

Gradually they gathered round them a scattering of expatriated bachelors, deeply attached to their furniture, who always delighted to show Eliza a new solitaire, while Piero composed.

Piero was the youngest among the bachelors, and his achievement of a transcendental family life lent him a certain augustness among them.

While through them he acquired a modified aspect of self advertisement; for they taught him that he who treads tactfully, may keep one foot in society and one in Fairyland.

Eliza abetted this innovation of compromise with her middle-class maxims. So Piero washed his face and wore tweeds which she chose for him.

Theirs was now a delightful life, Piero placed "Beauty" precisely in the palazzo; together they collected its antique forms, and together they would stand off and admire them in those nooks to which they had been appointed—and always Piero found everything "too exquisite."

Eliza was not neglected, Piero and an intimate artist designed costumes for her; they would stand her in the centre of the music room, and trip around her entranced with draping striped crêpe and monkey fur upon her; the attendant dressmaker bowed her head and said "*sicuro*," while Piero's manicured fingers depicted perfection.

There she stood, like a mummy resuscitated with a fictitious breath of flattery. The fearful tension of her eyes was bordered with very black fringes, and over the quivering tendons of her insteps was stretched expensive silken hose. Piero twisted her around and about —— like some marionette; while the dressmaker nodded again, "*sicuro.*"

Eliza took her headaches to lie for a nap of an afternoon, to stare through the pastel surface of the wall and the dim colour of the flower of love in the mist of the tapestry.

Of those rooms which she entered alone the planes of the walls seemed to turn inside out to withhold the fulfilment of life from her ———————— she could overhear the muted voices of the bachelors seeking the secluded study and the loggias.

When they returned to her table they stole into the atmosphere with their recollections, like soft cats, heavy with satisfaction.

After dinner they purred over ephemeral scandals in which the gentler sex is so inevitably involved.

There was no gusto in their laughter, no resentment of the frailty of woman, their comments on her charms were never warm.

For their eyes were preoccupied, as with the inner realisation of the wearer of a mask; while a bachelor would steal upon the insinuate silence with an anecdote.

"—— —— she invited the young attachés to dinner —— a shaft leading from a trap door in the ceiling to the roses banked in the centre of the dinner table —— and down slid Lady Pink —— but *only* Lady Pink —— ." The bachelor wafted his hands from his flanks, invoking Eve— but his gestures displayed the anomaly of an allusion to his own graces rather than hers. As of life so of art, they spoke with an unintentional aloofness, as those who speak in the language of signs to the deaf and dumb.

Despite the spiritual obligations, the soul of Piero flowed beyond Eliza's imagining. Flowed with the tropical mystery of an unnavigable Amazon, overhung by an exotic tangle of his smiles and hints.

Through all her comradely and inspiring traffic with them, Piero and the bachelors impressed Eliza as the incognito guardians of some holy bread. When they spoke they swallowed preparedly as if to rid speech of something incommunicably sweet and secret, which their mouths must never surrender.

Eliza's question of the bachelors' significance —— her curiosity, materialized to an almost palpable entity passing from Eliza to move among them, stroking their consciousness beseech-ingly —————————— they condescended to answer with conundrums of discretion.

Eliza had been reared by a great aunt who, steeped in melan-cholia, warned her of hell, and lauded the unconditional surren-der of being "sincere."

From this rudimentary religious influence she had graduated to spiritualism and the popular occult.

She cultivated her aura like a garden of unscented flowers.

But Eliza by dint of horoscopes and séances was reaching a higher plane ————— some plane on which psychic phenomena, like orgasms, so tantalisingly suggest themselves.

Her body became hollow ————— she could feel the wind of the spirit blowing about in it, stemming her blood and parching her skin.

The fearful tension of her eyes —————

There are crises in the life of the chaste woman, when the fet-ishes of savage ancestry and the Christian devil, together with all the weird personifications into which the unappropriated sex force transforms itself, fall upon her taut nerves to rend them in the stillness of the night.

After one such battle she had distinctly felt a hand and forearm "materialize" from out her abdomen.

- -

Now she could throw in the ballast of her mediumship against the loaded mystery of Piero and his bachelors.

She had long believed that Piero must have reached a higher plane having eschewed the devil in woman's flesh—and now she, herself had also reached a "higher plane".

- -

The clock of San Marco strikes one. Waiting on the remotest of Eliza's loggias for the poet who has written of "The Immaculate Vermin Of The Sugar Dove."

"- - - he should have come long ago—what keeps him?"

Piero, the inner muscles of his thighs twitching - - - paces the loggia.

THE STOMACH

There sat the mother.

Where the flesh should have been there was shawl—the wits of the aged go wool-gathering, dutiful relatives knit them into a frowsty comfort for the blinking, twitching, wheezing forgetter of many delights.

Her blind eye floated like a decaying fish in the dregs of her lucidity. There must have been parts of her even more terrifying than those that were exposed ——— in "out of use" there is ugliness.

Delicate and decent however were the appointments of the sitting-room, the cleared and garnished tabernacle for this bundle of human garbage.

Ladies of some culture—and some titled, asked the daughter little questions about mother, as if taking a dig at her flesh to see if she were still alive.

Virginia devotedly cosseted her mother, giving evidence that she had found no time for marriage. Every day a fostering coachman drove her with the aged gentlewoman slowly through the more fashionable streets.

Every desirable visitor she could muster into the half-conscious maternal presence would remember the even temperature of her sitting-room, the southern aspect, the cheerful flowers, the particular fleeciness of the wool which enwrapped her.

Virginia Cosway employed her leisure with the Arts.

Years ago a sculptor had chosen Virginia Cosway as model for *La Tarantella*, had taken her fingers between two of his own and slid them further down and apart upon her hip; then with accurate gesticulations he had inspired her with "the pose."

The famous statue had been standing for a quarter of a century in the public gallery visited by the processional tourists. Wrinkling a nostril and an under eye-lid, thousands of noses had lifted to it over catalogues.

The figure was over-lengthy on its pedestal, and the small head with its arched eye-brows sneered with a simultaneous invitation and repulse.

But because of the elevation of the statue, its significance for the spectator seemed rather to centre in the region of the hips, and also on account of the "pose" inspired by the Master, the outswung allurement, the momentary momentous projection of the stomach in the *danza española*.

The tourists stared at *La Tarantella* and supposed that she implied that there was a transcendental anatomy to be studied in the land of the Alhambra. The tourists were not allured by the tilted pelvis, each one dismissed it as being the concern of the next one. The tourists kept their mouths open to air their house of limitation in which they abode.

For a quarter of a century, the permanent physical adoption of that Spanish pose had defined the daughter's status—the authorised edition of Virginia Cosway issued by the Master for the international society of the élite parasites of the Arts.

She wore it as a tag of identification in the *grand monde*, where one must let off a rocket, to be rescued from the masses.

She performed her Hispano-abdominal ceremony at *les vernissages*, the private views, auctions of the Hôtel Drouot and the birthdays of new movements; it served her as a bass accompaniment to her spoken verdicts. It became familiar to the whole of Europe, and by middle age had brought an utter reverence upon her.

She had also accumulated her mythology; women who often wore mourning whispered how the heart of the Master had been broken. Callous women deprecated her shortsightedness on the occasion of his proposal. Elderly bachelors pointed her out as the great man's guiding star.

Only too early after she had refused him the sculptor had leapt to a rare and official celebrity, and Virginia found herself powerless to cap him with a husband of greater distinction.

So she clung to that trifle of her destiny she had restricted herself to accepting from him—the pose.

Important people would be enticed at receptions into the shadows of Spanish leather or Chinese lacquer screens, for a significant talk with Virginia Cosway the lifelong friend of the Master. There under the arc of the handshake, with a brief undulation of the hip, and the adjustment of the forefinger, the stomach outswung to its notable attitude, as if enticing aesthetic culture into her womb to be reborn for her audience.

This authoritative and challenging gesture became the formative process of her critique; this continuous resumption of her primal creation by the Master, who had, with his studio directions, hammered her into a posture in which she was to become fixed for life.

Her erstwhile suitor with due realisation that marriage is not the unique entanglement for the mighty, became grosser of feature and of cigar and continued to devote a cup of tea to her, whenever he was in the neighbourhood; for she not only was intimate with some of his wealthiest clients, but added very voicefully to that chorus without sound of which, the approach to our celebrities might not so easily be located.

Where Virginia went, always companioned by women of greater age and hereditary prestige than herself—as reinforcement—she expounded the gesture that had gradually attained to insolence, while conducting her well-attended inquisition of the muses.

The stomach had become an arbiter of aesthetics.

The mother grew daily colder in her woollens. ———

"Lady Beatrice, I should have delighted to spend Easter with you—but you see? My mother cannot spare me—I am a prisoner to my affections. A daughter has a sacred duty" ——— Virginia did something appealing with her eye-lids ——— and there it was again! Hand to hip ———

The old woman rolled her surviving eye on the stomach of her attendant daughter and only one of all the visitors distinguished among the wheezing and the rumbling these words like exhausted thunder.

"If only she would take it out of my way ——— even for a day. If only I could be left alone."

The daughter remained at her post. Artistic polemics prowled beyond the mother's doors.

Until of the mother, her soul and her lucidity, together with her eye swum into infinity.

After the funeral her friends said, "Do not grieve."

"I do not wish," the daughter answered, "to bury my dead."

Virginia Cosway bereft of her excuse, was left with Time as her consort. She gave forth sighs for her past sacrifice, which floated among her cultured acquaintances like whiffs from that protracted maternity of *outre-tombe*.

The stomach in its age was become fibrous and rigid.

And as it proceeded towards me, I would have sworn I could see, set in the wrinkled lids of its navel ———————————— a calculating eye.

THE THREE WISHES

The babies were all born in the same quarter of the same city—
two of them in the back streets—

Three boys.

The first looked up above him and stared, that first stare, without focus, without enquiry, without comment, into a pale silk
penthouse with vapoury wavy white frills.

Beside him a young woman with serenely braided hair was
winding white and pink and blue wool round the radius of a cardboard circle with a hole cut in its center.

Presently a fluffed and vari-coloured ball hung above the horizontal eyes.

About the time he was lifted from the scarcely perceptible soapi-
ness of his bath, to the fleeciness of a towel, warm from the fire-guard,
a brisk and scarcely middle-aged man would hurry into the room.

He would shut the door cautiously, not letting go of the handle
until he had turned it, and patting the pudgy thorax the baby was
arching forwards with his tiny fists clenched to it; cried jovially

"How's the king of the castle?"

Whereafter the shining solstice on the boat-like curves of the warm milk-bottle would fade comfortably into the irresistible hiatus of sleep.

+

The second looked up above him with the exact degree of detachment of the first, into a shadowy, dusty irregular bulgy fringe of battered kitchen utensils and worn-out lamps.

His pillow, under his left ear, was dimpled with a drying pool of yellow curd, to which flies mustered, from which they dispersed to scrape their legs and pattern the inedible surfaces of his linen with minute specks.

An old-young woman with dusty curls and a spot of grease on her gaudy bosom, was throwing bunches of old boots out of the case on which the basket-cradle lay, for the inspection of a couple of wandering workmen.

The boots of these men had worn down to their arrival, and they had come to look for work.

Boots are the civilized man's last foothold in society, without boots – – – – !

They were thus one of the stable sources of income to the parents of this second infant, who throve on the whole honestly.

If sometimes there might be a doubt as to the origin of any of their much behaggled purchases, the ragman breathed excusingly to himself

"Thou my God seest him."

And would always spit on the coin he received for them.

Under the scrap of burgundy coloured carpet for a cradle-cover, the ragman's infant rehearsed the battle of life with his feeding bottle, to which was attached an India-rubber tube aged to the colour of seaweed.

The tube had a nasty habit of flattening together and clinging to its own inside, when the mightiest spasms of insuction became powerless to imbibe the cold mixture of water and condensed milk.

Often the bottle would slip down the side-long niches of the cradle, head-up with its sustenance lying idle in the bottom.

A dish of yellow bone, worn like a Pierrot's frill by the teat, provided to flatten against the lips and prevent the swallowing of the tube, would keel over whenever the tube played serpent and sidle into the baby's mouth.

But it was this child's destiny that he should live. So nothing could choke him. And every once in a while the opposed and unguided gymnastics of the baby and the bottle would free some current of air and the tube sprang back to rotundity.

The nauseous-sublime liquid would gush surprisingly down the baby's throat, oftenest, at the time when quite worn out he was falling asleep, hypnotised by the regularity of his suctional reflex, into an illusion of satiety. His abdomen filled with what, outside him, was the atmosphere driving the stuffy sugary stench from his clammy swaddles up to his drowsiness.

+

The third was born in that addressless household, known as a den of thieves. The first vision of his looking upward is when propped upon his mother's knee, pale, in a public house, he squints at his girlish bonnet, puffed with transparent and unconvincing silk.

The offspring of a deliberate passion born into his parents' world of unaccountable luxury.

Already he wears bangles on his wrists; already he has sipped his drop of beer.

+

The first child, Ian Gore, went to a preparatory school for the sons of gentlemen.

The second child, whose name was Jacky Sider, went to board-school.

The third child, with his apple-y quality for his parent's eye, was prepared by private tutors, exceedingly slick with their hands.

He also had among so many lawless things, one lawful thing, a name.

That name was Hyde Park Hinderman.

+

Several of the earlier years of these three heirs were taken up with the pouring of the parents' minds, into their own. Years in no way notable except for the children's curious preference for the society of the lower animals.

Indeed, as none of these children were of vicious nature, the placid social relation to cats and dogs, and on rare occasions, elephants and tigers of Ian, Jacky and Hyde Park were identical.

They did not review these parentalised contents of their respective minds until that day on which each became conscious of his ego.

The ego no longer to be taken as a matter of course as undetached from its surroundings.

On that day the ego detached itself, and making a *volte-face* on the parental precepts, pronounced judgement upon them.

Ian Gore, on inspecting the chambers of his mind, finding himself stronger than anything that had been stored there, proceeded to break up the furniture. He denounced the fabricated truth of organised society as lies; precedents as corpses. He did not stop to question authority before he defied it. The moulding of the mind by a laboriously perfected system of education to the loftiest standard established by the human intellect, he objected to as pseudo-classic piffling. As for sportsmanship he defined the ball as the nincompoop's microcosm, and he doubted the beneficence of killing things that preferred to be alive anyhow.

Of good form—and Ian's father could be placed in the irreproachable minority—there was something clownlike about his soul, that urged him to pull faces at it; to stick out his tongue. He devised, for the future, how to frighten good form to death! Already he had appeared at dinner with a collar not quite fresh.

These decisions came completely into his mind as ideas, in conversation he summarised them with—

"It's all bilge," or, "You can't fool me."

+

For Jacky there had been no presentation of the highest standard of the human intellect, of sportsmanship, of good form.

He had been told that thrift was the moral motive of mankind. That three rags and an old fender equal one dinner, forty years of thrift, one old-age pension. That it was thrifty people that God, or was it the Prince of Wales, was most likely to stoop down to and pat on the back,

"Well done my good and faithful servant, Slow-but-Steady."

He did not think overmuch of the nincompoop's macrocosm; it was too likely to roll down the gutter; too likely to entice you under the wheels of a van.

His lively instinct was however, to get his hand into the pocket of that stooping God. For Jacky grew tired of the dusts of thrift. He was lured by the perfumes of brazen girls.

The abstract authority of the moral concept that Ian defied, took the concrete form of a policeman in Jacky's world. For Ian the policeman was only a faithful servant to be kept always in the same place, to be asked for various kinds of information.

Ian defied authority openly. He could. Belonging to the class in which authority was bred.

Jacky defied authority secretly, belonging, as he did, to that class for whom authority is "intended." For Jacky, slow of attention in the board-school, had found his eyes, his hands, to be marvellously dexterous.

He was, although good form had been presented to him as the fitness of smirking when answering his betters, not servile; not a coward. He guessed that betterness only meant advantage. He was going to "get at" advantage with his nerve.

He was one of those rare beings born to greatness, who see the world lying spread around them like an open gold-mine. Unlike the average man who sees nothing beyond his appointed pigeon-hole in which he hopes, by virtue of obedience to be allowed to remain safe "in that state to which it hath pleased God to call – – –"

Ian Gore was also born to be a great man. He first came to understand this when he discovered how infinitely more potential was the margin of his Latin verse, than the text. His hand and eye were also marvellously dexterous. He knew himself to be a draughtsman, and also that to mature his genius he must live upon a barge.

Mr. and Mrs. Gore had only one son to offer on the altar of society. This son refused. He wanted to revert to the beefy foul-tongued leading of a manly life; to drink beer with the husky dregs of a population. To limn souls that were not smeared over, smoothed out, made unrecognisable to the creator by the footling ritual of civilization. He did not care who, what, a man was. All he asked of him was to have "form," chunks of form, that the strong eye might wrestle with and master. The impulse of his art was to define volume.

His father pleaded, he would, "at least" – – – – – – – He insisted – – – – "first study art." Ian consented, after his inspection of an art school had suggested itself to him as a likely place for his initial rehearsals of "frightening good form to death."

+

In the meantime the more puny son of the criminal world had also conceived his ideal. An ideal so startling, so incompatible with the possibilities on his horizon, that he alone of the three, had it not been for an accident, would have stood a chance of failure.

Hyde Park Hinderman's desire was towards conformity. He yearned to prop himself against the pillars of society, in time to delicately detach himself and become one of such pillars himself. He was convinced that criminals were not good form. He longed for approval. In other words he was a snob.

It all began with his respectful admiration for a policeman's helmet. When he arrived at a definition of the exact adjustment between his parents' social status and the policeman's, there took place in him the spontaneous evolutionary modification of the parental type, so usual in the imaginative young.

He hung about the mission house, felt happy if he got patted on the head, and read their books. He was a pretty boy, with large blue eyes, a mixture of his father's grey blank ones, and the vague velvety black pansy ones of his decoying Mamma. An air of innocence was thus arrived at. The mission house felt itself to be in a responsible position.

His father said the boy had a white liver.

His mother was in awe of him. Somebody had once told her, "the child would be a judgement on her."

He would pore over the books from the mission house and then nag his parents about mending their ways. He tried to convince them that people didn't do these things. Sometimes he would cry on his mother's breasts – – "We're outcasts, outcasts"! She was like a deaf woman in a church.

Her husband would roar

"The bloody brat! Bitin' the 'and wot fed 'im. 'Ere we've bin all these years slavin' our lives out an' wot for I'd like ter know? To give 'im a persishun— Ain't 'e allers lived in luckshery? Round the swell pubs with his curls an' lace collars an' orl?

"Wot'ud 'is poor great grand-pa say I *dunno*. If 'e could only turn in 'is grave and see 'im now.

"'*E* was 'ung, that's what 'e was me boy in them days when they 'ung yer fer 'orse-stealin' 'e was. We got our pride, fumerly pride an' we don't make no mays aliongsez. Yer Ma's pa was the best safe-blower wot *never* was!

"An' 'ere's our own child, our only child we 'as bin lavishin' on. Our own 'Ide Park. Cottinin' on to the mission-house. Kissin' cops I shouldn't wonder! Gawd, it's more than a decent man can stand. Servile, that's what 'e is, servile. It's orfal 'avin' to say it of yer own son, servile!

"You'd let a lot of Toffs get away with *Everythink*! And let them *keep* it! Without as much as a thankye to yer.

"Jus' becorse they sing when they talks!

"Where's yer brains? Where's yer sense er justice? Where's yer self-respec'?

"Can't yer stand up in a fair fight an' take wot comes ter yer?

"Lor' blimme, yer might a bin born of a bank clerk! A bank clerk wot passes the cashier's safe, *hevery* day of 'is life, swelp me God, an' dies in the poor 'ouse, without a word of complaint.

"Ain't yer got *no* sense o' right nor wrong?

"Why I suppose if the Lord Mayor O'Lunnon left 'is front door open yer'd walk straight up an' ring the bell. Wouldn't yer now?

"Aow—don't cry, yer daddy didn't orter a' said so much. I didn't mean 'arf of it. There, me own lad, kiss as many cops as yer like. 'Taint nothing serious. You'll get all right, s'soon as yer voice breaks."

"I'm cryin', perpa," sobbed Hyde Park Hinderman, "Cause yer is a bad man."

This wilful misinterpretation of his reprovals exhausted the able burglar's compassion. He lifted his offspring by the seat of his pants, and chucked him downstairs.

+

The mission house and The Society for The Prevention of Cruelty to Children (all this society's wards are children who fail to reform their parents) took up this case.

Very little could have been done however, had it not been for that accident which was to help young Hyde in his laudatory design. The cops at last "got" his Pappa and Mamma and their sentence was for so long that it was hardly worthwhile for the son to wait for them to come out.

The mission house took him, and the mission house watched, how every day his eyes grew more innocent, his lashes pointed straighter up to heaven.

+

Mrs. Switheringham Bates first noticed him hanging round the preparation of lilies for the altar in the little chapel. She asked his history.

"Sad, sad," she said. A childless widow, she had often wished to adopt just such a pair of eyes as these.

"Criminals you say, dear me!" It was most annoying. "Criminals."

"And what," she asked Hyde some weeks later on another of her visits of charity. "What gave you the idea, er, what made you long – –"

"How long?" enquired Hyde willingly.

"I mean, what made you feel you would *like* to become converted?"

The child puzzled himself for awhile.

"I know," he answered brightly, "it was that orfal stale smell in the pubs."

"But what do you want to do – – with your Life – – Have you *thought*?"

"Oh mam, I want, I do so want to be good."

"Why?" asked Mrs. Bates suspiciously.

"Cause everybody what is anybody, anybody wot don't get chased around *is*."

This revelation of "goodness" surprised her into pondering deeply within herself; she was forced to admit it coincided with her own conception, exactly.

"And when you *were* good, what would you do then?"

"Make everybody what isn't good, good too," said Hyde staunchly.

"Why?" asked Mrs. Bates, almost threatening him.

"I want," said the boy, spreading wide his arms, "to make the whole world smell of flowers."

"Why?" snapped Mrs. Bates again.

"Cause," said Hyde Park ecstatically, "It would be same as here. An' I like it. I liii-ke it!"

"That boy," she remarked later, "has the most beautiful instincts."

"We begin to believe," said the parson, "that he has the vocation."

"And criminals, you say, extraordinary."

"Er – – What about his education?" she demanded irritably.

The parson looked her squarely in the eyes.

"The Lord will provide."

"But criminals; impossible!"

"You forget," he said, "To the Lord, all things are possible."

"The responsibility," she objected.

"The Influence," he encouraged her.

"The Taint?"

"I am convinced, that some ancestor – –"

"Ah, an ancestor?" She brightened.

"Was one of us. We have here, a pure throw-back."

"You think so?"

"I am convinced."

"I shall consult a criminolo – – – a specialist."

"I only hope," said the parson, pressing her hand, "He will understand this case."

+

Mrs. Bates did not return however, for some time. She was worried.

"You mope," said the new young doctor.

She told him of her loneliness, her love of youth around her. Piece by piece, he got the whole story of those innocent eyes.

"You fear, because the parents are criminals?"

"Yes."

"But excuse me, with you the boy would, would he not, be amply provided for?"

"I don't adopt by halves, I think I may say it would be—amply."

"He would get a first-rate education and what is more important, *plenty* of amusement I suppose?"

"Ah," sighed Mrs. Bates. "How I should love to hear him laugh.

"Of course as things *are* at present it is only fitting that he should remain a little too serious. But under other circumstances, - - - - - - I should discourage it."

"Oh certainly."

"The Parson thinks he has the vocation - - - but I should hardly care - - - a great fortune brings responsibilities, doctor. He would have to devote himself - - -"

"Precisely. But what about— What does the boy want?"

"He wants," said Mrs. Bates, "At present, to reform the world."

"There's scope for a career," the doctor laughed. "- - ways for spending your money which would hardly pass unnoticed. Should he make his attempt in good faith. He might after all land in prison."

"But what a different landing."

"Might influence the sentiment of the vote. Heard Debs got one million votes for presidency when he was *in* - -"

"But in America."

"Well he could run a newspaper."

"Dear man, it would cost him millions not to get bought up."

"If he went in for it in good faith - -"

"He would fail."

"They have," said the doctor, "all failed."

"I sometimes think great failure makes more fascinating men, than great success."

"They have more time."

"Such men understand women."

"Ah, they understand each other."

"It's true we have the eternal disadvantage."

"So ingeniously disguised."

"I am sure doctor, you will do very well indeed here.

"So you really persuade me that such an experiment would not end in calamity?"

"Calamity—but not in that particular calamity you might expect."

"Yet – – criminals?"

"With what you have to offer him, who would ever dream of crime? And there is one rule in heredity, dear lady, that is invariable. The impulse of the child is towards the negation of the parent. You cannot tell me you have never noticed this? – – – – In yourself – – ?"

"We never take for granted the things we prove. – – – Yes, I am, I admit it, only charitable because I wished from the first to supersede my mother's frivolity, my father's gree – –"

The doctor reprovingly,

"He amassed a very great fortune, Mrs. Bates."

"Why yes, one should only assess people at what they are worth."

"Which has made the experiment you are about to make, possible for you."

"Criminals." She harped plaintively,

"He might, you know, inherit the desire – –"

" 'The desire' is money. With that and an exaggeration of bad manners. The solution of the criminal may occur to you. There is no 'criminology.' "

"But when 'they' have small heads and – – – violate?"

"Ah, that's a different thing—pathology."

"Of course," said Mrs. Bates. "These parents have not killed—"

"—and murder is merely bad temper, given a cranium of normal proportions."

"Doctor you are a terrible man. What you must think of humanity! And yet you cure us."

"There you have it. That is indeed, in many cases, criminal. See, we are not so terrible after all, we criminals. Good night— And *don't* take things so scrupulously. There is only one duty, and it has never been done – –"

"You have made me feel so much brighter, doctor. It's stopped raining? *Good* night!"

+

Mrs. Bates, reacting from the doctor's philosophy, did consult a criminologist.

He was old, and the last bright patch had faded from his expectations.

He showed her charts. He shook his head.

He hoped for less than nothing of thieves' progeny.

The exasperation, that being a plain woman she always felt when choosing a hat, kindled her.

She had chanced on one more beautiful thing she coveted. It seemed as usual unsuitable. Again she renounced the idea of adoption.

Only, the next time she visited the mission house, Hyde was singing in the choir. It was an unfair ordeal for her: they had put him in a surplice.

The sight was *too* reassuring.

She gave orders for the records to be searched for his forbears.

A sexton was discovered on the distaff side, and this she felt justified her in taking the risk.

The parson regretted having been perhaps over persuasive, for Hyde Park Hinderman passed altogether into the hands of Mrs. Bates, to be known henceforth as Hyde Bates.

+

When the ego detaches itself from its surroundings, it leaves those surroundings littered about, waiting to regain significance from a revaluation.

So much disorderly building material, so much unfashionable stuff from which to select something fitting for the construction of the visible edifice of a personality, from which to shape the circumstantial garments of the spirit.

To the sensibility of Jacky Sider feeling of the stuff of his surroundings, it asserted itself to a grimly gloomy drop-curtain to the theatre of his future. Which it was urgent that he should lift.

It was jagged and faded, disintegrated and cubistic, it hung over him, pressed upon him, knocked against him.

His entourage of the ragman's shop fluttered dustily across his mind like a shredded fabric.

Rusted, twisted metals, battered rectangular inanimate—tables and chairs— The violated surface of the sawed-up corpses of trees, the denuded lewdness of pawned bed sheets: his father and mother counted them, fingered them, stacked them up with a sullen kind of joy. It appeared as if for them, these things were permits for the entrance to a shrine.

In the little back room where the clock ticked, there was a big bed and a candlestick of a youth and maiden under a big white china convolvulus dashed with gilt. In the back room there lingered in the day-time a certain volcanic peace.

Always after the day's haggling, the man and woman went to bed as early as they could. Yet this was the only hour their movements did not drag. After the meal of sausage and lettuce, they drew in the trestles which lurched under their soiled treasures outside the shop, with a febrile despatch.

They became like people about to go to the theatre.

All day long Jack saw them as animals who had learned to count. Sometimes when his mother said softly

"C'mon Jim, I've seen to the shutters," he saw them as angels, in the evening, on their way back to Heaven.

Jack "knew" what there is to be known, yet in the light of actual life, he did not know.

He was not bewildered by the strange convulsion of his breath when certain women passed him in the street.

But then they shone.

Their powder and their rouge seemed only the scintillating pulveresence in the radius of an arc-light.

They could not be covered. Their clothes were only added to them for the same purpose as the dog's feathers in the unsolvable riddle.

He knew of desire, and its promise of appeasement. The flesh of these women was of iridescent substance.

The man and the woman who had—most negligible of all the actualities, to the child—begotten him, were grey of hue and scrubby.

He could conceive of no magic that might spread a light on his mother's dusty curls.

They were there poor beasts, obviously, to feed him, that must be all.

And yet without realising, he knew their poverty to be blessed.

The neighbours sold more sightly goods, their shops were bright with paint.

But there were nowhere, among them, such concerted eyes, such irkless silences between a husband and wife, as in the rag-shop.

The rickety sort of balcony-attic in which Jack slept seemed to him the platform of a visionary railway station at which the express of the future was always overdue. He did not, like his parents to their room, retire to it; he was always starting out from it after blank uncalculated interims of sleep, sparsely sequined with dreams of what his ego had alone selected as compatible for his building stuff, from among the provisions of the rag shop: coins.

Dreams of coins.

Except for this, "home" merely tripped him into black pools of unconsciousness punctuating his hurry of life.

He must make up for his parents' lost time.

+

"Now you be off to school!"

"Aw rot! That man stuck up in the desk there, 'es 'arf a corpse a'ready. If I'm to look at 'im any longer, I'll grow like 'im. 'Es underpaid, that's wot 'e is."

"'Es doin' 'is duty."

"Aw, paw, 'e ain't doin' 'is duty. 'Es 'avin' me on. Wot th'great 'ell d'yer think I can learn from a man wots underpaid? Don't it prove 'e knows nothing? Would 'e stand for it if 'e 'ad any wits?"

"Well me boy, we can't hoil be millionhairs."

"Aw can't we? An' oo sez we can't I'd like ter know? Not nobody didn't. Oo is it 'as 'angs the little labels on the babies wot is allowed? Jus' so's nobody won't interfere with 'em, I serpose.

"Not 'arf! Hinglands' a free country hain't it? Or *hain't* it?"

"If yer wants ter be a millionhair yer'll *'ave* ter stick ter yer 'rittimetick, now then?"

"Yer can't," said Jack, "make no mistakes about money. Not if yer *love* it."

"Yer got ter count it."

"Bah, yer bin countin' all yer life, an' where's it got yer?

"Wot yer got ter do is to *'ave* money. The money will count itself. Never *yer* fear."

"Now do yer know wot yer talks like? Like a yid."

"Yer see 'ere, paw, I'm all fed up with this 'ere lack o' patriotism, everybody takin' it fer granted nobody can't 'ave any interlect, 'ceptin' ther bloody Jews.

"I'll show them!"

"Jacky, Jacky, 'ave a care, with orl yer persumpshun," warned mother Sider.

"It's right down dangerous to talk wot yer bin talkin' to yer pore par.

"D'yer know that there's other things wot's a'most as orful as Jews theirselves, an' them is crim'nals.

"'Ave a care that all this blither abart money don't lead yer ter crime, one day or 'nother.

"Fer it's money wot's ther temptation of ther devil.

"Think on yer pore ma, me dear, think er yer pore pa, and leave all that there evil to the gentry wot the Lord 'as born to it."

Jack, who at the mention of crime, had begun to hum, more than unconcernedly, sauntered out of the shop.

Jack Sider's values were not his mother's nor his father's.

In the back parlour of a not far distant pub, he stood conversing with his friends. A circle that had been much depleted by the removal of Hyde Park's parents; a circle that was on the watch for new talent.

"'E's quick, 'e is, and slim. It's a great thing, slimness in young 'uns, yer can use 'em in a variety o' ways."

"Oos tooterin' 'im?"

"Long Sloan, 'ere."

"Wot 'im! 'E's some tooter, I don't think! Look 'ow 'is young 'Ide Park turned out, that's a pretty bit o' tooterin' to my mind."

"Wot, Long? 'E's tootered some o' the best wot's never bin cotched. Yer ferget, that child o' Handrew's, 'e was always habnormal. There weren't nothing to be done with 'im. 'Is Par 'isself got reglar wore out with 'im, if it 'adn't been fer the strain, I betcher he wouldn't be *in* now."

"Well, young un do yer feel up to joinin' us on our privit 'scursion down ter 'Enly?"

"Gummy I do," said Jacky.

"An' looke 'ere. Yer only a beginner an' yer can't expec' tir divide up, not yet. That'll come. Say we give yer tew shillins fer yer evenin'?"

"O that'll come, will it? Yer don't say! Well it *as* come, mind yer, or I *'asn't*—

"This ain't no perfeshun where youth ain't no disadvantage, it ain't. Why I'm quicker than the lot o' yer. An' besides," he jibed,

"I'm still a pure one; I ain't got to 'ave no fear o' the perlice. They'd give me – – – O much more nir ten shillins, jus' fer yer address."

"Quick is 'e, quick is 'e? I told yer 'e'd be boss o' the 'ole gang before he was bearded. That boy," roared Long Sloan delightedly, " 'e's a compensation, that's what 'e is ter me, a compensation for all the disappointments that ever 'appened to me. Especially 'Ide Park."

+

It was not difficult for the Siders's son to be out at night. If the parental horizon was limited, he had the external liberty of children whose parents' lives are self-contained.

Having bred him and fed him the Siders assumed, except on such occasions as his nimble ambitions alarmed them, that as things went very well with them, they were going well with him.

The private excursion arrived at Henley; to be exact, right under the shrubbery of Mrs. Switheringham Bates's riverside bungalow, which had become known to them through her prodigal connection with the mission house. They had been able to ascertain the periods of her absences in town, and tonight they expected an easy job, avoiding the servants' quarters.

It was a still night. And as the stillness deepened, the slim one, hoisted on the shoulders of a senior, grasped a window sill.

In those days, to their hygienic experience an open window at night meant negligence and disoccupation. This gaping asunder of the cottage façade had met with them like a providence, determining their choice of entry.

Jacky had hauled himself onto the sill, enforced by the nether man's vertical arm, and peered into a yawning blackness—

It was at this moment intruded upon by a lighted candle that illumined the pane of glass like a moon.

His burglarous caryatid dropped from beneath him and his own unmistakeable silhouette remained where it was.

"What do you want?" asked Mrs. Bates, as one who addresses a servant, holding the silver candlestick still steadily.

"What are you doing on my window-sill—at this hour of the night? Who *are* you?"

Jacky's brain broke on the crisis. Into the rift there wedged itself, an associated idea.

Charity treats to the wholesomer plays have a highly educational value.

—"Somewhere where? In the dark. A boy looking in at a window – –" He had known all this before.

"When? Where? – – – –"

Then he remembered.

"Who are you?" asked the woman with the candle yet again.

"I'm," said Jacky Sider

"Peter Pan."

"But what—" she asked, so taken aback that this statement had no time to sound unnatural, "—ever do you want?"

"Jus' to 'ave one look into one o' them 'appy nurseries."

It was only lately that she had had a chance to be a mother—Hyde Bates was really here tucked downily into his bed—and the factitious maternity stirred that deep something within her, that stirs in real mothers – – whenever it does.

It was an entirely new and satisfying sensation, and she was not averse to staging its effect.

"Why you poor motherless creature," she cooed, raising the windows, and holding the candle to Jacky's face.

No his eyes were not upwardly angelic like "her" dear Hyde's—but shining now in his relief, to their usual warmth of liveliness, he looked, "just a loveable young rascal, all mischief, with not an iota of harm in him, the dear fellow."

Jacky with her robust aid stepped into the room, and Long Sloan was never to know this particular compensation again.

+

He felt as soldiers back from the trenches felt, in their beds, as though he were falling through softness.

This pastel room offered itself to him like a cheek.

Mrs. Bates led him to the other boy's bed. There where the prodigious lashes lay shrined, in something like lace. She could remember the Madonna as she bent above the bed, her hair which was loosened fell from her temples, veil-like. It was sparse hair and Jacky saw how it shone, not from itself like the women in the streets, but with a moderate shining that seemed to be applied to it.

"And now," she proclaimed, having brushed those lashes devoutly enough with her lips, "You see the happy nursery."

"Gawd," said Jacky Sider, as the sleeper in subconscious disturbance, turned and revealed the back of his head.

"It's a boy!"

Blue painted birds were everywhere about; he felt as though there must be a rush of them over his head, out of the room with him as he followed the mistress of the house downstairs, between the terraced frames of reticent gilt.

"Now," said Mrs. Bates, switching on the lights which fell first upon huge silver bowls filled with rose-coloured roses; the very silver which had lured him here with his friends, "How about a little supper?"

But it was as if a voice was driving insistently into his brain.

"When you had taken away all you could?

"What about all that was left?

"What about all there would always be left?

"What about *where* it came from?"

And he seemed to rise before himself, emptying the ocean with a thimble—like a personage in some old story he had been told.

"– – – A little supper?"

"I s'pose" said Jacky, looking round the room, "you couldn't never get more'n you wanted?"

"I never got anything I wanted," said Mrs. Bates, "until my angel upstairs – – –"

"An' 'ow've yer got all this 'ere, if yer don't want it?"

"Why, that? —Oh well you see my poor father was a very rich man, he left me all sorts of things. I hardly noticed.

"I think I had better show you," she said, contemplating the boy with a helpful air, "some pictures of all the other houses, this is only a cottage."

She reached out for a vellum album lying on the table.

"This is my place in town – – – and this – – – here is – –

"I have only shown you these," she added, when they came to her Villa in Biarritz, "because I wanted to tell you that with it all, my father was not a happy man.

"I look upon it as a very great lesson."

And Jacky, who seemed not to have heard, asked,

"Was yer father thrifty?"

"Thrifty? Well, yes, you might say he was thrifty; on a very large scale."

"A, very – – large – – –" repeated Jacky with autohypnotic concentration, "Oh." And at last, "Yes, I, understand."

Meditatively he began to stroke the puce brocaded velvet covering the chair on which he sat.

"That's very," smiled his hostess, "very old."

"Old?" he enquired, surprised.

"Ah," she said, "there are things to which age gives greater value, and other old things which have no value at all."

"Would you mind," said Jacky earnestly, "saying that over again."

"– – to which—" he repeated after her musingly, "—age— Yer mean its jus' bein' old stuff?—gives greater—value— And is value the same as wot is price?"

"It is," smiled Mrs. Bates benignly.

He ate in silence some more of the chicken in aspic she had given him. Their light of loveable mischief had dimmed to reflections more profound as he raised his eyes to hers.

"D'yer know, mam," he said, "Something must 'ave sent me to yer. To prevent me from going wrong."

She was all surprised. Youths, she reflected, seemed as a genus to have spiritual attributes she could never have guessed. She felt suddenly glad that she had on the outset of her discoveries secured, however, the very best.

This was very nice of course, but after all, nothing, compared to Hyde who had wanted—"To make the whole world smell of flowers."

Mrs. Bates was by nature a mono-maternalist.

"I've learnt more to-night," concluded Jacky, "than I never 'ave."

+

The atmosphere of the rag-shop was rather disturbed, on the morrow. A motherly heart having invited the tired lad to sleep on the library couch—he had lost himself from a picnic he had told Mrs. Bates, "dreamin' of Peter Pan"—and given him a goodly breakfast—

It was eleven o'clock before Jacky burst into his home.

He found it had shrunk. It was somehow smaller than himself.

"Go' mercy me," cried Mother Sider, "To think I might really 'ave giv' birth to a criminal – – at this time o' the mornin'."

She was frightened by some awesome change in her son, who seemed to be catching his breath.

"Muther," he demanded in a stormy whisper, " 'As it ever struck you how much *much* richer the 'onest ones is?"

"Rich, rich, I never 'ad nothing to do with it—'rich'!"

+

The ego of Ian Gore found nothing at all in his surroundings to utilise in the structure of the visible edifice of his spirit. Not even the coins that so much more properly came his way, than for Jacky Sider, could he make serviceable.

There was, according to him, "no intrinsic beauty within range of the parasites on the shop-keeper.

"The artist out of his own brain and his own sinews had made for his own spiritual indulgence all that has been appropriated by culture.

"A drop of his sweat transforms to fabulous fortunes—in the simulacrum of our understanding— The seventh wonder of the world of Croesus proceeds unaided out of his eye. Everything of *superlative* value must be formed from nothing."

His clean sweeping attitude to the world in which he found himself was that it had not yet been made. ——

Even the darling girls in the dust of urban spring must wait for seductiveness until they should be "made over" by him.

Nor was there any horticulture for his passions in the temperate zone of his parents' marriage.

There was no lurking penetralia of their home to intrigue his pubescent fancy to define. No warmth of shadow receding from the daily habitude.

Mr. and Mrs. Gore were reserved, as people who have no reserves. Their household gods were so sanctified that they had never known their names. Counterpoised and empty scales. Loving and respecting each other for having done a dirty thing, and for, that the bonds of matrimony had made of it as if it had never been. Ian's mother always spoke of "your father" as though he had something ominous about him, and concurrently a dispensation from Providence.

They both seemed only with the years to be scrupulously washing themselves away.

Like millions and millions of us, they were living off a literature that has worn down to asterisks.

Ian, in opposition to his beginnings in their polished vacuum, had been passed through the fine filters of many minds, with particular reference to the cooling quality of those minds, having received no inoculation of sensuality among the animated furniture that so unaccountably stood for his parentage, instinctively conjectured that he might rather to have been conceived of some circumstance virile and intransigent, like a boxing-match.

And it was this absence of conviction of continuity with anything antedating him that instigated him to create anew.

At the art school he found the first latitude for his rearrangements where the actual that had been lacking to him revealed itself malconformed by denutrition and inactivity.

The nude model as a self-condemning protest against the overclothed.

He regarded the poor bare man, sagging on his staff, with his eyes of a lizard that had known no sun, and the excrescences of his unproud knees confounding his symmetry.

And in this invalid desert of northerly light, the Hermes of Praxiteles had been raising himself in eternal commentary.

Ian was huge above the students, straddled there with his bronze head reared over his coarse garb of a house painter and in his eyes, like bloodstones, flickered sudden lights of violent suspicions; he would now and then turn from his scrutiny, to spit aside. He was chewing tobacco.

Then he spat himself out of the door.

When he returned he was holding high up from the ground something unrecognisable, and dangling limply, and damp. The rope was coiled loosely through his fist.

He stretched the clothesline across a corner of the studio, and shifted the wooden pegs into position. A pair of drawers and a cotton shirt hung from them, upside down. They had been washed by the porter's wife in the little back courtyard where Ian had found them.

Ian stood an easel up before them and began to draw.

The busy students became even more silent than before. Eccentric Englishmen, they suspected the disinterestedness of another Englishman's eccentricities.

Unconcerned as his movements had been it was most probable that he counted on attracting their attention.

They behaved as London behaves at the parties of the newly rich.

But the newcomer was drawing with authentic ardour, there was a virile litheness in the lines of dejection—he scattered about.

+

And when the Professor entered he could scarcely be said to have glanced at the isolated monomaniac as he strolled on his rounds of correction.

He would cock his head aside a student's and together they would wag, appraising the proportions of the lamentable being who hardly appeared able to hold together at all.

He talked a good deal of sensing the bourgeois structure beneath the masses, of noting how the leaning torso sagged into the pelvis.

When Ian felt that he was coming towards him he half abstract-edly lifted off the long leg he had been resting over the wooden stool, and drawing aside a little, waited with a certain attention.

The Professor surveyed the drooping garments almost cautiously; with Ian's drawing he was considerably more at ease.

"Well," he said, "I suppose you know what you are doing."

"That is my intention."

Ian drew towards the little man and pushed his eyes slowly into his, as if imparting a confidence.

"I feel," he rumbled ponderously, "for the contours of collapse, the bony structure to be, er, misleading.

"That is, that every issue, aesthetically should be kept—pure—absolute.

"If you get me?

"And that the degeneration of form, if it must be considered, be followed to its inevitable—ah—conclusions.

"That for instance, I can perhaps put it more clearly—the essence of drooping is a lack of inner support."

The professor nodded at every pause.

"That fluidic quality of your line, I like," he said.

"I aim, at—er—that particular sagging so to speak, of the stuff into the atmosphere," Ian answered.

The professor popped down the chalk he was holding with a sharp return to himself— He looked at the model and then at Ian.

"Anyhow," he said, "Next week we have a woman."

"Ah the bastard—" Ian mumbled after him, "—the bastard!"

It was as if he had been smudged horribly across his eyes with an intimation of something unformedly akin to the creature on the model's throne.

It occurred to him that he had never seen a woman unclothed.

Because the studio dust was somehow similar to the straggling hair on that body, it seemed so fearsomely to deprive that body of a divine right.

It was as if his mother in her chaste dress momentarily in his vision, foundered.

+

The sun through delicate shades was shining on Hyde as he awoke.

He was conscious of nothing except the vast living landscape of his body in which the faculty of existence never came to a frontier.

And yet the chest with the marble angels stood immovable only three yards from where he lay.

The bone of his brow and the spring of his nose between his eyes seemed to increase to a volatile mountain in which the mental nerves lay diffused in the strange numbness of this something infinite he projected.

The golden penetration of the sun through his eyelids, spread inwardly like supernatural light—

it liquefied him, and lifted him in imaginary ascension.

To his soul there were no limitations once he had shut his eyes.

TRANSFIGURATION.

Outside the window a dead man hung from a tree beside the track, and the wind moved in his trousers.

The scout-train with its watchful soldiers standing barefoot on the roof preceded us for a space of danger, shunted off somewhere into the steaming sunset.

We crawled along among the prodigious verdure, miraculously ejected in a thousand varieties from the same inch of earth that bound the cocos in spiral strangulation, and fell in tufted cascades in their rush towards the skies.

Now that it was no longer protected, our train bucked monstrously, jarring my spine with the reverberation of impact; the gliding locomotive had been driven leisurely upon by another – – – yet it was still twilight. The lights of an Indian farm in a clearing were not twinkling very brightly yet.

One of the extra soldiers who lay along his gun on the roof of a compartment rolled off and was crushed between the buffers; he was still a child and his gun was splintered.

"Do you come from far away?" asked the Mexican woman at my side.

"From Europe, New York, from Mexico City, and I have no salt."

In my lap, saltless, in white impotence to the appetite, lay six hard boiled eggs; the sullen light from the ceiling filmed in their slippery spheres, while contours like diagrams for constructing female heads in old art primers reminded me how Dan Leno had said: "Funny thing an egg – – – – it hasn't got any face."

"Come we will go to the Indians and beg some salt," said my companion.

Night pressed on the red glow of the torches held to the private parts of the locomotive that the train men were tinkering at blunderingly.

We pressed the palpable blackness that hit us back at every onward step, and arrived at a circle of human shadows. A woman with breasts under her insane hair challenged us, then she murmured to the circle and brought us back her gift.

I held my cupped palm out before me as I walked over the rocking flints, carrying the rough and turgid crystals carefully as a sacrament through the dark where the parted forest reared over the steel ribbons of the railroad.

Thick within the infinite foliage a sudden wooden seed would fall and stroke to a hush the close lying layers of leaves. In there, in the turbulent jungle entangled, lurked with their strange diplomacies of smell, species of beasts. How would it be to hack through these fortresses of vegetation? To move footloose among violent fowl and fantastic insects haunted by my primeval recognitions? To hold my peace with the stir of the forest, that sibilant silence – – – the inbreath of nature, drawing me in a panic of treacherous invitation?

The s-s-stir – – – every moment the Night should come crashing through with the incalculable tonnage of his invisible footsteps, to snap the cocos and tear the savage plants – – – – And something enormous, sentient, inimicable was striding now among the unholy vapours left by the setting of a murderous sun – – – – – the forestal Jove.

The flesh of the Mexican woman's face was baked onto the bone and must jar inhumanly to the touch. In her glaucous eyes the memories of her excitements shrapnelled like the flavour of the Chili pod.

Where woman meets woman in out of the way places her first concern is to tender a conversational passport of her chastity, so does the thin-lipped spectre of dishonour drive her buffoons before her even to the end of the earth.

My companion who had fallen thankfully upon half of the eggs and the crude salt, told me how she had had to leave her native town, owing to the misadventurous liaison of her son with a light woman. She was seeking to renew her impeccable occupation as a seamstress elsewhere. I could understand could I not? Her shame and her humiliation before the neighbours who had watched her flower and wither, a virginal tiger lily, before and after her espousals and widowing. And even as she tore the egg with her teeth, did she wrack that light body of her left-hand daughter-in-law for my approval.

Confident that I had now accepted her at a desirable valuation, clucking, and darting appraisals of the passengers on the train, she told me that the bad land of Mexico was populated by the devil's brood, and that I should save half a peso and probably my life by staying overnight at the apothecary's to whose good graces she would accompany me.

Every night we got off the train to sleep in some village for fear of the marauding bandits, and after the engine had been put to rights we pulled in at our station.

The streets were unlit and unpaved, only once did we come to a glimmer of light on the wayside. It was shining through the serried chinks of a bamboo structure. I loitered against it, and watched the shadowy pantomime of a small girl swinging a baby to sleep in a grocery box hung from the roof-beam. The petroleum light threw out its infinitesimal gossamer circles of hazy gold, and the streaks of the bamboos interposed their black notes or dissolved, as I moved my face from or toward the nebulous lullaby in silhouette.

As if he had sprung out of the mud beneath our feet, a male form now accompanied us; he had performed some ceremony of etiquette with my companion, and undertook to pick our steps for us to gain the eating house.

As he swept the broken flies from the table-cloth he eyed us with a Spanish cajolery, and when we were served he fell upon his food with the oversatisfaction of a man who has chanced on more than one good thing at once.

A repulsive complacence spread his fat face to a sensuous rhapsody; he looked a low creature, and the wares he was travelling with one surmised to be of inferior quality, but his behaviour as with even the spawn of the Latin races was suave and somewhat entertaining, and the Mexican woman warmed to it.

The apothecary, warned of our approach, opened his door to let the light fall across our path to guide us. His guest chambers were a couple of boarded partitions which had been knocked together casually and did not reach to the ceiling. Two little beds covered with horse blankets furnished the one I was to share with the seamstress.

She lay where the general light pouring over the top marked a new aspect of elation on her face, as she continued in her womanly way, the epic of her virtue.

The last banalities are enriched by an unfamiliar language, and it was a shimmering impression she engraved for me in her peon Spanish, of her girlhood spent in her father's bar-room. Of stacks of cut glass, coloured syrups, of gardenias, camellias. Of a Count with side whiskers, his phaeton and his Mexican horse of Greek proportions.

Far into the night my drowsiness was punctuated by the sting of a mosquito or a crisis in the seamstress' drama. For the whiskered Count who was sometimes a Baron, sometimes a deputy, seemed to fling himself into the story and out again through a clattering glass door.

There were entreaties, vows, objurgations, temptation by diamonds, and levelled pistols. And persistently, behind some sort of a carved white counter the seamstress marooned her virtue.

Through the following day we would stop at platforms where objects of ingenuous grace were brought to be sold, such things as willow canes gashed with patterns in the tradition of the Aztecs – – – And bronze girls offered their architectural bouquets from the white fields of tuber-roses shrining their coloured centres of tinfoil. Beauties that flew in at the window, and were spirited away as soon as bought.

Sometimes a surprise of Nature would curvet past the window to the flying perspective of the passing train. Flat on the stubbly land – – – a pond – – – a white sheet of sunlight sowed with frail and leafless flushed convolvuli stared at the colourless blaze of sky it reflected, in dazzling innocence – – – like a heavenly mirror studded with angelic eyes – – – cutting my breath with pure light.

But after noon the sky of the rainy seasons darkened and poured itself onto the earth, and when we came to our pitch black resting place we leapt from the foot board into a deep river of mud; the rain beat us onward to invisible retreats, and the damp voices of extinguished will-o'-the-wisps led us to travellers' inns.

I found myself in a high foul room where the dust cried out from the horrible stagnation of the ewers and basins of cheap hostelries; alone with the echoes of the planed corridors, the glassy eyes of the host, and the fearful iron of his bunch of keys. For in the black rain I had lost my seamstress who had engaged to house me as safely on this night as on the last; and now she might be scuttling about with her virtue seeking me in the night.

I plunged again into the deluge, and other invisible couriers preceded me to a second rooming house which I supposed must be the one my companion had indicated.

Here under a flickering lamp there huddled a maze of wooden stalls with strange darkness peering over the low partitions.

I insisted that another woman had got off the train and had been anxious for me to join her. But the native hostess disagreed with my arguments – – – I described her striped shirt waist – – – "Oh don't trouble yourself, I know who you mean, only," she neighed with shrilling irony, "she came here with a man."

I was overwhelmed with the indiscretion, for whichever wooden love-nest had been assigned to them, over its truncated walls, the accusative neighing of the hostess must strike the seamstress' ear. For I felt forlorn for her hours of protested proprieties which must now appear to her so wasteful. And I crept to my stall wishing that an insistent silence could somehow obliterate my unintentional meddling.

Next morning I met her crawling along the lean planks that across the meadow upon the rain-laden flowers bore their heavier burden of humanity – – – there passed us a great couple of spouses like Gothic gods side by side – – – and the seamstress as I bid her good-day – – – shuffled confusedly before me hiding her key spasmodically in her skirts like a symbol.

With the snobbishness of those who understanding all things forgive all things – – – I endeavoured with the perfect *sang-froid* of tact to put her at her ease. But a righteous change had come over my story teller, and she hated me now with the just and bitter hatred of women who know each other to be at last but women.

For the rest of the journey she shunned me with the triumphant reproach of a legitimate criminal caught red-handed by the detective of social convention. She flung me for what it was worth, the fictitious chastity of her nocturnal anecdotes, like a superfluous trimming she had considered fitting for my unprofitable companionship.

And so I watched her on the train when she was not looking.

On awakening from the travelling salesman's embraces she had opened her meagre valise and taken from it a kerchief of shining silk, and had changed to an open-necked bodice of soft stuff.

Reanimated by the man's cajoling evocations of her consumed adolescence for his convenience, from under the copper gleam of the kerchief which she had draped about her head, her mummied face reappeared in an indescribable richness of transformation.

Her shrapnel eyes had softened to a velvet tranquillity and from the battered pores of her skin a warm disclosing radiance flowed.

She sat pondering; glowing and blossoming with that essential virginity of the spirit which women reconquer only in the arms of those illusions they call their lovers.

Regally as a Madonna she breathed the incense of their initial innocence of Nature's salute. And the unfading pollen of love, broadcast on the universe, dusted her reviving flesh as she sidled, something wild that had been tamed, against her huckster of a night.

She kept so close to him as if she had found her home after bewildering wanderings. With the gesture of possession and the abandonment of rebirth she nestled in the shadow of the fat man of commerce who was shrugging away from her in his disgusted relief.

That which had been her transfiguration seemed to have coated her consciousness with a final filth. His ugly eyes polluted her with occasional lewd and downward looks of dismissal while he argued cost prices with a man seated on his other side.

By what glaring ethical impropriety had a fly-by-night amour with a stranger in a draughty railway inn invested this woman with such chastened and spiritual a dignity?

I was fired with the preposterous fantasy that if woman has been the pack mule for the transgressions of man it is because by some alchemy of her actions, she is within herself incapable of sin. She undeniably behaves in all contingencies as if assured of a transcendental sanction.

DRAMA

CRYSTAL PANTOMIME

Everything is a black background—in front a beautiful slim maiden dances—all very white—tentatively towards a witch—all very hazy smoke grey—who teeter away from and towards each other—the witch enticingly—the maiden doubtfully—the witch holds in her hand a crystal globe.

High above them a tiny beam of light, supposed to be reflected from the moving crystal, plays fitfully on the black background—as the dancing beam on a ceiling cast from a diamond or mirror reflecting the sun. And attracted to this dancing beam a "creature," a homunculus with propeller-like wings—as much like a blue bottle or a striped wasp as possible—bumps toward and away from the spot of light. This homunculus must be artificial, his wings whirring just like a fly's, and the motion of quadrille imitating the to-and-fro darting of a summer morning housefly—which is one of the finest rhythms observable.

The dance of the maiden and the witch ends by the maiden deciding to gaze into the crystal.

The crystal begins to grow larger and larger (the homunculus disappears) until the round spotlight which has taken the place of the crystal becomes the whole scene.

The scene is circular instead of square—and represents the interior of a crystal globe with its curved planes and depths.

The maiden is now to see her life in the crystal and it is the story of the maiden's future which is to be portrayed by the ballet. Only, as this maiden lived in the times when maidens waited at home while the youths went out into the world, it is rather the adventures of the young man that she will eventually marry—leading up to this, her future marriage, that the maiden will see in the crystal.

Her only appearances will be her meetings with him and her waiting—and at last her union with him.

****

The first scene is the village green—where little girls are dancing skipping rope and little boys are playing marbles while mixed groups play shuttlecock and battledore. The whole of the ballet takes place in a transparent crystal world—and the personages partake of this crystalline appearance, particularly their clothes and their hair. This gives an impression of ethereal beauty that cannot be equalled—and the ballet takes the spectators into an evanescent dream world so irreal and tenuous that it will take their breath away. The crystal shuttlecocks of bright colors are enormously big and the curves of the glittering skipping ropes are a great addition to the attitudes of the dance.

The shuttlecocks afford color motion up in the air—and the equally enormous glass marbles of the playing boys, a balance on the ground. The dance of the skipping ropes will be simultaneous to a leapfrog dance of the boys—the circular motion of the skipping ropes and the swift horizontal movements of the boys—who seem to fly across the stage when leapfrogging—as Nijinsky did in *The Spirit of the Rose*, giving an interesting modern rhythm. The subject of the ballet will appeal to everyone because, being so simple, the high-brows will enjoy it with that humorous compassion they afford for the souvenir sentiments and the general public will "get" it without effort. It is rich in possibilities as all simple eternal subjects are.

The maiden appears in this scene for she is the principal little girl with yellow glassy plaits tied with a blue ribbon. The little girls and the little boys mock one another in their play. But the principal little boy takes a shy notice of the little girl. He snatches her blue glass hair ribbon and offers the little girl his marble. The little girl scoffs at his attentions and, chucking the marble into the hollow of a nearby tree, dances off jeeringly while all the children dance and disperse. That is the end of the childhood recollection. The little boy looks at the blue ribbon he is holding and stuffs it into his pocket.

The scenes change while the crystal becomes cloudy. The nearer scenery is constructed of a transparent material like glass and the distant scenery is thrown onto the crystal planes by a kind of magic lantern—from the back if possible in order not to reflect on the dancers. The magic lantern scenery enhances the ethereal effect of unreal beauty.

****

The second scene is adolescence meeting at a country fair. One or two booths with fancy trifles which lend themselves particularly to bright glass colors—very much exaggerated in size—and diminished in number to give a decided decorating effect of composition—a little of the ridiculous that lends so much charm to ancient art and the sufficiency of a symbol to express a more complex actuality. There is at this fair an arbour of green glass trellis and climbing plant and in this arbour is a round table at which can be partaken of enormous glasses of vivid colored syrup.

The maiden visits the country fair chaperoned by her mother and grandmother. The grandmother is bent over a cane and dances with faltering steps. She wears a dolman cloak and ballet-dancer's legs. The mother wears a pork pie hat tipped over her nose, carries a lorgnette and her ballet skirt is a draped bustle with a tail of bunched drapery such as hung down the back of bustle skirts—but the skirt is absent—the movements of her dance give the poker-swan-like effect of the period—only her slim legs are also in tights—there is *no* skirt—with her hanging draperies she gives the effect of a gracefully slim-legged bird with its tail dragging.

There is a dance of ceremonies of meeting and introduction. The youth invites the maiden and her maternal ascendants to partake of monstrous syrups in the bower. This incident is very brief—the grandmother and mother dance off rigorously with the maiden—who glances back once—and sees the youth contemplating the blue bow he stole from her when a child.

****

Later: Twilight falls—the fair disappears. The maiden steals out in the dusk and dances to the hollow tree on the village green—

a dance of fireflies induced by moving lights—always with that together and apart dancing of insects in the air which gives the *leit-motif* to most of the rhythm of this ballet. The maiden has stolen to the hollow tree to look for the marble she had so long ago thrown away—it is the hour of sentiment and she is thinking of him. The fair is invaded by *amorini* who turn on the merry-go-round (a reproduction of the one in Paris with silver horses and mermaids). They fly away, the scene changes to a field of long grass. Several ladies are plucking fancy grasses—the cupids attack them from behind puffy little clouds in the sky—they run hither and thither affrighted, their arms outflung—under a shower of golden arrows—"the maiden" is hit. This scene is called "Ladies in a Love Storm."

****

The maiden has seen the youth contemplating her blue ribbon. She has been hit by cupid and she wants to have something to remember the youth by. So she searches in the hollow tree and finds the marble he gave her years ago—the marble bounds out on to the middle of the stage—where it appears as an enormous replica of itself with its coloured lines and twists. The maiden leans against the tree gazing at it—and gradually it evolves out of itself "the spirit of the marble"—it is a slim, a lithe sprite in all-over tights, coloured like the marble. He is almost incorporate with the marble. This dance must be danced by a very fine acrobat contortionist who can curve and squirm round the orb, push it with his pectoral muscles and when it rolls, remain with it by throwing his body and legs over his head. He must stand on his head on it, but otherwise his motion must identify itself with the circular rolling of the orb. This dance, for the maiden's eyes, expresses the personification of objects through sentiment—and that stirring of the imagination at dusk, that apprehends some living entity in the phenomena of Nature that please or arouse the dream-sense.

The old marble has become an object of palpitating interest to the maiden.

All this time the firefly quadrille continues as rhythmic accompaniment.

The scene changes—it is still dusk. There is a narrow high arch in a wall—through it one can see a fall of feathery foliage by artificial light—peculiarly beautiful green— There linger some Gypsy-like crass glass colored light ladies—beckoning to the youth— He is still gazing at his blue ribbon— The light ladies stroll up and down, pacing—their feet gripping the ground stealthily— This has still the together and apart rhythm of the insect quadrille— exactly as I have observed it outside a shady hotel in Paris. The youth remains oblivious— It grows darker for the light through the archway is extinguished and all that can be observed for a brief space is the rhythm of the pacing, stealthy, half-aimless, half purposeful legs— Then they disappear.

The youth looks up from his ribbon which does not entirely satisfy him—and out of the darkness where the light ladies have been a large, lashy, luminous eye winks at him and is extinguished— The youth is decided— He stuffs the blue ribbon, which symbolizes his conscience, into his pocket and throws sentiment to the winds.

He begins to dance in a defiant, distracted, disjointed, whirling motion—symbolizing the ebullition of youth—and in every direction towards which he whirls, a gigantic wild oat springs up right in front of him, until he dances in a perfect forest of them that absolutely impedes his movements— The scene fades— This is the dance of the wild oats.

Then follow the wild oats episodes.

The following scene is clear and gay—and the youth is dancing up to a quaint glass house—with two doorways side by side. From one doorway appears towards him a ravishing lady in a (blue or pink) paper crinoline. The sun is shining and the youth is about to clasp the lady when she pops back into the glass house and with a sudden shower of rain, her husband with a (pink or blue) umbrella emerges suddenly from the other door— The youth darts back— The rain stops— The husband disappears—the ravishing lady is again almost in his arms—when the same incidents repeat themselves. The youth, for his episode with a married lady, has come upon the old-fashioned barometer couple who predict the weather. Here we have again the to-and-fro movement in the dance rhythm. After the alternation of rain and shine has taken place a few brief times, the inevitable happens. So much sun and rain have induced a rainbow. The barometer house fades away and the youth is attracted to the spirit of the rainbow. A beautiful creature, all coloured like the rainbow. He is transported onto the rainbow—and dances (the two figures are suspended from wires) tip toe— A dance of wooing on the rainbow (which can consist of an arc of colored lights). When he is about to take her in his arms the (enormous) blue ribbon wafts itself in between him and the spirit of the rainbow—and arrests the dance. The youth falls off the rainbow onto the wet sand of the sea shore. But he has been dyed in the colours of the rainbow—and the mermaids mock at him— They sprinkle him with water to wash the rainbow stain away—and now he is all dripping wet— This effect he can attain by having long strings of transparent sequins hidden in pockets of his clothes which he can let out unnoticeably as he prepares to dance the short staccato dance of shaking himself dry—the dripping will sparkle as he dances and he will manage, by unclasping one clasp that holds them all together, to let them fall to the ground. He is now dry, and is free to turn his attention to the wooing of a beautiful mermaid with long green glass hair, who sits on a rock to comb it and he sits beside her, with her tail curled round his legs.

They enjoy a surprising spectacle—in the surf of the waves the mermaids are dancing—they are the genus of mermaids that have double tails—and on these tails they dance the trick dances that human beings dance with their legs— These dancers must also be suspended on wires in order to be able to move the tails with their legs inside them, the tails being much longer than their legs— This dance will be enchanting. The mermaids can stand on the tip of the one tail and twirl the other tail round it in pirouette. They will dance the Russian dance, their arms folded with one tail curved under them and the other tail flung violently out. The composition of the row of mermaids dancing in different attitudes on their double tails in their amusing curves will be most original.

The wooing of the beautiful mermaid is getting on finely. She coquettishly takes out her comb to comb her hair (the comb is enormous) when the youth, who is just about to embrace her, beholds the symbolical blue ribbon twisting in and out of the prongs of the comb. He leaps from the rock—all the mermaids fade away—and a huge blue wave with a crest of dripping foam hovers above him and remains stationary as a background to the next dance. In the shadow of this wave—some collapsed jelly-fish are lying on the wet sand—they gradually pick themselves up and dance, under the hovering curve of the blue wave, the dance of the jelly-fish with their crystalline domes and long floating colored streamers depending from them—they are all enticing the youth when the wave subsides—the jelly-fish fade away—and on a calm summer ocean appears the cortege of Venus in a shell drawn by horses like the white china figures I collect. The youth leaps on to the shell of Venus to which she beckons him and she points to the horizon—out on the horizon the youth sees the blue ribbon drifting—and the scene fades.

The next scene is moonlight— The youth has been lying asleep on the moss—and over him bends a dryad incorporated with a tree—the form of her ballet skirt repeats the form of the tree's foliage. She emerges from the tree and as they are about to embrace the blue ribbon floats in between them and the youth dances away—in his dance he is arrested on the point of tripping over something at his feet—it is the fairy ring—under a clump of white thorn bushes, through which the wires can be manipulated by a sitting figure, a group of exquisite marionettes dance beside a black glass pool surrounded by very luminous arum lilies—while the youth and the dryad dance a slow dance of admiration— The fairy queen is riding a fairy tiger reined with a daisy chain—when she sees the youth she descends from the tiger and dances to the youth and at last flies into his arms—and gets all wrapped up in the blue ribbon— The scene fades.

The youth is confronted by a towering column of narrow glass steps—and on its summit is a maiden bound—and round her feet curves the first curve of a dragon, with flames—tiny flames—darting from its tongue— The rest of the serpent-like dragon curves all down round the pinnacle of stairs— On either side of the maiden the sun and moon shed rays accompanied by stars—as in the old prints. The sun and moon with human faces. The scene is terrifically cold and pure in line and whiteness— even the flames of the dragon's mouth are blue like low burning gas jets. The youth dances a magnificent dance of courageous attack—always in the rhythm of to-and-fro—he darts towards the dragon—the dragon darts his head at him—the dragon draws back its head— The youth renews the attack—he has an enormous yellow gilt shield, sword, helmet and winged sandals like Mercury. At last he strikes the dragon— The pinnacle of stairs falls apart—giving an amusing cubistic pattern of white oblongs in the air at different angles to each other between the falling-apart blocks. The maiden descends, floatingly, to earth while the dragon falls apart to reveal nothing but the maiden's mother holding up her lorgnette— The maiden flies into the youth's arms—and after embraces he takes her blue ribbon out of his pocket— The scene fades.

The maiden and the youth are seated on a white china horse which gallops but never moves— Behind them every imaginable scenery passes in a brief space (cast by a magic lantern). They are on their honeymoon— The scene fades.

The crystal becomes clouded, only to light up again partially for a moment, to reveal a crystalline baby tumbling over and over itself swiftly out of the sky, while the blue ribbon, in momentous curves, with, as in old story books, "The End" written upon it, rises up to receive the baby as it falls.

THE PAMPERERS

Invisible	*Obvious*
Picked	*People*
Houseless	*Loony*

Porcelain breath — Sèvres bow — Gilded crimson — Curved flutings — Brocade — Tailored muscles — Whipped cream — Blue spirals — Salved lips — Salon — Debussy — Azaleas — Ancestors — Armorial complacencies — Ooze

Picked People melted by a distinguished method among the upholstery.

Tag Ends of Overheard Conversation

The social fabric is a curtain . . . and that warm garnet fold-shadow there, for souls' hide and seek. . . .

Decency shudders in the bare moment, taut between vestibule and auto . . . .

. . . . my crystalline lorgnette, . . . trees . . . at this season all are undressed.

The earth a poignant undertaker . . . .

I wish I had a wig darling.

. . . Observe the legs, the agony of the crucified . . . the tendons . . . delicate as Dresden china 15th century . . . ah yes! the troubles of the steam-heating plant . . . man from Milan knows his business . . . .

Oh Prince how charming of you . . . and what is your opinion of the sex question?

How simple . . . still I can't quite agree with you . . . we shall never give up wearing silk stockings.

SOMEBODY.	Ossy you know has discovered a genius . . .
OSSY.	. . . coming from the club . . . wonderful chap, see his predatory eye . . . picking up cigar ends . . . the grand passion . . . pockets full . . .
SOMEBODY.	Picasso uses all sorts of odds and ends.
OSSY.	No critic dare anticipate the masterpiece this man may stack . . .
SOMEBODY.	Mud larks and geniuses!
OSSY.	There's a revival in THE THING being a patron . . . I've got a Medici Villa somewhere . . . put the fellow in the stables here . . . heart's content . . . counting fags

Wait and see; fond of my dinner doesn't prevent me having an enormous respect for these creative sky-rocket-in-the-sewer chaps; *wait and see*
I've got flair . . . taken two of you to have got onto those cigar ends . . . *like that* . . . my God!
I'd forgotten Diana . . . Diana collects geniuses!

SOMEBODY.	She's got perfect toes . . . pedicured on a diamond footstool . . .
SOMBODY ELSE.	Bach played for her bath . . .
SOMEBODY.	Isadora Allen to dance her awake
S. E.	Bought a museum to wear at a ball
SOMEBODY.	Has to have the Daily Mail transposed into the Arabic for the autumn, British Journalese has a bite in it . . . superfluously supplements the morning frost . . .
S. E.	Steam from hot cocoa is so suggestive of breathing in the open
SOMEBODY.	But she has so many butterflies in her nightcap . . .
S. E.	Avoiding the vulgarity of looking expensive she waters the aloe in sack-cloth. Does nothing to her complexion, but a penny worth of ice
Has her own bran-mash prepared for her at the Ritz . . . reads Mahabharata through cotillions . . .

SOMEBODY.	So bored . . . has the most perfect yawn in Europe . . . virgin eyelashes, and abortive morals . . . why Di dear, we were just talking about you . . .
	(DIANA *turns off the light, sits on the pekinese which sinking still deeper into cushions notices nothing; and meditates in a fussy silence on the dial of a luminous watch.*)
	(*Two intimate* FRIENDS *sidle into the conservatory*)
1ST FRIEND.	*Can* I trust you?
2ND FRIEND.	*Did* I trust you?
1ST F.	Then I will tell you where I really was last week . . . at home with a black eye.
2ND F.	And where . . . ?
1ST F.	Oh, he was at home with a black eye too.
2ND F.	How ripping!
1ST F.	Delicious, we wore Longhi masks and had Watsiswinski play Handel on the spinet
2ND F.	Life can be very beautiful with a lover
1ST F.	The Wedgewood and the Venetian lustres are in splinters and the ceiling had to be repainted
2ND F.	It is your passion for danger, serves you your incontestable hold on our social

circle, whose criterion the intactness of porcelain, the watchword . . . "No china is ever broken here; here where the virginity of white carpets, sanctifies the passage of the correct"

1ST F.	Profundity of superficies
2ND F.	While to Stavinski's meteors the animal whines a million moons behind evening dress
1ST F.	Split passion to the forty gold pieces of a manicure set . . . and there it still is
2ND F.	Strew souls in fractions on dressing tables
1ST F.	Oh keep it up . . . disintegratedly above *those others* . . . what do you suppose they do . . . with insufficient money to do it with?
2ND F.	Nature looks after them . . .
1ST F.	When you consider what *our* régime has done to Nature
2ND F.	Diversion for our old age, in patching them up
1ST F.	Well, I suppose we're rotten . . . thank God, we're rotting soft
2ND F.	Double pile . . . or an intellect walking about on it . . .
1ST F.	Don't make me think . . . might drive me to anything . . .

| 2ND F. | Come Di's lit up again … Ossy's cocktails *Remember* … no china broken here … |
| SOMEBODY. | Diana dear, you might tell us where you *were* . . . while we were so patiently watching you? |

(DIANA's *chameleon rattles her emeralds.*)

DIANA.	Systematizing Futurist plastic velocity by the displacement of the minute-hand … *Ho capito.*
SOMEBODY ELSE.	Isn't she wonderful?
A MAN.	(*whose monocle has been hypnotized to idea associations by the luminous dial*) I don't know anything about Marinetti; I don't want to know anything about Marinetti but I respect him . . . he has a clean collar I am willing to accept the creed of any man who wears a clean collar
SOMEBODY.	Why the devil shouldn't Marinetti wear a clean collar? I don't know why Marinetti shouldn't wear a clean collar, all I say is . . . Marinetti wears a clean collar!
OSSY.	Di . . . if you half guessed what I've caught in the stables, you'd throw Futurism to …

DIANA.   Don't mean . . . that I'm out of fashion
                again
OSSY.   Since 1 P.M. . . . dispensing entirely with
                the middleman, we now have the genius
                served directly to the consumer
DIANA.   Let us consume . . .
OSSY.   (*to the footman*) James! just fetch the
                whatsisname out of the whatyoumecal-
                lems and don't let its feet touch the floor.

                (*The footmen carry in the* HOUSELESS
                LOONY *in his natural condition . . . on a
                throne chair with a step to it.
                The* LADY DIANA *has stood herself in front
                of a large light that hazes her yellow hair.*)

SOMEBODY.   Di will be able to put him at his ease!

                (*The importation fixes on her his fanati-
                cal eyes, set in the lewdest eyelids, the rest
                is stubbly.*)

DIANA.   There are only two kinds of people in
                society . . . geniuses and women.
LOONY.   I hang out with God and the Devil
DIANA.   (*continuing impressively*) I am Woman.
LOONY.   May be . . . (*sniffing her approach*) . . .
                but you smell like nothing-at-all; and

all that truck on you, makes me eye sneeze

(*Diana throws the emeralds, the chameleon and divers odds and ends vaguely in the direction of a Benozzo Gozzoli, and tries to imagine what a smell is like . . .*)

DIANA. I know . . . I knew . . . I have always known . . . you alone can see beneath the . . . beneath the . . . beneath the truck! I am the elusion that cooed to your adolescent isolation, crystallized in the experience of your manhood . . . (Oh do stop blinking at me, or I can't go on) . . . I am that reciprocal quality you searched for among the moonlit mysteries of Battersea Bridge.
I come to you with gifts those other women had not to give
I am measured by the silence of inspiration, tuned to a laudatory discrimination . . . made of the instigatory caress . . . I know the moment to press the grape to thy lip . . . put ice on your head; for I am the woman who understands . . . so *do* tell me what you are going to make with those cigar-ends?

LOONY.	I am going to make *Life* out of cigar-ends *Life*
	I must have Life . . . more life . . . I am Life . . . . my hair is full of life . . . my clothes are alive; but I am not satisfied.
	I will have more life . . . I will *make* more life . . . Life out of cigar ends
	When God made Life . . . he rested and saw that it was . . . good . . . the devil interfered, making it dangerous. But Life is more than this or that. Life is *amusing!* And you (*to* DIANA)—you make me laugh!
DIANA.	I am the merriment to float your leisure . . . And what do you do when you are not picking them up?
LOONY.	Sit in the pub arguing with my companion
DIANA.	You mentioned two . . .
LOONY.	One and the same . . . "God gives" and "the Devil to pay!"

(*The room fills rapidly with the* LOONY's *curiosity, the "taken for granted" advances to audience gravely noticeable.*)

Such are the secret dens of the terrorized. Look here, you woman-as-you-may-say, strikes me I've wasted a lot of

theoretic sympathy on the submerged . . .
you don't look half sorry for yourselves.
Why I've knocked a fellow down, out
there in the Grand "cause" he says "they
don't feel" says he . . . "they can't have the
same feelings as we have." And yet, and
yet . . . what would happen if one scraped
some of the nap off you?

SOMEBODY ELSE.   So you're stopping at the Grand?

LOONY.   There is no stopping at the Grand . . . the
Grand is all of "Out There" . . . I am the
grand man let loose in it. Out there
where no knick knacks nudge you into
minding your p's and q's . . . "my miraculous ambulance in spatial mystery"; out
there where there is everything to find . . .
the grand man is able to pick up anything he is able to see.

DIANA.   (*Sighs*) Oh! . . . take me with you, I am
the woman who can see.

LOONY.   You know not what you ask
Your aspirations are herculean
No human beings can be so polished, so
sequestered, so hermetically sealed . . .
but that they may still be able to aspire.
I am the apostle of Fraternity. I find my
brother in the most secluded coward . . .
But out there . . . they are not all as I am . . .

their sympathies have narrowed to their code. Were I to take you among them ... you would suffer ... even my protection would not suffice you.

You would be slighted ... you would be criticised ... considered soft.

You with your different way of sitting down, an unfamiliar manner of gulping food. Your most fervid conversation would lose itself as an impertinent silence among the debonair rumble of our caste. You would be witless and a bore; koh-i-noors for the cultured ear ... the crude realism of our Imagists would call up none of the emotions of the initiated in you ...

SOMEBODY.

I say Ossy ... we might be able to keep peace with 'em there.

LOONY.

Not at all, with you the art of ribaldry relies entirely on technique . . . dilettante . . . again the cowardice of the submerged . . .

Ours has the healthy spring of creative expression rooted in action . . . we coin nothing but the image and superscription of personal experience ...

My poor child (*catching* DIANA's *wrist as he descends from his throne . . . shuffling*

	the velvet). Dare you look . . . look . . . (*he looks for something he is surprised not to be able to find*) I was going to try to make you see the "Grand."
OSSY.	Oh Di, he wants a widow . . . James! draw the curtains.
	(*The curtains are drawn The gilded shutters thrown back*)—
LOONY.	(*to the grand outdoors*) What an idea to muffle It up like that Oh thou from whom all colds are caught . . . they're afraid of you catching cold! (*to* DIANA) Now my pretty house fly! Think of that mud . . . that bloody awful mud . . . in all the beauty of its bloody awfulness! A quality that escapes you? You have never felt it plasterly squelching between your toes, salving their parchment creak . . . cake coveringly for warm-footed nights, or sensuous slop cheek-spattering as a wench's spittle . . . from about the Rolls-Royce passing of the pitiably immune.
SOMEBODY.	He can talk about something!

LOONY.   Under the lemon-peel sunslip
                            Human bracchalian stretches
                            Cautiously draw near to the feverish at-
                                tainable,
                            The blood-shot calculations of an eye
                            Approximate spent ends
                            There are many on 'em
                            And there may
                            Be always more
                            Than man yet dares to wish for
                            I maintain
                            Though in those rare full hours of r-r-
                                round numbers
                            Perfection looms proportionate
                            The ever-widening cycles of our Future
                            Shall shed such transcendental showers
                                of ideo-fags
                            Shall muster the rear-forces of mentality
                            To sublimate
                            To boons that are
                            For man to pounce upon.
                            So in the low-geared meanwhile
                            The humble fanatic
                            Collects from where he can
                            Those battered finger-posts
                            To his ideal
                            Ashy iotas in the Balance of
                            The easier equilibrium of Life,
                            With patient love

To raise them where they lay
A tear of absolution
For the weak
Sucked to impersonality
By
The Zoroastrian mud.
While every here and there
The glowing ones . . .
Flare to the common call
Till numerously Enough
For Life
Fourpence for dinner, sixpence for love
My life!

Among the geometric static of your
   bric-à-brac
Your idle wills
Exile the unforeseen
The nice initiative of "nosing about"
Wilts to the barren orderly
Where bells and butlers
Places to put things in
Rob days of discovery
I ask *what* have you to find
Where can you pick things up?

(DIANA *indicating an ashtray, he reverently pockets half a manilla.*)

There, there! my good people . . . Don't ask me to say anything . . . but *forgive me.*

(*Retiring semi-despondently to his throne.*)

The grandest of us
Have phases of diminished elasticity
The most expansive
Periodically contract
Can it be possible I am getting narrow?

(*Looking with new interest at* DIANA, *who is still more preparedly posing.*)

And is it likely that women have other qualities besides their smell?

I have learnt something to-day
And in exchange
The spiritual explorer's
Footprints
Humanize
The shameless purity
of that padding on your floor.
Let them remain
For ever

	Encouraging
	Your tentative toddle towards other ends . . .
OSSY.	O . . . oo . . . oh . . . aah . . . aah! thanks offly . . . cocktail?

(*The* LOONY, *lifting each cocktail successively from the gold tray handed to him, drinks them all off with appreciation.*)

SOMEBODY.	Di dear! as you're still looking intense would you mind very much if we left him to you?
DIANA.	I have never met a genius I couldn't manage yet.
SOMEBODY.	You sure you're not getting let down on this one? The fellow uses the oldest-hat blank verse!
DIANA.	The cosmic form of the idea behind it!
SOMEBODY.	Well if you think a drop or two of sulphuric would help you at all . . . send to the chemist.

PICKED PEOPLE *evaporate.*

(*The* LOONY *has laid himself sublimely on a brocaded chaise-longue.*

DIANA *rather at a loss, as she remarks his drowsiness, plays a precocious trump taking off one shoe and stocking.*)

LOONY.

(*snoozily as he blinks at the little white thing blazing under the electric light*)
This little pig . . .
That little pig . . .
(*But falls asleep.*)

(DIANA *entirely at a loss, replaces the stocking and shoe . . . and calls—James!*)

DIANA.

Tell the men there is one thousand pounds for any one who will take that to a bath-room . . . and entirely clean it up . . . not boil it you know . . . but any other possible means . . . and oh yes, dress it . . . the Duke's will be about the right size . . . and then determinedly . . . you can bring it back to me.

AFTER THE IMMERSION

(DIANA *minus one shoe and stocking. The* LOONY *minus one shoe and stocking. They sit on the edge of the chaise-longue wriggling toes thoughtfully up and down . . .*)

DIANA.	You see after all they're very much alike.
LOONY.	(*anxiously*) I am losing my self-respect.
DIANA.	Oh not at all I assure you . . . you'll feel all right . . . it's only the first five minutes.
LOONY.	Look here my dear . . . (*resolutely drawing on foot gear*) . . . if you've mistaken me for a blooming canary bird . . .
	Well . . . I didn't size you up at first . . . For you're a woman you are—white . . . pulpy . . . wheedle-em-round your finger would you . . . ?
	not me . . . !
	You'd like to sap my brain to make a face cream of . . . tack a string to my jaw and pull it . . . "pretty, pretty" . . . say *Grand* louder for his precious!
	You've made a boss shot . . . a holy error . . . thought I depended entirely on me protective cake of mud . . . nothing inside but slosh . . . active because itchy . . . think you can drain off the creative impulse through a bath tube . . . just because you depend entirely on your tags and tatters (*tearing savagely at the Mechlin on her shoulders through which a miraculous white gleam bursts upon him . . .*)
	Ah . . . (*clenching his fists . . . to a superhuman brake . . . he sits down on the*

chair opposite her . . . smoothing his hair from his brow in sudden weariness)
Ah! you thought you'd got me that time?

DIANA. I maintain that any time will do.

SILENCE

DIANA. Stand up—Sir—and dress your soul for dinner. Throw out your chest and don't walk heels first . . . remember
It takes a genius five minutes to acquire what it takes five centuries to breed into us . . .
Those tirades about the Grand are *the* thing . . . dock them a bit . . . muddle people up more . . . But when you're not holding forth you must be like us . . . you *(hypnotically) are* like us . . .
No use picking up cigar ends— *Here . . .* are the whole cigars . . . *(handing him the box . . . the genius picks out a cigar entirely at his ease).*
Here the Grand is the infinitesimal . . . nothing so vulgar as the obvious.
When you talk to a Duchess treat her as if she were a prostitute at the same time hold fast to the ethics of property.

	Shown a picture . . . look at the left-hand corner . . .
	A book? Pass an innocuous finger-nail down the back of the binding.
	Turn everything upside down and inside out . . . and you'll get on . . . you've got to get on . . . I have just telephoned you to every daily paper in the kingdom and *now* . . . look at me with those *indomitable* eyes . . .
	(*turning to a step*) . . .
	Dear Duke . . . I must present Houston Loon to you . . .
	The great Vitalist
	. . . Europe raves about him . . . tomorrow . . .
DUKE.	A pleasure . . . ah I see . . . you've got a cigar . . .
	I'd just like to have your opinion on this Benozzo Gozzoli.
LOONY.	(*holding his nose carefully to the left-hand corner*) Are you sure it's a Benozzo Gozzoli? . . . By the direction of the scratches . . . you can't scratch a Bennozo Gozzoli from right to left . . . from the way he put the paint on . . . More probably a Genozzo Bozzolini.

My dear ... (*breathes* DIANA *devoutly*) ...
you'll *DO*.

THE END
OF THEM ALL

ROSA

by Bjuna Darnes

Rosa Trinklestein
Jeraboam Winered
  (*who would like to be Rosa's lover*)
Three Oafs
Seraminka, a maid.

Jeraboam Winered *sits in an armchair enfolding him like a middle-aged woman's breasts. His boots are magenta kid, and one is standing meticulously under his chair.*

Rosa Trinklestein *is reclining in antagonistic repose upon a Recamier sofa upholstered in purple and yellow stars, a red glass chandelier hangs from the ceiling. On the wall a single composite painting, Raphael's* Madonna *enshrined in a house of prostitution.*

ROSA *is juggling with three huge swords, a couple of pistols, and a slim knife for carving canvas-backed ducks. She has just left off kissing* JERABOAM'S *foot.*

JERABOAM.   I cannot count my stock—the flying pigs evade me— . . . I am getting tired.

ROSA.   (*deftly pinning the Madonna in the left eye with the longest sword*) I too have lived—have sat in a hansom cab and counted the tails on the horse.

JERABOAM.   Rosa why do you hate me so?

ROSA.   Do you suppose a ploughed field needs overturning?

JERABOAM.   Thank you!

ROSA.   Gratitude is pitiful—rather than be pitiful I would prefer you to twist your moustache.

JERABOAM.   Rosa you are cruel.

ROSA.   I am cruel but self-forgiving – – – it is not every woman that can (*catching a revolver in her teeth*) . . . do, this!

JERABOAM.   The iron is entering my brain I can feel it in my chest.

ROSA.   So you believe that it is her religion that teaches a woman to speak French?

JERABOAM.   You are so innocent—that is why your uncle seduced you at so early an age. (*he chokes with excitement*)

Rosa.	And for fifty years you have sat here kissing my hands; with the neighbours' noses on the window.
Jeraboam.	The neighbours are growing – – – growing – – –
Rosa.	Where we have kicked the turf.
Jeraboam.	We made the bed – – – the neighbours lie in it—
Rosa.	I have paid with fifty of the best years of my life for your one moment of absent-mindedness.

(*The* Oafs *walk in—they all look like* Rosa.)

1st Oaf.	(*grinning sheepishly*) I will tell my father about the swords.

(*The other* Oafs *shuffle their feet and pull their forelocks.*
Exit Oafs *sheepishly.*
Leaving muddy footprints on the carpet.
Enter Seraminka *with twins at her breast. The twins look like* Jeraboam.)

Seraminka.	What are you two doing to my sons— they are three months old and they catch flies. I cannot bear it. You two are doing

something to my sons. It is the quiet here—you have been so quiet for fifty years. (*She begins to dust swords and pistols feverishly as they flash round each other in the air.*)

JERABOAM. Seraminka—you need not dust – – – now.

(*A sword splits one of the twins at her breast in half.*)

SERAMINKA. (*vaguely*) What are you two doing to my sons?

ROSA. I am a devil—I am mad. Tell me, Seraminka what does your master do to a woman?

SERAMINKA. (*disdainfully*) I also have been admired. (*Exit*)

JERABOAM. I am getting tired – – – The neighbours are growing in the flowerbed.

(ROSA *stops juggling with the swords, plucks the one out of the Madonna's eye and lays them side by side over the* OAFS' *muddy footprints on the carpet.*)

ROSA. I have made a bed for us to lie on.

(JERABOAM *lays himself exhausted upon the swords.*
ROSA *as she prepares to lie down beside him glances at the dead baby.*)

ROSA.
Aah! – – – it was because you were not filled with a divine hatred. (*lying down beside* JERABOAM) This is not one of my sleepless nights.

JERABOAM.
(*biting her breast listlessly*) My God! How you do hate me.

THE SACRED PROSTITUTE

SOME OTHER MAN.	It's just the same with the higher qualities we hear so much about—in the comrade we hear so much about. I looked for modesty and found only fear; character and I found pigheadedness; intellect! It was short-hand lectures.
YOUTH.	But why bother about all that when they laugh so delightfully?
THE IDEALIST.	Woman for me is the maze of abortive experience deflecting me from the consummate nucleus—the unique affinity of whose existence no disappointments will ever be able to dissuade me. I went out to meet life open-handed with such good-will, without prejudice,

	without criticism—I scoured the streets—plunged into society—"touched pitch"—dissolved myself in amorous mysticism—yet, I have never been able to solve the problem of love. Woman!?! . . . Woman must exist—is it possible she belongs to somebody else?
ANOTHER MAN.	You bet she does—to some bully who beats her—the ethereal type always gets beaten—every pore of her skin cries out for it—no healthy man could resist—if only for that dumb reproachful eye—it's like hunting!
THE IDEALIST.	If women are bad, you are worse—perhaps if there were more men like me, the women would improve.
A MAN.	(*disdainfully*) Improve on *you*?
DON JUAN.	I am said to be supremely cruel to women, but no man has ever loved them as I have—my intuitive solicitude avoided *restricting* them by *over-valuation*. I have not insulted femininity by singularising with biased selectivism—the individual for my favour—picking my way, with alert precaution through the rose-garden of Love—I enticed those sleeping-beauties from their nests of illusion—and showed them

themselves. It is no fault of mine if they gave those selves to me and if, with my passing, very little was left. I played with their prejudices—I never found a prejudice that took more than twenty minutes to overcome. I squandered hours chasing their silly souls into the corners of their propitious mouths. I was gentle with them—and they fought me with the deceptive weapons of premeditated surrender. I maltreated them and they begged for more—no brutality I could invent was ever drastic enough to make them leave me of their own accord.

A MAN.

The only cruelty that woman refuses to submit to through man is any cruelty she may deserve.

DON JUAN.

The man who is unkind to women is the man of calculable possibilities—women feed on anticipation, race with the intractable—and are totally extinguished by the—attainable!

TEA TABLE MAN.

For sophistry—that beats all I've ever heard—our timid companion "racing with the intractable"—why her whole conception of man is as an escort on a crowded thoroughfare; "calculable possibilities" indeed—what is the reason for our organised society?—entirely for providing a safe radius within whose precincts *man* exhibits only so much of his brute reality as these delicate organisms can stand—why, half my life is spent in so pruning my natural tendencies that I may arrive at the degree of self-abnegation required by the modern woman, and to that end I pass my time in places where one spends money (the things we hanker after not being on the market), where I hope, by the strictest attention to the superficial, to stifle the aboriginal that lives in the middle of me—so far, I confess, it results in a double personality. But I congratulate myself that the obverse I show to women lets nothing through of what's on the other side.

DON JUAN.

Fearing that her kitty-yawns should turn to a shriek?—of terror??

TEA TABLE MAN.

Exactly. I am determined—cost me what it may—to keep her under the protection of her own innocence—

DON JUAN.

Do you keep her long?

TEA TABLE MAN.

There are a great many delightful women in my set, and I have the luck to be extremely popular. There isn't a day

passes that I haven't half-a-dozen different shopping engagements. The things
those women require! And they have
such confidence in me. Why, I help them
to buy their underclothes—all the intricacies of the feminine mind are woven
into frills and there's no limit— One day
it's cobwebs with patches of rosebuds
three inches thick, plumped about on
them—the next, something thick with
unexpected interstices of netting you
wouldn't dare to breathe on—and
through the lot, the palest ribbons chasing each other in and out, out and in.
Only once, while I was absent-mindedly
contemplating a vision of myself club-
bing a naked woman over the head in a
virgin forest on the counter, I asked my
companion if this decoration wasn't
rather superfluous as no one was ever
going to see it. Well, she turned quite
white—I cursed myself for a clout,
shocking her fragile sensibilities like
that—*no*, woman is not constituted for
knowing the truth. At night, after the
theatre which allows us to brush lightly
up against other people's passions, she
leaves me for her blue-silk bedroom,
where Veronal will put her to sleep.

	What would she *do*—if she only *knew* that all I wanted was to keep her awake?
Don Juan.	Try the Veronal on the canary.
Tea Table Man.	Realising that no offering is noble enough to lay at the shrine of this unimpeachable femininity, I am easily adapting myself to civilization—this accommodating contrivance that relieves us of all the onus of individual action. Am I not in duty bound to be grateful for being born in an age when it is unnecessary for me to live—all I have to do is to listen—there are still a handful of irrepressible creative outsiders to sin my sins for me, to pray my prayers for me. *Some* eccentric ass with a tune in his head can fill a *town* with what should have been *my* mating song—all I have to do is pay for a box and confess with a clap!

(*With a loud report* Futurism *arrives on the scene.*)

| Futurism. | Coward—pouah! Milksop! Poo-uuu-aaah! Tango Tout! |

(Tea Table Man *hits him in the eye with a violent potato.*)

FUTURISM.	(*furiously*) Blackguard! You nearly had my eye out! What man, I ask you, could look successfully at a woman with an only eye? (*pathetically to Procuress*) Why nobody would ever love me again. (*martially mopping his eye with a wet handkerchief*) I stand alone on the pinnacle of the passing moment, turning up my nose at the solar-system, hurling invective at the moon— chairs at the audience! (*calming down a little*) Has any-body got an intellect or a dog handy? (*no response*) I could have shown you a trick that proves the infallible superiority of animal instinct over human reason— There is nothing in life that is not best apprehended by the presentment of the nose! (*sniffs— like a GOD*)
A MAN.	Who the devil are you—to sniff like that?
FUTURISM.	(*staggered*) You haven't seen my name in the newspapers?
A MAN.	I don't read the newspapers—I read Greek.
FUTURISM.	(*boxing his ears*) Pastist! Feel a little of what it means to be alive! (*to the others*) Take that prurient cemetery and stand him in a draught. And *now*. (*pull-*

ing up his cuffs and turning his hands round about for the audience to inspect) You are sure there is nothing there? *(catches at the air with a superb gesture and holds it invisible between an eloquent thumb and finger)* Gentlemen —— The FUTURE.

(The men stare very attentively.)

ANOTHER MAN.	In all its sublime invisibility!
A MAN.	It looks exactly as it always did, so it must be what it always was.
ANOTHER MAN.	Impossible! You mean, what it always will be.
SOME OTHER MAN.	No—what it always is going to be.
FUTURISM.	I offer you a magnificent Future—entirely constructed on speculation. To prove that it comes up to my expectations, I have only to shove it into the Past—any bids?
YOUTH.	Coming—coming—coming—*when* is it going to come?
FUTURISM.	*(with an inimitable snap of the fingers back into the air)* Going—going—gone.
MEN.	A *prophet* has come among us!
A MAN.	And I mistook him for a conjuring commercial traveller.

PROCURESS.	My word—the women ought to see this.

(*The women are sent for and as usual flock round,* FUTURISM *"lascivating" them with his eyes.*) |
| WOMEN. | Only let us write our names with our life-blood in your autograph album!

(FUTURISM *hands them a tome labelled "Women I have had".*) |
| WOMEN. | But—? |
| FUTURISM. | It's all the same—I should have if I hadn't been talking so much— But perhaps I had better read you the proto-poem |

Tatatata ta ta ta ta ta ta ta ta ta
plum plam plam pluff pluff frrrrrr
urrrrrrrrrrrrraaaaaaaaaaaa
pluff plaff plaff gottgott gluglu
craaa craaa
cloc-cloc gluglu gluglu cloc-cloc
    gluglu
scscscsc——

Do you feel that you could get into a more intimate relationship with me than you are *now*?

WOMEN. (*inspired*) No. (*they sigh*)

(FUTURISM, *whose every gesture propounds vulgarity intensified to Divinity, slaps his bowler hat onto his head, crooked, and struts magnificently.*)

DOLORES. You seem to have successfully plumbed the feminine shallows. Could you tell us anything about this bare acquaintance of ours of hermaphroditic aspect—it calls itself Love.

(PROCURESS *herds all the women off the stage in order to spare them disturbing recollections.*)
(*Dolores draws* LOVE *forward.*)

MEN. Just looking at it makes no deep impression—but it's hardly seductive.

FUTURISM. Love is a feminine conception spelt "Greed" with a capital "G"—this is female, all right! (*drags off* LOVE's *roseate hood, dislodging a shower of golden curls*)

(FUTURISM *here declaims Futurist attack on love—most drastic.*)

(*When* LOVE *has had enough she runs away,* FUTURISM *after her, saying,* "My God, she has run away—I must just 'finish her off.'")
(FUTURISM *returns dragging* LOVE *across the floor by the hair.*)

FUTURISM.	(*demonstrating to men*) *I* just take them like this—tac-tac.
MEN.	That's all very well, but it's no consolation watching the other man doing it—good night! (*they go off*)
FUTURISM.	(*looking carefully around to see if they have all gone—lets go of* LOVE'*s hair*) Excuse me, I hope I didn't hurt you. I have to do that for the sake of my reputation. (LOVE *looks shaken but intensely interested.* FUTURISM *places her with gentlest care on the divan and kisses the nape of her neck.*) *Never* believe anything a man says about women, when there is another man present! (*looking unutterably sentimental*) I suppose you think I am a man made of iron, of absolute self sufficiency—*so* hard—
LOVE.	I don't think anything of the kind.
FUTURISM.	Too hard to want to be loved—while in reality, I have an infinite need of tenderness. Will you be *very* tender to me?

LOVE.	(*smiling whimsically and folding her hands in resignation*) Yes, dear.
FUTURISM.	(*quickly—afraid of being bored*) But love is not an emotion of vague sentimentality! Love *must* be atrociously carnal— will you be atrociously carnal—?
LOVE.	(*calmly*) Yes, dear.

(*Something in her tone makes* FUTURISM *look critically at her and then he starts again.*)

FUTURISM.	You are accustomed to the pastist man who talks to you about your soul—I shall not talk to you like that, but I shall reach your soul through the medium of your body.
LOVE.	Yes, dear?
FUTURISM.	Whereas the pastist man would have shaken hands and gone home, leaving you inconsummate—for women are only animals, they have no souls.
LOVE.	Yes, dear?
FUTURISM.	But you have just the sort of body I like—suave.
LOVE.	(*smoothing down her formless roseate garment*) How do you know?
FUTURISM.	The Futurist has x-ray eyes, and ears of steel— He can see everything without

looking at it, and stand any amount of noise—the evening breeze no longer reaches me, but the gentle vibrations of the *mitrailleuses* are still audible. (*loudly*) DARLING! (*gives her a thumping whack on the thigh*—LOVE *jumps*) A-a-a-a-a-a-h! You are just my type, for I have never seen anything like you before! (*very rapidly*) Will-you-love-me-will-you-love-me-will-you-love-me-love-me-love-me-love-me-me-ME—? ? ? I *must* have you—You see I have never had you before.

LOVE.   (*laughing*) But I don't want this sort of love—it's too quick. I only want love that lasts for ever and ever.

FUTURISM.   Do you know—*I* am a type like that—I could love for ever. In me there is everything—take out what you can. (*takes her in his arms and kisses her frantically, crying in between each half-dozen kisses*) Do-you-like-it? Do-you-like-it? Do-you-like-it?

LOVE.   (*passively*) Yes, dear.

FUTURISM.   (*flinging her away from him*) You are *fearfully* sensual!

LOVE.   *Yes, dear.*

FUTURISM.   You-deny-it!?

LOVE.   I *didn't* deny it.

FUTURISM.	Ah—I thought you would, and so I have no answer ready—dear, beautiful and divine little woman—you are the unique pleasure the warm gulf of intoxication from which one emerges—replenished—vital—like a formidable addition of Hannibal and the Alps—I need the brilliant chastity of your eyes to counteract the occasional sombreness of my nerves—I *must* have your soul.
LOVE.	But if I haven't got it—what is it?
FUTURISM.	Your soul is the ultimate profundity of your body—give it to me—and I will give you your little smile—I have seen you smile in my dreams. I have loved you so long, and I shall love you forever—I *wish* you would respond a little—I demand of the women I love to surround me with an atmosphere of *intense* sensuality.
LOVE.	You go too quick.
FUTURISM.	Too quick—! I've never spent so long on a woman in my life! Too quick! When my love is eternal and my train leaves in fifteen minutes— Hurry up! And love me! (*distractedly*) There is no time to waste—life has got to be *lived*— There's no time to stop to enjoy it!

LOVE.	(*relieved*) How did you find out that I'm really a woman?
FUTURISM.	How did I find out? Don't you realize I've dominated all the women of two generations who were worthwhile—except a *few*, who got off the train at the next station—I can tell women when I see them—beastly nuisances. You're the most feminine thing I've ever found—that's why I love you so—I don't believe *I'm* anything special to you, whereas if you were a Futurist you would be down on your knees before me. As you are, any ordinary man would do just as well.
LOVE.	Adopting your theories—I've begun to think they would. But as the value of sex is entirely fictitious, I find it makes it more precious to avoid promiscuity.
FUTURISM.	You take too long saying things. If you left out all the adverbs and adjectives and used the verb in the infinitive, I might have a chance to get what I want— before my train leaves. Why can't you love-me-love-me-love-me? I only want to make the little women happy— They *always* love me. All my mistresses are in lunatic asylums,—that's love if you like! Can't I make *you* happy?

Love.	What! In this atmosphere—you litter our couch with corpses.

(Pause)
(Futurism sits fixing her with theatrically amative eyes—Love smiles and wails like a cat on the tiles—her criticism.)

Futurism.	We men always carry woman in the back of our minds—when it isn't one woman, it's a hundred! But you are not one woman— You are *the* woman. *(strokes her face with infinite tenderness, gazing)* Little one—

(Love throws her arms round his neck with a gesture of surrender.)

Futurism.	Sweetheart—*darling*—loveling—STOP. You see, directly I begin to get sentimental you begin to like me—pou-ah!
Love.	This game of love is too bewildering for me—any possible move *I* make is bound to be in the wrong direction—it's not fair play.
Futurism.	This is not a game for fair play—it's a game of advantages.
Love.	In which the woman starts with a handicap of "vantage out"!

FUTURISM.	Women are so illogical.
LOVE.	So are you.
FUTURISM.	Futurism is diametrically opposed to logic.
LOVE.	But can't you see that you are being in-consecutive?
FUTURISM.	(*rapturously*) Ah—that's it—in-con-sec-u-tive, check-mate!

(FUTURISM *picks up* LOVE *and a handful of newspapers and stuffs them altogether into his pocket—which he slaps with a bang. In-mates and men gradually filter back.*)

MEN.	What have you done with her?
FUTURISM.	(*absent-mindedly*) Oh, everything—and nothing.
PROCURESS.	We are just going to have some amateur theatricals—if you care to stop?
FUTURISM.	I—dynamic—plastic—velocity—stop—!
PROCURESS.	The play is "Man and Woman".
FUTURISM.	Try putting glue on the seats.

(*The audience sit circle-wise on the outskirts of the hall to watch the performance.*)

DON JUAN.	(*confidentially laying his arm across* FU-TURISM's *shoulder*) My dear old chap, you

	have introduced a new tactic since my time. I must confess, I am surprised—you interest me! How is it worked?
FUTURISM.	New? I only wish it was. I am sacrificing my life to make things new—and only succeeding in making them *louder*. As for this, it's only the eternal axiom in waging the sex war—that "Man and Woman" are enemies. But that woman has one greater enemy than man—*woman*!
DON JUAN.	Ah, now it's recognisable—insult the sex, to catch the demonstrated exception?
FUTURISM.	Precisely. This dodge covers the whole field—hitherto you stopped short at maternity—we annihilate woman completely!
DON JUAN.	(*interested*) My dear Futurism, you know this *is* new—
FUTURISM.	Yes—if it were more than a bluff— But Nature is so uncompromising.
DON JUAN.	(*calls*) Mammy!

(NATURE *comes on, looking enquiring.*)

DON JUAN.	Oh, Mammy, you must help us. Futurism has invented a new game—we want to make our own children, evolve them from our own indomitable intellects.

205

NATURE.	Then do it— You can't expect me to help you with your intellects, they've raced far beyond my control.
FUTURISM.	Never mind the intellects—they're our business. Your affair is the children— you're the only person who understands them.
DON JUAN.	(*coaxing*) You always do what *we* want, dear, are we not your favourite offspring? In fact, you would be the perfect mother, if only you had restricted your family to *us*—we *don't want* a little sister—she's remained a child too long!
NATURE.	I have been looking into the feminist propaganda—and I am already seriously considering allowing her to grow up!
FUTURISM *and* DON JUAN.	Great Heavens! Anything but that!
NATURE.	I made you entirely independent, except for this question of reproduction— and you have shown no filial gratitude whatever—and to tell the truth, I'm beginning to feel rather out of touch with you—you're much too tricky and inventive—nothing ever satisfies you! I provided you with plenty of good stodgy bread and butter and you've been making jam while the fire burns— and now you've overeaten yourselves,

you want me to make you a perfect world—with no temptations. Well, I shan't—you'll just go on the best way you can—until you've learnt a little self-control.

(*She goes off in a huff.*)

FUTURISM.

There's nothing more to be got out of *her*!— Let's identify ourselves with machinery!

DON JUAN.

I shouldn't care about that—comparing myself to a machine, I feel extremely weak, to a woman, exceedingly strong— I *must* hang on to my cheaply bought self-respect. Let's hear some more about the latest amorous strategics.

FUTURISM.

Oh very well— Just hide behind the sofa. (*with an off-hand gesture he draws* LOVE *out of his pocket, scattering the newspapers, shakes* LOVE *out and stands her on the floor in front of him, taking her measure with a masterful eye as she pulls herself together*)

This is the sex war.

LOVE.

I suppose that means me—well, here I am— But I don't want to fight— It's silly— You are already victorious in being born a man.

207

FUTURISM.	Come along—you must pretend, any-way. Somebody's probably looking.
	(LOVE *hands him a pair of boxing-gloves—red flannel hearts—and puts on a pair herself with which every point made is emphasised by a psychological blow.*)
FUTURISM.	Don't mention anything I said to you last time—You wouldn't look half so silly in the end.
	(LOVE *stands perfectly still with her hands hanging down at her sides.*)
FUTURISM.	Mind (*bang*) it's you who are attacking me. I'm a perfectly peaceful person play-ing with cannons—until you come and worry me away from manly pursuits.
LOVE.	(*smiling*) All right—you protect yourself against yourself with any lies you like.
FUTURISM.	Thanks—I take cover behind you.
LOVE.	(*presenting herself with a bow*) The FIB of the Universe.
FUTURISM.	Then what are you telling the truth for—You *must* pretend to be real or I can't hit you—won't you kiss me?
LOVE.	Certainly *not*.
FUTURISM.	Certainly why not?

LOVE.	Because you would not be contented with a kiss, but reproach me for leading you on—to—nowhere.
FUTURISM.	I *promise* never to ask for more— Just one, if you don't I'll bother you to death till you do.

(LOVE *shrugs her shoulders—and kisses him.*)

FUTURISM.	(*hitting her*) It's all right— This is not cruelty, merely nervous reaction. (*with an intimate caress*) And now that you have given yourself to me—
LOVE.	What do you mean?
FUTURISM.	I mean that no true woman is immodest enough to kiss a man who is not her chosen lover! (*addressing the sofa*) That's the first round.

(*A yawn from the sofa.*)
(LOVE *and* FUTURISM *glare at each other amicably while adjusting their boxing-gloves.*)

FUTURISM.	I should get on much better if only you would come near enough for me to whisper to you.

(LOVE *approaches. He whispers into her ear for some minutes, while a pleased and furtive smile plays about her lips.*)

LOVE.

Old as time. You catch your little women with antique methods, reserving Futurism for "later on". All *those* rules were compiled by a defunct civilization—after all I can read! I assure you every time woman gives herself to man, it means a struggle between her pride and her desire. It's so stupid this appearing to succumb to diplomacy— I know you're going to win— You're too fundamentally dishonest not to, and I'm quite willing to be vanquished. But do fight me with new weapons—I do want to be amused.

FUTURISM.

(*volcanically throwing aside the red-flannel hearts*) Use your *Instinct*. You a woman and *can't tell* that all this sex war fake is *bunkum*. Can't you just *know* that I love you? Don't you *feel* that you are torturing me—that *all* I want is to make you happy and for you to believe in me? Why can't you believe in me? I know, it's my bombastic voice that has a meretricious ring in it? My meridional manners? And you *don't love* me because I am not handsome.

LOVE.	Oh, I don't mind *what* you look like—Let that confound the critics.
FUTURISM.	Dearest, I want to reduce you to a state of maudlin imbecility— Love *must* be swallowed whole. (*the electric light goes out*) Thank heaven.

(*They carry on the conversation in the low, sustained and intense tones of two people who are very much in love, of which only the following fragments are audible.*)

FUTURISM.	To be faithful to me—while I am never there - - - - - - - - - - - - - - - (*Silence*) - - - - - - - - *Now* do you believe me?
LOVE.	Nearly.
FUTURISM.	(*with passionate sincerity*) You can - - - - you can - - - - you do - - - - you
LOVE.	(*transfigured*) "Lord now lettest thou thy servant depart in peace".
FUTURISM.	- - - - do!
LOVE.	Good God. What am I doing— What am I saying?— Who am I talking to? (*quotes* FUTURIST *tirade against women*)
FUTURISM.	(*imploringly*) You can't hold me responsible for anything I said last week -Believe in me - - -

LOVE.	I ask nothing better than to believe in something— You – – – – – or myself.
FUTURISM.	(*briefly, his eyes blazing through her*) Do you – – – – – – – in yourself?
LOVE.	Sssssssssssh – – – – – – – if anybody's listening, this will end in a draw.
FUTURISM.	Still—there is a perfectly straightforward way of finishing this up.
LOVE.	Oh, come on.
FUTURISM.	It's very simple— You won't like it. Perhaps, after all it's the only way to make you believe in me—
LOVE.	What's it called—?
FUTURISM.	Just – – – BEING. (*taking fresh measurements with a thoughtful eye*) Do you feel much like a woman?
LOVE.	Not much—I don't think I could. I'm so well watered down with civilization.
FUTURISM.	Ah—you have never been galvanized by the force of undiluted masculinity— There isn't any left in the world except in me. Come here. (LOVE *approaches*) Do you want to know what it's like?
LOVE.	Awfully.

(*He puts his arm round her shoulders and they go and sit on the table—very close to each other—and for purposes of*

communication with their temples pressed together.)
(*Silence*)

LOVE.   I never knew how wonderful it is that hearts can beat.

(*Silence*)

FUTURISM.   What do you feel?
LOVE.   Very young—very foolish—very warm —very soft—in fact it's becoming a physical discomfort—the not knowing how to purr.
FUTURISM.   Can you remember anything?
LOVE.   Nothing whatever.
FUTURISM.   Can you realize anything?
LOVE.   Nothing but you—
FUTURISM.   *Now* what about the future?
LOVE.   The kitten's growing to be a panther— I'm sure she's dangerous—Oh, *do* shut me up in a harem, it's the only thing I'm fit for—I shall be jealous. But at least when you die, I shall be burnt alive on your corpse.
FUTURISM.   Bravo! (*playing with her finger tips*) And here?
LOVE.   Claws. (*she tears herself away*)

213

FUTURISM.	Where to?
LOVE.	I *must* just go and kill *all* the other women. Until I do, I can't feel safe.
FUTURISM.	You *touch* the other women, and I'll strangle you!
LOVE.	*Any* one of them might become the mother of your children.
FUTURISM.	You're OUT! (*slapping his knee triumphantly*) It's infallible—infallible— Did you hear that? (*he drags* DON JUAN *from behind the sofa, half asleep*)
DON JUAN.	(*rubbing his eyes*) Of all the elementary old-fashioned fool's games!
LOVE.	(*blinking her eyes*) It takes you a long way back!

(FUTURISM *rushes off*.)

DON JUAN.	He's disappointing—too primitive.
LOVE.	(*enthusiastically*) Oh, one of the most amusing creatures I've met.

(PROCURESS *comes on with* DIRECTORS OF THE WORLD BROTHEL.)
NATURE
REALITY (*a composite person called* WORLD-FLESH-AND-DEVIL *they are accompanied by two inspectors*)

PURITY
JOY
(*The inhabitants of the World Brothel flock round them.*)

PURITY.	(*inspecting*) What a mess!
JOY.	(*inspecting*) How very sad!
PROCURESS.	(*to directors*) We haven't succeeded in balancing accounts yet— You see, it is not yet decided whether the demand creates the supply, or the supply the demand.
REALITY.	Cut that! As long as you have them both, they will total up the same.
PROCURESS.	There's been a lot of fuss lately over the pathological and hygienic side.
WORLD-FLESH-AND-DEVIL.	Leave it to me to gloss that over—all we have to bear in mind is to keep the surface glittering.

ESSAYS AND COMMENTARY

ALL THE LAUGHS IN ONE
SHORT STORY BY McALMON

, and crackled a laugh that came out in sharp hard spurts
   of metallic sound.
Yoland laughed harshly disdainful.
And she smiled her glistening
mechanically glamorous smile into his eyes
            was laughing her unlubricated
laugh, steadily now – – – –
The jeer and taunt in her weird laugh – – –
         She laughed a warmer rusty
chortle now
         She smiled sphinxly
, and they shrilly shrieked laughter
            – – voice was higher and more abandoned than
usual. It shrieked, but rustily mechanical rather than human.
            Their jokes could not be heard
because of the laughter,
She gave an inebriated rasp of laughter

– – caused the other girls to shriek their shrill hyena laughter again.

       Yoland's cute crackling ripple

       sounded more subdued now

       because she had laughed too much before – – – – –

She was overcome with mirth and held her hand over her heart – – – – – – –

                          she explained—crackling

       Their laughter taunted like that of so many hyenas – – –

          jeering and laughing.

       Her rusty cackle of laughter sounded and Yoland's cute,

          inhuman laugh creaked after him.

       Chortling menacingly this time.

Her unlubricated rusty laugh chortled

Her laughter mingled with that of other girls to make hyena noises

Her teeth when she smiled, were the perfection of dentifrice and glistening beauty.

       She smiled enigmatically

       Though her smile seemed directed at me I knew she

          wasn't even looking at me.

– – to chortle a low metallic cackle

       She chortled cutely again

       , and she merely rattled her machine laugh,

       again to chortle dry rattling laughter

       "I love her laugh."

       Her laugh is cleared of emotions.

BRANCUSI AND THE OCEAN

The interpretation of Brancusi—
the analysis of the elemental.

An art engendered beyond the formidable naked subjectivity—
Here is no abstraction coerced to the domain of form—
Perhaps form arrested at its very inception—
a certain *élan* of primary embodiment—
has revealed to us the intriguing comparison of elemental
form—
evolved by the forces of nature—
and an elemental form whose evolution is submitted to the
process of the intellect—

Of a man comparatively young in years—whose concentration—such

sublime and imprecise

the friction of his aesthetic has brought to a white heat of featureless beauty—

the memory and anticipation of aesthetic fulfilment—

and he has got irrefutably that something that every one of them lacks—

the primary investigators of beauty.

At any race he has set a terrible precedent—that will be impossible to eliminate with either fundamental or accessory—

The form on which form is based.

And so elemental – – – –

that it actually connives with the atmosphere in any attainment of a prolongation of its direction

A song to the eye—

"who" used to take after *belle matière*—

Brancusi is one of the few moderns—whose art has survived its own impetus—its cosmic reticence—he has got none of that everything else that all his other contemporary sculptors have—

MY CATHOLICK CONFIDANTE

Confirming the near conclusion one sometimes comes to, that for most human beings traditional concepts remain more real than their actual experience, that it is *impermissible* to contradict tradition—my Catholick confidante, immediately upon describing the staircase fugue, gasped, as might one in regret for having desecrated an altar.

"Oh *no*! I shouldn't *say* that!"

For such, to question tradition is like denying God.

Confiding to me her own anguish she had offered this panic of her neighbour's as proof that "not she alone – – – –

– – – and listening was like looking through a microscope at a secret world.

She stood out among the working classes as the perfect exemplaire of wife and mother—her home, husband, children were well cared for—her terror of having another child—was financially sound—in her plan one addition to her family would have broken entirely down the civilised condition—to which as practical Idealists they clung.

The only safeguard she could imagine was entire chastity – – – – – –

The husband compliant; under stress of his inhibited electric virility—took to drink—

My confidante, finding her ultimation of chastity so unprofitable, with a look of absolute confusion—spoke these words of questioning affirmation—

"But the church says '*it's*' wrong!"

CENSOR MORALS SEX.

Censorship may be suitable to the haziness of the social morality and Censors might hold on to their authority for ever if censorship had not defeated its own aims. As long as any social misbehaviour is not official— When it becomes accepted behaviour—the Censor represents no electors.

There is no secret to be kept when "all" are in the secret.

The Censor is sufficient unto himself. Dare him to produce a single individual of the moral negativism—that he pretends he strives to protect—and he will be unable to do so. No one aspires to put any restriction on his own "amoral" sophistication.

The public to whom the censor defers exists only in its supposing that public to exist "somewhere" else.

The worst kind of sex maniac is the Censor (re: Sumner and Smoot). With their canine affinities—they can only sustain their sexual potentiality by sticking their noses into their neighbour's —————

Hitherto it has been said that a period of sexual liberty precedes a period of degeneration— The present tendency toward sex liberation should—understandingly and purely directed—inaugurate a period of *regeneration.*

If as Freud infers—Religion and Sex are interchangeable—why not reintegrate both giving the people an impetus toward the equilibrium they require?

Sexual myths become the masters of civilization.

CONVERSION

The obsessions prescribed by the Holy Church of Rome, are re-edited by the Psychoanalyst.

The Fathers and Freud successively established confessionals for neurotics, and it will not be long before they are fitted with domestic appliances.

Our Virgin Mary has resuscitated in the incest complex —————— it is refreshing to consider that "Our Mary" Pickford has also her devotees.

In psycho-analytic literature, at least, we are offered no escape from the post-natal womb of the Eternal Mother

And the Eternal Mother devours her literary kittens —————— invariably.

Once the Catholic convert has gone to —————— his Mother, his literature follows him in the filial *chute*

And now that the Psycho-Analytic convert has gone to his —————— mother complex ——————

The aim of the artist is to miss the Absolute ——— the only possible creative gesture ——— whereas the mystic impulse is to embrace a "ready-made" in the way of absolutes

And the Absolute of this new mechanised mysticism of the Psycho Analyst is the Unconscious.

So here we have "Psychoanalysis And The Unconscious" by D.H. Lawrence, where the *almost* lyrical prose of the *Women in Love* is also converted ——— to candy.

Thus: "But sweet heaven what merchandise. What dreams dear heart! What was there in the cave?

Alas that we ever looked!

Nothing but a huge slimy serpent of sex ———"

Which transposed to the economic style of "modernism" would run something like this ———

"Sweet heart   Alas   'Cave serpent ——— 'em' "!

Inevitably Lawrence like other converts whose reputation makes it imperative that they preserve their independence, compiles some ingenious terminology of his own and indulges in the well known *truc* of the distinguished disciple, in seeking a quarrel with his master.

With his *tour de force* ——— locating "I Am That I Am" in the Solar Plexus he has dangerously damned his own creative flux with a theory, and is already regarding the polarised navel of the infant Jesus through the eye of his pen.

He tells us that "Psycho-Analysis is out under the therapeutic disguise to do away with the moral faculty in man". My observation of every strata of society leads me to conclude that man has never exhibited the least inclination towards a moral faculty ++++++++++ ——— However what I really wished to say is that Mr. Lawrence has arrived at this rather obvious conclusion in the superficial dimension ++++++++++ Too late.

If Freud is not in the pay of the Jesuits, the omission should be immediately remedied. For he, contrary to Mr. Lawrence's assertion is in a fair way to accomplish—what the Fathers of the church so signally failed to accomplish—the purification of the race.

Already the élite in protest at the epidemic of psycho-exhibitionism among the merely cultured, are dropping "sex" entirely from their programme.

Psycho-Analysis has raised sex to the venerable status of a duty; and WHO ————— wants to do his duty?

GATE CRASHERS OF OLYMPUS—

The somersault of society dates from the day that a small Spaniard, P.O. Casse (*cf.* French breakage) so inevitably exhibited the portrait of a wine glass, "looking both ways at once".

Every new object to which he applied his disruptive aesthetic has had an extra crack knocked into it by his rabid opposers, i.e. disciples.

For although modern warfare is not responsible for our revaluation of values, modern art which is the actual cause is martialised to the extent that he who steals a stunt from its originator, does so, for the redemption of the aforesaid art.

I have heard that the original wine glass was broken by Braque, i.e. *cf.* break. Or at least that he broke another on the same day—

However I predict that the breakage of P.O. Casse will be canonised by the dealers—for he has successively broken a greater variety of objects, and with more rapidity than his most ardent opponents (i.e. disciples) could keep up with.

Example.

P.O. Casse broke a guitar—which prophetic pattern induced an aesthetic intimation comparable to what in other areas, the French call *frisson*.

This disjuncted guitar has in every "avant guard" every year, in every land re-re-re-represented the imminent intellectual revolt for one quarter of a century.

The same guitar—often seen believe me—broken at the same place—yet bearing a variety of signatures.

No head or tail of reason for this save that emancipation being contagious, if caught by the noncreative finds only the sexual un-confines in which or wherein to flower—

Magazine slogan—

Art is always "new" to the uninitiate—

GERTRUDE STEIN

Twenty years ago, people used to say to me, "the days when a genius could appear suddenly, and be unappreciated, are well and truly gone."

They said we were so very civilized, so blasé in the face of any conceivable surprise, that no-one could ever again leave the critics baffled.

Bizarrely, however, our culture is destined to find that any truly new thought will burst upon it like a fury. And it is to this destiny that the critics have once more succumbed in the case of Gertrude Stein.

For nearly twenty years, Gertrude Stein built up her œuvre, in relation to which our culture allowed nothing to see the light save the odd bit of bullying from the wittier journals.

She went on building her œuvre, in a manner which—despite established usage in such cases—I shall not call courageous (for only the most vulgar error could lead us to believe that the enlightened have need of courage in the face of the unenlightened), but rather serene. And the slight, contented smile with which she met the bullying to which she was subjected pleased me immensely.

She knew full well just how her brain's slightest act, once it had been deformed by ridicule, would land amidst the literature of her time like a chemical precipitate.

She has prodigiously dismantled the raw materials of style, and radically swept clean the literary arena, making new performances possible. Which has given rare courage to countless young people.

In America, many an author has gained renown by following one of the paths opened up by Stein's experiments. But Gertrude herself has been systematically undervalued in her own country, where for years now people have been crying out for a few properly American pioneers.

Well, here she is, the all-American pioneer! And once her unpublished manuscripts had been mined for all manner of riches, it was thanks to good old conservative England that this prophet from across the Atlantic was finally recognized.

Gertrude Stein is not a writer in any of the currently accepted senses of the word.

She does not use words to present a subject, but uses a fluid subject to float her words on.

I can point you toward what her art is made of by observing that you never hear anyone say, "I have read such and such a book by Gertrude Stein." People say: "I have read some Gertrude Stein."

I doubt any of her writings has appeared in French, especially as the essential feature of her work is its untranslatability into even its own language. For our obliging pioneer has reduced the English language to a foreign language even for Anglo-Americans.

And only her renown, which today is worldwide, and which she owes to the rude trials to which she has subjected the contemporary mind, could lead any audience to criticize what I have just said as a meaningless paradox.

Perhaps much of the opposition unleashed against Gertrude Stein stemmed from the fear of those people who claimed to be stunned.

If ever I let myself go so far as to understand all this—one fine morning I would no longer be able to—order my breakfast.

HAVELOCK ELLIS

About 1920 Havelock Ellis told me that in England where the mothers had silently put up with marriage, women were beginning to suspect marriage—they had enquired as to what their mothers had got out of marriage, and what they got out of it, said Ellis, "was *nothing*." Ninety percent of the women in England he assured me found no pleasure in marriage—"and when I put it at ninety percent I'm putting it quite low."

In 1912, a British "beauty" told me that she alone among all her friends—was not incommoded and thus horrified by her marital duty; they tried every way to avoid it – – – "and they're in love with their husbands, the finest handsomest men in England." She attributed her exemption from their "agony" to her husband having been attaché to the British Embassy in Paris – – – where he had *learned* – – –

That on Lord ———'s "first night" his bride enquired in ecstatic surprise – –

"Does everybody have such pleasure when they marry?"

"Everybody"—he actually assured her.

"Even the common people?"

"Even the common people—"

"Well all I can say is—it's much too good for *them*."

A woman told me the perfect consummation of marriage was *general* among the peasants of the Maremma, Italy.

In 1939—a woman—very superior type—(husband also)—who did housework—described to me how the wives in the tenement houses she had lived in ran out of their apartments screaming in apprehension to elude their husbands when they, "wanted to do it."

HISTORY OF RELIGION AND EROS

The secret Universe of omniscient creative impetus comprises the power-house generating our obvious universe.

From this power-house science has induced innumerable demonstrations of its mathematical abstract potency.

While Religion has aspired to convince us of its authenticity, its authority

RELIGION AND EROS

Since intellection outgrew the aboriginal simplicities it advanced through two seemingly irreconcilable channels

---

The mystic meditation of early Asia. The Scientific *research* of a younger Occident. Each a system for investigating the Power Universe to further man's, "Domination over all things," i.e., enjoyment of surprising revelations to be drawn into the open out of the unseen.

Difference of these systems:
The Asiatic mystic-scientist handled no laboratorial or mechanistic intermediary for probing the resources of the power-Universe. He found all needed experimental resources in the Mind-Body make-up of the human individual: an ego laboratory.

Inversely to the direct co-operation of the ancients, the occidental scientist interposes between himself and the Power Universe gigantic machinery, microscopic instrumentation to indirectly contact it. An incommunicative contact which compared to that of the ancients seems perilously like interference.

The oriental attained levitation.
The occidental flies a bomber.
The oriental aspiration contacted Power
the occidental, force:
The distinction:—

POWER: creative dynamism, consciously operative, solely constructive.[1]
In contacting power, lies immunity to the destructive *Religion's salvation.*
FORCE   merely a derivative of Power isolated, by limitation of intellect from its conscious motivation.

---

1   The agonies of life-into-death result from the undeveloped consciousness of other larger dimensions of our animation.

In force lies peril, destruction, fragmentation RELIGION'S DAMNATION.

RELIGION'S POWER OF GOD VERSUS REALISM'S BLIND FORCE wherewith man, mistaking destruction for dominion, furthers the ultimate menace to his perfectability.

Whatever transpired in the Ego-laboratory of mystic research proved so mysterious to the occidentals that finally they easily accepted it as the mystery to end all mysteries: the nothing-at-all.

Albeit to an observer from some cosmic distance the mystery would be cleared—

It is not prohibitive to man, as the complete microcosm, to train his intelligence on his components and gain control of their potentialities. To avail himself of his resources, akin to the atomic, electronic etc. in order to transcend the restrictions of his overt senses.

As the nature of phenomena apparent to us at present depends on the gamut of vibrations to which man, through his senses responds, in the course of his evolution this gamut extends – – –

Throughout the ages and still today a few human beings are born who exceptionally react to vibrational stimuli beyond the standard gamut. A simple, rational, electrical extension endowing them with quirks of perception comparable to telepathy, television . . . etc.[2]

---

2 Noticeably, so-called "supernatural" manifestations, by virtue of the similarity of their occurrence have always been regulated by laws as defined as those governing this world's accepted science.

THE EGO-LABORATORY

The religious concept that man is fitted to become consciously involved in the relationship of the perceptible to the imperceptible universe originated in occasional men of precursive genius being aware of Life as a Deific Electricity, proceeding from the *Absolute Status*, conveying to us our animation, our intelligence, our intuition.

It was the logical conviction of such men that increments from this infinite source of power would be at their disposal the more they adapted their organisms to draw upon it.

The mystic, closing his eyes, his ears, inverted the senses from the multiple outlets for contact, *concentrating* the various electric currents of mind and body to an unique current, of which, its intensity too great for reception in the concrete world, he sought, through meditation, to analyse the abstract potency.

This concentrated mind, inducing INTUITION found itself functioning, a little, within the realm of causation, a little aware how the laws of the self-rule of the Power-universe operate.

THE ELEMENTARY DISCOVERY

The rhythm of breath attuning the organism it aerates to the rhythm of the concrete world, the mystic noticed its interference with the concentration of the mind upon the abstract; each in-breath drawing the mind anew back to its concrete associations. His mind wandered — — — —

He determined to let his breathing drop out of the way of his *attention*—and succeeding, that rhythm modified; his breath subsided — — — —

– – – – – He felt his body sustained no longer by air but by something comparable to the ether, which, interpenetrating its atomic structure, liberated his organism from biological law hitherto insurmountable.

This lightening of the body, this etheric transmutation of the mind's instrument, liberated that latent faculty of the mind for reception of a transcendent form of radio transmission.

He found his perception, usually narrowed down to focus on the concrete world as intellect, when released from this focus, to amplify its contacts as it FLOWED BACK ALONG THE CURRENT OF ITS CONVEYANCE from the All-Conscious, whose medium may be likened to INTELLIGENTIAL ETHER.

At this stage of increasing potency his mind became reinforced as spirit; its ultimate dimension attainable being soul, indestructible component of the Absolute.

Subject to his new potency in spirit he found the etheric transposal set him free from the pull of gravity; permitted accelerated locomotion without muscular effort. He gained control of his own electric system, experimented with its use, the electronic transfer of his person through space, the projection of his mental perceptivity to a distance, etc.:

Released from the vibrational circumscription of the concrete whose laws are subordinate to the dominant LAW[3] of the Power-Universe, he came to understand that law by which the functioning of our usual universe may be modified,

3   law invoked in working miracles

(1) The structure of matter rearranged

(2) The materialising function of power

(3) The nature of the elements overruled by Power

(4) Electric life reconducted within the body[4]

The control of these psychic exercises operated from a cerebral centrum, named and located by the ancients.

Its contraction emitted a fine line of prolonged sensitivity into distance – – – its dilation incepted communication from the infinite knower. The supreme director from whom, the psychic scientist conceived, through increasing exercise of the spirit, full revelation of, and the cooperation with the unseen universe should eventually be transmitted to him.

Herein originated the PRACTICE of religion. EXERCISE OF THE SPIRIT incurring actual psychic gymnastics.

Exercise of the spirit induced ENLIGHTENMENT   ILLUMI-NATION   ECSTASY

The experience of illumination was incommunicable; could only, in description be hinted at. LIGHT was not primarily a synonym for wisdom. It indicated the perception of that other light, overtenuous for reception by the organ eye. Authenticated in the past through the research of the man-is-the-measure-of-the-Universe scientist in his self-circumscribed laboratory, this light, a lucence transpiercing the light of the world, is handed down to us in the symbol halo; now passed off as primitive decoration, while modern science makes use of the infra-red – – –

---

4   (1) of instantaneous healing
      (2) multiplication of the loaves and fishes
      (3) walking on the sea—calming the storm
      (4) raising the dead

– – – – allusion to God as "the father of lights" is not merely sublime poetry.

Above all in illumination the mystic abstractly perceived our impossible to blossom forth as *the* POSSIBLE.

CONTEMPLATION drew him far beyond his ego-electric exercises. In ECSTASY he at last tuned in on

THE CREATIONAL OVERTURE – –

– – – on beauty before its semblance descends

– – – on music before it in utterance descends

– – – on the source of presensate ecstasy whereof, to earth life, Eros alone brings some intimation.

However evasive of description their illumined experience, it imposed upon all illuminati an obligation: to impart to others the formula for its inducement.

An impartation involving the esoteric import of the CIRCLE.

Deific electricity coursing through a circle of mentalities, all concentrated on a like aspiration, increased the spiritual power.[5]

THE ELEVATIONAL MAGNET

Illumination effected our elevation of the spirit to that *other magnet* opposite to the Earth's attraction: a gravitation upward – – – – a sublime buoyancy.

---

5   Its corporeal counterpart is evidenced in the intensified animation of people gathered for a party.

Herein the origin of religious assembly perhaps indicative of consummate attainment being eventually only encompassable by *all men* as one whole   one circle.

Hence the religious insistence on the BROTHERHOOD OF MAN.

The eastern attitude of prayer, the joined palms, the soles of the feet pressed flatly together, precluding the ego-electricity from running off into the ground as in our bi-ped activity, constrained it, through circling and recircling, to vivifying accumulation sufficient for cooperating with the electric inspiration of Deity. The fingers tapered to point upward serving as antennae.

Study of the esoteric is not needful to prove the effectiveness of this *gravity upward*. Haphazardly we connect with it, when, for no apparent cause, at certain times we find ourselves suddenly light as air skimming the pavement, where oppositely at some recent hour, our leaden legs seemingly bored into the earth a tonnage of onerous animation, under a like leaden lunge of the brain to the tug of the terrestrial center.

To the mystic our human world of phenomena as we experience it at present compares to a sculpture-picture, a radio-television broadcast in three dimensions, issuant from the Deific designer; while to the non-mystic this projected image of the actor assumes his entire identity, dynamism, origin and permanence whereas

MAN IS A COVERED-ENTRANCE TO INFINITY

Contemporary man presumes his life to begin, come to an end, with his body. His intelligence to be manufactured by the brain; he being unaware of the currents in cosmic power conveying to man his apparent *esse*; unaware of the brain being merely an instrument of reception and transmission.

Seemingly this psychic system of scientific investigation, tending toward total depreciation of the tangible universe, being too acutely specialised for working out the dual abstract-concrete imperative of our intended evolution,[6] short-circuited – – –

A strange inertia settled upon the Orient. Exercisers of Spirit sat, incessantly asleep, in public places, their finger-nails growing through the palms of their hands.

———————

To the earliest disciples, the mystic system proved often communicable. But all systems of spiritual exercise come to a crisis incurring decrease of comprehension. The snap-back of human consciousness from the take-off of inspiration: the *stretch* of consciousness into the imperceptible universe still depending, to some degree, on the contemporary stage of evolution in the *concrete world*.

———————

Later students misinterpreted the scientific-mystic teaching as an exhortation to make the mind a blank; to immobilise the flesh.

———————

Books of mystic instruction, written in code, conveyed nothing of their real significance to the uninitiated. Held by the purist to be supremely authentic, one, apparently an account of many battles, precisely and reiteratively enumerating the hordes of warriors en-

6   As indicated by Christ in saying:—"I come not to take them out of the world but to keep them from the evil."

245

gaged, had the trick of turning into a mathematical treatise on the control and alternation of rates of vibration involved in various psychic operations. At which point in perusal the student's cranium *seemed* to open up, very like a certain Picasso cubist head, for abstract instruction to pour into it. Not oral. Communicated thought. Not the student's thought.

The thought of DIRECTIVE INTELLIGENCE   Religion's VOICE OF GOD.

While modern science successfully harnesses intangible phenomena inducted from the invisible Universe, the layman unquestioningly accepts the astounding results. Presented with any claim of mystic science his faith immediately reverses. He behaves as if he had never even *heard* of anything but solids.

His "keep-off-the-grass-of-the-infinite" is self-protective – – – the brain is cautious.

The mystic, in contemplation received lightning impressions of the inconceivable – – – – as of the universe timeless, dimensionless, "turning inside out" in process of creative revelation – – – passing during the eternal moment through itself – – – identifying the microcosmic with the macrocosmic in the energy of the atom,

The absolute momentum causative pulse of Life, of Breath, of procreation – – – construed for him by conscious magnitudes, living equations.

The Brain is cautious – – –

The characteristic result of encroachment on the frontier dividing the abstract from the concrete being explosion. Even as the modern scientific extraction of force from Power produces explosion, cerebral encroachment may cause explosion in the mind. Inasmuch as the mind is not kept tensile. Restricting speculation as to the larger resources of existence with the irreflective assumption that the evolution of man is completed; whereas he should measure his mental capacity in conformation to his travel of transition since, sequent to chaos, a miniscule incipience of life first quivered in an ocean. He does not keep in balance with time through realization that his destiny is to fare onward, at least as far as he has come, which realization would preserve his equilibrium, even on impact with the "*unknown*."

EROS

Human emotion is become excessively confused owing to the scission of sex from religion.

Sex presented to the purity of youth as at once beatitude and secret filth

Religion, as sole security and total prohibition

Sex! This word, at last, so overflows with misassociations. To clarify its future significance, sex must be renamed. Meanwhile, for "sex" let us substitute *Eros*. Somehow the sound of the Greek cupid survives unsullied; unlike longer words derived from it.

Eros became identified with "Sin" when the uninitiated misconstrued the asceticism of ancient Asia's students of psychic science; mistook an *automatic transmutation of virility* for drastic mortification of the flesh, thus dragging a metaphysical dis-"connection" into the domain of physical interchange – – – repression.

The oriental quarrel with "Desire" coincides with the incipience of Exoteric Religion.

Exoteric religion originated in a fusion of ancient seers' determination to mystify such as might degrade the psychic technique to destructive demonstrations—origin of Black magic, and the "outsider's" *own* misinterpretation of religion's dicta.

Any disciple, by nature unadaptable to transformation of his auto-electric potency, could, as anyone to-day, simply not imagine what that would be like.

In trying to make it out, he substituted the mutilation of impulse for the transformation of impulse. Incapable of purely mental relaxation he strained against a biologic process. How could he understand "having no desire" to mean "desire vanished of itself"?

To this is due religion's war against the flesh. It may seem to the layman, that perhaps, according to atomic physics, there is no actual flesh.

A true mystic genius would never have snubbed the Creator with derogation of "the Flesh"—for also our desire, not of our own contriving, is from the Creator broadcast to us— He had merely ceased to function within range of our *desiderata*. He would have no more imposed chastity on the common man than would Bach have forbidden him to play the concertina.[7]

Rather, the ancient must have understood the electric incitement of Eros – – –

"They twain shall be one flesh," described the sense of a tangible bond, a vibrational co-identity of perfectly married people, as if the Eros union bequeathed to them a continuous reciprocal radiation that distance does not disrupt.

_____

7 The esoteric "career" of chastity was aimless, save for those having what the Church still alludes to as "the Vocation".

"Whom God hath joined together let no man put asunder," undeniably confirms the derivation of Eros from the divine abstraction, delimiting the self in the peace of participation, of being no longer contactless in a mysterious universe.

The "man of flesh" phrase in evolution is giving way to the "man of electronic vitality" largely through the accelerated life-tempo characteristic of the United States.

His manner of being in a state of transition, with Eros most evidently involved.

Due to this evolutional transition, for the modern human the merely fleshly approach to Eros becomes inconclusive.

The approach to Eros of the future subordinates mere flesh to vibrational co-ordination promoting release of the intrinsic electrification inducing Eros-Bliss.

A co-ordination imposing on the individual, as in psychic science, self-control, inversely to the bursting (again explosive) excitement induced by the filth-bliss confusion of the sin-centuries.

It is no longer a *sub rosa* rumour that numerous devotees of Eros—at present are disappointed.

How mysterious his own potentials remain to man. Adolescents are motivated by an ardent anticipation of Eros, while intellect is unaware of the sensate manifestation towards which their ebullience urges them, for when successfully experienced it overly surprises with the realisation that one, in his ordinary state of consciousness, could never imagine, or even subsequently, evoke.

Between the brain and the spirit lies some intermediary sentience receiving the broadcast of our instincts.

ELECTRIC EROS

Even as there exist scaled approximations in the universe, such as a once-assumed structural similarity of astronomic constellations to the invisible atom, so, comparable to the mystic's electrical suffusion by the infinite *élan*, Eros is also an electric release (The "*Flesh*" again, like the terrain, an instrument.) Safety valve for an electro-neural system in its stress of sensitizing the human organism. Eros recharges the electric battery of the nervous system.

Further similitude to mystic principle: the release of Eros is the closing of the circle of all emotions fused to one emotion in instantaneous consummation. A flash of attainment to infinite sentience, resulting in perfect relaxation. Replica in reduction of the mystic's ecstasy in illumination.

Connective likeness of mystic electrics to the electric charge of Eros was either suppressed or forgotten.

The serpent in Eden is symbol of the extreme imposture – – –

The substitution of "sex-morality" for humane morality.

Compare the demoniacal tortures inflicted on sentient human beings all through the ages, in the guise of religious correction, to the intimate doings of two fair adolescents coerced by the glow of the moon – – – search diligently for any wrong they have wrought upon their *fellows*; yet not long more than a century since Religion stuffed them each into a barrel lined with excruciating points of nails, and rolled them, sanctimoniously down-hill to death.

IMMORALITY CONSISTS IN CRUELTY—   IT HAS BEEN THE PRETENSE OF CRUELTY TO ENFORCE MORALITY.

The explanation of this anomaly reverts to the risk of "explosion" on the frontiers dividing the secret from the overt realities.

Eros is the one transmission from the power universe to cross those frontiers unmodified—metaphysically intact, yet available to sensate experience.

Even as esoteric religion, esoteric Eros exploded in the human mind, leaving a debris of sadism to infiltrate religious institutions.

Originally erected around a prop of sublime significance, such institutions, the prop long since, through misinterpretation, withdrawn from them, are becoming meaningless; as though a spurious agitation had been "touched off" on the disappearance of a serene reality.

In apology for this loss of power—incomprehension through our spiritual disability was camouflaged in the scapegoat personification of Satan, changing all God's beneficiencies to man, to menaces.

CONFUSION OF SATAN WITH EROS

The channels of discard discharge coursing alongside the avenues of Eros, an anomaly challenging our aspiration to purity (Purity—consciousness concerned only with the beautiful outcome of functional life) to ignore disintegrated human psychology with the filth complex – – – sanitative for the aboriginal—but with the coming of modern plumbing the Kingdom of Satan is submerged.

Freud, training a bright light of analysis on such psychological terrain, illuminated all but a blind spot, THE ELECTRIFICATION OF BLISS—that terrain, exploited by his followers, is become an infinitely extensible maze of introversion in search of Eros – – – the little man who isn't *there* – – – – –

Freud is unnecessary to the future. His utile achievement lay in his solution of the problem, "To mention or not to mention." By making it, aided by the scientific aegis – – – fashionably polite to mention. Clearing a way out for inhibition.[8]

---

8   Contradictorily a pamphlet by Radó reveals an unpredictable side-track toward insanity.

THE LIBRARY OF THE SPHINX.

While the sphinx retains her secret, who shall reveal the unconsummated significance of the asterisk—

Notwithstanding that the secret of the sphinx is not conveyed in words—the asterisk is an assumption that the secret is possessed by each of us and therefore need never be mentioned—

the asterisk is the signal of a treasure which is not there.

Is it possible asked the sphinx of the sphinx—

have we not also that pornographic literature, distributed under the rose—

Exactly—it is that very pornographic literature—which has exposed—

The secret—that the sphinx does not know her own secret—

Impossible—it would have been remarked upon ere now—

—Not so—for the sphinx has never spoken. The passive sphinx who has put up with everything—has never given a sign—

It was my womanly modesty, said the sphinx—

Not that—said the sphinx, it was your corroding misapprehension that the other women were not with yourself, in the same case.

"Woman—" said Havelock Ellis to the sphinx, "put up with what she got and she got *nothing*!"

I dared not lose my literature—sobbed the sphinx—it was so lo-o-o-vely!

Your literature—let us examine it your literature—

It was written by the men—

And the sphinx never gave a sign.

Even James Joyce in the introspective finale of Mrs. Bloom to his cosmic day—writes—"'would he give me' if I let him 'retire' on my 'bases'"

but said the sphinx, there was in this case a biological interference to account for her sacrificial suggestion—at the same time—you remember that at Gibraltar under the blue bedspread of the sky it was a lawn kerchief that substituted the sphinx—

And evidently Mr. Bloom had had to essay other methods—recollect that she soliloquises his tongue is too flat or something!

Still—the Blooms are doubtful—on more propitious days of the month they may have

Let us make the absolute descent from Parnassus and examine the opus par excellence wherein the secret of the sphinx claims to be positively *shredded* of its veils — — —

That little x x x x tuber Frank Harris—cun-t INKER

How minutely he describes the geographical aspect of the Venusberg—it was not given to him to witness Vesuvius in eruption—the spasimal larva - - - - -

So he absolves his manhood with the "love juices" of expectation – – –

Frank Harris who entered the seventh heaven with a syringe in his pocket—

Oh let him be said Peter on shrugging at his authorship in his record— The Lord is merciful to scrubby-looking men—he has given the compensation phobia.

D.H. Lawrence who has come nearest to defining the psychic experiences of passion has plainly revealed that he is not cognisant of the mechanistic processes by which those psychic experiences can progress into appeasement.

He is checked by the ominous darkness that settles upon the protagonists of his love passages—together with the herculeanization of their spines and thighs.

The pre-orgiastic consciousness replunges into the primeval bog of protoplasmic slime – –

Women in Love perhaps is the only book that has invested the flesh with a semblance of the august—or the virile male impetus with grandeur—that buck rabbit!

But the contingence of the immature girl child and the buck rabbit persists in reality throughout the relations of all the men and women in the book—for his women who are in love he returns to the irrational psychology of the female—

Gerald is a normal man—but the ultimate impression of him that exasperates his mistress—is the eternal child crying in the night—she is able to derive no satisfaction in her comforting of this crying child —— and at last she – – turns him loose in the snow!

All the women in the book are, as is usual in novels, attempting to intellectualize a content for the vacuum of their sensation.

The primary phenomenon of our new "liberated" literature—is the superiority complex of the male as regards his intimate relation with the female,

If the sphinx had spoken a word—

but no—

So Lawrence along with the others—

In *Sons and Lovers*—

—tumbles a maiden on the bank of a river—she is dressed for out of doors—it is a virgin too—the civilized safeguards of the toilet are not included in the love nest of clay—anxiety is not the best cantharide of nature—

The psychologic depth of —— is disgust at the maiden's lack of passionate response to satisfy Lawrence's public— That the maiden was not satisfied—has probably even—caused them surprise – – – on one side of the channel.

And to turn to the Archangelic D'Annunzio himself—in *Il fuoco*, the one-sided record of the best advertised love affair of a century—

How do the lovers stagger about in a mist—in a state of *débile* hysteria—we are to conclude as the result of a series of revivifying galvanizations of the nervous system.

If our erotic, romantic, and realistic literature has presented the gentle reader with an interminable procession—of ladies "possessed" in floods of delight—the instantaneous beatification of the female by the (always) condescending male—where may we ask did those authors live? In some sublime refuge from our daily life? So ill do these records tally with the confidences made, in the hospital, the home and the nunnery – – *or the sanatorium.*

Nor must be omitted another type of man in literature, a rare and an apologetic man—such as for instance the heroes of Aldous

Huxley, whose intellect overpowers their virility to their erotic discomfort—but again there is no inference that the surrounding beauties would not be wholly beatified if only they did not think too much—to be able to "let themselves go".

Strangely enough the only current literature that discourses upon the disappointments of hymen as an accepted fact are the third rate Parisian erotico-comic papers, which appear to be prepared exclusively as popular excitants to lubricity—perhaps they are employed as the villain in the piece to offset the satisfactory heroes or the shadow in contrast to which the libidinous light shines the brighter. Also, in the soggy atmosphere of T. S. Eliot is embedded the typist who fresh from the embraces of a stray acquaintance—

turns on the gramophone

and swallows her hairpins

(I am not quite clear in *my* recollection of the latter line)

Mr. Eliot has observed the typist and her combinations drying on the roof with the same disrespectfully acute ray of observation that he turns on classicism and pessimism alike.

The lover who was worsted by the gramophone probably had a uniform conception of either.

Practically the whole of our psychological literature written by men might be lumped together as the unwitting analysis of the unsatisfied woman. The episode of marital relations in Evelyn Scott's narrow house is perhaps the most accurate presentation of the average intercourse under the realist's microscope. Exceptionally there is no *parti pris*—it was not written by the dominant male.

Nor is it only the written word that has connived in the deception of the beatific possession; there are also monuments to the purely literary conception, using literature in the sense in which the French use it, as for instance: the Apache has his "literature" meaning, a tradition that has become fictitious. In public he must snatch the choicest morsels of meat from his mistress's plate— cuffing her on the ear therewith— He must drag her across the floor by her hair—should he omit to do so she would desert him— these "garnitures" of his social status are as fixed in their laws as the order of precedence in a coronation ceremony—

One such a literary monument is the conception of "*La fille de Joie*". And there is no married woman to whom the beatific possession is so repugnant as to the *fille de joie*.

She was joyful indeed. Emma Goldman has seen inmates of an American house of prostitution—pushed screaming towards the chambers of "joy" where the more "eccentric" patrons awaited them. In England where everybody that is outside Debrett's has an inferiority complex, her face is petrified with a complex of such profound inferiority that it is unfathomable by even the most probing imagination. In Germany—the nearest she comes to joy—is when she can wile away an hour of leisure in the, from her inevitable point of view, purifying atmosphere of a pederasts' café.

The traditional career of the *fille de joie* was as transitory as is very joy itself—she drank champagne and died in hospital—

Other of her joys were bribing the police—being examined in indescribable circumstances for venereal disease, being threatened into supporting a *maquereau* and contracting syphilis.

Yet who would suggest that the night life of the metropolis is not entirely joyful—he is too drunk to notice—

When he comes to himself in the morning he will congratulate himself on joy he has erotically administered to a *fille de joie*.

There is another literary hoax—the hoax of the *gros gaillard*.

The big strong man as the best lover.

Alas the exercise of force destroys the ephemeral sensations—

Nerves are not ponderous—

Inversely—the woman who scratches her face will feel pain—the woman who gets her head blown off does not.

THE LOGOS IN ART.

In the distances of space our greatest aesthetic interpreter was not an artist until he became an acrobat

Picasso that aesthetic acrobat—

Greek the spirals of form move round the limbs—orderly to the omniprevalent calculation of the relation of surface to centrality.

The movement of the object is provided by the so strictly retained attention of the eye—

The perfection of statuary is a challenge to the congruent disposal of the atmosphere—

The church—that ungainly edifice that so *impoliment*—shuts out the divine "view"

The dual subjective in Pictorization—subjective conception—and subjective projection—

The possible extension of their relativity. The significance of form is profound according to its dual relativity to the finite and the infinite—of a metre to its rhythmic conformity to finite and infinite rhythm.

It is a pauper aesthetic that falls to the stacking—inclining and laying of linear extensions—

It is the unpresentable in presentation that causes it to exceed replica—

Bas relief that movement is intercepted to prolong itself in lateral intensity—in lieu of a forwarding *passagère*

The movement is carrying itself into the Eye instead of progressively out of our sight.

The new Zig Zag decoration was the most conducive to the premature symptomatisation of intoxication

When the rectangular falls down on its job= —

Our home will be "on" the Cinema—

Screen

There has been *some* good modern setting in—*nouvelle vierges*—and the first one has ever had

Still there is a sublimity that lacks the sublime—

that penetrates these readopted proportions of elevation—

Apparently because the proportions of their superficies are too great for their purpose—leading as they do to no altars— For there is no *common-sense* reason why a straight line should not have the same significance in the twelfth and the twentieth century—

The logos is insinuated Modern art—because there is a certain renaissance—evidently the masters they follow were of healthier contagion than those of some previous generations—
And there is no renaissance without breath—
The breathing upon of the logos—

_____

But by what way does the logos inform contemporary art—according to the laws of chance—

THE METAPHYSICAL PATTERN IN AESTHETICS.

The pattern of a work of art is interposed between the artist's creation and the observer in the mode of a screen formed by the directing lines or map of the artist's genius.

This is the essential factor in a work of art.

The old masters presented the esoteric plan of their individuality superimposed upon a "subject".

The moderns present the map of their individuality without the secondary reconstruction of the pictorial coherence of our customary vision.

Every time we recognise the work of any given master it is by the singularity of this map of his aesthetic system. Never by the subject.

It would be a *reductio ad absurdum*—the ability to judge a work of art by the subject it represents.

If the pictorial aspect were the fundamental entity of a work of art, a new subject by a known master would be unattributable; "So and so" paints girls in sunlight —— tomorrow he paints a man in a subway. By what law do we recognise the individuality of the master?

By the identity of this metaphysical pattern with his personal aesthetic. This knocks mere subject out of the reckoning as an indispensable element in art.

The intention of the modern movement is to liberate art from the convention of pushing this individualistic aesthetic structure to a final pictorial conclusion.

The modern has chosen to exteriorate the "God in the machine" without the ceremonies of the graven image.

The stages of progress towards the presentation of the purely metaphysical structure of an aesthetic creation have been marked various degrees of subject in dissolution and subject in process of crystallization influenced by the artist's perception of phenomenal dynamics.

The picture in which the transpiercing of the pictorial subject by the metaphysical pattern is most completely revealed is the El Greco landscape lately loaned to the Metropolitan Museum. Here the "intention" of the moderns has been forestalled to the extent that the aesthetic pattern projects itself beyond the subject matter.

The same is to a subtler degree noticeable in the rhythmic arabesques to which he induces his religious figurations.

In all the masters we can track this formative metaphysique to within their spatiality, volume, and motor idiosyncrasies of technique, however compactly incorporated in objective reproduction.

MI & LO

I.

Form

lo

Does form result from seeing unform repeatedly? For the first man I see is formless, in that he has no recognisable form. But the second man I see is recognisable as having the same form as the first man I have seen.

.

mi

Not so. For the one half of the first man I see is the replica of the formation of the other half of the first man I see. Thus, instantaneously he takes form.

The intention of his form being endorsed by its duality. Form is the union of identicals.

lo

The first half being the question to form and the second half the answer of form.

mi

Form being thus a token of the truth in which the question and the answer are incorporate and inseparable: truth being the question that answers itself—as immortality existing as a question in man's mind, is answered by its confirmation in the macrocosmic mind of god.

lo

Then are the first halves of the microcosmic forms in the human mind and the second halves in creative god-head?

And is this the elucidation of "man in his image and likeness"?

But where occurs the macrocosmic element in this monad?

mi

Inasmuch as to the duality of this man-form indicated by right and left inheres the infinite intermediate, which, as cognisable from the fourth dimension, makes possible the one half of a man to be at an infinite distance from the other half of a man. In the recession of boundary during the process of thought, while the intellect encompasses phenomena with its convergent apparatus, comparable to sight, and compresses duality to the third dimensional unification.

lo

Then man is an instrument for imposing form upon phenomena. Man *IS* auto-conscious.

mi

Man is not the conceiver of form. The phenomenal universe provides exercise for the tenacity and increase of perception toward its ultimate reception of macrocosmic forms.

Form is a signal reconnoitred by the intellect on its march upon the illimitable.

lo

Then it is the confinement to form that incites the intellect to exceed itself.

mi

Form is the expressive encroachment on the increate from which— Appearance with its several significances derives.

From the untraceable precedent all form emanates; as sentry to the presence of creation.

lo

But may not intellect be the mold of phenomena?

mi

The mind and phenomena fit each into the other with exactitude; that is so.

If it were not, phenomena, to which the mind does not fit, become unbounded, would flow out of cognizance.

The encompassment of phenomena by the mind is the resistance of the mold for the conservation of the form.

lo

But a mold is an inverted form for the containment of a (so far) unassembled form, whereas phenomena already have form.

mi

The mold has been taken originally from the form. And after all the concavity of the mold is but the continuity of the convex form.

Any regular or irregular scission of any element will constitute a form in its mold: the confrontation of inner and outer—

II.

mi

Life we may say to be animation—and the source of animation can be disclosed.

The source of all animation is the unique force of the universe—every human body is animated by the whole unimaginable tonnage of the force of the universe.

An incalculable ocean of impact—an impact that should crush the body to infinitesimal fractions of smithereens.

lo

How then is such crushing tonnage of force available to the human body—

mi

When it arrives at contact with the body—it runs down the nerve centre of the brain and the spinal column and provides energy for the whole organism; the surplus runs into the ground, the spinal column acts as a lightning conductor to the universal force which continuously coursing through, continuously animates.

lo

But how does this force gain entrance—

mi

Through the pineal gland considered of such great importance by certain ancient sages.

Its outlet into the ground as a continuity of its course through man provides the much discussed attraction to the earth—or gravity—

It is for this reason that the body in recline can harbour a greater vitality—by placing the soles of the feet together, and thus establishing an extra self-enclosed circuit of energy—the same is true of the circuit enclosed by placing the palms of the hands together and it is not for nothing that out of the dark mystery left by an enlightened past—that the attitude of prayer has come down to us—a circuit of the arms and hands for the greater retention of the divine animation.

This is understandable inasmuch as the animated force disperses at the end of the spinal nerves—to, in the perpendicular event, bifurcate through the feral motor extensions—

In the supine event, force, which in the fourth dimension has impetus four ways at once, traverses the body horizontally which (but this is too intricate to explain in third dimensional formulas) produces—slumber. Not being pushed forward in sleep you give up your cooperation with active time.

lo

But I can lie awake or be most animated horizontally?

mi

In both conditions then are animated degrees of progress. Yet you will agree with me that in the erect position there is a possibility of, tendency, to stay awake indefinitely—while in the horizontal position there is no possibility or likelihood of staying awake for ever— Generally speaking the erect position tends towards awakeness and the horizontal position tends towards sleep.

lo

How can we divine whether a fourth dimensional cognizance would be for the benefit of man—do you who so much insist on its superlative importance—envisage it as a prototype of heaven—might it not precipitate us into an unbearable because inadaptable hell—

a hell produced by our inadaptability to its functions—

an unease infinitely unsupportable—

No—for all the great mediates such as Christ have insisted on just the opposite—

And all would-be expounders of the fourth dimensional condition have laboured to convey their knowledge to us, uniquely through their great desire to render service to men.

They were overwhelmed by the reality to them so easy of access—and so totally inaccessible to the rest of mankind—

Perfect Being—is so easy if, "you know the trick"—

It is so true that only the muddy patches in our minds hold us to the third dimension.

Morality is not a behaviour but a discovery.

A christ can arrive at morality because when he has given all; he has still got all for himself.

lo

But again what is morality?

mi

Morality is the impulse to supply the necessities of the soul.

lo

And again what is morality?

mi

Morality is to give all you have and still possess all.

lo

But is not this giving, a pouring of water through a sieve?

mi
Truly—from him that hath not shall be taken away.

III.

mi
The creative man is one whose consciousness is deepest within himself—

lo
But the creative man is one whose consciousness travels farthest—

mi
As the deepest roots put forth the highest branches.
But the consciousness of the uncreative man—hovers at a slight distance from himself and from the outer universe.
He is never quite in contact with his own mind—or the minds of others—

lo
Can man put forward an irrefutable conclusion of the existence of God?

mi
Yes for it is irrefutable that there be a sum total of the multiplication of all things.

God is the correct solution of the mathematical problem of the universe.

lo

Is there an irrefutable conclusion as to the existence of the soul?

mi

I think therefore I am— But further—I can think about what I think.

That is the testimony of the soul.

If man had no soul he could not be the observer of his own existence—

It is impossible for existence to be severed from the cause of existence.

If man were only the human phenomenon—he would be merged with the phenomena coincident to his state of existence.

There would be nothing to hold him off them as the spectator.

If man was merely a physical phenomenon—all conditions in which men may find themselves—would be at all times and for all people the ideal condition—that is the inevitably suitable condition.

If I am born a hungry and ill-treated child—I could find no discomfort in these conditions.

For I physically should be that thing in myself—a hungry and ill-treated child—the hunger and the suffering would be as much an integral part of my physical existence as my arm and my leg—it would be part of my make-up—there would be no element in me to reject it—

But the soul with its ideal prerogatives knows very well that that is not the way to live—and sets up an effort at rejection.

There would be no third dimensional suffering if we were not connected with a fourth dimensional soul.

The flesh cannot say be the flesh *we* suffer—because the flesh is the flesh— Yet the flesh and the soul can say to one another—we suffer.

Sensibility explores the nervous system and reports to the soul.

Yet the soul cannot suffer. Yet it is the audience without which the body has nothing to which to convey its suffering—

And happiness is inherent to the soul—the flesh cannot be happy without contact with the soul—but happiness is in the soul—

Pleasure is an operation of the body to allow somewhat of the joy of the soul to filter through it.

As it is possible to cure suffering so it is impossible to cure happiness.

You can say be happy although you have not got the love you desire—you cannot say be unhappy because you have got the love you desire.

Happiness is then the rightful condition—the condition "expected" by every human soul—because there can never be any *need* for its illumination—

It is the thing that must ever of necessity be rightly, "allowed to remain."

There is some mistake to the declaration, "Man's inalienable right to the pursuit of happiness"—happiness pursues man—and man in his unconsciousness is continuously running away from it.

Conceptions of events are more intense than the events *per se*. Because conceptions gain intensity from having no duration in time—while the event itself is prolonged and disintegrated by reason of its duration in time.

If I read of a woman starving to the point of death I get an intense concrete impression all wrapped up in the parcel of one moment of the agony of starving to death— I may weep over the social injustice—at the least it entirely holds my attention.

But if I myself experience the process of starving to death—I go through none of this agony of mind—there is no similarity between the simple poignancy of conception of starving and the complex protractedness of the inside information on starving to death—

A thousand and one things are occupying my mind—I notice that my shoulder blades are bobbing through my jersey dress.

I remember all the unfinished beefsteaks I have ever left on a plate.

The sight of canned food in shop windows takes on a sudden and under all other circumstances non-existent glow—an *aspect féerique.*

Death—it is the only thing that at the moment is happening in my mind.

I have no waste energy for bemoaning social injustice for I am overwhelmingly aware that it would be as impossible to extract a peso out of anybody as to travel to the moon.

The man who is starving to death—feels nothing but an awful fool—

And the inevitable law of compensation steps in—

When one becomes too weak to stand up—the relief of lying down becomes so tremendous that it is almost worth the starvation to be able to indulge in it.

IV.

lo

But you may say that the blind back of man is the shutter on the fourth dimension.

But I say that that it is the arresting plane on which the universe like a cinema on the screen, through the medium of the senses, projects itself.

mi

But the universe is of the third dimension—and therefore still the shutter on the fourth dimension.

lo

But take away that shutter and the projectiles of phenomena traverse the man, who is then to all intents and purposes "not there."

mi

I have said that man is the medium for knocking phenomena into shape. So if he was no longer limited by the blind back he would be rounded out to the fourth dimensional contacts.

It is possible that the fourth dimension would equal zero if we were unable to retract to the third dimension in order to have something focussed to compare it by—

lo

On the assumption that God without his creation would cease to exist.

V.

mi

Morality is the accurate mathematics of life.

lo

But what is morality?

mi

Morality can only be attained through a perfect understanding, domination and utilisation of the senses.

Any man who has lied has inserted a two for a one in the calculus of his life, and therefore his life-sum must add up wrong.

He cannot present an accurate computation either to himself or the cosmic mathematician.

Yet in an illogical society there is often the necessity for a temporary lie for the sake of ultimate truth.

In the ultimate analysis morality is clarity.

VI.

lo

Do you believe that any extra-ordinary consciousness can be obtained through what is known as meditation—and if there is any demonstrable value in what is known as enlightenment? Or illumination?

mi

It is extremely difficult to distinguish in meditation where physical phenomena end and lucidity begins.

The first semblance is that of exceeding the confines of the body—the feeling of the dissolution of the physical load—but the reality of this is difficult to disengage from the results of the cessation of visuality.

Be that as it may, it is undeniable that the un-use of the eyes—in a state of complete wakefulness—sets up a sublimation of sight outwards to an intensity of sight inwards.

Life originates in the fourth dimension and is projected into the third dimension. It has been explained that a man aware of the fourth dimension, if enclosed within a room without exits, could get out of the room.

That is because he in the fourth dimension—can follow the procedure of the universal involution.

The introspector is aware that he is connective with infinite distance—

That is he can in the third dimension be aware that life is un-limited in what we call space—although it appears to be limited in time.

He is aware that life *que lui est disponible*—is unlimited—but that the three dimensional organism at his disposal can only make a limited use of it.

And all men of ample consciousness find third dimensional phenomena to be barriers to the following of their consciousness up or back to its source.

If there were entities whose conscious rhythm coincided with the intervals of atomic matter and time—it would be possible for other entities and another universe with different phenomena to inhabit the identical space occupied by ourselves—

A universe superimposed upon this universe.

Reality is the seal of the creator on nothingness.

The introspector in trying to catch the process of his mind is conscious of a certain restriction—not of the property of his mind but of his manipulation of it. He is insistently disturbed by the oppression of not being able to avail himself of all there is there.

This is a good deal owing to the slowness of intellectual process—the protractedness of educational exercise—and the paucity of events or aims in individual life. It is also caused by the absorption of information through single-sensed organs—in which the impression is flat instead of globular—

A globular impression.

VII.

mi

It were erroneous for one by whom all things are understood to encumber himself with an opinion—

lo

Yet is not that understanding an attainment to the consummate point of view? Is not point of view opinion?

mi

In so much as opinion is the defence of a situation? Whereas he who understands is he who immovably identifies himself with – – –

lo

Therefore, he who incalculably replaces himself.

mi

To the end of all understanding—submission of identity to the continuity of Truth.

lo

?

mi

Truth is that evidence the intellect ignores in the interest of its *libre arbitre.*

lo

But is it not in pursuit of evidential Truth that the intellect exercises its *libre arbitre*—

— — — — — — — — — — — — — — — — —
— — — — — — — — — — — — — — — — —

Is Truth the concept inviolate to controversy; a single silence amid a loud diversity—

mi

Truth is the question that answers itself. Truth is the creative formula.

VIII.

lo

What is perfection?

mi

The maximum reciprocity between conception and realisation.

lo

A conception that allows no realisation.

— — — — — — — — — — — — — — — — —
— — — — — — — — — — — — — — — —

mi

Perfection occurs within that zone where it is possible to advance but not recede.

lo

In advance there is degree but in perfection there is no degree

— — — — — — — — — — — — — — —

mi

In perfection the infinite dissimilarities are reconciled.
Extrospection. The infinitrospector – –

In meditation the mind unbuilds itself for a divine re-edification.

lo

It is not easy to determine the junction between introspection to neurosis.

— — — — — — — — — — — — — — — — — *Introspeculates* — —

mi

Yet all the evolutional "odds" are on the neurotic for it would seem that it is in the as yet unsown fields of consciousness that he loses himself.

lo

And the genius finds himself.

IX.

mi

There is a degree of knowledge that reaches no farther than death. We exist for as long as we can imagine ourselves. All that secedes from the Absolute—asserts the only independence. The Liberty to be perishable.

The death of the body, of reason, of the will of affection— All these deaths added together amount to no more than the death of beauty—

the fall of man

The struggle of man—

floundering between his descent into the microscopic universe for which he has discovered a mode of introduction and an intuitional ascent towards the cosmic.

The phenomenon of vibration is an emission from the macrocosm or divinity to humanity.

It is amusing that microbes have an aspect of diabolism. Mediocosm = man.

X.
Lust

mi

I doubt whether the new Promiscuite would admit the authenticity of lust.

Lust being perhaps as far as the Purist can conceive of it—an insane attribution to a sane *impulse*.

The miasma of traditional taboo rising to the brain at the onset of desire—the complement of shame imposed on the right to realisation—a mental congestion that obfuscates the directitude of virility.

lo

But may there not be some perspicacity in this presentation of an abandonment of the reasoning self to a swollen eroticism?

mi

It is the paradox of morality that the only human passion that has been tabooed is the amatory passion. The sole passion that is not destruction—the only passion that can do no harm to anybody—the only passion that can disseminate comfort and consolatory relationship—

The law of the world moralist actually is—

Thou mayest kill—wholesale

But thou *shalt not* enjoy

One would think that suffering sold easier—that there was a greater profit to be culled from pain—that the moral merchant-combine should so consistently endeavour to withhold rapture from the market—

THE OIL IN THE MACHINE?

Hear the evangel of the new era—
The machine has no inhibitions
Man invented the machine in order to discover himself
Yet I have heard a lady say, "*Il fait l'amour comme une machine à coudre*," with no inflection of approval.
   It is the oil in the machine to which the mystics referred as the Holy Dove ——— And what could we make of the sort of pulpy material the Padre Eterno made engines out of
   We spasimal engineers
Whose every re- act -ion of grace is an explosion in consciousness.

TUNING IN ON THE ATOM BOMB

Serene, amid scintillas of sunlight gilding our narrow garden, writing of the danger induced by extracting force from Power, suddenly, seismically was I overcome by an eccentric sense of guilt; as though speared by an echo of some forgotten wisdom sunken in ancient time, forbidding all revelation of some perilous secret.

Excentric guilt! I did not *know* the secret.

A causeless accusation as if of defying some unknown taboo detonated in my brain, a shattering terror of the limited incarcerated within the illimitable—

Longing to regain serenity I struggle to regain serenity, to refocus a tremulous perception, to recapture my easeful surroundings—to see "Nature" as before my inexplicable shock? explosion blast? despite a dawning premonition it might no longer prove to be enjoyable ——

Indeed, the lively foliage of the garden had concentrated to a mirage of but one branch, bronzed by some unnatural blast, a mummied relic of previous appearance to arraign me as dupe of molecular pretence to forms of reality.

I faced a glaucous continuity of evacuated space, a universe constructed of intangibles crushed one upon another like endless proportionless strata of inexistent glass, reflecting nothing (*néant*).

Nonentity of force, of pressure, more pressure; inopposable pressure upon the soulless branch it was driving into the visual locale, through my brain and out into the limbo ever present to man's blind back.

My usual warm appreciation of the concrete world disintegrated in a global disappointment – – continued in endless chain-reaction of terror transpiercing me.

I could feel the former ulcer in my body revert to its origin, a sensate sore in cerebration—nauseous nucleus of fear.

Jam packed into an instant the linked infantile panics diffused by ill-mated parents—the consequent catastrophes of maturity shrouded in lethal anxieties—rearose – – – from dreamy hollows, long since sealed by my inconquerable optimism due to the fascination of existence – – – – – – anxiety . . . . an inexhaustible fount of terror involving force in fear of itself.

Turned loose on an Infinity, forever emitting one, now, meaningless apparitional phenomenon after another all common to our historic earth.

Thought, no longer reasonable, confronted with the prestidigitation of an unreasonable universe, changed to mere confusion.

Temperamentally content to enormously appreciate the world as it is patterned for us; unable to imagine what part was mine in this over-all alarm I miserably supposed my unfounded distraction to be symptomatic of insanity. But I was not inclined to give in—consent to it when I had not invoked it.

However onerously, I would go on as usual—struggling through a sort of double life half my conscious *esse* belabouring the other half with blows of inordinate apprehension—of what, I could not even guess—while dropping smiled "darlings" to my daughter who responded, "What makes you always so damned cheerful?"

Before the mysterious onslaught, I had been about to look through the New Testament to locate, in chapter and verse, the inspired utterances of Christ. Such as

"The Spirit" (all conscious Power) is everlasting life; the letter (derivative unconscious force) is death. (This being only one *significance* of this cosmic saying)

Resolute, I returned with my manuscript to the lately inconducive garden seat, determined to proceed with my writing, taking for granted my former confirmations survived the unaccountable transformation.

I searched the scriptures for the divine citations – – – – – and at once it was as if the very roots of the supreme knowledge were being torn up and the leaves of the tree with threatening verses in celebration of doom printed upon them, scattered in the patient face of humanity, lashing it, blinding it – – – a ruthless tornado of castigation; the breath of a god whose raving majesty consisted in correcting his creature, purely for *being* as created.

All I seemed allowed to perceive in such darkened scriptures were authorized specifications for Inquisition. In a black-out vision—phantasmagoria of the exoteric religious debacle—my mind submitted to some abnormal pressure, brought into focus with that of the Inquisitor, was forced to concede his interpretation alone to be logical.

In line with such gospel very Eternity deteriorated to an ultimate dimension of hopelessness from which there is no escape, even the suicidal, for man accounted endlessly responsible for not having formed *himself* in his own unlikeness.

There was nothing to seek in this shattered scripture – – – nothing to write with thought defeated.

For weeks, I resisted, a misery so mysteriously baseless, slowly reducing to tremulous fear the terror that appeared to invade me from something endlessly surrounding me—till it faded to the annoyance of neurosis – – – – – – this lessening

UNIVERSAL FOOD MACHINE

I. Universal Food Machine

Open radiators at regular intervals along the streets to temperate the rigours of winter—and as an integral part of the architecture heated shelters for those anonymous creatures who seem to come from nowhere and to be going nowhere.

Also automatic distributors of some luscious soup most carefully composed of the essential elements of perfect nurture, and so savoury that it stimulates the more subtle faculties—together with exquisite croutons to furnish the necessary sensation of solidity that is needful for the ease of the digestive organs. How much would be saved by calling in the vast sums in disseminated charity and pooling them for a national distribution of general welfare. How easily would such an overhaulment occupy the millions of unemployed.

What a reduction in the donations for hospitals.

Halt says the practical moralist—would you encourage thriftlessness and idleness—but what has become of thrift in the face of unemployment—and idleness is abnormal—a paralysis of the nervous system resulting from blind education.

As by all the laws of psychology—the equality clamoured for by the socialist is an obvious impossibility—and as such equality is the desire of a type of mind whose experience has been too rude a familiarity with the elemental necessities of life—and therefore with little apprehension of those aesthetic necessities of leisure.

The trend of politics tends towards a levelling down—but what is there impractical in the conception of levelling up—

There may be an inevitable social ladder—and consequently a lowest rung—but it is a matter of merely humane decency that that lowest rung should be shifted higher up.

For surely we have sufficient knowledge to discern that human life constrained to concentrate on the preservation of the body alone—has no value—and the more we shall come to realise that the body is merely an instrument—we shall realise the moral obligation of setting society on such a basis as will provide.

II. War

We speak a great deal about the end of War— We desire the end of War— You will nowhere find an individual who prays for War. Yet War would not come upon us if it were not invoked. By whom is it invoked? It seems impossible that it should be so—and yet it is so— War is not a scourge of destiny which falls upon us independently of our will.

Yet look around us at the peoples of belligerent nations on the eve of hostilities.

One side must surely show some signs—of an atavistic ferocity—but no—save for those   —differences that mark the race—and at a long distance disappear leaving the opposing peoples looking so exactly the same—

You will find the same farewells to affection in deference to duty. The same stern-jawed youth facing the same horror—turning his back on the same amenities of life both youths have.

III. Effluvia of decomposition of the Spirit

All evil thought, all cruelty, the paralysed vitality of loneliness, the crushed vibrations of drudgery and the bewilderment induced by enigmatic injustices are broadcast through our universe and received by the collective human organism. Think not that all the agonies such as for instance those sustained in War end with the dying of the bodies which endured them, for they are "on the air" and like a poison gas enfeeble the survivors. The decomposing bodies are buried to avert contagion, but the decomposition of the spirit, impalpable to our senses, is an inconfinable and a lasting corruption.

Yet History reveals our race intent on the manufacture of so dangerous a psychic chemical that the world in the end will succumb to its effluvia if we cannot succeed in evolving an ethical antidote.

Scientists are beginning to experiment with the vibrations of the brain while these and similar vibrations have been known to the mystic from time immemorial to be as effectual as the vibrations of light and sound.

Therefore when Christ commanded us to do unto others as we would that they should do unto us, it was as a primary measure of spiritual hygiene.

We cannot draw a fully wholesome breath from an atmosphere laden with enforced anguish. For suffering of itself is charged with lasting forces of destruction—leaving us a heritage of insecurity and disaster that accumulates affliction, and as an invisible ray, darts out disease and mortal confusion.

WILLIAM CARLOS WILLIAMS

Williams has overwhelmed the earlier impressionism of surface
with a new impressionism of the structural Entire: his pen a probe.
Analysing, for us, the components – – indigenous and historical—of an unwitting majority, he draws unprecedented deduc-
tions from Everyman's impacts which are forever
"kindling his mind (more
than his mind will kindle)"
As an observer Williams's complete integrity of meditation
reaches that ultimate exactitude which alone refreshes poetry
with unexpected marriages of words – – – – – giving his verse
the enduring individuality of his
"Chronic hills"

NOTES

STORIES

THE AGONY OF THE PARTITION

(6:150)

"The Agony of the Partition" is an incomplete work that includes a clean portion in Loy's hand, replete with word counts; this section is numbered one. Sections two and three are drawn from additional handwritten fragments. Most of the story is contained in a single archival folder, but some pieces that extend the end of section two were located in a file labelled "Unidentified Fragments" (6:183). It appears that Loy intended to write more about the rooming house that is the focus of "Agony"; a sample additional segment is included for further reference at the end of the editorial notes.

The surname "Bundy" makes a brief appearance here, and is central to "Hush Money," a story Burke dates as written between 1917 and 1922. Within the notebook containing "Agony" there is a letter drafted by Loy to *Harper's Bazaar*, asking if the editors might be interested in publishing her poem, "Aid of the Madonna". A version of Loy's poem "Property of Pigeons" is also included. "Aid of the Madonna" was first published in *Accent* in 1947 and "Property of Pigeons" appeared in *Between Worlds* in 1961 (*Lost LB* 209–10).

PAGE 5

The title "The Agony of the Partition" may be "The Agony of the Partition."—Loy writes it both ways in the manuscript—*ed.*

PAGE 6

After "heart beat on my" the next page reads:

to be or not to be inserted?

It was evident, as I sat up, alert, that someone in the next room had chosen the spot corresponding to mine, to rest against the partition.

projected on to the stage only

an emotional abstract of

the plot

A contact so ethereal,

"which Mrs. Nome . . . decoded" is a later addition, and is followed by "(into language?)"—*ed.*

All honorifics—"Mrs. Nome and Mrs. Moppet"—are "Mrs" in the original—*ed.*

"at law without evidence" was "at law argued"

"of any claiming" was "of any especial"

"claiming. I might have been" was "claiming or"

In the margin next to "contact" reads "?"—*ed.*
"to lean against" was "to lean up against"
After "against" reads: "(the partition?)."—*ed.*
"hardly registered the passing of a" was "hardly recorded a"

PAGE 7
In the margin, next to "lock, a glimmer of light" reads "OK"—*ed.*
"converse. After" reads "converse; After"—*ed.*
"carrot" was likely "carrots"
"orangutan, approached" was "orangutan, approached in a state of
   august enquiry—"

PAGE 8
"rooms—her critical sneers, her undue familiarity—" reads
   "rooms. Her critical sneers. Her undue familiarity."—*ed.*
After "undue familiarity" was "'And her foul language! You can't
   imagine what I've been called.'"
"'foul language. Do'" may be "'foul language: Do'"—*ed.*
After "'servant?'" was "And her foul language. 'Do you allow this
   woman to treat me like a servant?' the plaintiff wailed"—in the
   margin next to this sentence reads "?"—*ed.*
"did not stir" was "had not stirred"
"but proudly astonished" was "but astonished [into an] with unusual pride - -"
"appealing to her." reads "appealing to her,"—*ed.*
"curls wrapped in an emerald scarf" was "curls sheathed in an
   emerald cloth"—next to this amendment reads "or square?"—
   "square" is unclear—*ed.*
"as they thought" was "in a twinkling"

After "alone – – –" was "for where I lurked they could not / empty kitchen" and "see me"

" 'I seem to have been' " was " 'I seem to be' "

In margin next to "Irishwoman" reads "colleen"—*ed.*

Before the second section of "Agony of the Partition," a page reads:

> I asked her how she could make such an idiotic exhibition of herself with such a mother—
>
> 'Why she didn't go to you for advice – – – Cassy said "Not much—I mean to manage this affair *my* way"—
>
> She managed it all right – – getting her pregnant was his way of showing annoyance his excuse—just that he'd never had to bother—because this girl he lives with can't conceive—
>
> "He said," [and] the blonde's voice grated more shrilly on Mrs. Nome's tension—
>
> "I hope she kills herself and the baby too"
>
> "She," the voice fell slobbering in her throat – – wanted to keep it to remember him by—
>
> "My poor sweet child" cried Mrs. Nome—
>
> "My poor sweet child – –"

PAGE 9

II.

After "fell lower" a long wavy horizontal line is drawn in the text—*ed.*

" 'her Nature, although denied' " was " 'her Nature, had been' "

" 'denied me' " reads " 'denied (to?) me' "—*ed.*

After " 'cling to her' " was " 'like a slowly waning essence' "

"With these few words" reads "These few words"—*ed.*
"affair, whose" reads "affair, with whose"—*ed.*
After "discrepancy" reads "(or disparity?)"—*ed.*
" 'I love him' . . . erotically" is a later addition
"Shaken with my" was "Shaken with the enormity of my"

PAGE 10
"erasure of feature: the unfaded" was "erasure of feature—due to
    the veil of insomnia that dims the unfaded"
After " 'him to her' " reads "?(at the fair)."—*ed.*
"My bruises . . . 'violent with me' " is a later addition

PAGE 11
"moaned the girl . . . chair—" is a later addition
" 'had been such friends' " was " 'had been friends' "
" 'over and over again I told her' " has a couple of variants, including
    " 'I kept on telling' "
" 'never seen.' Mrs. Nome seemed . . . back her up" was " 'never
    seen.' continued Mrs. Nome"
"That face they brought" reads "That face she continued they
    brought"—"she continued" may belong to the line above—*ed.*
After "surprise." a small gap is left before the next paragraph—*ed.*

PAGE 12
" 'into her room against' " was " 'into her room so hardly' "
" 'grief—should have been her wedding-day—that' " reads " 'grief
    should have been her wedding-day; that' "—*ed.*
" 'lightning overthrow, sheathed' " was " 'lightening overthrow, re-
    taining in their sheath? coat of lava' "

" 'contractile' " was " 'contractive' "

" 'as if she were too heavy to fall' " is a later addition

" 'an insane levitation' " was " 'an impossible levitation' "

After "looking as she always did, perplexed" reads:

> Walls withhold (see notes)
>
> The partition had not that mercy; hung with spy-paper it came to function as a seismograph, and at once a sound-track for cataclysms that would suddenly converge on Mrs. Nome at impredictable intervals along the otherwise unbroken tenor of her isolation. Time, for her, a clock that had stopped, only recalled itself to her attention, when, crazily, its alarm would "go off".

The next page reads:

> It seemed to me as if riotous armies invaded a vacuum;—the shadowy brain of Mrs. Nome, while besieged by foreign terrors—only awaiting their recession, to reform her obstinate vision of her daughter's soul.

"for convincing" was "to convince"

In the margin next to " 'After she got rid of the baby' " reads "OK"—*ed.*

" 'all night, every night, dragging' " was " 'all night, dragging' "

PAGE 13

"projected as it were in television" was "projected in television"

"clapboard; in her aerial colouring, a place" was "clapboard; a place"

"alcohol, with Cassandra" was "alcohol, Cassandra"

" 'And they actually had' " was " 'And they had' "

Above " 'mix with decent people' " reads: "insert all the Mops friends here or previously?"—*ed*.

Another available variant of " 'after that low crowd … like them – –' " is " 'She'll never again be able to mix with decent people. After those common – – –' "—*ed*.

After " 'readapted' " reads:

> Ira's scream of resentment—paralysed the partition—"the dirty, the mean—hypocritical cad – – that's the lowest thing I ever heard—absolutely the lowest – – – –"
>
> "Cassandra was not speaking of the Moppets—you know she loves to chat with grocers' wives and bell hops—scrub women; anyone, she used to spend half her time that way—" Mrs. Nome repaired forgetting, perhaps subconsciously indicted, she had not used that kindling word – –
>
> "The Moppets are simple, jolly people—and whatever *you* may see in her, Ma Mop is fundamentally kind."

III.

The heading "Mrs. Nome" is Loy's own; a paragraph above this heading reads:

> *The Agony of the Partition*
>
> The blonde and the baroness sipped their tea. In sparse phrases they discussed "men"; like icebergs scanning the horizon for something to collide with. Touched on abortion with a precision of surgical instruments. Frequent as their lips to their cups, the word "rich" hissed from one to other on the air ultimatum in acquiescence—

After "vindicatory" reads "?"—*ed.*

"occasional effusion" reads "occasionly effusion"—*ed.*

"in an angelic" was "in angelic"

"fastidiously selected the" was "fastidiously the"

PAGE 14

"Mrs. Nome perhaps" reads "Mrs. Nome (bowed her soul) perhaps"—above "(bowed her soul)" reads: "somewhere else" —*ed.*

"plausibly suspected"—"suspected" is unclear—*ed.*

"fleshly bond between mother" reads "fleshly bond (between) of? mother"—*ed.*

"This, she had modified," reads " 'This, she had modified' "—*ed.*

Above "the young, withholding" reads "OK bits. Mrs Nome."—*ed.*

After "disgust?" reads "x apropos—cf [*possibly* "of"] some former observation"—*ed.*

" 'pregnant'—to *her*" reads " 'pregnant'—To *her*"—*ed.*

"Mrs. Nome, repudiated mother" was "Mrs. Nome, the repudiated mother"

"in an amazed agony" was "in agony" and "in amazement"

"her the conceptual" was "her conceptual"

PAGE 15

"Mop seemed to be discreetly" was "Mop seemed always to discreetly"

"bed-pan" was "bed"

"she might carry" was "she might be carrying"

After "offertory" reads "?"—*ed.*

"biological gods" was "sly gods"

"hilariously angry; each, although obviously at odds, fully" reads "hilariously angry, each, although obviously, at odds, fully"—*ed.*
"Nome wondered, was this" reads "Nome wondered 'was this"—*ed.*
After "affection" a long line is drawn across the page—*ed.*
After "ideological" reads "?"—*ed.*
"gloriously all pernicious" was "gloriously pernicious"
After "embroilment" reads "?"—*ed.*

PAGE 16
" 'The Most Beautiful' " was " 'the most beautiful' "
After " 'brought about' " reads, on the next line, *"Wraith of Love"*
—*ed.*
Another draft fragment reads:

> If only I could get rid of my mother
> [*long line across page*]
> But however melted in sorrow, it would seem the partition still remained, it must still *resist.*
>
>   Iva Cooper had not had her say, because "All that was low enough—but this disgraceful affair with Martha this is *too* much. She's crazy to get rid of you—so that common girl with her stub neck, her spotty face can come and live here. I'm [her] Cassy's room-mate aren't I? I wouldn't stay a minute with the [ridiculous] filthy creature. Cassy finds great qualities in her—hidden qualities, to you or me they would not be evident—qualities so rare she has to spend [the] her nights with her to enjoy them.
>
>   You've seen the disgusting way they lie all over each other on the divan, from 8.oc in the evening until 3 in

the morning—and then when we have left for home, how Cassy suddenly runs back—

[*along margin of same page*] But—moaned the partition I'd taken a room by myself—and Cassie implored me to forgo the deposit—she wanted me here with her – – she [wanted] longed for the chance to make up to me for her former unkindness— A staccato "yes"—pinged upon that partition—she wanted your fifty dollars—

The next page includes:

"Oh I'm sure there's nothing lesbian in it" – – – interfered the partition, faintly serene – – – "Naturally, you have to pretend, being her mother, I quite understand that—losing the man you love" mused the partition [faintly serene] "is a queer death, you die away with him—yet [you] continue to be torn by the pain that has slain you—your life, which was his he has taken with him—the only illusion [for recovering] of resuming it, is to cling to those others who knew him also, talking about him reconstructs him, retrieves a little of his, your, living breath – – – when Martha and Cassandra whisper together for to us so long long hours on that conferential sofa—they are only co-operating with Time in their protracted healing – – – that sofa is [the] a salvage rock of reminiscence for [their] their love's ship-wreck . . ." [However] All the same Mop insists that Martha had begun to get over Gurney—but her confidences with Cassandra have, awfully, revived it – – – – –

(6:154)

Burke claims that "The Crocodile without any Tail" was written in 1926, when Loy's youngest child, Jemima Fabienne Cravan Lloyd, was seven. Loy devised narratives to teach her daughter languages; stories were first told in French, and then repeated in English (*BM* 372–73).

"The Crocodile without any Tail" is a typed manuscript with numbered pages; pages one and three have two identical copies. Some corrections are made throughout, but most are indecipherable, as they are blacked out with type. Variations in spelling have been edited by relying on the most prominent usage; for instance, "Mamma" is "mamma" at the outset, while "the crocodile" is "the Crocodile" by the end of the text. "School master" and "singing master" are both hyphenated and not; the hyphens have been dropped here.

PAGE 18
"grass" was likely "flowers"

PAGE 19
" 'to attach a Christmas tree' " reads " 'to attach a Xmas tree' "—*ed.*

PAGE 20
"eat its porridge" was "eat hi"
"Mr. and Mrs." reads "Mr and Mrs"—*ed.*

"Happy Go Lucky" was "Happy go Lucky"
"which to live, and a large" reads "which to live. and"—*ed.*

PAGE 21
"began to rain. The" reads "began to rain, the"—*ed.*
"come and live were" reads "come and live there were"—*ed.*

PAGE 22
"see a singing master. They" reads "see a singing master they"—*ed.*

PAGE 23
"up his head and opening his mouth" reads "up his and opening
his mouth"—*ed.*

PAGE 24
"looked exceedingly" reads "looked as exceedingly"—*ed.*

GLORIA GAMMAGE

(6:164)

This short story is a sketch based on the American writer and
wealthy socialite Mabel Dodge Luhan, here named Gloria Gammage. Dodge was one of Loy's closest friends and influences in Florence, where Loy moved in 1907 (*BM* 119–22). Loy writes "Mabel" in
large hand near the top of the last page, which also yields an instance
in which the name of Mabel's first husband, the architect Edwin
Dodge, can be discerned beneath "Antony," Loy's male protagonist.

Most sheets of this handwritten manuscript conclude with a total word count for the page in question. While reading as a complete narrative, the piece begins mid-sentence, suggesting that a portion may be missing at the outset.

PAGE 25

Prior to the first paragraph, the manuscript reads: "ermine of her cloaks,—and feathers soft as her lashes—isolated her from the prevailing light—"

"Gammage" reads "Gammadge" in the first instance only—*ed.*

"hurry" reads "[*torn page*]urry"—*ed.*

"weeded in" was "weeded by"

"accesses of surfeit it was" reads "accesses of surfeit was"—*ed.*

"surfeit was" was "surfeit were"

After "personality" reads, partly crossed out: "(she picked up Esau and a couple of his sunset glows and stuffing them beside her in the car—off home with him.)"—*ed.*

All honorifics—"Mr. and Mrs. Gammage"—read "Mr and Mrs"—*ed.*

"out at official" reads "out official"—*ed.*

"Mr. Gammage advising" reads "Mr. Gammage—advising"—*ed.*

"who's whos ruminated" reads "who who's ruminated" and was "who who's stare"—*ed.*

"glass ambush" was "the impregnable glass ambush"

"biology" was "anatomy"

PAGE 26

"emptiness" was "intuition"

"that her instincts" was "those instincts"

"marriage and the social prestige" was "marriage at Palms"

"budge" was "move"

"conscious of the men than most women who are" reads "conscious than of the men most women = who are"—*ed.*

"into conscious" reads "into consci[*torn page*]"—*ed.*

"irritations of longings" was "irritations towards actions"

"cannot sensitize" was "cannot clearly sensitize"

Loy draws a line between "sensitize—" and the paragraph that follows—*ed.*

"eyes searching" was "eyes roving"

"seemed to" reads "[*torn page*]eemed to"—*ed.*

"get under" was "get her fingers under"

"alike" reads "a[*torn page*]ke"—*ed.*

"fuller interpretations" was "higher interpretations"

"of the 'whole vitality' . . . fuller interpretations—" is underlined in Loy's text—*ed.*

PAGE 27

"only woman" was "only person"

"blown herself up for" was "blown herself for"

"ostracism" was "isolation"

"bizarre ingredients" was "bizarre material—"

"inquisitive soul" reads "inquisitive soul.)—"—*ed.*

"amplitude and" reads "amplitude of and"—*ed.*

"when she was bored" was "when she was tired"

"Between her and Felicity" was "Felicity"

"provenance income" was "provenance and income"

"there had" was "had long their"

"degree of social parity" was "degree of parity"

"were with the" was "had with the"

"slower sociable" was "slower men"

"she phones" was "she calls"

"thrown her" was "thrown away"

"because they have no emotions" was "they have no emotions"

"types with which she" was "types she"

PAGE 28

"says her husband" reads "says her husbands"—*ed.*

"covered in priceless lace" was "covered with lace"

"delights to drop hot" was "delights in dropping hot"

"and is listless to her husband's wooing" was "and is not listening to her husband's persuasions"

"no man's land of meaning" was "no mans landing of significance"

"anxious" was "determined"

"leaving Gloria" was "and leaves Gloria"

"to strike the population" was "to strike terror into half the population"

"Gloria, knowing" was "But Gloria, knowing"

"has invoked" was "has inadv"

"pale in significance" reads "pale into significance"—*ed.*

"an enormous overdose" was "an overdose"

"The commotion" reads "[*torn page*]e commotion"—*ed.*

"in her extensive household" was "in her household"

PAGE 29

"finds Antony" was "finds Edwin"

"mooing around" reads "mooing [*torn page*]round"—*ed.*

311

(6:160)

"Hush Money" is prefaced by a note in Loy's hand which reads: "Daniel is Mina Loy when she went to see her father who was dying—". Burke counters this claim by pointing out that when Loy's father Sigmund Lowy died in England in 1917, Loy was residing in New York, and hadn't seen him for five years (*BM* 248). Although "Hush Money" remains fragmented and incomplete, it was clearly important to Loy; on meeting Freud in 1922, Loy gave him a copy of this story which the psychoanalyst duly read and pronounced "'analytic'" (*BM* 312–13).

In "Hush Money," as in "The Three Wishes," Loy uses a "+" to indicate a break between some narrative fragments; she also conducts careful word counts throughout. The surname "Bundy" reappears briefly in Loy's "The Agony of the Partition".

PAGE 30
All honorifics—as in "Mr. and Mrs. Bundy"—are "Mr and Mrs" in
     the original text—*ed.*

PAGE 31
In original, a blank line exists between "ashes." and "Mrs. Bundy
     was appointed"—*ed.*
After "her keys" reads the following passage, crossed through:
          There was another daughter who said nothing, she had of-
          ten desired death [but considered it her duty for fear of

criticism to stay] but considered that to be a shirking of duty, for one of them must "stay" with father and mother.

She stayed.

Daniel left.

"seventh male nurse" was "male nurse"

After "male nurse" was "who was seventh in the series"

"prescribed for rotten patches" was "prescribed for him"

"still more" was "still greater"

"persuasiveness" was "persuasions"

"The poor half imbecile" was "he got positively"

After "approach" was "And had in the wordy"

"expert insults" was "expert verbal insults"

"which forced" was "which co"

"for protection" was "for their last protection" and "for their last ambush"

"justification—the truth—" reads "justification the truth"—*ed.*

"necessity for peace" was "necessity with his sons"

"Her next" was "In her"

"was incredible—a cheque" was "was a cheque" and reads "was incredible a cheque"—*ed.*

After "consciousness" was "had been eased as by confession"

After "indulgence" was "Daniel had gone out into the world most ill-prepared—he had [great notions] what his mother had called great notions of himself, which in his brilliant recurrent beginnings, were justified but died on the ebbs of"

PAGE 32

Above "Daniel stayed with filial superstition" reads: "the drawers and cupboards of her [other locks on her] personal furniture had been broken open and could not shut again—Mrs. Bundy rattled her keys."—*ed.*

Between "two male nurses" and "expounded" was "was an excellent reminder of what a marvellous work of [nature] evolution the lowest form of civilised being, is in reality—"

"expounded at such" was "expounded in his"

"was restless, he" was "was restless, Daniel"

"was a mumbled" was "was his father mumbling"

"And yet Mr." was "And Mr."

"a very marked horror of bad women" was "a marked horror of the bad woman"

There is a blank line between "women—" and "The patient"—*ed.*

"The patient" was "Mr. Bundy"

"once at Daniel" was "when he saw"

"'are catching on fire'" was "'have caught on fire'" in both instances

"begin smoking" was "begin smoking too early"

"as in this case" was "as in this instance"

"a glowing" was "a speck of"

"fitful and reflective reactions" was "fitful and haphazard" and reads "fitful and reflective reflex reactions"—*ed.*

"was only fidgety and ill"—"and" is in brackets, and the whole was "was wonderingly fidgettyly ill"—*ed.*

Between "at ease" and "Daniel" is a blank line in the manuscript —*ed.*

"planted as saplings" reads "planted saplings"—*ed.*

After "eaves" reads "to shade its conclu[*unclear*]"; possibly "couching"—*ed.*

Before "Mr. Bundy next to him" was "Mrs. Bundy's mother had w"

PAGE 33

"Conversation between" was "That conversation between"

"husband and wife" was "husbands and wifes" and reads "husband and wifes"—*ed.*

"game of tennis" was "game of ball"

"served the ball" may have been "batted the ball"—*ed.*

"to his wife—the wife" was "to his wife's bat, to make it easy for her"

"the wife retaliating" was "the wife would"

After "potato" are two pages, with single vertical lines drawn through them, that include the following:

> had stayed at home, [it was like passing] she was like a chilly draft from an open tomb.

———

[Sometimes David]

The home was pleasanter than it had ever been, the [intermin] incredible warfare [that against 2 allies who fought each other, in this way somehow as they—while they opposed each the enemy, the aspiring generations whose aspirations they bomb barricaded with their envy and shot across at them with their commands]

———

[The] In which commanding officers [made war upon] fought each other and wounded their soldiers like enemies

with their commands had been *greatly* simplified by the sub-
traction of Mr. Bundy and Mrs. Bundy now that she held the
supreme command was more amenable to circumstances.

There was a great deal of talk about heredity, and the
youngest sister had written a noble letter to a youth with
adenoids, giving him back his freedom, the youth in an
equally noble letter, had pointed out that nothing would
make any difference to him.

A certain amount of form or plot had come into life,
with this first definable event in their career of 'poor dear
father's nervous breakdown, they all felt that they knew
better how to handle things now that things were no
longer [rea] vague.

[The psychology of the interior less chaotic]

The withdrawal of the mannequin to his spare bedroom,
[being had left] had cleared a lot of psychological space

A certain amount of order had come into chaos.

"the holiday" may be "a holiday"—*ed.*
After "disordered one" there is a short line across the center of the
    page; the "+" is not Loy's—*ed.*
"In them" was "seemingly m"
"He had lost the thread of his life's discourse" was "He seemed to
    have lost the thread of his conversation" and "life's discourse"
    was also "living discourse"
"father's repetitive reminiscences" was "father's reminiscences"
"reminiscences as he could" was "reminiscences often rea"
"pouncing" was "jumping"
"on a remark—for his" reads "on a remark, say of [*unclear word*]"—

for his—*ed.*

PAGE 34

"mother's opposition—that" reads "mother's opposition that"
—*ed.*

"the frantic nightmares" was "the frenzies rare"

"He leant over . . . and wept" is a later addition

"He leant over" was "Daniel leant over"

After "audience—" was " 'O course I do—' "

" 'convinced 'im—as' " was " 'convinced 'im—that' "

" '—and lookin' ' " was " '—she' "

" 'as though she feels' " was " 'as though she ad' "

PAGE 35

" 'down in the morning so' " was " 'down so' "

After " ' 'arf a hour' " was " 'after studying years of stuff' "

" 'They can't know' " was " 'They don't know' "

" 'about people wot' " was " 'about their patients' "

" 'you'd a got' " was " 'you'd ave' "

" 'as finds out what's the matter' " was " 'as finds the causes' " and
" 'what's wrong' "

" 'wouldn't believe—why' " reads " 'wouldn't believe why' "—*ed.*

"entrances steady as blind eyes" was "watching rigid set like blind
eyes"

" 'You take it from me' " is a later addition

" 'be so nice' " was " 'feel so nice' "

" 'they 'ave to' " was " 'Like to want' "

" 'they just 'appened to rot away' " was " 'lettin' themselves just gently decay' "

Crossed through, the end of the manuscript reads:
> Daniel was young and as he had [had] been allowed no other pleasures, extremely sensitive.
> [When David passed through the house he would sometimes run across
> When David]
> In the house David would sometimes pass his [elder] sister—the sister that

INCIDENT

(6:162)

Alongside some handwritten notes, "Incident" consists of two typed manuscripts of five and six pages respectively; both are signed "Mina Loy" and have very occasional annotations, although the five-page text is slightly more refined and is therefore the document used here. Distinctions between the used manuscript and its alternate are noted below.

The focus of this piece—an experience of arrested circulation—bears a distinct resemblance to a climactic moment in *Insel*, a novel Loy is believed to have written in the thirties. In her notes, Loy suggests that "Incident" was a "petty accident" that took place in Geneva when she and Emily Balch—"as usual in teasing argument, due to our opposite temperaments"—were rushing "to tea with the George Herrons." Loy visited Geneva in 1919 (*Salt Companion* 13). Emily Greene Balch (1867–1961) won the Nobel Peace Prize in 1946, in honour of her work for the Women's International League for Peace and Freedom; George D. Herron (1862–1925) was an American Christian socialist activist.

PAGE 36

"Suddenly, I found myself 'nowhere.' 'Fool,' I anxiously" was "Finding myself suddenly 'nowhere,' 'Fool,' I anxiously"

In longer script, about two thirds of the page are empty after " 'nowhere' "

PAGE 37

"conveyance" was "conveyance or communion"

"bluish base" was "dark bluish base"

"fascinated me" was "pleased me"

"conveyed to one" was "conveyed to me"

"a shaft" was "a cylindrical shaft"

Above "cylindrical" Loy writes "or funnel shaped spiralling," and, on the alternate typescript: "like a tornado or funnel [like] shaped"—*ed.*

PAGE 38

Above "just as I could *hear*" reads "*see* as cylindrical"—"cylindrical" is crossed out—*ed.*

"tornado-like thunderous onrush" was "thunderous onrush"

"at once ceasing to be cognisable by me" is bracketed by hand in alternate typescript

"At the same time, the click becoming" was "The click becoming"

"leg, lifted" was "leg lifted"

PAGE 39
"public square!" was "public square." (correction made to both
typescripts)

(6:163)

"Lady Asterisk." is written on the verso sides of an illustrated volume of Italian religious art and artefacts dating from the fifteenth
to the eighteenth centuries. Across the bottom of one fresco Loy
has written: "Bits for incident in Book". The slender narrative
frame involves a dinner party of the elite, and encompasses scraps
of conversation (and possibly streams of consciousness) in which
the narrative tone dominates. The structural disjointedness of the
work is compounded by the fact that the same volume includes
notes for "The Apology of Genius," a poem Loy first published in
The Dial in 1922 (*Lost LB* 77).

The story makes passing reference to Maurice Dekobra (1885–
1973), the French writer widely viewed as a subversive who was
well known in the inter-war period. The Irish writers George
Moore (1852–1933) and George Bernard Shaw (1856–1950) are
also mentioned.

PAGE 41
"mistress at the prime minister's" was "mistress looked over"
"Mrs. Birthright" reads "Mrs Birthright" in all instances—*ed.*

"prefer to remain" was "prefer to stay in London the"
"Pure" was "So perfectly pure"
After "this table—" was "Ah dear lady I prefer to remain where I
    am— I never want to"

PAGE 42
"had caused" was "She had caused"
"apostles of England" was "apostles of the"

PAGE 43
"enforcing chastity" was "enforcing morality"
"They have solved the sex question" was "There is no more sex
    question" and reads "solved sex"; this phrase could also be
    "They have no solvent sex question"—*ed.*
"all you have to do is to keep" was "if only you keep"
Before "And cocktails" was "And when you have taken a cock-tail
    or two—"
"but they take all the kick out of love philtres" was "but you can-
    not taste the love philtres"
"a coal forest" was "the coal forest"
"without an effort!" is a later addition
After "Everything's changed—" was "I would"
"slant on political" was "slant on ideals of political"
After "stable—" reads "X"—*ed.*

PAGE 44
"Dekobra bagged his Bolshevist" was "Maurice Dekobro got [*un-
    clear word*] Bolshevist"
"Dekobra" reads "Dekobro"—*ed.*

"thank you!" was "thank you?"

"up and stamped"—"stamped" is unclear—*ed.*

"all this humbug"—"humbug" is unclear—*ed.*

"knew how to write" was "knows how to write"

"generations of women" was "generations when women"

"And now he himself" was "Anyhow George Moore"

Beneath "last Bustle—" was "McDamage"—the final third of this
page is left blank—*ed.*

PAGE 45

"of the upper classes is the study of the lower classes through
art." was "of the wealthy is the appreciation of the lowest classes
through art—"

"a grimace" was "the grimace"

"A critic who" was "A philosopher who"

"they are in" was "they have in"

After "But tradition—" was "No one w"

"If the" was "The"

IN MAINE: GREEN'S COLONY

(6:161)

This handwritten script begins with a title page reading "In Maine:
Green's Colony". While the page numbering is irregular, the chronology of the story can be deciphered via Loy's regular word
counts. These calculations indicate that the beginning and end of
"In Maine" are missing; the extant text begins on a notebook page

numbered four, and concludes with two suggestive fragments. Loy's drawings and designs are scattered throughout, as are excerpts from another text that suggest that "In Maine" may have been composed in the late twenties or early thirties.

PAGE 46
Above the "4" in the upper right corner of the first page of text, Loy writes "perhaps"—*ed.*
"eye of your own" was "eye of his opposite"
"There they are" was "Maine"
"they are always shaking" was "when they are always"
"to behold itself . . . its consciousness" is a later addition

PAGE 47
"neighbour's grass plot" was "neighbour's back path"
"lodger's room" was "guest's room"
"atmosphere than the rest" reads "atmosphere. it the rest"—*ed.*
"dangerous—to incur the enmity" was "dangerous—to make enmity"
"but John" reads "bit John"—*ed.*
After "clean American" was "that in France, is known as the Satyr—through a very different process, is known as the *vieux marcheur*"—the last four words are not crossed out—*ed.*
"who fumbles" was "that paw"
"desperation of dissolution" was "desperation of adolescen"
"to such a word" was "to the word"
"my impression" was "but my impression"
"down the other" was "out of the other"

PAGE 48

"confidant" reads both "conversant" and "confidant"—*ed.*

"passion for Lucy" was "passion for Mary"

After "for Lucy" was "Lucy was all that Maine stood for"

"typified. She" reads "typified she"—*ed.*

"Although" was "But"

"within and not without" reads "within a not without"—*ed.*

"at a little sweeping, a little shaking out" was "at sweeping, shaking out"

"I do like Lucy" was "I do like Mary" in the first instance

"fleeing beauty" may have been "flying beauty"—*ed.*

PAGE 49

"A short conversation" was "It w"

" 'her' warm young life" was " 'her' vitality"

"idiotically delightful" was "really idiotically delightful"

"achieved his" was "achieved a further"

"Yes! More,"—"More," is unclear—*ed.*

"I do" was "Lu"

"If she were sick I would nurse her" was "If she were sick I would take her straight up to my house— Mind you that's a clean thing to do."

PAGE 50

"—could have done" was "—that"

"damage. As things were" reads "damage, as things were" and was "as it was"—*ed.*

"at once" was "soon"

"many couplings" was "most couples"

"Mr. and Mrs. Granger" reads "Mr and Mrs Granger"—*ed.*

"—there was" was "—As yet there was"

After "account for" was "I began to feel that if only I had had the [good] strange fortune to be caught in the nest by a man from Maine I might have been a 'better' woman but a worse writer— When to my surprise"

"incognito Freud" reads "incognito [*unclear word*] Freud"—may be "Mr"—*ed.*

"unveiled. The worthies" reads "unveiled, the worthies" and was "unveiled, were the"—*ed.*

"in banishment" was "in banishing"

"breasts preferred to have" was "breasts to have"

"taken murky refuge" was "taken refuge"

"lurks even" was "lurks everywhere since it lurked in those"

"planet—" was "planet—had never left"

"driving back" was "driving home"

"hoofing up" was "kicking up" and reads "hoofing up cloud" —*ed.*

"relieved himself of his" was "relieved himself of the"

"unpronounceable" was "inarticulate"

"*élan vers l'idéal*" reads " 'élan vers l'idéal' "—*ed.*

After "neighbours" a long line is drawn across the page—*ed.*

PAGE 51

"village. Where every" was "village. So clever"

"watched—where everyone" reads "watched, where everyone" —*ed.*

"mothers watching" was "mothers waiting"

"grandparents slept lightly" was "Pappas slept" and "fathers light"

"nightly by the window of the den" was "nightly in the den"

After "the den" was "by a bright oil lamp by the window"

After "without shades" reads, partly crossed out, "without [*unclear word*]"—*ed.*

"learning the danger" was "learning that danger"

"Straher sang" was "Straher told"

"no matter where else—" reads "no matter where else,"—*ed.*

In the margin, at the end of the paragraph beginning "This black magical" reads the following list:

1. In Maine.
2. Static
3. Annoying Mrs Bundy.
4. Passivia
5. The Stomach
6. Life and Death.
7. Transfiguration.
8. Triple Extra.
9. Songge Byrde
10. Passivia.
11. The Brother in Laws—*ed.*

"village post office" was "villagers"

"we could descry" was "we could already descry"

PAGE 52

"chaw" may be "Shaw"—*ed.*

"this post office" reads "thes post office"—*ed.*

"monocle and his" was "monocle, Lucy, and his"
"arrival—at such time" was "arrival—with a marvellous facility for being in two places at once—"
"was actually telling" was "was telling"
"to patting John Straher intimately on" was "and patting John Straher on"
"enquired" reads "enquiring" and was "enquired"—*ed.*
"And had been directed to" reads "been directed the only" and was "been told that"—*ed.*
After "description—" was "was"
After "saw her" was "she had brought a basket of wild raspberries"
"raspberries as her official" was "raspberries to welcome"
After "nobody" was "in seemingly"
"branchlike" was "clawlike"
"work-ridden arms and hands" was "work-ridden hands"
"It was widely known" was "It was known"
"once lain low with measles" was "once had measles"
"a letter of thanks from" was "a letter from"

PAGE 53
"Though this underworld" reads "Those this underworld"—*ed.*
"underworld" may have been "back world"—*ed.*
"could never become" was "never took away"
"mystery which spurred" was "mystery which I shared"
"I passed" was "I could"
"everyone" was "every acquaintance"
"and of each" was "and was s"
"It cost me" was "It took me"

After "discover" was "and then from one of our own party"

"said my informant" was "said John"

"really well. And as" was "really well. He called up a few loiterers to help"

"it was more than one's life was worth" was "one's life wasn't worth it— Once s"

"they could remember" was "they remembered"

"or at least" reads "or a least"—*ed.*

"These degenerates" reads "These *degenerates*"—*ed.*

"a few filthy" was "the few filthy"

"they were hunched"—"hunched" could also be "humped"—*ed.*

PAGE 54

"Their major impulse was murder then minor rape" is a later addition

"their lives were spent in one long loathsome lust" is a later addition

"In one infested lair" reads "[at] in on one infested"—*ed.*

"good sport to be alive" was "good sport mer"

After "with their" reads [*torn page*] ge sized"—"ge sized" is crossed out—*ed.*

"They only" reads "[*torn page*]hey only"—*ed.*

"kill and fornicate" was "kill"

"I asked and asked" reads "[*torn page*] asked and asked"—*ed.*

After "enthusiasm—" was "only we cou"

"only a very genuine succession" was "only a succession"

"walking stick" reads "wa[*torn page*] stick"—*ed.*

"a little—in case" reads "a little—[*torn page*] in case"—*ed.*

PAGE 55

"A peaceful" was "What a peaceful"

"its own heat" was "its temperature"

"in heaven—" reads "in heaven—."—*ed.*

"It was impossible" was "It was a day on which"

"they seemed" reads "the seemed"—*ed.*

"at the outpost" reads "as the outpost"—*ed.*

"napkin tied over" was "napkin over"

"from Wonderland that ended Alice's dream" was "from Wonderland after Alice's dream"

"but she had not" was "but her"

"aspect, her human" was "aspect, her complexion"

"called good day" was "said good morning"

"any strange children" was "any children"

"distant hill" was "distant hollow"

"Nobody starting" was "Nobody peeping"

After "hedges" was "When I came to the third house"

"the sun—its meadows" was "the sun—in a hollow"

PAGE 56

"under an apple tree" reads "under apple tree"—*ed.*

After "daisies" reads "A shingle path led / or gravel"—*ed.*

"* * * * *"—denotes about 500 missing words—*ed.*

Before "Everything around" reads "knows the difference—"
—*ed.*

After "far off—" was "and the Lord be thanked for that"

"schoolmaster for her kind" was "schoolmaster for the likes
of her"

"nodded to him" was "nodded to all that he said"

"*****"—denotes missing words—*ed.*

"hand invited me" was "hand to spy my approach had cleared a space"—"hand" remains crossed out—*ed.*

"the indescribable" was "the disreputable"

"of her poverty" was "of poverty"

After "her poverty" was "And we sat down."

"not clean, those" was "not clean like the houses i"

"wither—sometimes" was "wither—we"

"onto the flyblown"—"onto" appears crossed out—*ed.*

MONDE TRIPLE-EXTRA

(6:167)

"Monde Triple-Extra" parodies the class and gender politics of a very modernist sort of celebrity—see, for instance, mention of "*la petite* Duchesse de Da Da". These concerns echo Loy's satires of Futurism such as "The Pamperers," and suggest that this story was written in the late teens or twenties.

Loy's handwritten corrections can be found throughout the typescript of "Monde Triple-Extra," and the visible edits are documented below; the majority are indecipherable, as they have been blacked out with a heavy hand.

PAGE 57

"left corner" was "left hand corner"

PAGE 58

"harem or a" was "harem"

"For as the" was "For the"

"soldier beside" was "soldier next to"

"must fall" was likely "must die"

"so had each eager lady dismissed" was "so did each eager lady dismiss"

"those ladies attending upon" was "the ladies attendant on"

"a firmness" was "such firmness"

"and fluent curve of rosy thigh" was "such fluent curve of ivory thigh"

PAGE 59

"wandering fingers" was "long white hand"

"*geste négligent*" reads " 'geste negligent' "—*ed.*

PAGE 60

"a skirt revealing" was "her skirt which revealed"

"weary of—). And her loose" was "weary of) whose loose"

"cloud in a wind" was "cloud in the wind"

"thither. And as" was "thither and as"

"made of a metal" reads "made of a mettle"—*ed.*

"moon. While the" was "moon while the"

PAGE 61

"under that name" was "in that name"

"the wand; allowing" was "the wand allowing"

"alabaster, enrapturing" reads "alabaster, enraptured"—*ed.*

"Adoration" was "adoration"

"from her with the mop" was "from her the mop"

PAGE 62
"Youth is occasionally incapable" was "Youth in the majority is
 incapable"

NEW YORK CAMELIO

(6:177)

This character sketch was probably written in the late twenties or
very early thirties; it is embedded in a notebook otherwise domi-
nated by another story and a few drafts of a poem called "The
Widow's Jazz" that Loy read aloud at the Paris salon of American writer Natalie Barney in 1927, and published in 1931 (*Lost
LB* 95–97).

Loy has titled both pages of the handwritten manuscript, which
wittily demarcates in miniature many of her writerly concerns,
including failed romance, abjection, excess, and self-dissolution.
The protagonist's name is variously written as "Cameleo" and
"Camelio"—"Camelio" is used in the title.

PAGE 64
"The woman is meditating" reads "the woman is meditating"
 and "the woman . . . how" appears to be a later addition—*ed.*
"of life that drew man out" was "of desire that drew Life out"
"Do you" was "Now do you"

"behave yourself" was "control yourself"

"profile of" was "profile like"

"Camelio has—Camelio" reads "Camelio has [a] Camelio"—the
dash is uncertain—*ed.*

PAZZARELLA

(6:171 & 172)

"Pazzarella" is modelled on Loy's relationships with the leaders
of Italian Futurism, Giovanni Papini and F. T. Marinetti, with
whom she became close in 1913 while living in Florence (*BM*
151). There is ready evidence for this supposition: a "Mafarka"
appears in Loy's story, and Marinetti published a novel entitled
Mafarka the Futurist in 1910. Additionally, under the title of her
handwritten draft, Loy writes: "Parody of Gio's Work"; above
it she notes: "Dedicated to the great Tuscan—the most sympathetic of misogynists." Lastly, some of the content of "Pazzarella"
overlaps with that of Loy's well-known poem sequence, "Songs
to Joannes," which is widely believed to refer to Loy's ill-fated
romance with Papini (*Lost LB* 53–68).

There are two available manuscripts of "Pazzarella": one handwritten, one typed. The differences between the two are slight,
and where three pages are missing from the typed version, the
sense is readily continued via reference to the handwritten draft.
At the top of the typescript, Loy has pencilled a note correcting
the spelling of her female protagonist's name; "Pazzerella" is used

throughout, but Loy has written "should be / spelled Pazzarella / Pazz / meaning slightly / mad woman".

The letters in this narrative are translated from the French by Martin Crowley; the original versions can be located in the editorial notes below.

PAGE 67

" 'My affection' " was " 'But my affection' "

PAGE 68

Above "embraced me ceremoniously" reads, by hand, "or ceremonially?"—*ed.*

"to my mind." reads "to my mind-.-"—*ed.*

PAGE 69

" 'No—you trust' " was " 'No—no you trust' "

" '*You* have chosen me!' " was " '*You* chose me!' "

" 'me after all—' " reads " 'me after all—.' "—*ed.*

PAGE 70

Above "those intelligent eyes" reads "or so recently awakened?"— note also that "intelligent" is in parentheses—*ed.*

" 'hardly relevant,' " was " 'hardly advisable' "

After "freedom again" there is a gap in the typescript from pages nine to eleven; the sense continues seamlessly in the handwritten draft which is used here

After " 'world—' " was "etc." followed by a blank space occupying about a quarter of the page—*ed.*

"I had prescribed" was "I prescribed"

PAGE 71

Typescript resumes at "out of mere contrariness"

PAGE 72

"'I in no way'" reads "'I, who in no way'"—*ed.*

"'yourself—outraging'" reads "'yourself. outraging'"—*ed.*

"*in extremis*" reads "in extremis" and was "in the extremis" —*ed.*

"'your flesh—'" reads "'your flesh—.'"—*ed.*

PAGE 73

Above "'illuminated lovers'" reads "illumined?"—*ed.*

"'at its goal—'" reads "'at its goal—.'"—*ed.*

"'affinity—'" reads "'affinity—.'"—*ed.*

"'takes nostalgic leave'" was "'takes a nostalgic leave'"

"'*humblest*'" was "'humblest'"

"'And, doesn't exist—'"—Loy leaves these quotations intact in the typescript, rendering the speaker uncertain—*ed.*

PAGE 74

In the typescript, after "'I shall murder you'" there is no break before the next paragraph—*ed.*

"'a brute—'"" reads "'a brute—.'""—*ed.*

PAGE 75

"'or a theoretical ethic'"—"theoretical" is written by hand into what appears to be a blank space in the typescript—*ed.*

After "'theoretical ethic?'" there is a gap in the typescript of two pages; again, the sense continues seamlessly in the handwritten draft, which is used here—*ed.*

"'Futurist ethics'" reads "'futurist ethics'"—*ed.*

After "'postponement'" was "'The public may learn if it waits long enough.'"

"'have been kept waiting'" was "'are kept waiting'"

After "'always waited?'" was "'Has nothing to wait for— / She has always been waiting'"

"Mafarka" has been changed to "Brontoloni"; later in the script, Mafarka is the name to which Loy returns, and hence is used here—*ed.*

PAGE 76

After "'she blushed?'" the bottom of the page is torn off, and a line or two of dialogue may be missing—*ed.*

"'rather that not being'" reads "'rather (that) not being'"—*ed.*

"'Not for anything.'" was "'Not for anything on earth.'"

After "'spleen induced'" reads "(?)"—*ed.*

The letter, in the French original, reads as follows:

Homme unique,

Tu ira a la guerre, des maintenant je suis hors de ta vie—reduit aux elements primitives de l'offense et de l'attack. Et si la nuit [sans] sous les etoiles sur la terre dur tu te souviendras jamais de quelques heures divinement voluptueuses à Florence; ce serait pour te reprendre pour ta faiblesse. Avec la guerre la femme la femme n'a rien à faire—cependant il y aurait pu être quelque chose pour

moi à faire, j'aurais pu, maintenant que la moitie du population mâle sera exterminée j'aurais pu avoir un fils de
toi mais Mafarka me l'a interdit.

L'instruct à beau crier.

Je t'envoie mon amie dans un baiser parce'que tout
comprendre est toute pardonner.

Amant parfait, estce qu'on t'en leverai tes—non mes
"riccioli"?

Tuo——

Pazzarella—

PAGE 77

"this advantage: it effaces" reads "this advantage it effaces"—*ed.*

The French original reads:

"Amour j'ai medité pendant trois jours entiers—je t'adore
et je me sens trop vide de toi. Je m'en fiche du futurism.
L'enfant de nous deux est celui dont l'avenir à besoin tu ne
me donnerai pas raison mais moi j'ai raison. Si tu peut
eparguer une demi heure de ton inébriante vie interieur
a cette travaille importante, je viendrai à toi n'importe ou
tu te trouve— "

PAGE 78

"two of us—you won't" reads "two of us you won't"—*ed.*

The second portion is as follows:

– – – "si tu me preterai l'argent pour le voyage nous aûtres
sont tous sans le son pour le moment si tu est du même je
vais le mendier quelque part. Dis moi si ou non—si non

ca m'importe peu— je peut me passer aussi d'être la bien-faitrice de l'humanité.

Tu n'a pas besoin de discuter ceci avec tes compagnions debonnaires—c'est une chose je prends *trés aux serieux*."

" 'journey—we are' " reads " 'journey we are' "—*ed*.
The last letter, as rendered in French:

Geronimo,

Tu est le seul homme assez [fort] homme pour me dominer absolument le seul assez fort pour me tenir entierement pour soi-même—le seul Helas—qui est assez dur pour m'écraser—

Tuo Pazzarella

A l'amant absent—au fraicheur de ta salive.

Salut.

After "Salut." the remaining two thirds of the page is left blank; a long line is drawn crossways through it—*ed*.
Typescript resumes with "She had right on her side"
"no money. That" reads "no money, that"—*ed*.

PAGE 79
Below "inspiring" reads "find word for sucking in"—*ed*.
"silken gown" was "silk gown"

PAGE 80
"*podere*" reads "Podere"—*ed*.

PAGE 81

"spread about us" was "thread about us"

"shrill surprise, had not split up" reads "shrill surprise, split up"
   —*ed.*

PAGE 83

" 'irritate you; to the point' " was " 'irritate you to the point' "

" 'I could imagine' " was " 'I could image' "

PAGE 84

" 'only an intellect—' " reads " 'only an intellect— .' "—*ed.*

" 'your animator' " was " 'your animation' "

" 'enjoy me—in' " reads " 'enjoy me,—in' "—*ed.*

In margin, next to "newborn seraphim" reads "? plural ?"; above
   the same reads "a? or s"—the "m" of "seraphim" is underlined
   —*ed.*

PAGE 85

" 'when you are suffused' " reads " 'when you, suffused' "—*ed.*

PAGE 87

" 'super-refinements' " reads " 'superrefinements' "—*ed.*

" 'your tastes' " was " 'your faster' "

PAGE 88

" 'I observe' " reads " 'I observed' "—*ed.*

PAGE 90

"preciously bound" was "precisely bound"

339

"'Listen—' And the word" reads " 'Listen— ' and the word"
—*ed.*

"eternal non-impartation" was "eternal silence" and "incommunicativeness" as well as two other unclear words, possibly "intranslation" and "unimparting?"; in the margin reads "? frustration"
—*ed.*

"secret she imagined she had" was "secret she had"

"'it to you—'" reads "'it to you—.'"—*ed.*

PAGE 91

"'Woman—'" reads "'Woman— ?'"—*ed.*

"Of every instinct" was "Every instinct"

Above "petrified humanity" reads "humaneness?"—*ed.*

PAGE 92

"'don't know—'" reads "'don't know— .'"—*ed.*

"'Maybe that is your life?'" was "'May that is your life?'"

"I admired" was "and I admired"

"compromises of my lips" was "compromising of my lips"

PAGE 94

"*litterateurs*" reads "'litterateurs'"—*ed.*

"*Pazzarella de le Scala di Pietra*" reads "'Pazzarella De Le Scala Di Pietra'"—*ed.*

PAGE 95

"*laisser aller*" reads "'laisser aller'" and was "laisser aller"—*ed.*

PAGE 96

In the margin next to the paragraph beginning, "In the divine manner" Loy has pencilled: "Something missing here before the end"—*ed*.

"inspiration. At once" was "inspiration at [*possibly* "it"] once"

"begotten of it" was "begotten it"

"'everything,' partakes" was "'everything,' she partakes"

PAGE 97

"my heart—" reads "my heart— ."—*ed*.

"However that may be" was "However, that may be"

PIERO & ELIZA.

(6:173)

"Piero and Eliza." is a manuscript that consists of five typed and two handwritten pages, and concludes with Loy's signature. A title page reads "Piero and Eliza," and offers a compact, blunt plot summary ("florentine old maid & fairy"), as well as the name "Gino Sensani". The same sheet includes a reference to "The Stomach" (1921) which may be a companion piece to "Piero and Eliza"— both stories involve an artist, his beleaguered "muse," and an unusual focus on the abdomen.

Burke reads this short story as fact, and describes how Loy knew the openly gay Italian artist, Gino Carlo Sensani, between 1907 and 1910—the first years she spent in Florence. According to Burke, Florence was then a refuge for expatriate American and British artists and homosexuals; many of the latter were escaping the backlash after the well-publicised Oscar Wilde trials of 1895 (*BM* 108–09).

PAGE 98

"vermouth" may be "vermouths"—*ed.*

"a greenish white" was "the palest green"

"insolent interrogation" was "absolute interrogation"

"an arrogant crimson blot, and" was "a stain of arrogant [*unclear word*] crimson, and"

PAGE 99

After "*ambiente*" reads, in pencil, "(or setting)"—*ed.*

"inhibitions" was "complexes"

"palazzo" reads "Pallazzo" in all instances—*ed.*

"Gradually" was "Slowly"

PAGE 100

"While" was "And"

"one foot in society and one in Fairyland" was "one foot in [wonderland] society and one in wonderland"

"palazzo; together" was "palazzo, and together"

"antique forms, and together" was "antique forms: and together"

"Piero twisted" was "And Piero twisted"

"love in the mist" reads "love i'the mist"—*ed.*

After "tapestry," a handwritten page shows a variety of notes for the upcoming clause beginning "while a bachelor" including: "Sometimes a bachelor would steal upon the insinuate hush with an anecdote—"; the same page also contains notes reading: "The young attachées she had invited to dinner—" and "were [said D] gathered round a shaft— etc.—"

PAGE 101

"like soft cats" was "like a soft cat"

"For their eyes" was "Their eyes"

"while a bachelor . . . an anecdote" is a later addition

"mask; while a bachelor" was "mask. Sometimes a bachelor"—in the left margin was, heavily crossed out, "heard"

"The bachelor wafted" was "Dorsay wafted"

"anomaly" was "paradox"

"than hers" was "than to the anecdote" and also "than to the ladies'"

"spiritual obligations," was "spiritual obligation"

"Eliza's imagining" was "her imagining"

"comradely" was "pally"

"bachelors impressed" was "bachelors seemed"

"sweet and secret" was "sweets and secret"

"bachelors' significance" reads "bachelor's significance"—*ed*.

PAGE 102

"Eliza had" was "Eliza and"

"séances was" was "séances is"

"like orgasms" was "those unachieved orgasms"

"parching" was "urging" and "urging on"

Typescript ends with "stillness of the night"

Above "one such battle" reads "Morrison"—this word appears at the top of the page and may be a heading, marginalia, or an adjective describing the battle in question—*ed.*

PAGE 103

"The Immaculate Vermin Of The Sugar Dove" was "The immaculate vermin of the sugar dove"

On the back of the last sheet, Loy writes, "progressive— / introduction / of further relationships—"

THE STOMACH

(6:178)

"The Stomach" is a six-page typescript. "Florence" is pencilled next to the title, and "July 1921" is typed at the end. On the title page for "Piero and Eliza." (another story that focuses on artistry and, ultimately, the abdomen), Loy writes: "The Stomach— Sargents portrait of – – – –". Beneath this incomplete statement, a lighter and possibly different hand reads: "Isabella Stuart Gardner?" Isabella Stewart Gardner was an American art collector and philanthropist; John Singer Sargent painted her portrait in 1888.

Originally, the mother figure of "The Stomach" was a father; in her handwritten edits to the typescript, Loy changes the parental gender in each instance. Along with all of the pronouns, these changes include "aged gentleman" to "aged gentlewoman"; "paternal presence" to "maternal presence," and "protected paternity" to "protracted maternity".

For a discussion of "The Stomach" in relation to modernist mythologies of sexual conquest and the body, see Tim Armstrong, *Modernism, Technology, and the Body: A Cultural Study* (Cambridge: Cambridge UP, 1998, p. 117).

PAGE 104
"there was shawl" was "there was knitted wool—" and also "knitting"
"Delicate and decent" was "How delicate, how decent"

PAGE 105
"chosen Virginia" was "used Virginia"
"Cosway as model for" was "Cosway for"
"*La Tarantella*" reads "'La Tarantella'" in all instances—*ed.*
"elevation of the statue" was "great height of the figure"
"inspired by the Master" was "inspired by the master"
"*danza Español*" reads "'danza espanola'"—*ed.*
"they abode" was "they preferred to abide"

PAGE 106
"issued by the Master" was "issued by the master"
"*grand monde*" reads "grand monde"—*ed.*
Beside "*monde*" in the left margin, in faint type, reads "each"—*ed.*
"*les vernissages*" reads "'les vernissages'"—*ed.*
"Hôtel Drouot" reads "Hotel Druot"—*ed.*

"talk with Virginia Cosway" was "talk with Virginia the"
"undulation of the hip" was likely "undulation of the hips"
"forefinger, the" reads "forefinger; the" and was "forefinger the"
   —*ed*.

PAGE 107
"age and hereditary" reads "age hereditary"—an "and" is written
   in the left margin—*ed*.
"herself—" was "herself"
"eye on the stomach" was "eye on the obtrusive stomach"
"only one of all the visitors" was "only one of the visitors" and was
   corrected by Loy to read "alone of all the visitors"—*ed*.

PAGE 108
"prowled beyond" was "prowled around"
"together with her eye" was "together with her blind eye"
"*outre-tombe*" reads " 'outre tombe' "
After "eye" is written, by hand and crossed out, "through"

THE THREE WISHES

(6:179)

"The Three Wishes" is a complete, handwritten manuscript of fifty-
one pages; aside from some minor edits, the text is very clean. The
original title, heavily crossed out, appears to have been "Three of
Them."; alongside it reads "By *Mina Loy*." The pages are numbered
throughout. Pages 48 and 49 are missing from the file in Loy's pa-

pers labelled "The Three Wishes," but exist, intact, in another folder entitled "Unidentified Fragments" (6:183). As in "Hush Money" (c. 1917–22) and "In Maine: Green's Colony," Loy here regularly uses the mark "+" to denote breaks in narrative flow.

Eugene Debs (1855–1926) receives brief mention in this story; a founder of the International Workers of the World, Debs remains one of the most famous socialists in American history. Debs ran for presidency of the USA five times; on the last occasion, he conducted his campaign from prison, where he was serving a sentence for speaking out against American involvement in World War I.

PAGE 109
"back streets—" reads "back streets—."—*ed.*
"white frills" was "white borders"
"turned it, and patting" was "turned it round again"
"clenched to it" was "clenched to his ribs"

PAGE 110
"bulgy" was "bulging"
"battered kitchen utensils" was "battered utensils"
"would always spit" was "would spit"

PAGE 111
"worn like a Pierrot's frill by" was "worn by"
"teat, provided" was "teat, like provided"
"falling asleep, hypnotised" reads "falling asleep; hypnotised"—*ed.*

PAGE 112

"knee, pale" reads "knee; pale"—*ed.*

"unconvincing silk" was "unsatisfying silk"

"the placid social relation" was "the social relation"

PAGE 113

"Of good form—" reads "Of good form,—"—*ed.*

"irreproachable minority—" reads "irreproachable minority: – "—*ed.*

"there was something clownlike" reads "there was + something clownlike"—*ed.*

PAGE 114

"kinds of information" was "kinds of aid"

PAGE 115

" 'it hath pleased' " was " 'it has pleased' "

"Mr. and Mrs." reads "Mr and Mrs" in all instances—*ed.*

"limn souls that were" reads "limn souls " that were"—*ed.*

"suggested itself"—"itself" is either crossed out or underlined—*ed.*

PAGE 117

" 'got our pride' " reads " 'got out pride' "—*ed.*

" 'Our own 'Ide' " was " 'Our own little 'Ide' "

" 'might a bin' " was " 'might be' "

PAGE 118

The sentence beginning "The mission house" reads: "The mission house and The Society for The Prevention of Cruelty to Children, all this society's wards are children who fail to reform their parents, took up this case."—*ed.*

"'Criminals you say, dear me!'" reads "'Criminals' you say, dear me!'"—*ed.*

After "enquired Hyde willingly" reads "?"—*ed.*

PAGE 119

"own conception, exactly" was "own, exactly"

PAGE 120

"'a criminolo – – –'" was "'a criminologist'"

"'He will understand this case'" was "'he will understand your case'"

The "+" between "'case'" and "Mrs. Bates" is not in the original text, although Loy leaves a space between these paragraphs—*ed.*

"'would get'" was "'would getting'"

PAGE 121

"'I should discourage it'"—"'I should'" is crossed out in text—*ed.*

After "'Oh certainly'" was "said the doctor"

"'make his attempt'" reads "'[*torn page*]ake his attempt'"—*ed.*

PAGE 122

After "reprovingly" reads "(sententiously?)"—*ed.*

"'Which has made'" was "'Which makes'"

"'Criminals.' She harped" reads "'Criminals' She" and was "'Criminals' she"—*ed.*

PAGE 123
"'And *don't*'" was "'and *don't*'"

PAGE 124
"pressed upon him" was "pressed against him"

PAGE 125
"he saw them" may read "He saw them"—*ed.*
"convulsion" reads conv[*torn page*]sion"—*ed.*
"of all the actualities" was "of the actualities"
"magic that might spread" was "magic to spread"

PAGE 126
"realising" was "knowing it"

PAGE 128
"far distant pub" reads "far distant Pub"—*ed.*
"'quicker than the lot'" reads "'quicker that the lot'"—*ed.*

PAGE 129
"town, and tonight" reads "town, tonight"—*ed.*

PAGE 130
"Jacky had hauled" was "Jacky was hauling"

PAGE 131
"he looked" was "he was"

PAGE 132

"And he seemed . . . had been told" is a later addition

"said Jacky, looking round the room, 'you'" was "said Jacky, 'you'"

PAGE 134

"and given him" was "and she had given him"

"'with it—"rich"'" reads "'with it,—"rich"'"—*ed*.

After "+" the last three quarters of the remaining page is torn
    away—*ed*.

A scrap between pages, largely crossed out, reads:

> Leah Sloan—is a thief
> artists model
> the artist approves—
> of her stealing—

"The ego" was "But the ego"

PAGE 135

"coins that so much" was "coins so much"

After "shop-keeper" a long horizontal line is drawn across the
    page—*ed*.

"'simulacrum of our understanding'" was "'simulacrum of under-
    standing'"

"'out of his eye'" was "'out of the artist's eye'"

"of their home" reads "of the[*torn page*] home"—*ed*.

"Their household . . . their names" is a later addition

Before "Counterpoised and empty" was "They harmonised in
    perfectly"

PAGE 136

"years" reads "yea[*faded page*]"—*ed.*

"had" reads "ha[*scratched out letter*]—*ed.*

"reference" reads "refer-[*torn page*]"—*ed.*

"rather to have" was "rather have"

Above "antedating" reads "ceding?"—*ed.*

"Praxiteles had been raising" is "Praxiteles ha[*torn page*] raising"
—*ed.*

PAGE 137

"courtyard where Ian had found them" was "courtyard"

"busy students became" was "busy students were" and "busy students now"

"disinterestedness" was "disinterest"

"most probable" was "just possible"

"They behaved" was "So they behaved"

"the parties" was "the flamboyant parties"

The "+" between "about" and "And" is not in the original, although
Loy leaves a space between these paragraphs—*ed.*

"And when the Professor" was "When the Professor"

"isolated monomaniac" was "monomaniac in his isolation"

"wag, appraising" was "wag their" or "wag them"

"bourgeois" reads "bourg"—*ed.*

PAGE 138

"that he was coming" was "him coming"

"lifted off the long leg" was "lifted the leg"

"over the wooden stool" was "off the wooden stool"

"attention" reads "attenti[*torn page*]"—*ed.*

" 'I suppose you know' " was " 'you know' "
After " 'a woman' " Loy leaves a blank line in the manuscript
—*ed.*

PAGE 139
"It occurred to him . . . woman unclothed" is a later addition
"except the vast" reads "except th[*torn page*] vast"—*ed.*
"chest with" was "chest of drawers with"
"three yards" reads "three yds"—*ed.*
"volatile mountain" was "floating volatile mountain"
"lay diffused in" was "lay buried under"

TRANSFIGURATION.

(6:180)

"Transfiguration." consists of an incomplete typescript that has
been edited in Loy's hand; many paragraphs throughout end
with a pencilled "x"—perhaps denoting that they have been
checked and approved. It is likely that the story draws on Loy's
1917 journey from New York to Mexico to meet Arthur Cravan,
whom she married shortly thereafter (*BM* 251, 255).

A boxer and a fond purveyor of outrageous impromptu performances, Cravan wrote for and published the little magazine *Maintenant* in Paris (1913–15), and came to New York
in 1917, where he met Loy. Cravan has been hailed as one of
the earliest proponents of Dada; a sample of his writing and a

discussion of his relationship to the movement can be located in *The Dada Painters and Poets: An Anthology* (Robert Motherwell, ed. 2nd ed. Cambridge, MA: Belknap Press of Harvard UP, 1981).

Dan Leno, who is briefly referenced in "Transfiguration." was a music-hall comedian and performer who lived and worked in England in the latter half of the nineteenth century.

PAGE 140

"Outside" was "Out of"

The sentence beginning "The scout-train" was "The scout-train preceded us for a space of danger with its barefoot soldiers standing watchful on the roof; shunted off somewhere into the steaming sunset."

"inch of earth that bound" reads "inch of earth: that bound"—*ed*.

"Now that it was no longer protected, our train" was "No longer protected, and our train"

"a compartment" was "one compartment" and "our compartment"

PAGE 141

"while contours" was "their contours"; "while" is unclear, and could be "which" or "white"—*ed*.

"reminded me how" was "and I remembered how"

" '– – – – it hasn't got' " reads " '– – – –'t hasn't got' "—*ed*.

After " 'face' " reads an incomplete amendment that begins "And then as I said staring at"—*ed*.

"my companion" reads "my [*torn page*] p [*torn page*]"—*ed*.

Above "We pressed" reads "breasted"—*ed.*
"with breasts" was "with disparted breasts"
"dark where the parted" was "dark. [*new paragraph*] The parted"
"over the steel ribbons" was "over steel ribbons"
After "of the railroad" was "on either side"

PAGE 142
"sun –" reads "sun, –"—*ed.*
"clucking" was "with clucking"
"appraisals of the passengers on the train" was "appraisals on the
    train"

PAGE 143
"good thing at once" was "good thing at a time"
"even the spawn" was "even the sprand"
"entertaining, and the Mexican" was "entertaining, the Mexican"
"warmed to it" was "warmed to it [*three or four unclear words*]
    myself"

PAGE 144
"bar-room" reads "Bar-room"—*ed.*
"punctuated by the sting" reads "punctuated, or by the sting"
    —*ed.*
"as soon as bought" was "as soon as they bought"

PAGE 145
"pitch black resting place" was "pitch dark resting place"
"of his bunch" was "of bunch"

355

"into the deluge" was "into the [*unclear word*]"—could be "high go"—*ed.*

"For I felt" was "And I felt"

PAGE 146

"like a symbol" was "as a symbol"

"my unprofitable companionship"—"companionship" is pencilled in by hand

"salesman's" reads "sales-[*unclear letters*]'s"—*ed.*

"Reanimated . . . copper gleam" was "Reanimated by the man's cajoling evocations for his convenience of her consumed adolescence, from under the copper gleam"—above "the copper" Loy has pencilled a second "under"—*ed.*

PAGE 147

"against her huckster" was "against huckster"

"she had found her home" was "she had her home"

"coated her consciousness" reads "coat [*torn page*] consciousness" —*ed.*

"ethical impropriety" was "ethical a"

After "a transcendental sanction" there is a blank line, and then the manuscript continues:

> The inhabitants of the Isthmus of Tehuantepec filled the third class carriages stacking the wooden seats with embroidered human clusters.
>
> The women gave me coffee in a cocoanut bowl exclaimi

DRAMA

(6:155)

Loy's ballet consists of a single typescript of sixteen double-spaced pages with very few handwritten editorial changes throughout; these are noted below.

PAGE 151
"teeter" was "tot-titters"

PAGE 152
"while mixed groups play shuttlecock and battledore" is a later, handwritten addition
After "a balance" reads, in type and in the midst of an otherwise blank half page, "(Follow with page 3)"—*ed.*

PAGE 153
"*The Spirit of the Rose*" reads "the spirit of the rose"—*ed.*
"from the back if possible in order" was "from the back in order"

PAGE 154
"poker-swan-like effect" reads "poker-swan like effect"—*ed.*

PAGE 155
"all-over tights" reads "all over tights"—*ed.*

PAGE 156
"youth remains" was "youth, remaining"

PAGE 157
"The barometer house . . . spirit of the rainbow" is in brackets in typescript—*ed.*
"arms the (enormous)" reads "arms the (an enormous)"—*ed.*

PAGE 158
Above "transparent sequins" reads, in handwriting, "or plastic drops (better)"—*ed.*
"long green glass hair" was "long yellow glass hair"
After "his legs" reads, in handwriting, "It might be better to keep the rainbow stain on the youth's body / he can still dance himself *dry*"—*ed.*

PAGE 159
"the dance of the jelly-fish" reads "'the dance of the jelly fish'"—*ed.*
"domes and long" was "domes along"

PAGE 160
"yellow gilt shield, sword, helmet" reads "yellow gilt shield (espinal yel) sword, helmet"—*ed.*

PAGE 161

Crossed out at the end of the typescript, also in type, is the following:

****

On a wire a stiff figure, like the ones in "Cartesian" bottles, only carrying a bunch of colored air balloons—symbolizing desire—whirls round and round in the crystal ball with a small child after him—only for a brief moment— Then the first scene evolves.

THE PAMPERERS

"The Pamperers" was first published in *The Dial* in 1920 (69:1), and was the inaugural work of the "Modern Forms" section of that periodical. Only a fragment of the published text exists in Loy's papers. The play was published a second time in the *Performing Arts Journal* in 1996, where it was edited and introduced by Julie Schmid. With some minor adjustments to punctuation and layout, it is *The Dial* version that is used here.

While most critics concur that "The Pamperers" was written in 1916, Schmid suggests that Loy may have started writing it in 1915 ("Mina Loy's Futurist Theatre," *Performing Arts Journal* (18:1) 1996, 1–7, p. 5). Susan Gilmore contends that as late as 1917, Loy described "The Pamperers" as a work in progress in an interview she gave to *The New York Evening Sun* ("Imna, Ova, Mongrel, Spy," *ML: W & P*, 271–318, p. 281). According to Burke,

Loy gave some thought to staging "The Pamperers" in 1916, shortly after starring in Alfred Kreymborg's *Lima Beans* opposite William Carlos Williams (*BM* 214, 222). For additional critics who date the play as a product of 1916, see Virginia Kouidis, *Mina Loy: American Modernist Poet* (Baton Rouge: Louisiana State UP, 1980, p. 16) and Janet Lyon, "Mina Loy's Pregnant Pauses: The Space of Possibility in the Florence Writings" (*ML: W & P*, 379–402, p. 397).

In "Little Lusts and Lucidities: Reading Mina Loy's *Love Songs*," Jeffrey Twitchell-Waas argues that in "The Pamperers," Loy satirises not Futurism *per se* but rather, the Futurists' betrayal of their own radical ideals (*ML: W & P*, 111–130, p. 113). With that satirical impulse wholly in view, there are a number of references— veiled and overt—to cultural figures in "The Pamperers". Loy's friend and the founder of Italian Futurism, F. T. Marinetti (1876– 1944) merits direct mention, as does the Florentine Renaissance painter, Benozzo Gozzoli (1421–1497). The French composer Claude-Achille Debussy (1862–1918) appears in an introductory list; "Watsiswinski" or "Stavinski" likely refers to the Russian-born composer Igor Fyodorovich Stravinsky (1882–1971). "Isadora Allen" is a nod to the founder of modern dance, Isadora Duncan (1877–1927), who Loy befriended during her early years in Florence, 1907–10 (*BM* 110–11). Loy wrote a long poem about Duncan in 1952; a segment from that work appears in *The Last Lunar Baedeker* under the title "Songge Byrd" (238).

(6:175)

Loy attributes "Rosa" to one "Bjuna Darnes"—a none-too-subtle spoonerism of the name of the American writer Djuna Barnes (1892–1982). Loy and Barnes met in New York around 1920–21 and maintained their friendship in various locations around the globe, including Berlin and Paris, until Loy's death in 1966 (*BM* 295, 313, 362). Loy infamously features in Barnes's *Ladies Almanack* (1928) as Patience Scalpel, who has a voice "as cutting in its Derision as a surgical Instrument" (Champaign, IL: Dalkey Archive Press, 1995, p. 12). While it is tempting to read the weapon-wielding Rosa as Loy's instigation of or riposte to Barnes's parody, her papers yield little in the way of evidence, as only one undated typescript of this play exists. "Rosa" concludes with Loy's characteristic self-attribution, "MINA LOY".

PAGE 183
"*magenta kid*" reads "*magenter kid*"—*ed.*
"*Recamier sofa*" reads "*recamier sofa*"—*ed.*

PAGE 184
"stock" reads "stoch"—*ed.*
"So you believe" reads "SO you believe"—*ed.*

PAGE 185
"fifty of the best years" was "fifty years"

PAGE 186

"my sons. It is" reads "my sons it is"—*ed.*

"I am mad. Tell me" reads "I am mad tell me"—*ed.*

THE SACRED PROSTITUTE

(6:176)

In a letter to Carl Van Vechten dated December 27th 1914, Loy writes: "I am going to send you—a part of the Love-Sex Review—'The Sacred Prostitute'" (Beinecke, Van Vechten archive, Loy correspondence folder). This play was written when Loy was living in Florence, and had befriended F. T. Marinetti and Giovanni Papini, key proponents of the Italian Futurist movement—hence the starring role allotted to the character "Futurism" throughout.

The file for "The Sacred Prostitute" contains both a typescript and a handwritten draft. Differences between the two versions are predominantly related to punctuation; more substantial distinctions are noted below whenever they contribute to the overall understanding of the gestation of the play. All other annotations refer to Loy's handwritten editing of the typescript. The first extant page of the written draft is marked "4" on the upper right-hand corner, and it is from this page that the typescript begins. A note midway through the typed manuscript indicates that seven pages of the original text are missing. While the handwritten version shows a corresponding gap in pagination, in the typescript, the pagination continues unabated. As there is no discernible break in sense, this note may be a narrative device to indicate that "Man and Woman," the play within the play that might fill that gap, will not be included.

"Sacred Prostitute" is typed at the top right-hand corner of each page of the manuscript, but no title page can be located in Loy's papers; as such, critics have tended to use Loy's letter to Van Vechten as the definitive phrasing for the title. For dating and discussion of "The Sacred Prostitute," see Virginia Kouidis, *Mina Loy: American Modernist Poet* (Baton Rouge: Louisiana State UP, 1980, p. 16); Janet Lyon, "Mina Loy's Pregnant Pauses" (*ML: W & P*, 379–402, p. 395); Julie Schmid, "Mina Loy's Futurist Theatre" (*Performing Arts Journal* (18:1), 1–7, p. 3), and Burke (*BM* 186).

PAGE 188

Unlike the typescript, the handwritten draft begins *in medias res* with an unattributed line prior to those spoken by Some Other Man, reading: "passion?—it's merely neurosis."

In the handwritten draft, the sentence beginning "It's just the same..." reads: "It's just the same with the higher qualities we hear so much about—in the comrade, the intellectual companion."

"dissuade me" was "dissuade me from"

PAGE 189

In the handwritten draft, the page beneath "Woman!?!..." is badly torn; the discernible writing that follows has been elided from the typescript, and includes the following phrases: "She harried the delicacy of my sentiments—with coarseness— /

disinterestedness with cubi / signs [*possibly* "sighs"] of Eros— / store—a."

"Woman must exist . . . to somebody else?" is in handwritten, but not typed, draft—"somebody" was "someone"—*ed.*

"on *you*?" was "on *You*?"

PAGE 190

In handwritten draft, "more than twenty minutes" was "more than half an hour" in the first instance

"man is any cruelty she may deserve" was "man is the cruelty that she deserves"

PAGE 191

"(the things we hanker after not being on the market)" reads, in the first instance in the handwritten draft, "(we all know the things we most hanker after are not on the market)"

PAGE 194

"I could have shown you" is "I could have shewn you" in hand-written draft

PAGE 196

In handwritten draft, "autograph album" was "autograph-book" in the first instance

After "the proto-poem" the handwritten draft reads: "(*De-claiming with **super** magical intonation*)"; here the proto-poem includes an extra line of "ta ta ta" (13 in total) between "frrrrrr / urrrrrrrrrrrrraaaaaaaaaaaa" and the line beginning "pluff plaff plaff"

PAGE 197

Above the last "h" of "(*they sigh*)" reads "N," and the "h" is crossed out—*ed.*

"bare acquaintance" reads "bare-acquaintance"—*ed.*

In the handwritten draft, from "Futurism *here declaims*" to "'finish her off'" is an addition on a separate, single sheet of paper. On that page, after "(*most drastic*)" Loy writes: "P.S. Haven't got it here to translate / later on will do." What follows this note are the lines, "When love has had enough . . . I must just [go and] 'finish her off'"—this section appears to be an incomplete prose summary inconsistent with the style of the drama throughout. It is included in this volume as a stage direction, but in the typescript, it reads as if Futurism were speaking the whole aloud—*ed.*

PAGE 198

"*dragging* Love *across the floor*" reads, in handwritten version "*dragging [in] Love by the hair*"—"*across the floor*" is a later addition

In the handwritten version, before "*I* just take them" Futurism states: "*I* don't waste time over women—"

PAGE 199

"leaving you inconsummate—" was "leaving you—unaccomplished—" in first instance in handwritten draft

PAGE 201

"replenished—vital—like" reads "replenished-vital-like"—the dashes used here are consistent with the handwritten draft—*ed.*

In handwritten draft, "spent so long on a woman" was "spent so much time on a woman" in the first instance

Between "fifteen minutes" and "Hurry up! And love me!" the handwritten draft includes the following addition: "The Futurist has to spend his life on trains—they alone have the requisite velocity for our indomitable energy—"

PAGE 202

"why I love you so" was "why I loved you so" in first instance in handwritten manuscript

"entirely fictitious" was "entirely factitious"

"I find it makes it" was "it might make it" in first instance in handwritten draft

"All my mistresses" reads "All my ex- [ex] mistresses" in handwritten draft

PAGE 204

After "*watch the performance*" the next page in the typed manuscript is unnumbered, and reads: "7 pages of manuscript missing"; at this same point in the handwritten manuscript, the pagination goes from 22 to 30—*ed.*

PAGE 205

"insult the sex" was "insult to sex" in typed draft; handwritten manuscript reads "the sex"

"this *is* new—" reads "this *is* new—."—*ed.*

PAGE 206

"while the fire burns" was "while the sun shines" in the handwritten draft in the first instance

PAGE 207

In handwritten text, "out of *her*!—Let's" reads "out of *her*! – – – –
– – – let's"

PAGE 208

"must pretend, anyway" may be "pretend anyway" (note: the
handwritten draft reads: "you must—pretend—anyway")—*ed.*

"*every point made*" was "*every psychological point in*" in handwritten draft in first instance

PAGE 209

"leading you on—to—nowhere" reads as such in handwritten version; typed draft reads "leading you on-to-nowhere"—*ed.*

In handwritten draft, "true woman is immodest enough to kiss"
was, in the first instance, "true woman would kiss"

PAGE 210

"Why can't you believe in me?" is drawn from the handwritten
version—*ed.*

PAGE 211

In first instance in handwritten draft, "there – – – – – – – – – – –
– – – – (*Silence*) – – – – –" was "there – – – – – – – there – – – –
Silence"

In handwritten draft, the dashes between "You can," "you can," "you
do," and "you" are extended ellipses

" 'thou thy servant' " reads " 'thou they servant' "—*ed.*

"What am I doing— What am I saying?" was "What am I doing—What am I doing" in first instance in handwritten draft

PAGE 212

"something— You" is taken from handwritten draft; typescript
reads "something – – you"—*ed.*

"perfectly straightforward" was "perfectly honest" in the first instance in handwritten draft

"believe in me—" reads "believe in me—."—*ed.*

PAGE 213

"Nothing but you—" reads "Nothing but you—."—*ed.*

PAGE 214

In handwritten draft, "It's infallible—infallible— Did you hear
that?" reads, "it's—infallible – – infallible (*running to the sofa*)
Don Juan—did you hear that"

"amusing creatures" was "delightful creatures"

ESSAYS AND COMMENTARY

ALL THE LAUGHS IN ONE SHORT STORY BY McALMON

(6:151)

Loy and the American writer Robert McAlmon were friends, and
in 1923, McAlmon's publishing house, Contact Editions, printed

Loy's first book, *Lunar Baedecker* [*sic*]. Burke argues that Loy is the model for Gusta Rolph, a character in McAlmon's 1923 account of writers in Greenwich Village entitled *Post-Adolescence* (*BM* 293–96). Loy also appears in *Being Geniuses Together* (1938), McAlmon's portrayal of the expatriate artists' community that lived in Paris in the twenties.

McAlmon wrote many short stories that could be the unnamed focus of "All the laughs," but in terms of its content, Loy's piece bears a distinct resemblance to "The Laughing Funeral" of *Post-Adolescence*. "All the laughs" has a title page in Loy's hand. Although it appears to start *in medias res*, this speculation is complicated by Loy's use of a comma at the outset of the occasional line throughout. The handwritten text is formatted like a prose poem; in spite of the vagaries of Loy's margins, every attempt has been made to preserve the integrity of her lineation.

PAGE 219
"sphinxly" reads "sphynxly"—*ed.*
"– – voice" was "and – – voice"

PAGE 220
"she explained" reads "[*torn page*] she explained"
"taunted like that" was "taunted as"
"metallic cackle" reads "metallic cuckle" and could be "chuckle"
    —*ed.*

(7:188)

Loy and the Romanian sculptor Constantin Brancusi were associates in Paris in the twenties and thirties (*BM* 328, 386). In its unabashed admiration for the artist's aesthetic approach, "Brancusi and the Ocean" recalls Loy's poem "Brancusi's Golden Bird," which was first published in *The Dial* in 1922 (*Lost LB* 79–80).

The rough, handwritten document of "Brancusi and the Ocean" includes a draft of a poem entitled "La descent des Ganges". A more complete version of this poem is published in *The Last Lunar Baedeker* as "Descent of the Ganges," and Roger Conover dates it as most likely written in the late 1930s or early 1940s (*Last LB* 252, 327).

PAGE 221

Before "The interpretation of Brancusi" was "To arrive at an intellectual—of Brancusi's sculpture" and also "To interpret Brancusi / Ai"

"beyond the formidable naked" reads "beyond the / the formidable naked"—*ed.*

"intriguing comparison"—"intriguing" is unclear—*ed.*

"comparison of elemental form" was "comparison of the elemental form"

"evolved by" was "that has evolved through"

"an elemental form whose evolution" was "an elemental form that evolves"

"is submitted" was "through the"
"such sublime" was "such colossal"

PAGE 222
"white heat" was "white head"
"the memory" was "Is like the memory"
"irrefutably" was "implac" and "undeniab"
"primary investigators"—"investigators" is unclear—*ed.*
After "of beauty" reads, largely crossed out:
> La descent des Ganges

> In the divine cascade
> of whispering stone
> the goddess hostesses—
> immutable invitation
> to the frail ribbed ascetics—
> and holy elephants

"its own impetus" was "its impetus"
"got none" was "got nothing"
"his other contemporary" was "his contemporary"

MY CATHOLICK CONFIDANTE

(6:183)

Like "Havelock Ellis," this short sketch offers an example of Loy's
fascination with the cultural constraints placed on human sexual-

ity. A title page in Loy's hand identifies the piece as "Katherine's Confidences," but the heading on the manuscript proper reads "My catholick confidante".

Loy returns to this sketch in a more direct fashion in a set of rough notes that accompany her essay "History of Religion and Eros" (6:158). These notes describe the couple in question as Irish, and very much in love, until the husband begins beating his wife after taking to drink as a "consequence" of the Catholic directive that they abstain from non-procreative sex. Here Loy states that the wife spends the family savings on an abortion at one juncture, and that she eventually leaves her husband.

Loy sets this second version in New York in 1939; it concludes with the following meditation on prostitution, sex, and Christianity:

> In an ideal Society prostitutes would be [appreciated] as the kind ladies – – – – "Sex" would be consecrated by the church— The law [would be on] alert for any resurgence of sadism – – –
>
> In an ideal society prostitution might disappear— But the [m] [point] supposition sometimes occurs to me that society pretty much in status quo would be [of] very differently tempered—if our intelligence toward its component: the human forces—were changed by a christianly clarification—[all the] the primary transformation needed is of our attitude of mind.

PAGE 223

"for most human beings" was "for human beings"

"in regret for having" was "who should having"

The sentence beginning "Confiding to me her own anguish" caused Loy difficulty; she dedicates a whole page to its drafting, which reads as follows:

This woman's

[The anguish this woman revealed to me—]

[The confidences of this woman]

Her remark had been made to [in confirmation of the anguish] of her own anguish— —

[She had been]

Confiding to me her own anguish her [remark had been made] reference to her neighbours was made to prove she was not the only one - - -

Confiding to me her own anguish she had [made] her reference to her neighbours [was offered as proof]

Confiding to me her own anguish, she had offered this picture of her neighbours as proof that "not she alone - - -

And listening—was like looking through a microscope revealing [the] a [the] secret world - - -

After "secret world" Loy leaves the remaining two thirds of her page blank—*ed.*

Before "She stood out" was "Among the"

373

"her home, husband, children" was "her children"

PAGE 224

"in her plan" reads "in her planned"—*ed*.

"in her plan one addition to her family" was "one addition to her family"

"broken entirely down" was "broken down"

"the civilised" was "their civilised"

"condition—to . . . they clung" was "condition—"

"The husband compliant; under stress of his inhibited electric" was "husband, as a result of the unnatural dam on his electric"—a note at the bottom of the page suggests that Loy also considered writing: "The husband compliant, [being like his wife] holding as she,"—*ed*.

"confidante, finding her ultimatum of chastity so unprofitable, with" was "my confidante with"

After " "*it's*' wrong" " reads "It, the"—*ed*.

CENSOR MORALS SEX.

(6:166)

Loy's "Censor Morals Sex." makes brief and oblique reference to John S. Sumner and Owen Reed Smoot. Sumner led the New York Society for the Prevention of Vice, which charged the editors of *The Little Review* with obscenity for publishing extracts from Joyce's *Ulysses* in 1920; Utah Senator Owen Smoot was a well-known campaigner for censorship in this same period. Loy attended *The Little Review* trial (*BM* 287–89), and it is believed that in 1923 her own book, *Lunar Baedecker* [*sic*], was confiscated at the US border due to its explicit content (see *Lost LB* 224, and Sandeep Parmar, "Not an Apology: Mina Loy's Geniuses." *The Wolf* (17) 2008).

"Censor Morals Sex." is a single handwritten page embedded within the manuscript of "Mi & Lo". Although many of the sentences remain incomplete, the piece is free of Loy's usual corrections and revisions, and is written in a neat hand. Only four editorial notes apply: firstly, "social morality" reads "social moral"; secondly, a colon has been added after "re," thirdly, "their neighbours," reads "his neighbour's," and lastly, "interchangeable—why not" reads "interchangeable why not".

CONVERSION

(6:153)

"Conversion" consists of a typescript with numbered pages; after the title reads, in type, "by MINA LOY," and Loy's name appears again in capitals at the end. The essay is prefaced with a sheet that reads, in Loy's hand: "Critique / of D H Lawrence / Psycho-Analysis / & the inconscious [*sic*]". The script contains three discernible handwritten changes: the "Psychoanalyst" of the first sentence was "Psychoanalyst: ?" and "neurotics and it" was "neurotics it"; lastly, "So here we have" was "And here we have". French words and the title *Women in Love* are in single quotations in the original. Loy's numerous spellings of "psychoanalysis" and its variants are pre-served, as are the oddities in her punctuation.

Lawrence's *Women in Love* was published in 1920, and the film star Mary Pickford was at the height of her fame between 1910 and 1930. In a good article on "Conversion," Suzanne Hobson contends that it was "probably written between the mid-1920s and 1930s" ("Mina Loy's 'Conversion' and the Profane Religion of her Poetry." *Salt Companion.* 248–65, p. 249).

GATE CRASHERS OF OLYMPUS—

(7:188)

There exist half a dozen drafts of "Gate Crashers of Olympus—". The first is a poem entitled "Review" and dated 1925. The poem begins as follows:

In the beginning Picasso
broke a wine glass—
disrupted a guitar
As his things were very nice
They have now gone up in price—
    Thus has the soul of man become a triangle

The next two drafts are rough and incomplete; one is entitled "The Misunderstanding of Picasso". Included here is a conflation of the fourth and fifth versions. The sixth is written in a truncated telegram style (replete with the word "stop" between phrases), and appears to be an outline for the whole; this version follows the editorial notes below.

PAGE 230

Before "The somersault of society" was "Society turned somersault" (note: in alternate version, "The somersault of society" is "The somersault of morality")

"P.O. Casse (*cf.* French breakage)" reads "P.O. Cassse—cf. (French Breakage)"—*ed.*

"revaluation" was likely "revolutionised"—*ed.*

"revaluation of values" reads "revaluation values"—*ed.*

"is the actual cause" was "is responsible"

"is martialised" was "is to"

"to the extent" was "to that extent"

"I have" was "However I have"

"was broken" was "was not broken"

"same day" was "same aftern"

"the dealers" was "the art dealers"

"successively broken a" was "successively broken more"

"and with more" was "and in"

After "with" reads, in the margin: "X Although [they] in every article to which he applied his disruptive ingenuity"—*ed.*

PAGE 231

Before "disjuncted" reads "disjected?"—*ed.*

Each "every" in the sentence beginning "This disjuncted" was an "all"—so: "all 'avant guards,' in all years, in all land" "yet bearing" was "but bearing" and "still bearing"

The sentence beginning "No head or tail" follows the first sentence of the text in one draft, but consistent with the telegram-style outline below, is included here at the end—*ed.*

"to flower—" was "to persist"

The sixth version reads as follows:

Somersault of society dates from day small spaniard PO Casse, cf. french breakage.) inevitably exhibited portrait wine glass looking both ways at once. stop.

Other [New] objects to which Casse applied [his] disruptive aesthetic—had extra crack knocked into [it] by rabid opposers. i.e. disciples. stop. War not responsible [revolutionised] moral revaluation, modern art martialised extent "he who steals stunt originator, does for redemption said art." stop. Heard original wine-glass broken. Braque or another [one] same day—stop—[prefer] predict P.O. Casse canonised by dealers—[for has] succeeded breaking greater variety objects quicker succession than most ardent opponents. i.e. disciples possible keep up with. stop.

[Perhaps 25 years] [Quarter century] P.O. Casse broke first guitar, prophetic pattern purveyed one [of] aesthetic intimation[s] compare what other areas french call frisson[s]. stop. Found disbanded guitar all years all countries re-re-re-represent latest [aesthetic] intellectual revolt all avant guards during quarter century—stop

—Trace misuse communal guitar instigation new promiscuity stop general interchangeability rectangles circles calculus inversion. stop

Blast human limbs preposterous directions created public carelessness as where other portions an along thrown to—stop. May account women now doing duty what hither to [*unclear words*—possibly "refill" and "as"] accident and men hurl challenge what formerly submitted [to as] urge stop

No head tail reason this except emancipation contagious caught by noncreative finds only un-confines sex [to] [in] [in] where flourish.

GERTRUDE STEIN

(6:156)

Loy and Stein became friends in Florence in the period 1910–1913 (*BM* 129–31). Loy is described in Stein's *The Autobiography of Alice B. Toklas* as the giver of "a delightful lunch" and as an individual who fully understood Stein's literary innovations (Harmondsworth: Penguin Books, 1981, pp. 144–45). In 1924, Loy published two articles about Gertrude Stein's writing in *The Transatlantic Review* ((2:3) 305–9; (2:4) 427–30). The first of these pieces includes Loy's poem "Gertrude Stein," wherein Stein is described as "Curie / of the laboratory / of vocabulary" (*Lost LB* 94). In 1927 Loy was invited to introduce Stein's work to a Paris salon run by the American writer Natalie Barney (*BM* 360–61). This short essay is Loy's introduction, which consists of a typewritten script in French; on the back of page three, in Loy's hand, reads: "Lecture on Gertrude Stein". The original text is included below, and was translated for this volume by Martin Crowley.

Due to slight tearing of the pages, uncertainty exists about the phrases and words "once it had been," "of her time," and "indicated". Additionally, after the paragraph ending "chemical precipitate" was another that has been excised because too incomplete. What remains reads as follows: ". . . presents Gertrude Stein, as I have indicated, as the Madame Curie of language. For her deep . . . carry thousands of tons of material for . . . word."

Original Text

Il y a vingt ans qu'on me tennait ce propos, "que le temps . . . bien mort où pourrait surgir un génie pour être méconnu."

On disait que nous sommes à un tel point cultivés, et blasés . . . vant toute surprise que nul ne pourrait désormais dérouter la . . . ritique.

Mais c'est la destinée bizarre de notre culture que toute pensée vierge éclatera parmi cette culture comme une folle furieuse. Et à cette destinée la critique s'est soumise une fois de plus dans le cas Gertrude Stein.

Pendant près de vingt ans, Gertrude Stein a construit son œuvre, autour de laquelle tout ce que la culture permettait de paraître était quelques brimades dans les Revues humoristes.

Elle continuait à construire son œuvre, je ne dis pas courageusement, comme c'est en pareil cas l'usage de le dire; car c'est de la plus basse méprise que de supposer que les conscients ont besoin de courage devant les inconscients,—mais avec sérénité. Et son petit sourire de contentement au sujet de ses brimades m'a . . . nfiniment plu.

Elle savait très bien comment toute action de son cerveau, . . . éformée par le ridicule, devait tomber parmi la littérature . . . mps comme un précipité chimique.

. . . s présente Gertrude Stein, ainsi que je l'ai précisé . . . mme la Madame Curie du langage. Car dans ses profondes . . . des milliers de tonnages de matière pour . . . mot.

Elle a prodigieusement désintégré la matière brute du style, et d'une façon radicale a balayé le cirque littéraire pour faciliter de nouveaux spectacles. Ce qui a donné un courage inouï à d'innombrables jeunes.

En Amérique, maints auteurs ont atteint la renommée, en suivant une des nombreuses voies entr'ouvertes par les expériences de Stein. Mais Gertrude elle-même a été systématique méconnue dans son pays, où depuis des années on réclame à tue-tête quelques initiateurs proprement Américains.

Eh bien, la voilà, l'initiatrice toute Américaine! et après que làbas ils ont puisé dans ses manuscrits inédits toutes sortes de richesses, de formes nouvelles, elle a été reconnue, cette prophétesse d'outre-Atlantique, par la bonne vieille conservetrice, l'Angleterre.

Gertrude Stein n'est pas écrivain en aucun sens du mot accepté jusqu'à présent.

Elle ne se sert pas des mots pour présenter un sujet, mais d'un sujet fluidique sur lequel laisser flotter ses mots.

Je peux vous indiquer la consistance de son art en remarquant que jamais on n'entend dire "J'ai lu tel livre de Gertrude Stein." On dit: "J'ai lu *du* Gertrude Stein."

Je me doute qu'aucun de ses écrits n'a paru en française, surtout que c'est l'essential de cette œuvre qu'elle est intraduisible même dans sa propre langue, car c'est cette plaisante initiatrice qui a réduit la langue anglaise en langue étrangère même pour les Anglo-Saxons.

Et c'est seulement sa renommée, aujourd'hui mondiale, due aux dures épreuves auxquelles elle a soumis l'intelligence contemporaine, qui empêcherait n'importe quel public de me reprocher ce que je viens de dire, comme paradoxe insensé.

Peut-être que beaucoup de l'opposition déchaînée contre Gertrude Stein venait de la crainte des gens qui se disaient ahuris.

Si jamais je me laissais aller à comprendre tout cela—il arriverait un beau matin où je ne saurais plus—commander mon déjeuner.

HAVELOCK ELLIS

(5:101)

In the years preceding World War I, Loy grew interested in the burgeoning field of sexology, or the scientific study of sexuality of which Freud remains the most famous proponent. Loy's reading included the work of British sexologist Havelock Ellis, who attempted to objectively interrogate, among many other topics, homosexuality (*Sexual Inversion*, 1896) and women's sexuality (*The Sexual Impulse in Women*, 1903). In the incomplete paragraph preceding this fragment, Loy describes Ellis as a "towering authority on sex." Alongside this paragraph, Loy writes "Sex / Havelock Ellis / Lady Howard Ellis de Walden". By the time Loy wrote "Havelock Ellis," there had been three Barons Howard de Walden with the surname

"Ellis"; it seems likely that Loy refers to the wife of Thomas Evelyn-Scott Ellis, 8th Baron Howard de Walden (1880–1946), who may be the unidentified "Lord" of this piece.

In the notes for Loy's "History of Religion and Eros" (6:158) there exist two alternate versions of "Havelock Ellis," one of which is titled "Eros"; both are included below. A brief reference to Loy's conversation with Ellis arises also in "The Library of the Sphinx."

For more information on Loy and sexology, see chapter four of Cristanne Miller's *Cultures of Modernism: Marianne Moore, Mina Loy, & Else Lasker-Schüler* (U of Michigan P, 2005); Paul Peppis, "Rewriting Sex: Mina Loy, Marie Stopes, and Sexology" (*Modernism/Modernity* (9:4) 2002, 561–79), and Rowan Harris, "Futurism, Fashion, and the Feminine: Forms of Repudiation and Affiliation in the Early Writing of Mina Loy" (*Salt Companion*, 17–46).

PAGE 235
Alongside the first paragraph, in the margin, reads the following:
We were becoming quite good friends when I mentioned *a propos* of I forget what—when one thinks of when they succeed in releasing atomic energy—there's enough in one's little finger to blow up the dome. (opposite the dome?) [The blue] clear blue young eyes of Havelock hardened—"You're mad," he hissed and spoke to me no more.

"suspect marriage" was "shy clear of marriage"
"they had enquired" was "they had discovered that what [*unclear word*] to"

" 'was *nothing*' " was " 'was zer' "

"a British 'beauty' " was "a famous British 'beauty' "

"she alone among" was "she among"

"was not incommoded" reads "were not incommoded"—*ed.*

"her marital duty" reads "their marital duty"—*ed.*

"duty; they tried every" reads "duty and tried [*unclear word*] every"—*ed.*

The quotations around " 'and they're in love . . . men in England' " are not in original—*ed.*

After " 'men in England' " reads "From this same super-privileged set I got the story"—*ed.*

"That on Lord" was "When"

PAGE 236

"he actually assured her" was "he assured her"

" 'common people?' " was " 'common people?' she enquired."

" 'Even the common people—' " is followed by "he" and the whole is crossed out—*ed.*

Under " 'Well all I can say' " reads "in 1915"—*ed.*

" '*them*' " is underscored twice and reads " 'them?' "—*ed.*

"A woman told me" was "A woman who returned from the Maremma told me"

"who did housework" was "who earned her"

    Eros

    Of all rackets arising from the [*unclear writing*]
    in the racket of Eros the greatest is the invitation of the
    printed page.

Compare this hospitality to chance illustrations popping up from the Book of Life

A charming Catholick woman describes to me how the wives in the tenements can be seen to run[ning] screaming out on to the landings of the stairway in terror of their husbands' natural insistence on conjugal rights.

– – – – only less boisterous was the aversion of two British society women circa 1912. In both cases these women adored their handsome and distinguished husbands.

A strange gamble – – – Eros. At this same time it was reported to me, that among the (I gathered otherwise rather miserably situated Italians living in the Marremma the perfect consummation of Eros was almost 100 per cent.

At the very same time—[Lady X] An english woman on the morn of her honeymoon enquired of her husband Lord X,

"Does everybody experience such divine pleasure when they marry?" "Everybody" he answered. "Well all I can say is, it's much too good for the common people."

On a separate, single sheet of paper:

Havelock Ellis told me that, in England "women were suspicious of marriage (2) they asked what their mothers had got out of marriage—(1) and where their mothers had put up with it in silence—what they got out of it" said Ellis, "was nothing." 90 per cent of the women in England found no pleasure in marriage to offset the pain of childbirth, "and when I put it at ninety per cent" he assured me "I'm putting it low." We were getting along so well when apropos of "what" I cannot remember I alluded to an article [*beneath* "an article" *reads* "a statement"] I had read—on atomic theory [that] there is enough atomic energy in one's little finger—that if released could blow up the whole of the Boulevard Montparnasse. The clear blue "youthful" eyes of Havelock hardened "You're *mad!*" he hissed and spoke to me no more—

HISTORY OF RELIGION AND EROS

(6:159)

There are two folders of handwritten notes entitled "History of Religion and Eros"; one contains the twenty-page-long, typed essay included here. The manuscript has very occasional amendments in Loy's hand, and the footnotes are Loy's own. The final footnote refers to Sándor Radó (1890–1972), an influential psychoanalyist who moved from his native Hungary to the United States in the thirties.

A statement that appears midway through "History of Reglion and Eros," namely "MAN IS A COVERED-ENTRANCE TO INFINITY," echoes a line from Loy's poem "O Hell," which was first published in *Contact* in 1920, and reads: "Our person is a covered entrance to infinity / Choked with the tatters of tradition" (*Lost LB* 71).

The essay also explores many of the same themes as "Mi & Lo," Loy's philosophical dialogue believed to have been written in the thirties. Burke dates "History" as a product of Loy's years in New York's Bowery District, 1948–1953 (*BM* 422–23).

PAGE 237
"i.e., enjoyment of surprising" reads " enjoyment of surprising";
    "i.e." is drawn from a handwritten draft—*ed.*

PAGE 238
"these systems:" reads "these systems"—*ed.*
"The Asiatic mystic-scientist" was "The Asiatic-mystic-scientist"

PAGE 240
"that increments" reads "that increment"—*ed.*
"it aerates to" reads "it aerates? to"—*ed.*

PAGE 241
"this etheric" was "this ethenic"

PAGE 242
"a fine line" was "a five line"
"through increasing" reads "though increasing"—*ed.*

PAGE 243
"our impossible" was "the impossible"
"*the* POSSIBLE" was "the POSSIBLE"
"impartation" was "importation"

"attraction: a gravitation" reads "attractio a gravitation"—*ed.*

PAGE 244
"with it, when" reads "with if, when"—*ed.*

PAGE 245
"Exercisers" was "exercises"

PAGE 246
"phenomena inducted from the invisible" was "phenomena in inducted from invisible"

PAGE 247
"his destiny is to fare onward" reads "his destiny is to go onward"—
on the back of page 9 of this manuscript, Loy has written
that on page 13, where this phrase occurs, "fare" should be substituted for "go"—*ed.*
After "*'unknown'*" in typescript, about four fifths of the remaining page is left blank—*ed.*

PAGE 248
"our desire, not of our own contriving, is from" was "our desires, not of our own contriving, are from" and reads, "our desire, not of our own contriving, are from"—*ed.*
"vibrational co-identity" was "vibrational co-identify"

PAGE 249
" 'man of electronic vitality' " was " 'man of electric vitality' "

In the margin next to "Between the brain . . . our instincts" Loy writes in large hand: "?)"—*ed.*

After "our instincts" about two thirds of the remaining page is left blank—*ed.*

PAGE 250

"humane morality" was "humanie morality"

"intimate doings" was "ultimate doings"

"IT HAS BEEN THE PRETENSE OF CRUELTY TO ENFORCE MORALITY" was "CRUELTY ENFORCED MORALITY"

PAGE 251

"incomprehension through our spiritual" was "comprehension (through) our spiritual"—a large, pencilled question mark exists in the margin next to these changes—*ed.*

Next to "CONFUSION OF SATAN WITH EROS" Loy writes "or Substitution of Satan for Eros"—*ed.*

"channels of discard discharge coursing" was "channels of discord coursing"

"challenging our" was "challenging ours"

"to purity (Purity—consciousness . . . life) to ignore" reads "to purity to ignore (Purity – consciousness . . . life)"—*ed.*

"extensible maze" was "extensible able-maze"

PAGE 252

In footnote, "toward" was "to word"

THE LIBRARY OF THE SPHINX.

(7:190)

"The Library of the Sphinx." brings together five of Loy's abiding preoccupations: modernist literature, psychology, sexuality, the asterisk, and lastly, the claim made in Oscar Wilde's *The Picture of Dorian Gray* that women are "Sphinxes without secrets." The latter two of these interests are specifically discussed in the introduction to this volume. Loy's "Lady Asterisk." and "Havelock Ellis" share direct points of reference with "The Library of the Sphinx."

Loy makes many casual allusions to modernist figures and works of literature in this essay, including Joyce, Eliot, Aldous Huxley, and D. H. Lawrence, whose *Sons and Lovers* (1913) and *Women in Love* (1920) receive special mention. Less familiar references involve the sexologist Havelock Ellis (see editorial notes for Loy's essay of that name); Irish-born editor Frank Harris, author of the multi-volume, scandal-making autobiography, *My Life and Loves* (1922–27); Italian author Gabriele D'Annunzio (1863–1938) and his novel *Il fuoco* (*The Flame of Life*, 1900); American writer Evelyn Scott (1893–1963) and her first novel *The Narrow House* (1921); and lastly, anarchist activist Emma Goldman (1869–1940).

Although she observes that she is working from imperfect memory at one juncture in this text, Loy recalls Joyce better than Eliot: in the "Penelope" episode of *Ulysses*, Molly Bloom describes how her husband has kissed and ejaculated upon her backside, and these practices may be what Loy refers to with her paraphrase "if I let him 'retire' on my 'bases'". The line may also refer to the fact that Molly and Bloom sleep top to toe at the end of the book. As Loy further conjectures, Molly does indeed complain that Bloom has a tongue too flat to perform satisfying oral sex. However, Loy tells us that in *The Waste Land*, the typist puts on the gramophone, dries her combinations on the roof, and swallows hairpins; while the first of these three actions is accurate, in fact, the typist dries her laundry out of her window, and does not swallow hairpins, but less dramatically, "smoothes her hair with automatic hand" (l. 255).

Evidence that Loy planned "The Library" exists in another folder in her papers, where a torn sheet bears the heading "*Sphinx*." followed by a list that includes "Women— / Sex / Sin. Novels etc. / Lawrence / Joyce / D'Annunzio. / Huxley— / Frank Harris"; beneath this list reads: "Look up— / Sherwood Anderson / — Waldo Franck [*sic*]—" (7:188). Fragments in the "The Library of the Sphinx." folder suggest that Loy intended to write more about the American writers Anderson (1876–1941) and Frank (1889–1967). As numbered by Loy, pages five to fourteen of "The Library of the Sphinx." remain; the last, incomplete portion of the handwritten script is included at the end of the editorial notes.

PAGE 253

"Notwithstanding that the secret" was "Notwithstanding the secret"—"notwithstanding" has been altered, and is not entirely clear—it may read, "Notwithstated"—*ed.*

"assumption that the secret" was "assumption of the elucida solution of the"
"by each of us" was "by everyone of us"
"us and therefore need never be" was "us but is not allowed to
be"
"asked the sphinx" was "said the sphinx"
After "rose—" reads two long dashes, like an extended "="—*ed.*
"Impossible" was "But"
"been remarked" was "been noti"

PAGE 254
"misapprehension" was "assumption" and "delusion"
"that the other women" was "that every other women"
" 'Woman' " was " 'But woman' "
After "nothing" was:

>I dared not lose my litera-
>I am about to speak—
>At last I speak—
>said the sphinx
>['They'] 'We' are no longer interested—they have found
>   their solution—
>of my secret—?
>Jazz—said the sphinxes – – –
>to keep on jumpin'!"

In the margin alongside the above, Loy directs herself, "insert
somewhere else," and this she does: this passage is almost identical to part of the dialogue in "Lady Asterisk."—*ed.*
"lo-o-o-vely" was "lo-oo-o-vely"

Before "*Even* James Joyce" reads the title: "*I. The library of the Sphinx.*"

All honorifics—"Mr. and Mrs. Bloom"—read "Mr and Mrs" in the text—*ed.*

" ' "would he give me" if I let him "retire" on my "bases" ' " reads " "would he give me" / 'if I let him "retire" on my 'bases" ' " —*ed.*

"interference" was "reason," "procrastination," and then "reason"

"to account for" was "for"

"suggestion" was "act" and "offer"

"suggestion—at" was "suggestion—on"

"recollect" was "You recollect"

"Let us make the absolute descent" was "Let us descend"

"be positively *shredded*" was "be *shredded*"

"That little" was "That nasty"

"the geographical aspect" was "the ascent"

"of the Venusberg" was "of Vesuvius"

"the spasimal larva" was "the spasmodic. He"

PAGE 255

"So he absolves" was "He absolves"

"seventh heaven with" was "seventh with"

"on shrugging at" was "when he looking up"—"at" is unclear and may be "off"—*ed.*

"to scrubby-looking" was "to ugly scrubby-looking men the flesh shrinks from"

"nearest to defining" was "nearest to explore"

"psychic experiences" was "psychic introspection"

After "only book" was "(a censored book—that has given the flesh" "the flesh with a" reads "the flesh a"—*ed.*

"or the virile male" was "or made the virile male"

"returns to" was "resorts to"

"derive no satisfaction" was "find no compensation for"

"novels, attempting to" was "novels to"

PAGE 256

"The primary phenomenon" was "The first phenomenon"

"male as regards his intimate relation with the female" was "male
  as regards the female"

"relation with the female" reads "relation the female"—*ed.*

"spoken a word" was "made a sign"

"best cantharide" was "best natural cantharide"

"depth of —— is disgust" was "depth of —— reason"

"maiden's lack" was "maiden's unr"

"response to satisfy" reads "response satisfy"—*ed.*

"revivifying" was "healthy"

"may we ask" was "may we asked"

"authors live?" was "authors life?"

"daily life?" was "daily life where the"

"nunnery – –" reads "nunnery. – –"—*ed.*

"apologetic man" was "apologetic type"

"heroes of Aldous Huxley" was "heroes of (chrome yellow man)"

PAGE 257

"erotic discomfort" was "social discomfort"

" 'themselves go' " was " 'theirself go' "

"Also, in the soggy" was "Also, the soggy"

"of T.S. Eliot is embedded" was "of T.S. Eliot's poetry"—"T.S." was "W"

Next to the material on Eliot, along the margin, Loy writes: "The Case of Cupid and Cupid versus Venus and Venus."—*ed.*

The sentence beginning "Mr. Eliot has observed" reads "Mr. Eliot has observed the typist with the same disrespectfully acute ray of observation that turning on classism and pessimism alike,—with which he observed her combinations drying on the roof."—*ed.*

"a uniform" was "an equal"

"Practically the whole" was "The whole"

"psychological literature written by men might" was "psychological literature might"

"The episode of" was "The scene of"

"Exceptionally there is" was "There is"

PAGE 258

"also monuments to" was "also those monumental traditional monuments"

"in the sense" was "in the French sense"

"for instance: the" reads "for instance, The"—*ed.*

"become fictitious" was "become tradition"

"should he omit . . . desert him—" is a later addition

"a literary monument" was "a monument"

"And there is no . . . *de joie*" is a later addition

"the chambers of 'joy'" was "the amorous chamber"

"everybody that is" was "everybody has"

"Debrett's" is unclear—*ed.*

"her inevitable point of view" was "her point of view"

"disease, being threatened into supporting" was "disease, supporting"

Under "a *maquereau*" reads "a *man*"—*ed.*

PAGE 259

"night life of the metropolis" was "night life another"

"to notice—" reads "to notice—."—*ed.*

"When he comes to himself" was "Rest assured that when he
comes to himself"

"he has erotically administered" was "he has administered"

"*fille de joie*" reads " 'fille de joie' "—*ed.*

After "*fille de joie*" was the heading "*Sphinxes in Tête à tête.*"

"Alas the exercise" was "Alas exercise"

"blown off does not" was "blown off will"

After "does not" and largely crossed through is the beginning of
the next instalment in Loy's "The Library of the Sphinx." It
reads as follows:

Sphinxes in Tête à tête.

The irate husband ordered her to "go [to the doctor]
and find out what is the matter with you—"

Doctor – – – I do not enjoy the er marital—er – – – The
doctor.

No *nice* woman, my dear lady *ever* enjoys it.

Blessed is the peace-maker. For he does the best he can.

The fast married woman that horrified the hotel—"[I
have many lovers – although] I cannot enjoy 'it'—you see,

it gives me inflammation of the womb - - - yet I have so many lovers because - - I don't know why—

But I *adore* to see them taking off their boots—or something - - -

The German baroness—

I feel nothing at all—during that time I think of what I shall order for next day's dinner.

THE LOGOS IN ART.

(7:188)

Loy deliberated about what to call this handwritten piece; slight variations in the title include "The Logos in the Arts." and (possibly the first) "Logos in Art." The fragments here are part of a longer work, of which 1, 2, 6, and 7 are the numbered pages that remain. "Logos" can mean word, speech, discourse, or reason, and is often conflated with the divine; Loy's text is thus tied to her ongoing explorations of aesthetics and metaphysics.

PAGE 260
"Greek the spirals" was "The spirals"
After "centrality" reads "or encircle the limbs drawing the eye - -
    etc."—*ed.*

PAGE 261
"conformity to finite" was "conformity to inf"
"*passagère*" reads " 'passagère' "—*ed.*

Above "The new Zig Zag" reads "*Logos in Art*"—*ed.*

"falls down" was "fell down"

"Cinema" reads "(Cinema)"—Loy may have wanted this word excised—*ed.*

"Screen" has a long line through it—*ed.*

"*nouvelle vierges*" reads "Nouvelle vierges"—"*vierges*" is unclear —*ed.*

Beneath "penetrates" reads "permeates"—*ed.*

"because the proportions of their" was "because their"

"too great for" was "too great or p"

"their purpose" was "their adaptation"

PAGE 262

Above "The logos" reads "*Logos in Art.*"—*ed.*

"than those" reads "that those"—*ed.*

"of some previous" was "of previous"

"breathing upon of the logos" was "breathing into of the logos" and also "breathing of the logos"

"inform contemporary" was "inform the"

THE METAPHYSICAL PATTERN IN AESTHETICS.

(6:165)

Describing "The Metaphysical Pattern in Aesthetics." as "a prescient essay on modernist abstraction," Burke dates it at 1923, which is the same year that Loy published her first volume of poetry, *Lunar Baedecker* [*sic*] (*BM* 325). This piece consists of a typescript of two pages; the folder in Loy's papers contains no handwritten or additional drafts.

PAGE 263
" 'subject.' " reads " 'subject!.' "—*ed.*
"*absurdum*—the ability" reads "*absurdum* the ability"—*ed.*

PAGE 264
"graven image" reads "graven ikage"—*ed.*
"subject in dissolution" was " 'subject in dissolution' " and reads
    " 'subject in dissolution"—*ed.*
"In all the masters" reads "I all the masters"—*ed.*

MI & LO

(6:166)

The American poet Marianne Moore labelled Loy "a sound philosopher"; by rather stark contrast, the English poet Edwin Muir expressed concern about Loy's philosophical tendencies, which he described as her willingness to " 'intellectualis[e] life without . . . coming to conclusions' " (*BM* 222, 336). "Mi & Lo" allows us to test these two assertions; the work is Loy's attempt at a Socratic dialogue in which different parts of her one self—the "Mi" of Mina and the "Lo" of Loy—play both roles.

Burke suggests that Loy wrote "Mi & Lo" in the thirties, and sent it to her son-in-law Julien Levy for inspection (*BM* 376). The manuscript is over sixty pages in length, of which only four pages have been typed. Although a set of notes suggest a plan, much of the text is in very rough form; the dialogue frequently disappears in favour of circuitous arguments, tangents, and convoluted, incomplete notes. As in other works—particularly "Transfiguration."— Loy repeatedly puts a large "x" next to sentences or sections of this manuscript. An additional portion of "Mi & Lo"—centring on Christ's relationship to the Jews—exists in a folder of Loy's longer autobiographical work, *Goy Israels*, which is also thought to have been written in the thirties (2:30).

The most comprehensible and complete portions of "Mi & Lo" are included here, or about half of the entirety; emphasis has been given to the sections that are part of the dialogue proper. On occasion, Loy does not identify her interlocutors, and their names have been added whenever a change in speaker is discernible. The ten distinct sections are not numbered by Loy, but indicate a break in either theme or in the continuity of the script; where headings arise, they are Loy's own.

PAGE 265
"Does form result from seeing unform repeatedly?" is pencilled along the top of the typescript
Next to "union of identicals" reads, in handwriting, "Argue re Picasso"—*ed.*

PAGE 266
After "the answer of form" reads, by hand, "Re often giving an unexpected answer"—*ed.*
Above "a token" reads "or symbol"—*ed.*

"inseparable: truth being the question that answers itself—as" was "inseparable: as"

"immortality existing" was "immortality ousting"

"existing as a question" reads "existing a question"—*ed*.

"the macrocosmic mind of god" was "the mind of god"

"microcosmic forms" reads "micosmic forms"—the "cro" is crossed out—*ed*.

"is this the elucidation" was "as this education"

"monad?" reads "(monad)??"—*ed*.

"indicated" was "signalled"

"cognisable from the" reads "cognisable the"—"from" is crossed out in text—*ed*.

"fourth dimension" was "plus-dimension"

From "In the recession . . . of thought, while" is an addition pencilled into the typescript; "thought" is crossed through—*ed*.

Next to "In the" Loy has written: "[*unclear word, possibly "él-ogement"*] *pendant le procès de* [*unclear word, possibly "la"*] *penser*"—*ed*.

"unification" was "encumbrance"

PAGE 267

Above "Then man" reads "or (the intellect of)"—*ed*.

"Then it is the confinement" was "Then it is untraceable the confinement"

After "of creation" reads, by hand, "(creative ideation)"—*ed*.

PAGE 268

"The encompassment" was "While the encompassment"

"The encompassment . . . has form" was attributed to "lo"

"phenomena already have form" reads "phenomena already has form"—*ed.*

"concavity of the mold" reads "concavity of the mould"—*ed.*

After "outer—" was "the 4th dimensional aspect of"

After "outer—" appears a torn page that reads as follows:

mi

> In the face of a social non-provision, the grab-hazard pleasure of the masses is a poor, defiant and unlovely pleasure shoo'ed into the shadows of civism.

lo

> Yet are not the movie and radio concerns for the provision pleasure.

mi

> Only and always the imparticipatable pleasure of mythologies.
>
> The assurance of the mob that the gods have leisure to love

The typescript ends here; all else is handwritten

II.

A title page between I. and II. reads, "Power / force animating Body— / Electric Prayer / etc"

The first line of this page follows on from another, and reads, under "mi": "No for the fourth dimensional aspect of life is myriad—"—*ed.*

"whole unimaginable tonnage" was "whole universal tonnage"

PAGE 269

"the nerve centre of the brain" was "the brain"

"and provides energy . . . surplus runs" is a later addition

"Its outlet" reads "Its onlet"—*ed.*

"mystery left by an" was "mystery of an"

"has come . . . animation" is written along the margin of a page, and is a later addition

PAGE 270

Above "This is understandable" reads "The philosophy of a civilisation dies when a race has forgotten the interpretation of its geniuses."—*ed.*

"understandable inasmuch" was "understandable for"

"bifurcate" reads "bifurcated"—*ed.*

"feral motor extensions"—"feral" is unclear—*ed.*

"(but this is too . . . formulas)" is not bracketed in Loy's draft —*ed.*

"this is too intricate" was "this is an almo" and "a go"

Next to "slumber" reads "???"—*ed.*

"Not being pushed" reads "(not being pushed"—*ed.*

"Not being . . . time" is a later addition

"In both conditions" may be "to both conditions"—*ed.*

"then are animated" may be "there are animated"—*ed.*

"erect position" was "upr"

"stay awake indefinitely" was "stay awake for ever"

"possibility or likelihood" reads "possibility if likelihood"—*ed.*

"tends towards" was "indicates" in both instances

"might it not" was "may it not"

"inadaptability to its functions" reads "inadaptability of to its functions"—*ed.*

PAGE 271

"for all the great" was "for none of"

"mediates such as Christ" reads "mediates as christ"—*ed.*

"would-be expounders"—"expounders" is unclear—*ed.*

"laboured to convey" was "laboured to make the"

"to the rest" was "to the w"

"a christ" is Loy's spelling

PAGE 272

After "be taken away" reads the following:

> *Of Genius*
> Genius is honesty
> talent is theft.
> Education is the training for intellectual thievery.
> What is faith—
> faith is the ability to set in operation, forces of whose existence you have no guarantee except through their (results effects)
> Morality is not a device but a birth-right
> Morality is as impersonal as criminality
>
> *Psychological Distance*
> There is a distance
> or rather a proximity at which number is heterogeneous.

A thousand bugs at sufficient distance if focussed by a
magnifying glass would present one bug to the power
of form.
There is a distance at which number is homogeneous.
proximity produces diversity
distance produces uniformity

III.

"consciousness is deepest" reads "consciousness deepest"—
"deepest with" may have been "is closest to"—*ed.*
"within himself" was "to himself"
"hovers at a slight distance" was "hovers between distance"—
"slight" is unclear—*ed.*
"quite in contact" was "quite sure of"
"with his own mind" reads "of his own mind"—*ed.*

PAGE 273
"correct solution" was "correction answer"
From "I think therefore I am" to the end of section three is attributed to "lo" in original—*ed.*
"coincident to his state" was "coincident with the"
"make-up—there" reads "make-up there"—*ed.*

PAGE 274
"Yet the flesh and the soul can say to one another—we suffer" was
"But the flesh can say to the soul we suffer—"
"without contact with the soul" is a later addition, and is preceded
by "?"—*ed.*

"to cure suffering" was "to destroy suffering"
"to cure happiness" was "to destroy happiness"
"there can never be" was "there has"
" 'Man's inalienable' " reads " 'Man's alienable' "—*ed.*

PAGE 275
"weep over" was "weep of"
"simple poignancy" was "simple and"
"conception of starving and" was "conception and"
"complex protractedness" was "complex vagueness"
"on starving" may be "in starving"—*ed.*
"The sight of" was "the beauty of" and "the aspect of"
"shop windows"—"shop" is unclear—*ed.*
"takes on a sudden" reads "take on sudden"—*ed.*
"*aspect féerique*" reads " 'aspect féerique' "—*ed.*
On either side of the sentence "Death—it . . . mind" a line is drawn
    across the page—*ed.*

PAGE 276
"universe is of the third" reads "universe of the third"—*ed.*

PAGE 277
"But what is morality?" is attributed to "mi" in the original—*ed.*
"who has lied" was "who lies"
"for a temporary lie" was "of a lie"
"sake of ultimate truth" was "sake of truth"
The sentence "Yet it in . . . ultimate truth" is repeated; the second
    variant reads: "Yet in an illogical society there is [often] the ne-

cessity often presents itself for the temporary lie for the sake of ultimate truth."—*ed.*

PAGE 278

"physical phenomena end" was "physical phenomena begin"

"cessation of visuality" was "interruption of sight"—only "interruption" is crossed out—*ed.*

"wakefulness—sets up" reads "wakefulness sets up"—*ed.*

"aware of the fourth dimension" reads "existing in the (or aware of the fourth dimension)"—"existing in the" is crossed out—*ed.*

"without exits" reads "without issues (exits)"—*ed.*

"get out of the room" was "get outside of the room"

"he in the fourth dimension—can follow" was "he has control of his fourth dimensional potentiality"

"he is connective with infinite distance" reads "he (has connectivity is) connective"—*ed.*

After "be aware" reads "(find other word)"—*ed.*

PAGE 279

Beneath "the three dimensional" reads "BLIND BACK"—*ed.*

"ample consciousness find" was "ample consciousness are"

"third dimensional" reads "3rd dim"—*ed.*

"back to its source" reads "back to its share source"—source appears to be a later correction—*ed.*

"inhabit the identical" was "inhabit our"

Beneath "nothingness" a line is drawn across the bottom of the page, followed by: "It is the nature of infinity that it is infinite at every point."—*ed.*

"educational exercise" was "educational impressions"

PAGE 280

"he who immovably"—"immovably" is unclear and could be
  "immeasurably"—*ed.*
"submission of identity" was "the submission of identity"
"*libre arbitre*" reads " 'libre arbitre' " in first instance—*ed.*
"amid a loud diversity" was "amid diversity"

PAGE 281

A circle is drawn around mi's statement "Truth is the question . . .
  formula" followed by a series of four wavy lines across the
  page—*ed.*

PAGE 282

After "finds himself" about two thirds of the remaining page is
  left blank

IX.

After "asserts" reads "?"—*ed.*
"death of the body" was "deaths of the body"
"together amount to" reads "together (brought to a whole) amount
  to"—*ed.*

PAGE 283

"towards the cosmic" was "towards cosmic"
After "cosmic" reads "?—for which he has not i.e."—*ed.*
"macrocosm or divinity" was "macrocosm into the"

After "Mediocosm = man" Loy writes: "Mediocosmic? Can this word be used."—this note to self appears to mark a break in the philosophical dialogue. The next six pages include a set of rough notes organised under the following headings: Vengeance, Truth, Religion, Propriety of Words, Miracles, Poem, Spirit, Meditation, Christ, Masses, Anomaly of Equality, Revolution, Hindu, and Beauty—*ed.*

Under the heading "Miracles," Loy briefly continues the Mi/Lo dialogue as follows:

lo

Yet god is ever-changing—

mi

Unchanging in changeableness.

There is no process in the working of a miracle.

It is operated in the fourth dimension. No miracle ever happens in the third dimension: only its effect is apparent.

"conceive of it" was "conceive it"

After "*impulse*" reads "(longer word)"—*ed.*

"complement of shame" was "complement of educational"

"a swollen eroticism" was "the swollen bestia"

PAGE 284

"law of the world moralist" was "law of the sex"

"mayest kill—wholesale" was "might kill—"

"should so consistently endeavour to withhold" was "should have to withhold"

THE OIL IN THE MACHINE?

(6:168)

"The Oil in the Machine?" is typed, signed with Loy's name in capitals at the end, and dated 1921. Three discernible changes have been made to the script: "And what could we make" was "And what the hell could we make"; "pulpy material" was "pulpy materials," and "re- act -ion" was likely "reaction" in the first instance. It is possible that Loy intended that the phrase "to discover himself" be in quotations, but only one faint, handwritten mark remains at the outset of the phrase. This piece is discussed in *Modernism, Technology, and the Body: A Cultural Study*, wherein Tim Armstrong suggests that it is indicative of Loy's tendency to resist a simple equation between the human body and the machine (Cambridge: Cambridge UP, 1998, p. 115).

TUNING IN ON THE ATOM BOMB

(6:181)

The manuscript of "Tuning in on the Atom Bomb" consists of five pages of occasionally edited handwriting. Two additional versions of the first page indicate that this is not Loy's first draft; the differences between all drafts are fairly minor, and one alternate version is included below. The entirety is prefaced by a small sheet of paper reading: "Tuning in on the Atom Bomb – – – / Page I–V."

References to nuclear warfare, "our narrow garden," "my daughter," and an ulcer date this work as a product of the forties: the USA dropped atomic bombs on Japan in August 1945, Loy shared residences with her daughters Joella and Fabienne in New York from 1937–48, and Loy was diagnosed with an ulcer in 1940 (*BM* 388–90).

PAGE 286
"Excentric" is Loy's spelling
"perception, to recapture my easeful surroundings" was "perception, on easeful surroundings"

PAGE 287
After "molecular" reads "(?)"—*ed.*
After "glaucous" reads "(?)"—*ed.*
"anxiety . . . ." was "anxiety . . . ."—Loy goes out of her way to cross out the eleventh full stop—the entirety is a later addition—*ed.*
"imagine what part was mine in this over-all alarm I" was "imagine, I"

PAGE 288
"apprehension—of what, I could" was "apprehension—I could"
After "saying)" reads "(announcement) (dictum)?)"—*ed.*
"manuscript" reads "mss"—*ed.*
"the lately inconducive" was "the inconducive"
After "transformation" reads "? (transmutation)"—*ed.*
"tree with threatening" reads "tree—(the letter) with threatening" —*ed.*
"phantasmagoria" reads "(phantasmagoria"—*ed.*
"religious debacle" reads "religious (? word) debacle"—*ed.*

"some abnormal pressure" is a later addition; after "pressure" reads "(?))"—the second bracket is unclear—*ed.*

PAGE 289
"accounted endlessly responsible" was "accounted responsible" "of neurosis– " reads "of neurosis.—"—*ed.*
At end of manuscript, upside down at the bottom of the page reads: "German Consulate MU *83523* ══ — "—the number may be "8o3533" or "8.3523"—*ed.*

Tuning in on the Atom (alternate draft of first page)

Serene amid scintillas of sunlight gilding our narrow, green garden – – writing of the sordid consequences invited by extraction of force from Power
Suddenly
Seismically
was I overcome by an eccentric sense of guilt – invoked by an echo emitted by some forgotten wisdom sunken in ancient time punishing revelation of perilous secret – – – –
– – – I did not know the secret!
Causeless accusation as if, for defiance of some unknown taboo detonated in my brain – – –
shattering terror—inobviously brought about, of sickening incarceration of the limited within the illimitable.
Longing struggle to regain serenity – – endeavour to refocus perception

UNIVERSAL FOOD MACHINE

(6:182)

"Universal Food Machine" is an undated political commentary composed by hand in a single notebook. The thematic concerns—hunger and war—suggest that this work is a product of the World War II period, when Loy was living in New York City, and was increasingly writing about the homeless people who inhabited her local streets (see "IV Compensations of Poverty (Poems 1942–1949)" *Lost LB*, 109–46). The piece is prefaced with a title page that includes the following three subheadings: "Universal Food Machine," "War," and "Effluvia of decomposition of the Spirit"—the order and phrasing of these titles are preserved here as a means of structuring and relaying Loy's draft composition.

PAGE 290
"Universal Food Machine" begins *in medias res*; the top of the first available page reads:
    . . . as is now the case for [gas and water and] gas—with open radiators"—*ed.*
"Open radiators" was "with grids here and there"
"for those anonymous" was "for the wayfarer and"
"to come from nowhere" was "to belong nowhere"
"Also automatic" was "And automatic"
"composed of the essential" was "to with the essentials"
"essential" reads "essentials"—*ed.*
"stimulates" reads "stimulate"—*ed.*
After "vast sums" was "nec spent"

"charity and pooling them for ... general welfare. How" was "charity. How"

"the millions of unemployed" was "the hoards of the unemployed"

"would you encourage" was "you would"

After "idleness" reads "(?)"—*ed.*

"but what" was "but where"

"of thrift" was "of thriftles"

PAGE 291

"of politics" was "of thought has"

"levelling up" was "levelling higher"

"surely we have sufficient knowledge" was "surely the time has come"

"human life constrained to concentrate" was "human life that is constrained to the"

"and the more we" was "for it"

On the first page about war, Loy begins:

> Prophecies
> Speculative Prophecies.

> _____

> [How can war come to an end while there remain within us [a] the egoist]

> _____

> Speculative Prophecies

The end of War.

"the end of War" was "the abolition"
The blank space between "those" and "—differences" is Loy's

PAGE 292
"and at a long distance" was "and that from"
"find the same farewells to affection" was "find only sad leavetak-
    ings"
"in deference to duty" was "in the name of deference to duty"
"both youths" was "each y"
"all cruelty" was "cruelty"
"for instance" was "for instanced"
"its effluvia" was "its deadly effluvia"
"Therefore when Christ" was "And so it is"
"would that they" was "would be done by"

WILLIAM CARLOS WILLIAMS

(7:190)

This short, handwritten commentary about Loy's friend, the
American poet William Carlos Williams (1883–1963), is included
in a file entitled "Notes on Literature". The upper right-hand mar-

gin of the page reads, "mailed 5th of June *1948*," and the entirety is signed by Loy. The quoted lines are from Williams's long poem, *Paterson* (1946–58). Three amendments are made to this otherwise very fair copy: Loy corrects a misspelling of "marriages" (it was "marriges"), and replaces two words: "new" becomes "unexpected" and "beauty" is changed to "individuality".

MINA LOY was born in London, England in 1882. A key figure in the history of modernism, her writing commanded the attention of Ezra Pound and Yvor Winters in *The Little Review* and *The Dial* respectively, era-defining journals that published Joyce's *Ulysses* and Eliot's *The Waste Land*. Aligning herself with Futurism, Dada, and Surrealism, Loy influenced pivotal figures such as Marcel Duchamp and Djuna Barnes.

SARA CRANGLE is a Senior Lecturer in English and a director of the Centre for Modernist Studies at the University of Sussex, UK. Her books include *Prosaic Desires: Modernist Knowledge, Boredom, Laughter, and Anticipation* and (with Peter Nicholls) *On Bathos: Literature, Art, Music.*

COLEMAN DOWELL BRITISH LITERATURE SERIES

The Coleman Dowell British Literature Series is made possible through a generous contribution by an anonymous donor. This endowed contribution allows Dalkey Archive Press to publish one book a year in this series.

Born in Kentucky in 1925, Coleman Dowell moved to New York in 1950 to work in theater and television as a playwright and composer/lyricist, but by age forty he turned to writing fiction. His works include *One of the Children Is Crying* (1968), *Mrs. October Was Here* (1974), *Island People* (1976), *Too Much Flesh and Jabez* (1977), and *White on Black on White* (1983). After his death in 1985, *The Houses of Children: Collected Stories* was published in 1987, and his memoir about his theatrical years, *A Star-Bright Lie*, was published in 1993.

Since his death, a number of his books have been reissued in the United States, as well as translated for publication in other countries.

FOR A FULL LIST OF PUBLICATIONS, VISIT:

www.dalkeyarchive.com

SELECTED DALKEY ARCHIVE PAPERBACKS

ARNO SCHMIDT, *Collected Novellas.*
  Collected Stories.
  Nobodaddy's Children.
  Two Novels.
ASAF SCHURR, *Motti.*
CHRISTINE SCHUTT, *Nightwork.*
GAIL SCOTT, *My Paris.*
DAMION SEARLS, *What We Were Doing*
  and Where We Were Going.
JUNE AKERS SEESE,
  Is This What Other Women Feel Too?
  What Waiting Really Means.
BERNARD SHARE, *Inish.*
  Transit.
AURELIE SHEEHAN,
  Jack Kerouac Is Pregnant.
VIKTOR SHKLOVSKY, *Bowstring.*
  Knight's Move.
  A Sentimental Journey:
  Memoirs 1917–1922.
  Energy of Delusion: A Book on Plot.
  Literature and Cinematography.
  Theory of Prose.
  Third Factory.
  Zoo, or Letters Not about Love.
CLAUDE SIMON, *The Invitation.*
PIERRE SINIAC, *The Collaborators.*
JOSEF ŠKVORECKÝ, *The Engineer of*
  Human Souls.
GILBERT SORRENTINO,
  Aberration of Starlight.
  Blue Pastoral.
  Crystal Vision.
  Imaginative Qualities of Actual
  Things.
  Mulligan Stew.
  Pack of Lies.
  Red the Fiend.
  The Sky Changes.
  Something Said.
  Splendide-Hôtel.
  Steelwork.
  Under the Shadow.
W. M. SPACKMAN,
  The Complete Fiction.
ANDRZEJ STASIUK, *Fado.*
GERTRUDE STEIN,
  Lucy Church Amiably.
  The Making of Americans.
  A Novel of Thank You.
LARS SVENDSEN, *A Philosophy of Evil.*
PIOTR SZEWC, *Annihilation.*
GONÇALO M. TAVARES, *Jerusalem.*
  Learning to Pray in the Age of
  Technology.
LUCIAN DAN TEODOROVICI,
  Our Circus Presents . . .
STEFAN THEMERSON, *Hobson's Island.*
  The Mystery of the Sardine.
  Tom Harris.
JOHN TOOMEY, *Sleepwalker.*
JEAN-PHILIPPE TOUSSAINT,
  The Bathroom.
  Camera.
  Monsieur.
  Running Away.
  Self-Portrait Abroad.
  Television.
DUMITRU TSEPENEAG,
  Hotel Europa.

  The Necessary Marriage.
  Pigeon Post.
  Vain Art of the Fugue.
ESTHER TUSQUETS, *Stranded.*
DUBRAVKA UGRESIC,
  Lend Me Your Character.
  Thank You for Not Reading.
MATI UNT, *Brecht at Night.*
  Diary of a Blood Donor.
  Things in the Night.
ÁLVARO URIBE AND OLIVIA SEARS, EDS.,
  Best of Contemporary Mexican
  Fiction.
ELOY URROZ, *Friction.*
  The Obstacles.
LUISA VALENZUELA, *Dark Desires and*
  the Others.
  He Who Searches.
MARJA-LIISA VARTIO,
  The Parson's Widow.
PAUL VERHAEGHEN, *Omega Minor.*
BORIS VIAN, *Heartsnatcher.*
LLORENÇ VILLALONGA, *The Dolls' Room.*
ORNELA VORPSI, *The Country Where No*
  One Ever Dies.
AUSTRYN WAINHOUSE, *Hedyphagetica.*
PAUL WEST,
  Words for a Deaf Daughter & *Gala.*
CURTIS WHITE,
  America's Magic Mountain.
  The Idea of Home.
  Memories of My Father Watching TV.
  Monstrous Possibility: An Invitation
  to Literary Politics.
  Requiem.
DIANE WILLIAMS, *Excitability:*
  Selected Stories.
  Romancer Erector.
DOUGLAS WOOLF, *Wall to Wall.*
  Ya! & *John-Juan.*
JAY WRIGHT, *Polynomials and Pollen.*
  The Presentable Art of Reading
  Absence.
PHILIP WYLIE, *Generation of Vipers.*
MARGUERITE YOUNG, *Angel in the Forest.*
  Miss MacIntosh, My Darling.
REYOUNG, *Unbabbling.*
VLADO ŽABOT, *The Succubus.*
ZORAN ŽIVKOVIĆ, *Hidden Camera.*
LOUIS ZUKOFSKY, *Collected Fiction.*
SCOTT ZWIREN, *God Head.*

FOR A FULL LIST OF PUBLICATIONS, VISIT:
www.dalkeyarchive.com